THE DEADMAN'S TRIBE  BOOK 5

I0779175

brave ENOUGH

NICOLE CRAIG

Ebook ISBN 979-8989214488

Paperback ISBN 979-8989214495

ASIN B0FPWKBJCZ

Developmental Editing by Sara-Jane Higgins (Plot to Polish Author Services)

Editing by Steph White (Kat's Literary Services)

Proofreading by Vanessa Esquibel (Kat's Literary Services)

Internal Formatting by Kat Wyeth (Kat's Literary Services)

Cover Design by Deranged Doctor Design **www.derangeddoctordesign.com**

Nicole Craig

Visit my website at https://nicolecraigauthor.com

Join my Reader's Group at https://www.facebook.com/groups/362438775117 0522

Printed in the United States of America

First Printing: October 2025

DEDICATION

People said you couldn't.
They said it behind your back.
They said it to others when they knew you'd hear about it.
They even told you to your face.
They made you feel like you shouldn't.
They made the most basic things seem impossible.
They made you scared to try.
But you did it anyway.

Even then, they didn't stop trying to make you feel small.
Well...

They don't get to win.
So you did it again.
And again.
And again.
You never stopped.
I fucking love that about you.

1

JANUARY 19, 2024

Midas

"Nova, I need an optimized path to get inside the school grounds!" Midas shouted. He ducked as debris from the corner of the building showered into his scalp-cropped brown hair. Yeah. Probably should be wearing his helmet, but he hated being able to see it on the outskirts of his vision. He'd take his chances.

"Parameters?" the AI requested.

The sound of helicopter rotors distracted him, getting louder by the second. Looking up, he stood with his back tight to the wall as it skimmed into view. It was a green helo, which meant it didn't belong to the men firing at him. The cavalry had arrived. Unfortunately, that meant he was likely to have a visitor he wasn't particularly interested in seeing right now. He just couldn't catch a break, could he?

Ignoring the helo for now, he dared another look around the corner of the building, this time nearly losing a soulful brown eye to a chunk of the building's square edge shot out by a bullet. "Fuck!" he yelled, leaning tight to the building once more.

Between the deafening thwap-thwap of the helicopter's blades and the echoes of close-range gunfire, he brought his watch up to his mouth to answer Nova's female voice. "Consider distance from my location to the school, the most current grid layout of the city, stationary objects, and factor in time of day. Project movement of mobile targets based on precedents set with previous movements made, ignoring the helicopter directly above my coordinates unless considering it as a possible distraction for the soldiers or as an escape route."

"Calculating."

A voice tinged with an Afrikaans accent came out of nowhere, along with a rope that dropped from the belly of the helo. "Too late to crash this party?"

Midas looked up and was saved from a reply because a man had already flung himself through the bottom port, a dog strapped to his front. When the body hit the ground, the newcomer gave the rope a yank, and it retracted back up inside the helicopter, which then took off.

He glanced over at the man, his fraternal twin, whom he hadn't seen in person in almost six months. "Who invited you?" Midas grumbled.

The blond flung his arms wide. "No one invited me, bro. Heard there was a party, so here I am."

He began unhooking the canine, a golden Egyptian street dog he'd rescued from Sallum two years ago. She'd been a hot mess when he found her. Starving, mothering two pups, flea-ridden, and beaten by the men who used her as a guard dog at their warehouse, she'd imprinted on Nemo when he fed her a tube of peanut butter, and her devotion was absolute.

"Fashionably late and making an entrance, as always."

"Correct." Nemo's superhero smile and the wink of his baby blues gave a lightness to the mess he'd inserted himself into.

"I see Gem hasn't taken you to the surgeon yet to get that twitch in your eye fixed." Sometimes he wondered what the little pixie saw in his brother.

Free of her safety harness, Scheherazade made short work of greeting Midas, standing on her hind legs, ears perked, and nosing his belt for treats. He gave her head a solid rubbing between the ears. "Sorry, girl. No treats right now. Didn't know I'd be seeing you."

The dog chuffed her disappointment, licked his hand as if to say, "That's okay," and then moved to heel at Nemo's side.

"She loves me, tics and all."

"Someone should give her a physical. And a rabies shot. And a free head-shrinking session."

"Nah. Gem's fine. No one's playing doctor with her but me." Nemo looked around. "Speaking of medical play, where is Tuberculosis? Shouldn't he and his subbie be helping you?"

Midas snorted, half in humor and half in disbelief at his brother's cheek. "If Steel hears you calling him TB's submissive, you're going to be on a leash, naked, with a red-hot ass, and tied to a pole in the Arctic Circle."

"That was oddly specific. Hey! But then at least I can tell Santa in person what I want for Christmas."

Shaking his head, Midas muttered, "You are so broken." After chancing a look around the corner of the building, the brothers returned fire on the men who had spotted them, then Midas filled Nemo in on his teammate's whereabouts. "TB and Steel got hung up about three blocks south. I've been relegated to scout because *somebody* decided to hook up with a cat burglar, get all respectable, and then abandon my ass to hang in the wind so that he could work with the enemy."

"One, Gem says hello. Two, I will never be respectable. And three, Mythos is not the enemy. We're on the same side." Nemo glanced at Midas. "Thought for sure Waters would have replaced me by now. Kinda makes me all warm and fuzzy to know the boss thinks

I'm irreplaceable." Nemo cleared his rifle from his shoulder. "What's the situ?"

Midas pulled his desert-colored balaclava up over his face to study his brother. It was hard to believe they were twins, even fraternal ones. They truly looked next to nothing alike.

Nemo stood just under six feet tall and weighed in at just under two hundred pounds, looking the part of a footballer. Aside from his Captain America good looks, he was golden tan year-round from being outside, covered in tattoos, and pierced everywhere. Rumor had it, he'd even pierced his dick, something that made Midas shudder over how painful that had to have been.

Midas was his complete antithesis—pale from spending most of his time stuck in a computer lab, although lately he'd been leading more projects and getting outside more, tattoo- and piercing-free, and built like a rugby player.

"Nobody briefed you?" Midas asked. His voice came out rougher than he'd intended, but his brother had that effect on him since his defection to Mythos.

Nemo sighed. "Calm down, grasshopper," he cautioned. "I know the basics. One of the Mythos compounds was attacked before it could be completely evacuated, their guards were immobilized, and we're going in to find the last five kids and the teacher. I meant, why are we *here* and not *there*?" He gestured at the gated compound down the street.

"Can't get there from here." Midas grunted. "No clue who these fuckwitches are. Nova's working on scenarios."

On cue, Nova came online. "I have calculated five possible routes to the compound, organized from shortest to longest distance of travel."

"It's fucking three blocks," Nemo muttered. "We can see it from here."

Midas rolled his eyes. "Yes, but can you see if there are more shitweasels lying in wait? No, you can't, so we look at options." He dipped out around the corner, and a hail of bullets hit the edge of the building, a chip hitting him in the face and scratching him under the eye. "Fuck this noise! I'm so done with this bullshit. Nova!" he barked. "Reassess and reprioritize the list in descending order of threat level."

"Calculating." After two seconds, the AI returned. "The least level of threat is to continue to the east three blocks, then alternate one block north and one block east for one half mile, make your way to the river, then use the tributary to access the compound."

"What the fuck? That means heading away from the target," Nemo murmured.

"Yeah, not what I was hoping for." He turned his attention back to the AI program. "Nova, what is the estimated time of arrival to the compound with that trajectory?"

"Using that route, it would take an estimated nineteen hours and forty-two minutes to access the compound."

"What the ever lovin' fuck? Why so long?" Nemo asked.

"There are an estimated seventeen hostile targets," she continued. "All scenarios using the combatants of Midas, Steel, and TB suggest that stealth and patience are the prudent option. This includes waiting for nightfall to access the grounds."

Nemo grabbed Midas' wrist and spoke into the watch face. "Add Nemo in with those combatants."

"Great," Midas muttered. "That'll increase the time frame." With a gentle shove to Nemo's shoulder, he moved his twin over. "Waiting for nightfall is not an option, Nova. Reassess for alternative ingress."

"Query. 'Alternative'?"

"Ways we can enter the property that are not normal. Things other than doors, windows, over the walls, or other ways that are obvious entries for a human. Speed is of optimum importance."

"Understood. Calculating."

Frowning, Nemo smacked him on the shoulder. "Why the rush? The people in the compound have been cut off for four days. There're kids in there. We need to have the least amount of risk. I don't like it, but they can make it one more day."

"No, they can't," Midas corrected him. "No water. No electricity. No clue about food, given the extensive damage to the buildings. Five kids under the age of around ten. The only ones left were an elderly teacher and the last Mythos guard. At his last report, he was bleeding out and knew we wouldn't make it in time to save him, and he said the teacher was unconscious. That was two days ago, and he hasn't answered a call since. They can't afford nineteen minutes, let alone nineteen hours."

"This doesn't make any sense. What the hell would these guys want with five orphans and a nun?" Nemo wondered. "Did they capture any of them?"

"Yeah. Another teacher. We found her about six hours ago. Wasn't pretty. No sign of the children."

"Fuckers," Nemo whispered under his breath. They were quiet for a moment. Nemo uttered another expletive. "They've got to be Salieri brethren."

"Nothing else makes any sense," Midas replied. "The kids aren't orphans of any political significance, and the facility isn't government-run."

"But it doesn't make sense," Nemo said. "How did they know where the compound was? And why would they want the girls back, given their paradigm of sacrificing all the females in the line? There's got to be a better way to staff their mines than recapturing kids we took back from them."

The AI's voice interrupted their discussion. "I have managed to find an alternative route, but it will be a difficult entry."

With a snort, Midas shook his head. "When isn't it, Nova?"

"On November seventh, you made an uninterrupted ingress—"

"It was a figure of speech, Nova. It meant, 'It's always difficult.'"

Nemo grinned. "She needs more tweaking."

"That sounds so wrong." Midas sighed. "Sarcasm isn't easy for a machine."

"It's not easy for a lot of humans either."

Midas redirected the conversation. "What's the plan, Nova?"

"Along the eastern wall, approximately twenty-five yards from the northern corner, there is a drainage gate. It is large enough that the average adult human can move through it if they crawl. Entering through this tunnel will allow combatants to enter without detection, as all opposing forces appear to be at the south end of the compound, guarding the front gate."

He heard Nemo groan. "Better not be full of sewage."

Midas grinned. "Not the first time you've crawled through shit to get somewhere."

"Yeah, but that was when I was in a hurry to get *out*. I never would have done it to get *inside* somewhere."

"You love this shit—pun intended. You're not happy unless you're getting dirty."

"I just hope Demon's got enough penicillin for everybody." A finger poked Midas in the chest, then gestured to Scheherazade. "If my girl here gets sick, I'm kicking the shit out of you."

The dog barked as if adding her agreement.

"Nova, please tell all combatants to meet at the drainage tunnel along the south wall, and tell Cerberus we need a distraction in order to get there. Something to keep the gatekeepers busy."

"Copy that, Midas."

The two men waited in silence. The dog sat, on alert, at Nemo's heel. After a few minutes, a new male voice dropped into the channel. "Prepare for the boom."

"Fuckin' Cerberus. Why are we always 'preparing' for shit? Just do it already," Nemo mumbled to himself.

"Still not getting along with Gem's ex? Figured you two would be bros by now."

Using his pocket scope, Nemo got down on his knees and peered around the corner of the building as delicately as he could. "He's not her ex. Yes, we've hugged our shit out, metaphorically speaking, because I'm not into threesomes. And no, we're not 'bros.' We're never going to be 'bros.' I already have a brother, one I'm quite fond of," Nemo admitted. "One that I miss, even if he is pissed at me."

Darting a look to his right, Midas saw that while Nemo's focus was on the gate down the street in front of them, his tight posture and expression said he meant what he was saying. Immediately, Midas felt bad for sniping at him and used the man's given name to show he was sorry. "Sawyer... I..."

"Nothing needs to be said, Kash." Nemo returned the respect as he moved back to safety and glanced over at his twin. "You're my brother. I love you. I know you love me, too, even if I'm a pain in your ass." He gave Midas a smack on the back of his shoulder. "Now, focus, my young Padawan. If I'm not mistaken, our three-headed-dog friend is about to make things go click-click-boom in a most delightful way."

There was a hollow sound, like a firework coming out of a mortar. Mouth agape, Midas couldn't believe what he was seeing. A canister flew from somewhere behind and to the left, trailing rainbow-colored smoke. When it finally hit the ground, the canister rolled until it hit the gate, but it didn't explode. It merely lay on the ground, puffing out multicolored mist. After a minute or so, it stopped smoking. Foolishly, one of the younger soldiers stepped forward and picked it up off the ground to look it over. Still, nothing happened. Several of the guards gathered a little closer. Finally, there was a loud pop as the flash bang grenade canister exploded.

The young man who had been holding the canister clutched his face and dropped to the ground in agony. The sound of five muted thumps was followed by five flying objects toward the gate. As soon as the objects landed, Nemo grabbed Midas by the arm and hauled him toward the opposite corner of the building. "Time to go!"

A chain of five loud explosions sounded, followed by screams from some of the men at the gate. Using the distraction, the two men and the dog took off, ran three blocks east, then turned left and ran for what was the northeast corner of the compound. When they hit the southeast corner, Midas spared a quick look at the main gate, noticing it was still shrouded in smoke and chaos from the modified grenades, then put all his focus back on his brother and the dog, who were easily fifty yards ahead of him. Nemo, that fucker, was still faster than fast.

TB and Steel were nowhere to be seen. Midas tapped his watch to call out to them on their comms. "TB! Where are you?"

TB came over the speaker. "I'm a little busy here."

"Well, get unbusy. We need you at the northeast corner of the compound. What's your ETA?"

"Hopefully, less than ten minutes. We managed to grab one of the soldiers. We're securing him now, and Medusa is coming to collect him. Go ahead. We'll catch up shortly."

"Copy that." Midas turned to his brother. "Ready?"

"Let's get dirty," Nemo replied.

Since he didn't speak German, the typical language for K9s, Nemo'd trained her in his native tongue of Afrikaans. "Scheherazade, *lei die pad!*"

Instantly, the dog's whole demeanor changed. She'd made huge strides since being rescued. She went from a tongue-lolling, ears-perking goofball to a working dog in the span of the four words uttered. Nose twitching, she headed into the tunnel, her small frame easily fitting inside the clearance. Nemo followed her, able to fit through if he crawled on his hands and knees. Midas was pretty much reduced to crawling on his belly, given his larger frame.

"Thank goodness it's dry," Nemo called over his shoulder.

"Yeah. It doesn't look like anything has come through here in ages. Pretty much clean as the day it was built. Bet Mythos cleaned it and rerouted the drainage to use this for a possible escape route." He switched gears. "Nova, is the end of the pipe clear of targets?"

"Confirmed. All heat signatures are around the main gate, but there are a few in buildings on the main thoroughfare of the compound's western side."

It took just a few minutes to traverse the pipeway. However, as they approached the end of the tunnel, Nova stopped them. "Correction, Midas. Some of the targets from outside have joined those who were inside the gate. They are doing emergency triage on those affected by Cerberus' diversion."

"Scheherazade, *stop*," Nemo commanded.

Luck, or more likely, smart thinking on the part of Mythos, was with them. Blocking the opening of the drainage pipe was a rusted-out pickup truck parked near a garden shed. Neither looked like they had been used in some time, but Midas knew that with Mythos, looks were often deceiving. The pickup might look like shit, but it would run like a brand-new machine. The sagging roof and peeling paint of the shed were camouflage for whatever was actually inside. Mythos was more than adept at hiding what they didn't want people to see.

A sudden sound of gunfire broke into his thoughts. Another explosion, bigger this time, rocked the ground, and the sound of collapsing concrete reached them.

Cerberus piped into the channel, "That was not me, gentlemen."

"Well, that's not good," Nemo quipped.

Quickly yanking his balaclava into position, then lowering his goggles, Midas watched as smoke poured out of a nearby building. His brother did the same, then pulled a specialized dog version from his belt, putting them on Scheherazade.

"The building they hit is not the one we've been told is our target. That tells me they don't know where to look. We don't have long before they hit it simply by guesswork. Nemo and I are headed in. TB and Steel, you'll have to catch up when you can."

The building they were headed to was directly catty-corner to the one that had been taken down. To his right, his brother covered him from possible enemy fire as Midas took off from the relative safety of the pickup truck to a wooded area directly south of their current location. Once he arrived safely, Scheherazade took off after him at a dead run, followed closely by Nemo, with Midas providing cover. The men had done this so often in their years of working for Tribe that even with Nemo's recent switch to working for Mythos, it came as second nature.

A glint came from an upper right-hand window in the nearest

building, and Midas realized the guerilla soldier was tracking Nemo. He raised his weapon, fired, and heard the quick scream of the man behind the glint and then nothing.

"Nova, we had a surprise guest in the northeast corner. Sweep the buildings again for heat signatures."

"Nemo?" A voice came through the ear comm. It was Midas' team leader.

"Yo, Waters!"

"I've lost Midas. He's offline. Where is he?"

"To my left."

Nemo flicked his brother's body cam. In return, Midas pinched the top of Nemo's ear.

"*Doos,*" they said in sync with each other.

He marveled at how some things would never change between them, no matter how far apart they were, or how long it had been since they'd seen each other.

"Okay, he's back now," Waters confirmed. "I need you two to take cover and wait for TB and Steel."

"Copy that," Midas replied.

The two brothers used their movement technique to hide behind another truck parked in front of the closest building. Gunfire followed them.

"You know, hunkering down behind a truck that's probably got a full tank of petrol is probably not our smartest move," Midas yelled over the noise.

A voice came over the comms that wasn't out of breath, but it definitely belonged to someone hauling ass. "Midas! Nemo! We're coming at you through the pipe. We're going to need cover to get to you."

"Roger that, TB," Midas returned. He looked at Nemo, and his grin got bigger. "I barely fit through that thing. Can't wait to see how he gets through."

"He's so gonna get stuck. New nickname. Winnie-the-TB." Nemo snickered.

Both men chuckled. TB was six foot seven and two hundred forty pounds. He was all muscle, but his size often made normal activities a challenge, which made for great humor to the rest of his teammates.

Again, without thinking, Midas dropped to one knee, just behind the rear passenger tire, taking the low position. Nemo squatted just under the passenger side mirror, ready to take the high position over the hood. Scheherazade moved between his legs.

A barrage of bullets began again, although now it was above them and toward the tunnel, following the new moving targets.

"This is fucking crazy!" Midas groused. "I don't care who you are, it takes a special kind of twisted to bomb a fucking school, then guard it."

"Ah, brother, where's your spirit of adventure? Kids and women in a bombed-out building. This is the day we were made for."

"No, we were made for stealing stuff. We got caught doing that, and now we're here, about to get caught with our dicks hanging out."

A grumpy voice came over the comms. "Not enough ear bleach. Please put that shit away."

It was a joke, of course, to try and get Midas' mood to relax, but he didn't want to tell his team leader that it wasn't working. Nemo's unannounced arrival was making him grumpy. Just over fifteen months ago, his brother had left Tribe, a company the twins had worked at together for five years previously. Occasionally, he saw his brother on video chat when their two groups worked in parallel, or even together, but Midas was still salty over his leaving.

Nemo had left Tribe and his brother because he'd met and fallen in love with a woman who worked for Mythos, a group Tribe had been working with loosely, when they ended up helping with the rescue of TB's woman. Nemo had to follow her if they wanted to be together because her contract wasn't up for a few more years, and she felt obligated to stay to help stop a globally organized crime group called the Salieri that operated like a cult. Nemo, also, was under a contract of sorts, but he'd been given permission to leave for reasons Midas never understood. Well, to be honest, he'd never been told what the reasons were, and probably never would be.

Midas didn't begrudge him falling in love, but he was definitely jealous. His twin had always been a playboy, playing loose and fast with any woman who was willing, and there had been a lot of willing women. Now he was committed and happy. Midas had always been the steadfast one. The dependable one. If either of them were to end up with someone, it should have been him, so yes... definitely jealous. And lonely.

For years, Midas and his teammates had assumed that relationships wouldn't be possible for them. After all, they were "dead." Ghosts. Graves marked their untimely deaths under accidental circumstances, and the world went on turning. No relationships with friends, family, or lovers meant no vulnerability. Tribe had already tragically lost one member that way. They hadn't been about to do it again.

However, things had changed recently. One by one, his team had fallen in love with some amazing women, and the relationship rule got booted from the "company manual." That left Midas as one of two remaining singles in the group. Hardly surprising, really. He left their offices the least, tied to his computers, until recently, when he was tapped to run the ground operations on projects. The closest he'd been to a woman in years was Nova, his AI creation, and she was only "female" because he'd given her a female voice. Hell... she was the closest he'd come to female companionship *ever*.

Shoving that thought back into a box, locking it, and pushing it aside, he realized that as pissy as he was at this moment, this day was clearly about to go up shit creek without a paddle, a life vest, or even an actual kayak. Pissy wasn't even going to begin to cover his mood when this was all said and done.

"I've got eyes on the dynamic duo," Nemo yelled above the gunfire.

The two newly arrived were barreling toward them when suddenly, an explosion hit directly behind Steel, the Latino man of the pair, causing him to stumble. The giant man with him stopped and fired a spray of bullets to hopefully prevent getting shot while he backtracked the few steps to pick his friend up off the ground.

"Incoming," came a woman's voice over the comm.

"Medusa, what do you see from up there?"

From her helicopter above, the pilot spit out, "Four assholes loading a mortar. Angle suggests it's aimed directly at the area of the truck. I'd get the fuck out of the way, boys. I'm on my way toward them, but it's still not a good idea to be there."

They heard the rotors of Medusa's helicopter above their heads and sprang into action, both moving down the road inside the compound. They'd made it about twenty-five feet when there was a boom in the distance.

"Watch out," the woman yelled. "I didn't beat them to firing. Inbound!"

A loud explosion hit, the aftershock propelling Midas into his brother, who collided with a tree along the dirt roadway. Scheherazade went flying, but into the open area of the dirt road. Immediately, she was back up on her legs and racing to Nemo, her tongue washing his face.

"Easy, girl. I'm okay," he shouted.

"Maybe you are, but I'm not." Midas shoved his brother off of him with a grunt. "You really should be a softer landing pad."

"That's what happens when every inch of me is muscle."

Bullets started up again, narrowly missing the two sniping brothers as they crab-crawled into a recessed brick doorway of a commissary with a massive picture window. "Well, this isn't good," Nemo observed.

"No, it's not. I give it ten seconds."

Bullets immediately sprayed the window behind and above them, glass nicking Midas' face. Nemo covered the dog with his body to protect her. A rapid glance up showed Midas that the shooters were out of sight, probably in a building catty-corner to them on the second or third floor.

"Your AI is slipping, bro," Nemo chastised. "Didn't you ask her to search for heat signatures?"

Midas grunted. "They could be shielding themselves. Nova, how are we on finding those targets?"

"All I am finding is a single signature in the far southeast corner of the original building."

"Only one?"

"It is larger than a standard signature for an adult."

"People huddled together in a small, confined space?" Nemo suggested.

"Likely." Midas looked at the dog. "How's our girl?" Midas felt a slimy lick on his hand at the bottom of his gun. A quick scratch to her jowl and he was back in focus mode.

"She's got a cut on her ear, but otherwise, I think she's okay."

Midas tapped back into his watch. "This channel remains open to all until the project is complete. We've got opposition above us. Second, maybe third floor. We're sitting ducks as soon as we leave the shelter of this building. From the drainage pipe, I could see curtains fluttering in the second window from the corner. Asshats have no clue about countermeasures, but that doesn't make them less deadly." He checked his rifle magazine, then checked his brother. "You okay?"

"Yep."

"Make yourselves small and duck out of the way. Here I come," Medusa informed them.

A hail of bullets rained down in the middle of the dirt road in a straight line, kicking up dust and debris, followed by a green heli-copter flying low to the street. As it approached the building in ques-tion, the bullets flew up the side of the building and sprayed into the windows where two men had just appeared to take shots at the men below.

TB and Steel sped from the trees, then took shelter behind what was left of the truck that the two brothers had been behind a few moments ago.

"What's the plan, Midas?"

"Waiting on the compass."

Nova's voice came online again. "After the second building to the south is a narrow alley that comes alongside the back of the identified building. Schematics show that the first door on the left goes into the main entryway. There are four doorways once inside. One on the west wall leads to the kitchen, one to a closet, and one to a small classroom on the east wall, and one to a hallway on the south wall, which leads to a set of stairs. Those stairs lead to additional classrooms on the second and third floors. A final set of stairs on the third floor will lead you to the roof. The heat signature is located in the small classroom."

"Roger that," Midas replied. "Okay, you heard her. Nemo, you have point. TB, you have our six, so let us know when we're good to move."

2

JANUARY 19, 2024

Midas

A QUICK ASSESSMENT OF THE STREET SITUATION HAD TB AND Steel assuming positions behind the truck, much like those Nemo and Midas had assumed earlier. Providing the necessary cover, Steel called to the brothers to head out. With Scheherazade tight to Nemo's side, they began to head toward the alley, ducking into recessed doorways as they went, covering each other as they moved.

"Watch out!"

A single shot fired, and a body leaned out a window and hung there by the waist. A rifle clattered to the street. Nemo pulled back his gun and looked at his brother. "That's thirteen, big bro."

"Really? You're counting? How many times over the years have I saved your ass?"

"You're wasting your breath, Midas," TB yelled. "Nitwit can't count that high."

Nemo shouted, "Hey! T-Rex! Pipe down. With your big head and little, tiny arms, I'm amazed you can even hold a rifle."

"Get some original material, Nerfherder!"

"All right, ladies," their team leader growled over the comm, "put the claws away and get moving. Focus on what's in front of you. Remember, we have no idea what you're going to find in there."

"ETA on our exit vehicle?" Midas asked.

"Demon, Loki, and Gilgamesh are a half mile out. Once we know what you've got, they're on their way in. They ran into a little trouble of their own and are just mopping up."

"Christ, who's driving?"

Their team leader chuckled.

Nemo spared a quick look at his brother, who glanced back at him. "Shit. Loki. That's worse than TB driving."

TB grunted. "At least it's not Medusa."

Her voice came over the comm. "I heard that. Just for that, it's on like Donkey Kong when we're safe."

Steel groaned. "Waters must be letting her hang out with Kubrick."

TB grunted.

Nemo grinned at his brother. "And you know what that means. Mario Kart Wars. Awesome! You lost last time. You get to be Princess Peach."

Midas grumbled something about wishing he'd strangled him in the womb. His brother was his blood, but he was also a royal pain in the ass, had absolutely no filter, and was totally inappropriate at all times... even in the middle of a firefight. He made it difficult most of the time, but... in his heart, he loved him.

Steel posted himself on the far side of the door to the entryway, eyes above, rifle at the ready in case someone came at them from the windows, with TB watching at the mouth of the alley looking for soldiers to come at them. Nemo was at the door, rifle slung across his back, mini battering ram at the ready, while Midas stood along the far wall, rifle aimed at the doorway to follow on Nemo's six. Scheherazade was poised to enter through the door.

Midas counted down on his fingers.

Three! Two! One!

With the clenching of Midas' fist, Nemo slammed the door with all his might once, twice, and on the third bang, the door went off its hinges and hung only by the bottom two. Scheherazade flew in, barking up a storm, Nemo right behind her. Midas followed, with Steel yelling at TB to make his way down the alley to them. Once TB was through the door, Steel followed, staying in the doorway as their lookout.

"Medusa," he yelled, "you got me?"

"You're covered, Steel, but you might want to cover your ears and heads. I'm dropping now."

They all hunched down as they heard the whistle of a missile and then felt the shock of it hitting the building next door. "That should keep them scrambling for a few minutes. Hurry up, gentlemen, my dance card is getting full."

TB looked up at Steel. "That woman has a case of B.A."

Steel smirked. "Badass?"

"No. Bad attitude."

The men gave a quick set of smiles all around, then stood and scanned the room. It was empty but totally destroyed. Shelving had fallen over, support pillars were showing fresh cracks, beams were split and groaning, and in some spots, they could see through the ceiling of the first floor up to the second and third floors.

The men split into pairs, Steel and TB heading up the stairs to clear the upper levels, or what was left of them. Nemo cleared the closet, then he and Midas did the same for the kitchen. The four men reunited in the main entryway, ready to enter the schoolroom.

"Nova," Midas called, "how's our heat signature?"

"Unchanged, Midas. It is in the northwest corner of the room."

In the same formation they used to enter the building, the men battered down the door and went in. Standing in the doorway of the enclosed space, they marveled at the destruction. The only thing left in one piece was a heavy oak cabinet that was probably used to store supplies.

"Fuck my life, how is anything in here alive?" TB whispered.

"Scheherazade, *soek*," Nemo commanded. He slung the battering ram over his back opposite his rifle and withdrew his pistol from his holster at his hip.

The dog yipped and put her nose to the rubble. Unerringly, she headed to the cabinet and alerted.

Nemo picked his way across the room to the dog, with Midas just behind him and to the right. TB swung around to the far wall behind them, and Steel remained in the doorway. "*Goeie meisie*," Nemo praised.

Nodding at Midas, he trained his pistol on the door, and Midas whipped it open. A collective gasp from inside the cabinet was followed by whimpers of fear.

Nemo barked, "Waters, we have five friendlies."

"All right, people," the team leader ordered. "Loki is about a click away. He'll block the alley. Medusa, we're going to need eyes in the sky to get them loaded."

"Roger, Waters."

A grumble came over the line at her joke. "Not funny," Waters mumbled.

"I'll make sure to blast his music while we Mario Kart, then," she snipped back.

"You're fired."

"You're not my boss. You can't fire me. You try it, and next time, we'll leave Midas home with Kubrick."

"Then I'd see you in hell," he quipped back.

All they heard on the other end of the comms was laughter. Over the last few months, the two had become close since they were the recognized team leaders of their respective groups. They were constantly going at each other. Medusa had absolutely no interest in

Waters, and vice versa, but if Midas hadn't known better, he'd have thought they were brother and sister.

By now, Nemo had lowered his pistol and holstered it. Five little girls, ranging from a baby to around ten, were huddled together, crying and shaking.

"Hello there, little ones," Midas said. He got down on one knee. "Do you speak English?"

The eldest girl nodded.

"Everyone okay? Anyone hurt?"

The girl who had just nodded was awkwardly holding a baby in one arm, while the other arm was bent at an odd angle and clearly broken. Clutching the sleeve of the girl with the broken arm was probably the youngest of the children, other than the baby. She had a gash at her temple that had bled and was now scabbed over. She was the quietest of the bunch, crying without sound, looking stunned, and likely suffering a concussion. The two other girls, who appeared to be twins, were dirty, had minor cuts and abrasions, but other than being petrified, they seemed okay.

"Demon, we've got at least one broken arm and one possible concussion. Other minor injuries."

"Roger that. I'm ready. Give me the broken arm first, if you can."

Catching movement out of the corner of his eye, Midas saw TB bend down to touch something. His eyes drew to a sensible shoe attached to a leg encased in shredded tights and a polyester knee-length skirt. The rest of the body was underneath a student desk and some rubble from the ceiling. TB looked over at Midas and shook his head.

"Team leader," Midas reported, "one deceased. Adult. Female. No child bodies that we can see."

"Copy that, Midas. Loki is blocking the alleyway. Get them out of there."

Nemo grabbed the baby from the eldest girl, and then Midas lifted her and the one with the head wound into his arms. The little one had her thumb in her mouth, big, rounded eyes, and a death grip on his sleeve. The two were probably sisters. TB grabbed the twins, and Steel returned to the door as their lookout again.

Bullets rained in the street toward the opposite buildings. Up above, Medusa's helicopter laid down cover fire. As fast as their legs would carry them, the men ran out of the school building and into the alleyway. When Midas got to the back of the truck, he quickly handed over the girl with the broken arm, then the second child. In an assembly line, the men handed the children to Midas, who handed them to Demon and Gilgamesh, who loaded them toward the front of the vehicle. By the time the baby was on board, Demon was already working on the first child.

The men were attempting to help cover Midas loading the truck when he felt a tug on his arm. It was the little girl who had been sucking her thumb. The one holding onto the other girl he'd carried to the truck. "Miss Mouse," she whispered, tears streaking down her face.

"What, sweetheart?" he asked. He could barely hear her.

"Miss Mouse." The child whimpered.

Midas thought back to the woman under the rubble. "Is Miss Mouse a toy or your teacher, little one?"

"She's our teacher," her older sister said from the back of the truck.

Midas looked down at the crying child, then back to the girl getting her arm splinted. "I'm sorry, girls, but Miss Mouse won't be coming with us."

"You can't leave her," the girl in the back cried. "She saved us."

Midas grimaced. "I'm sorry, but she's too hurt to come with us. Someone will find her." He hated lying, but he didn't have time to placate the child's fears.

"No, that's Sister Mary," she corrected him. "Sister was killed in the first big boom. Miss Mouse is still inside. She was over by the wall and shoved us all into the cupboard. Then she went to do something, and she never came back."

Midas swore, then looked at TB, who shrugged.

"Waters," Midas spoke into his comm. "One more possible friendly. A teacher. We need to go in and look."

"Not a lot of time, Midas," their team leader warned. "Our hostiles are regrouping."

"I'm not leaving without checking," he came back. "What does she look like, sweetheart?"

"Brown hair, tall."

"Anyone's going to be tall to her," TB murmured under his breath.

"Is she young or old?"

"She looks like a Disney princess."

"Three minutes, Midas, that's all you get," Waters directed.

"Fuck, we can barely get into that room again and back to the truck in three minutes," Nemo grumbled.

"Keep chatting like a coffee klatch, and it's going to be two. After that, I'll have Medusa leave your lazy asses behind."

Midas shared a look with his brother, who looked at the dog gazing at him.

"Scheherazade, *soek!*" Following his command to the dog, Nemo went after her in a loping gait back into the school building. Midas was next, then TB, with Steel in tow as cover. TB was grousing the whole way. "I didn't see another body. She's probably dead."

"I'm not leaving a person behind if there's one alive," Midas growled. "Fan out."

The men canvassed the outer room one more time, but no body was found. Scheherazade, finding nothing, went back into the classroom where the children had been, and seemed to be concentrating heavily on a large pile of rubble that had come down on top of a bookshelf. She alerted.

"Fuck!" Midas yelled. "Over here."

Rifle slung over his shoulder, he began to grab chunks of concrete off the bookshelf and threw them behind him. The three other men joined in.

"One minute, guys," the voice over the comm said.

"I think it's less!" Medusa yelled. "We've got unfriendlies, count of twenty, and coming in fast. Several have grenade launchers the size of a cow."

"Let's hustle, guys," Waters ordered.

"Incoming!"

"What is so fucking special about these particular kids?" TB mumbled.

The rebels launched a barrage of grenades at the building. The walls shook, concrete and dust showering down from the ceiling on the men as they covered their heads. "Almost there. She's under this bookcase," Midas confirmed.

As the last of the debris on top of the shelving was cleared, beams began creaking above. "Midas, there's no time," TB warned.

"Shut up and lift! Put that Frankenstein strength to better use than flapping your grouchy mouth."

Nemo and TB crawled up to the top of the shelving unit and the pile of concrete beneath it and began to lift the shelf. "You're going to have to drag her out, bro," Nemo told him. "Too much weight on the bottom of this thing to toss it clear."

Midas prostrated himself on the ground and shone his penlight underneath. There she was. A mass of brown, tangled hair, skin, and clothes covered in concrete dust, her head turned away from him. "Miss, can you hear me?" Silence. "Miss, are you hurt?" Still silence. In the darkness beneath the shelf, he couldn't see if she was breathing or not. "Pulling her out."

Just as he was about to do so, another blast hit the building, this one bigger than the last. "Dammit, Medusa, a little warning next time would be nice!" TB growled.

"Sorry, but we've got problems. We need to get those kids out of here. Loki, take off. I'll take care of the guys."

"Copy, Medusa." They heard the truck roaring away amidst the gunfire being exchanged and the grenades.

"Do you see stairs, Steel?" Medusa called out.

"Cleared the roof once. Heading there again." Steel went running to the doorway and up the stairs.

"Your three minutes are long past, Midas. Out. Now. Teacher or no teacher."

"We are not leaving her." Midas grunted and pulled on the arm closest to him. "TB, I really need you to dig deep and get that bookcase higher. She's pinned."

"Fuck," he growled, then did as Midas asked. A giant heave later, the bookshelf was about two inches higher, and Midas pulled again. She began to come free. As soon as her body cleared the rubble, TB and Nemo let go of the bookshelf, the resounding crash echoing in the room. More concrete dust came down from above as another mortar hit the building, and the walls shook.

"Medusa, what's the plan?" Midas barked over the comm.

Medusa's voice came in static-filled and broken. "Get... the roof... come out... land."

"Can you land on that little space?"

TB looked at Midas like he was speaking a foreign language. "Did you seriously just fucking ask Medusa if she could land up there?"

"Forgive me, Daddy, for I have sinned," Midas grouched.

TB grunted. "Not into age-play, muppet brother. Bondage. Which I'm going to put you in if you call me Daddy again."

"Save your fetishes for another time, gentlemen," Waters relayed in their ears.

"Pardon my incredulous question, but I don't particularly want to get my ass shot off after rescuing those kids, then coming back in here for the teacher," Midas complained.

He gathered up the woman in his arms, not even checking to see if she was breathing or worrying about injuring her further. There was no time. Nemo and Scheherazade led the way, followed by Midas with the teacher, and TB bringing up the rear.

It was only a few seconds after they got to the doorway of the roof where Steel waited when they heard the hail of bullets coming down onto the streets and the deafening sound of the rotors of the helicopter. All Midas could see through the narrow entryway was a footbar, then the doorway of the helicopter.

"Next stop, Madame Tussauds," Medusa intoned. "Have your tickets ready for the conductor, gentlemen."

Steel looked behind the chopper, knowing that Medusa's eagle eyes were on what was in front. Nemo ran and jumped inside with Scheherazade next to him, then looked to the east and west before motioning to Midas to follow him through the door. TB served as his escort, vaulted in across the doorway from Nemo, and both men reached out to Midas, pulling him up by his biceps and hauling him with the woman still in his arms into the helicopter. As he laid her across the bench seat, Steel brought up the rear, shooting at their assailants to cover his own ass. Medusa was already taking off before he was even inside or had the door closed.

"Fucking Christ, woman, how many times do I have to tell you not to do that?" he yelled.

"Apparently not enough!" she yelled back. "Quit whining like a little girl. We're in the pipe. Buckle up."

"How's it going, boys and girls?" Waters asked on the comm.

"Hairy as Sasquatch, but I'll get them out."

"Excellent, Medusa. Loki's already past the checkpoint and hauling ass to the rendezvous. Keep in touch, and we'll see you there."

"Roger that."

It wasn't until that moment that Midas finally looked down at the woman he'd pulled from the rubble. Her back was arched oddly. Gently rolling her to her side, he noticed the backpack she had on for the first time. Odd. His eyes traveled up to her face, and he inhaled sharply.

Whoa. Disney princesses got nothing on this woman!

He moved to where her head lay, gently raising it and praying she didn't have a neck injury. He slid underneath her, placing her head on his thigh. "Nemo, triage!" he hollered.

Nemo knelt down at the woman's side and began checking her over. His normal playboy-comedian style went away with a snap. "Massive head contusion, probably from concrete falling, possibly even the shelf hitting her." He pulled up an eyelid. "Pinpoint pupils. Likely concussed. Out cold, but she's breathing." He began running his hands down the rest of her, and when he got to her ribs, he began to unbutton her blouse.

"Really, dude?" his brother questioned.

"Shut up. Her skin is on fire, even through her shirt. I need to see."

Sure enough, when the shirt opened and bared her skin, her entire left side was a mass of bruising and cuts. Definitely cracked ribs. A number of them by the naked eye.

Nemo continued his triage. "Ankle completely swollen, possibly broken."

"Cover her up."

Nemo began to rebutton her shirt. "Awwww, somebody feeling possessive?"

Scheherazade stood up on Midas' knee and cocked her head to look at the woman. She gently licked the hand lying across her middle. "*Goeie meisie*, Zade," he complimented her. He looked down at the woman and noticed that there was movement behind her eyelids. "Come on, Miss Mouse, open your eyes."

There was a groan, a minuscule shift in his embrace, and her eyelids tried to open. Scheherazade reached up and licked the woman's cheek. The swath of her big pink tongue cut through the dust and grime. She really was a beautiful woman, even covered in dirt.

Another groan, and the eyes opened further. A beautiful golden brown flashed out at him from under her half-opened lids and eyelashes.

"Hello, there, *heuning meisie*." He smiled. "Welcome back to the world."

Her eyes promptly closed, and she passed out again.

"Well, bro"—Nemo clapped him on the shoulder—"nice to see you've still got it with the ladies."

"Go play with yourself, fuckwitch."

The men all laughed at Midas' favorite swear word, stolen from Waters' girlfriend.

A sharp bank was made with no warning. "Sorry, guys. Enemy incoming. Hang on to your junk."

Medusa employed evasive maneuvers and dropped them quickly from their current altitude. Midas felt his stomach up in his throat until it had time to settle down. Someone swore under their breath, probably TB. For being such a big guy and a tough dude, he really hated getting in any vehicle that Medusa was driving or flying.

"What's your ETA, Medusa?" The boss' voice came back over the comm.

"Should be to you in thirty minutes if I can shake our boyfriends. Looking dicey though. Might be longer. Gonna have to fly around the original flight path."

A glare on his face for Medusa, Steel burst in on the comm as he planted his ass in the copilot seat. "A small group of hostiles ahead. Gonna have to head north, then back around."

"Roger that. Keep us posted."

"How are the kids?" Midas asked.

"Don't know yet. They should be steaming in here any moment. Haven't heard that we need buses, so they must be okay in general."

Scheherazade laid her head and one paw on the woman's shoulder, as if protecting her from anyone who might want to take her from Midas. The remainder of the ride was silent except for the sounds of the helicopter and the gentle chuffs from the dog.

3

JANUARY 24, 2024

Mouse

SHE WANTED TO OPEN HER EYES, BUT THE BRIGHT LIGHT THAT radiated behind her closed lids was painful. Her body felt compressed and weighed down. It was uncomfortable. It felt like her fingers were twitching, but she couldn't seem to lift her hand. What was going on?

She heard noises around her, but they were no longer the noises of bullets, shelling, screaming, crying, and the building falling. It was more like rustling and, every once in a while, whispered voices. Everything sounded like it was underwater.

With what little strength she had, she opened her eyes.

"Well, hello there, *heuning meisie*. Glad to see those pretty eyes."

"The children—" She winced. Her throat was sore. Not only that, but her voice was too loud, and the lights were too bright.

"Shh. The girls are safe," the soft voice said. It sounded kind.

Sympathetic. "You look like you're in pain. I bet the lights are making your head feel like it's a tin drum inside. Let me turn them down."

The lights began to dim until all she could see was a soft glow across the room where a wrought iron table lamp sat. The walls appeared to be an eggshell color, but there was normal furniture in the room, at least as far as she could see. She tried to turn her head, but it hurt too much. She did manage to make out dark-colored curtains drawn over the window, the small gap between the panels letting her know that it wasn't dark outside, nor was it sunny. Beneath her fingers, she felt soft material rather than scratchy hospital sheets. She was partially propped up in a comfortable bed against soft, fluffy pillows. Where was she?

"I'll be right back. Just going to get the doc to let him know you're awake."

She was frightened, and she didn't know who this voice was, just that it was male. He had an odd accent she didn't think she'd heard before, but despite him being a stranger, and the surroundings unfamiliar, his voice was soothing.

"Please." She sounded like a fairy-tale frog, ragged like gravel on gravel. "Don't leave."

Now, why did she say that? For all she knew, this person, despite his kind voice, could mean to harm her.

A dark figure came toward her from the foot of the bed, and he grew more distinct as he got closer, but her eyes still hurt from even just the little bit of light in the room. Not only did her head feel like the tin drum inside that he'd mentioned, but it felt like someone was hitting it repeatedly with a hammer. She whimpered in pain.

"Shh, *heuning meisie*, I'll stay. I'll just text him, all right?"

He flipped his wrist, revealing a watch. After typing a quick message on it, he sat down on the bed at her left side. "Close your eyes. I promise I'll stay right here with you."

She did as she was told. For several minutes, they sat quietly in the dim light. When she heard a second person arrive, she reopened her eyes to find another man had entered the room, this one as tall but not as broad. When he approached the right side of the bed, he stood just off the foot.

Her mystery man introduced him. "This is Demon. He's our medic. He's just going to check you over quickly. You've got some bad injuries." He twisted so that his focus was on the standing man. "She seems extra sensitive to light and volume," he informed the medic.

The man called Demon hummed to himself. "Typical with head injuries. It will get better with time." When he came closer to her, she saw he had bright-green eyes and dark hair that was long, pulled into a knot at the back of his head, but shaved on the sides. Reaching over onto the side table, he grabbed some items and held them up so she could see them. "Can I check your blood pressure?"

She nodded but winced when she felt both pain and nausea at the movement. The doctor also had an accent, although it was slight. It sounded like it might be Scottish or Irish.

After taking her blood pressure, he pulled a penlight out to look into her eyes. She hissed at the bright light. "Sorry. You've been in and out for about six days, though I doubt you'll remember any of that. You definitely have a concussion. You have some severely bruised ribs and a badly sprained ankle as well. In some ways, you might have been better off if the latter had broken, but either way, you're going to be on bed rest for a bit. Are you hungry?"

She started to shake her head, then remembered how awful she felt when she moved it even the slightest. "No," she croaked.

"Okay." His eyes flashed over to the other man, then back to her. "You were severely dehydrated. I gave you fluids with an IV. If you promise to drink on your own, I'll take the IV out." His head nodded down at the hand closest to him.

"I promise."

The man named Demon considered her carefully, then began to gently unhook the IV. Once it was removed and a bandage placed over where the cannula had been, he gathered all the materials and spoke to the mystery man next to her. "You sitting with her?"

"Yeah, I've got my laptop. We'll be good."

The look the doctor gave her caretaker seemed loaded with a private conversation. After a long pause, he finally gave instructions. "Eight ounces of water every two hours. No exceptions. When you're ready, soft foods to start. Otherwise, rest. No moving without help, even to the bathroom. Don't want to risk reinjuring the ribs or the ankle." The doctor turned to her caretaker. "Nemo will take over when you need a few minutes."

The man grunted, as if he wasn't happy with that, but he said nothing.

"Rest," the doctor said to her. It sounded like a threat more than an instruction. "If you don't want him to help you with something, let him know. Medusa will be happy to come in." With that, he left.

She felt her mystery man shift next to her. "I'm sure you have lots of questions. So do we. Right now, just rest. You need to feel better before we get to anything else. You're safe. The girls are safe. Everything else can wait."

With relief, she closed her eyes and immediately fell into the blackness.

WHEN SHE WOKE, IT WAS CLEAR SOME TIME HAD PASSED. THE room was dark except for a shaft of light from the hallway, and the blinds were pulled and turned so that just bits of moonlight shone through. To her left was a bulky shadow, the shape of a man, with what appeared to be a laptop open, his glasses reflecting the blurry contents of his screen as his fingers flew across the keyboard. The turn of her head on the pillow caught his attention. Movement? Sound? He set the laptop down to his left on another chair and leaned forward.

"We meet again. How's your head now, *heuning meisie?*"

She swallowed hard, closing her eyes tight. The drum, cymbals, and hammer were still there and still at work.

"I thought as much. Let's get some water in you. Might make you feel better."

She opened her eyes at the sound of him reaching for the insulated cup on the nightstand next to the bed. When she tried to sit up, he set the cup back down and put a gentle hand on her shoulder. "Don't move. You'll hurt yourself." He reached over to the corner for an extra pillow. Ever so gently, he put an arm around her shoulders, easing her slightly forward, and slipped the pillow behind her. "Better?"

She nodded, watching him through half-raised lids. The pain was slightly better when she did that, versus opening them wide.

"Good. Let me help you with this. You went about twenty rounds with that bookcase, so your body is feeling the effects. Movement is going to be difficult for a while, I'm guessing." Equally as gentle, he brought the cup to her lips, making sure the straw didn't poke her.

After a few sips, she backed off from the straw. Swallowing hurt.

He pulled the cup away and set it back on the table. "Doesn't feel good, huh?"

"Sore," she confessed.

"Probably from yelling for help for an extended period of time. Tell you what. He just said eight ounces of fluids every two hours. He didn't say what form it had to come in. Let's try something else."

He stood up and stretched, his T-shirt pulling up slightly as he reached for the ceiling, and in the dim light of the laptop screen projecting their way, she got a glimpse of tight abs above his belt. Wow.

With a twist toward the left and the right, he groaned. "Crap chair. Gonna bring the recliner in here later. Be right back."

When he came back into the room a few minutes later, he had another insulated cup and a spoon. He took the lid off, dipped the spoon inside of it, and then raised the spoon to her lips with a couple of ice chips on it. Without thinking, she opened her mouth, closed it around the spoon, and dragged the ice further into her mouth. It felt heavenly as she held it there, letting the water melt and slide down her throat without having to swallow.

He waited, seeming to know exactly when the ice chips had melted, and he scooped another few chips from the cup and brought them to her mouth. They continued like that until the chips were gone, and she closed her eyes in exhaustion.

"Can I ask you two easy questions, *heuning meisie?*"

Eyes still closed, she nodded, then wished she hadn't. A whimper came out of her, and she grimaced.

"I promise, only two. Don't feel bad or scared if you can't answer them, okay? You took a really bad knock to the head, so it's possible everything's jumbled around in there right now."

It sounded like he was smiling as he spoke, so she tried to open her eyes a little. He was more difficult to see now that he wasn't in the light of his laptop screen.

"Okay, question one." She felt the bed dip slightly on her left side, and she noticed that he was now leaning on his forearms on the bed itself. "My name is Midas. Can you tell me your name?"

She opened her mouth, but nothing came out. Her hands fisted in the bedsheets, and her eyes opened wide, despite the pain. She couldn't remember! Why couldn't she remember her name? Panic began to well up inside her, and it must have shown in her face because she suddenly felt a slight pressure on the top of her hand and a light squeeze.

"Breathe, *heuning meisie.* Remember what I said. Don't feel scared. Things are jumbled. It'll come back to you." The squeeze remained constant until she calmed. Then he let up on the pressure, although he left his hand atop hers.

"Okay, let's try question two. This one will be easier, I promise. What's the last thing you remember?"

She looked up at the ceiling and closed her eyes. It hurt to concentrate, so she blurted out, "Mary. Lamb?" It was all that would come out. Her voice sounded funny to her.

"Mary had a little lamb?" he asked to clarify.

She gave a single head nod.

"Okay, that's good." He squeezed her hand again, gently, then let go to grab his computer. He typed a few things, hit a single key, and put it back down, focusing all of his attention on her. "Now, don't talk. Just go back to sleep. When you wake up, we'll see what we see, okay?"

She reached out to touch his arm. "Girls?" she rasped.

His hand settled on hers. "Everybody's fine. Two of them saved your life. If it hadn't been for the brave little one, we wouldn't have known to go back in for you because you were so buried."

All she could manage to say was "Okay?" It was so exhausting and painful to talk.

"She had a cut to her forehead. It looks like it bled a lot, but head wounds do. Once we cleaned her up, it was nothing serious. Her sister had a broken arm, but the baby was untouched, surprisingly. The twins had just bumps and bruises, lots of concrete dust, but they're clean, fed, warm, and happy right now."

She closed her eyes in obvious relief, but as he pulled away, they sprang open again. Her hand grasped at his and squeezed with every ounce of strength she had. "Where?"

"Easy there, *heuning meisie*, that grip is going to break my hand," he teased. "They're here with us. My brother, Nemo, is with them. They're probably watching that movie about the fish with a broken fin. The one he's named after."

She closed her eyes again, humming quietly.

"That's it. Go back to sleep. Best thing for you right now. I'll be here when you wake up."

"*Heuning meisie?*" Her mouth struggled to form around the unfamiliar words.

"Very good. It's Afrikaans. It means 'honey girl.' Your eyes. They're the color of honey."

Her hand slipped from his arm. With that, she drifted off into blackness, feeling safer, more secure. The last thing she remembered was the ghost of a touch to her forehead.

4

———————————

JANUARY 24, 2024

Midas

HE KNEW THE EXACT SECOND SHE FELL INTO SLEEP, BUT instead of returning to his report, he stayed sitting beside her.

When it came time to assign someone to watch over her, Waters probably would have asked their interrogator, TB, but Midas argued that the giant wasn't nicknamed "Total Bastard" for nothing. He was big, grumpy, and impatient. Their Information Specialist scared pretty much everyone, except his woman, Flame. Instead, he argued he'd be best to get the information, and since he also did all the IT work, he could quickly search the information as she gave it to them. What could be better?

He wasn't sure if Waters bought his argument though. Hell, he wasn't even sure he bought it. He had to admit that his fascination with Miss Mouse was something he was uncomfortable with, and yet, he couldn't help himself. The madness had extended to putting her in the guest room of his apartment rather than one of the vacant ones Tribe had.

Her breathing had dropped into slow, even breaths, so Midas opened a new window on his computer, encrypted the chat, and tapped in his boss' code.

W: What have you got?

M: Not much. She doesn't remember her name.

W: I'm sending Nemo up there. I need to see you in person about a couple of things.

Midas tipped his head back against the wall and groaned silently. Yep. Looked like his ass-reaming for disobeying orders within the chain of command was set to begin shortly. This was not going to be fun.

M: I'll be there shortly.

He closed out the chat box and gently banged the back of his head three times on the wall. This was going to suck big, hairy cape buffalo balls, and it would probably be just as dangerous.

Nemo arrived twenty minutes later, Scheherazade in tow, with a burger bag from a fast-food joint down the block. Midas adjusted the covers around the woman in the bed and then gestured out the door. He didn't want their conversation to wake her up.

When he left the room, he closed the door so just a sliver of space existed between it and the doorjamb. He wanted to hear her if she woke up and was scared about being alone.

"Since when do you eat that shit?"

The blond sat down at the breakfast bar, opened the bag, and unwrapped a burger. Taking the meat out of the bun, he tossed it to Scheherazade. "I don't. She does."

With a shake of his head, Midas ran his hands over his closely cropped hair. "Dog's stomach has got to be rotten."

"Dude. She lived on the streets in Egypt, surviving on garbage. A cheeseburger is the least of the poisons I could give her. She deserves a reward."

"Whatever. I have to meet with Waters. She wakes up periodically and tends to be very disoriented. When she woke up a few minutes ago, I warned her that someone else would be here. She doesn't really talk much. Not sure if it's because it hurts to talk, if she's scared, or what. Just don't frighten her, okay? Be slow with her."

"Dealing with women isn't really something I'm a novice at, big bro."

"Don't remind me," Midas grumbled. "If I'd had to haul your ass out of one more alleyway or parking lot, I probably would have given up and left your ass there." He felt his temper escalating.

"Nah." Nemo waved him off. He fed another burger patty to the dog. "Although. You should have. And long, long ago."

"You're fuckin' right, I should have."

With a quizzical look on his face, Nemo clearly felt the tension coming off him. "Well, luckily, you don't have to worry about it anymore."

"No, I don't. Everyone knows your history. The fact that Gem hasn't kicked your ass out already is a miracle."

There was a pause before Nemo spoke again, a coldness in his voice that people rarely heard. "All right." Nemo crumpled up the paper bag and tossed it onto the countertop. "Let's get this shit out and dealt with. Say what you need to say."

Realizing there were no more yummy burgers in the bag, Scheherazade padded off down the hallway to the woman's room, nosing the door open enough to slink through. She was incredibly perceptive when it came to emotions, and it was like she knew the brothers needed privacy.

"I've got nothing to say to you," Midas said.

"Oh yeah, because you being all accusatory and judgy says every-thing's cool between us. What the fuck has crawled up your ass?"

"I am not doing this with you right now."

"If not now, then when? Over a conference call with everyone in the room? Every time I've been on the screen, you can barely raise your head to look at me. Your teeth are grinding so hard I'm able to hear them over the speakers. Just spit it out."

"Fine. You want to know what I'm pissed off about? You left, Nemo! You left with no warning. You sent me a video to say goodbye and ran off with some piece of ass—"

He got no further because Nemo's fist connected with his jaw. Midas actually staggered with the blow.

Chest heaving, Nemo stood with his hands clenched into fists at his sides, muscles straining with absolute control to stay in place. "Gem is not some 'piece of ass' to me, and no one knows that more than you do."

Immediately, Midas felt his anger deflate. All that was left was horror at what he'd said about Gem because of months of being hurt over Nemo's departure and, if he was honest, jealousy. He didn't want Gem. He just wanted what Nemo had with her. And with Nemo gone, Midas felt as if there was a huge hole in his life. He didn't have anyone to protect anymore. He should be relieved, but he wasn't.

"Shit." He closed his eyes and hung his head. "I'm sorry. You're right. I know you better... and Gem."

His brother's fight mode dropped, and he rushed to hug him. "Dude, you're my brother. I love you. But I was just holding you back, and you know it. You needed me to leave to become the best you can be. You're going to be a perfect follow-up to Waters."

Midas' mouth opened, and he sucked air into his lungs in shock.

Nemo cocked his head to the side, his face incredulous. "You didn't know?"

"I..." He felt like he couldn't breathe. "Why?"

Nemo looked guilty. "I assumed you knew. Maybe you weren't

supposed to." He put a hand on his brother's shoulder. "Relax. It's not happening tomorrow. Both God and Waters have a few years left in them. But making sure you're ready isn't exactly an overnight job. It's why God told Gem she shouldn't leave Mythos, and that she and I had decisions to make. The right ones. My leaving was the right decision, and he knew it. If I'd stayed? You'd never be ready, still trying to bail me out of jam after jam. Minus the women. I'm one hundred percent Team Gem."

Midas scrubbed his face with his hands and turned his back on his brother. "This is too much."

Nemo slapped his shoulder twice. "No, it's not. You'll be awesome at the job, and you'll get to boss everyone around. You were always bossy," he teased. "You'll eat that shit up."

The younger twin turned on his heel and walked down the hall to the woman's room. Midas followed, watching as his brother entered carefully and quietly.

She was awake, her hand on the head of the dog who had crawled up into bed with her. When Midas entered the room, her relief was obvious. It made him stand up a little straighter, and his chest expanded at the thought that she'd missed him. "Hello, *heuning meisie.*" Out of the corner of his eye, he felt his brother stiffen at the nickname. He ignored it. "How are you feeling?"

"Sore."

He nodded. "I'm sure you are. Do you need to get up before I leave?"

She hesitated.

"I'll call Medusa to come help you, okay? I need to leave for a couple of hours, but I'll be back." He gestured behind him to the foot of the bed. "This is my twin brother, Nemo, and the owner of the dog."

She looked between the two men, confused.

"I know. We don't look a lot like twins. Thank goodness."

Nemo smacked his chest with the back of his hand, and he winked at her.

"He's going to hang out with you until I come back. He's an ass, but he'll take good care of you." He turned to Nemo. "Demon ordered eight ounces of fluids every two hours. Swallowing from the straw bothered her sore throat, so we switched to ice chips. And keep the lights out. They hurt her eyes."

With a final look at the woman and a reassuring smile, he left the room to head downstairs to see his team leader. Secure in the elevator, he sighed. This was really going to suck. He inhaled deeply to a count of five, let it out slowly on a count of five. He could avoid the man, but the sooner he faced him, the sooner it would be over.

5

JANUARY 24, 2024

Midas

ONCE OUT OF THE ELEVATOR, HE PASSED CHERRY AT HER massive reception desk. He gave her a nod, and she returned it. Looking back at her screen, keys clacking, she sang, "Someone's in trouble." Then she gave him a teasing smile.

Midas shook his head. "In his office?"

"Yep." She popped the p. "And God is already on the line with him."

"Fuck me running," he whispered. Waters, his team leader, he could handle when the man was pissed. But God? The big boss? Even with never having seen the man, he was scary as fuck. He was likely to go supernova on him.

"Yeah, better get out the lube, sweet cheeks, because your ass is about to get reamed. He was pissed."

"What was I supposed to do? Leave her there to die?"

"Midas, I know you couldn't, the team knows you couldn't, even

Waters knows you couldn't. God? He's another story." She tipped her head toward the hallway. "Better get in there before he starts throwing thunderbolts."

"That's Thor."

"Tomato, tohmahto. Go. I'll be in with tissue to wipe your tears and a mop and bucket to wipe up the blood from when he tears up your asshole."

"Ugh. You've been hanging out with Kubrick too much."

"Go." She shooed him with her long nails—a deep, glittery green this week—and flicked her fingers. "Quit stalling. It's just going to be worse the longer you leave it."

Grumbling to himself, Midas went to the door and stopped just outside it. Breathe in five count, breathe out five count.

Suddenly, a voice yelled from behind the door, "Quit being a pussy and get in here, Midas."

Waters was watching through the security camera. Cherry was right. He was fucked.

Midas turned the doorknob, stepped through the door, closed it behind him, and sat in the chair at the round table where Waters worked. "Still not working behind your multi-thousand-dollar desk?"

Waters grinned. "Nope. Kubrick made me a total table convert. I use the desk for other things." He raised his eyebrows up and down once, an evil grin across his face.

God chimed in, "All right, girls, quit talking about Waters' sex-furniture that I appear to pay for. Midas, what the hell?"

Okay. They were going there right away. He could play the game. Pretend he was clueless and make them spell it out, but that would just take more time than he wanted to be sitting in this office. Best to just get it over with. "What would you have had me do? I was told there was a woman inside. I was supposed to ignore that? We made it out safely and sort of on time. No harm, no foul, and we saved another person. I call that a win."

"It was reckless."

"It was right." Waters backed up his teammate.

"Shut the fuck up, Waters. You were just as pissed at the time as I am now. I expect you to be the levelheaded one. Ever since you met Kubrick and became the eyes in the sky, you've gone soft." Waters ducked his head so his boss couldn't see him laughing on the laptop camera.

Both Midas and Waters knew the big boss wasn't really mad. He just didn't like it when they took needless risks.

"Sometimes risks are worth it."

There was a snort over the intercom, followed by the crunching of a caramel apple sucker, simultaneous with the unwrapping of another one. Great. He was actually pissed off after all.

Through the noise, God said, "All right, aside from the fact that you disobeyed a direct order and went back into that building, then proceeded to belay a revised order because it didn't fit your timeline, we now have *six* orphans in our midst. The woman is a bit trickier."

"Why?" Then he realized why. "We know the girls are children of Salieri members. You think she's one too."

Waters nodded. "Yes, but maybe a wife, a daughter, a sister, something."

He froze. "Why?"

"According to the staff who managed to flee before we got there, Sister Mary is the only teacher who remains unaccounted for. She refused to leave until all the children were gone, and there was a woman, recently arrived at the school, who stayed behind with her and the Mythos guard who died. Based on our description of her, she was not, technically, a staff member. She was more of a resident who was helping out."

Inside, Midas was burning lava hot. He rose from his seat and paced back and forth in Waters' office from his chair to the window, both hands on top of his head, fingers laced, rubbing them back and forth over his scalp as he stared out the glass at nothing in particular. He heard low murmurs behind him, Waters conversing with God over the speaker, but he wasn't processing what was being said.

Hanging his head, he kept his hands laced along the back of his neck because he was afraid if he let go, he'd break something, and most of the things in Waters' office now had to do with his film director girlfriend, Kubrick. Closing his eyes, he began counting inside his head to try and level himself out emotionally. He hit two hundred fifty before he was back in control of himself, then unlaced his fingers and forced his arms to relax at his sides. Only then was he able to return to his seat at the table.

"You ready now, or do I need to get you a rawhide bone to gnaw on?"

"I'm not a dog," Midas grumped.

God snorted over the speaker. "You deal with this, Waters." He clicked off.

"All right, let's get this done. I didn't expect she'd remember her name. Did she remember anything at all?"

"She said the last thing she remembers is the nursery rhyme 'Mary Had a Little Lamb.' Fuck if I know what that means."

Waters tapped his pen repeatedly against the tabletop before scratching a note on the legal pad to his right.

"You know," Midas began, "they have an app on your phone to take notes on. You'd kill less trees."

"Yeah, I know. Prefer the old-fashioned way."

"Jesus, you and Kubrick are going to kill me. When the earth dies, we'll know exactly where ground zero was."

"Hey, we recycle. We just prefer to write shit down. I was that way before I met her."

"I know. It's part of why you're so stupid-perfect for each other." He knew he sounded like he was complaining, but it wasn't irritation he felt. It was envy.

Redirecting their conversation, Waters said, "Mythos is hanging out for a bit while we sort through the Cairo project. I'll have Nemo ask the oldest girl, Shakira, about the nursery rhyme. Maybe she can shed some light on it."

Midas shifted in his seat. "When she woke up, they were the only thing she asked about. If they were okay. Where they were. Everybody settling in okay so I can reassure her?"

"Yeah. Gem and Nemo have had them most of the time during the day, getting them hopped up on junk food and kids' movies. They like to watch *Snow White* a lot. Apparently, they think Miss Mouse and Snow White are the same person."

Puzzled, Midas said, "They look nothing alike."

Waters shrugged. "Kids. Who knows? One thing that's been nice is that Scheherazade has been a big help for them. We can add therapy dog to her list of special skills." Waters got a faraway look in his eyes, and a soft smile crept across his face. "It's kinda cute. When the little one tries to crawl away, she grabs her by the seat of the pants and drags her back to the rest of the kids."

"She's a mama to the core, that dog. Always was protective of her pups too."

"Only bad thing—aside from the sugar high—is if I hear 'Heigh-Ho' one more time, I'm cancelling our streaming services and getting them all library cards."

As their resident psychology expert, on top of his computer skills, Midas was concerned about the girls' mental state. "You'll survive. Treating them like normal, everyday kids is the best thing for them. Gem and Nemo know what they're doing since kids are sort of her thing with Mythos. It's been almost a week since the extraction. Any side effects showing up from the attack?"

There was a brief pause while his team leader studied the pen he held. "Nightmares."

"Not unexpected. How bad?"

"The baby, Paris, is with Flame and TB since she's so close in age to Axel, but I'm guessing she's probably too young to have any issues. I don't know about Shakira and Ona, the other sisters Nemo and Gem have staying with them. You'll have to ask Nemo. He hasn't said anything, but then again, he might not. You know the Mythos crew. Quiet unless directly asked." Waters shrugged. "I just know about the twins, Liliana and Catalina. They're staying with Kubrick and me." His cheeks seemed to tinge a bit pink at the admission.

Waters and Kubrick took in two of the girls? He had so many questions. He decided to stick with a safe one.

"The twins get back to sleep okay afterward?"

"After a bit. I feel bad for Kubrick. She already deals with my nightmares, which, granted, are obviously less often now that we're together, but now she's dealing with all three of us and our shit. She's good about it, and luckily, the girls seem to gravitate toward me at night, subconsciously knowing I understand, maybe? With the two of them sleeping in our bed with us, I've been getting kicked all night long for the past several days. Luckily, I don't need that much sleep due to my Navy days."

While surprised that they were allowing the kids in their bed, Midas smiled at the forced frustration and grumpiness in Waters' voice. Despite the verbalized complaint, he didn't sound all that upset about it, which created more questions.

"Liliana's actually been okay. But Catalina... even when she naps, they're bad."

"I can try and talk with them, if you think it will help. Otherwise, I'm sure we can find a therapist who will work under the table."

Waters nodded. "Mythos offered too. They have a couple under contract, but the trouble is, they're overseas, and that would mean taking the girls away. Kubrick's already attached. She has a break from filming for a few months, and she'd take them herself, but that would mean we'd be apart, and... well, we've seen how well I do with that."

Midas had to grin. Waters was referring to a location shoot his film director girlfriend had been on in China, where the man had lasted all of a day and a half before he'd been on a plane to her side. They'd been the least "committed" couple prior to that, together all the time yet still managing to lead separate lives. It looked like watching over the twin girls was causing a shift in the level of their relationship.

"Mouse has had a few as well. They seem to vary in intensity. She doesn't mention them the next day, so I wonder if she even remembers them. She doesn't wake up from them, either, but she does settle down when I go in to check on her. Her rumblings are inarticulate, so no clue what they're about, and that also means no clues as to her identity. Who does the staff say she is?"

"They don't know."

Frowning, he leaned forward in his chair. "What do you mean, 'They don't know'?"

"They don't know who she is. She was basically found on their doorstep about six months ago, bruised and bloodied, no identification, nothing other than her backpack, which had a change of clothes in it and a couple of paperback novels."

"She didn't tell them who she was."

"Couldn't. She didn't remember."

Midas frowned, talking through his thoughts. "So the amnesia isn't from a bump to the head or the trauma of the attack on the compound." He paused. "I can try and search her through facial recognition, but she's pretty banged up. Might be better if we waited a couple of days for the swelling to go down. Better chance of success. I can search the missing persons databases. She sounds American, which narrows things down somewhat, and it means she could have had a passport at some point. Depending on how long she's been overseas and how she got there, she might have school or employment records, which would increase the search parameters. Demon already took fingerprints when we moved her into my guest room, so I could run those while watching over her."

There was silence from his boss and an assessing stare.

"What?" Midas asked, nonplussed by the pause. "What's the problem?"

"You're planning to continue working from her room?"

"Well, yeah. What's the difference if I work on the computer in my office or from a laptop in her room? It's not like Nova doesn't already travel everywhere with me to assist. Killing two birds, as it were. I work, and she's protected."

Midas felt himself fall deeper under Waters' scrutiny as the man sat back in his chair, twisting his pen around in his fingers. Finally, he asked, "Why does she need protection inside Tribe?"

Shit. What did he say to that? "Well, she can't exactly take care of herself right now. And since I was supposed to be gathering information from her, it just made sense to stick close so I could process it immediately as we received it. We talked about this."

"No one ordered you to put her in your apartment and stay with her twenty-four seven."

"Are you saying you want me to stay away from her?"

"No. As a matter of fact, I don't."

"Then what the fuck is this interrogation all about?"

"Something's not right about her."

Midas felt himself start to puff up like a cobra at his boss.

"I'm not saying she's the enemy," his supervisor cautioned. "I'm just saying there's something here that we can't see. My spidey senses aren't just tingling. They're burning."

Midas sighed and ran a hand over his scalp again. "I get it. As soon as you said she showed up there with no memory, a million scenarios started running through my head. None of them are good, and none of them end well, but I can't help but think that she's on the up-and-up. Her first thought when she opened her eyes was for the girls."

"Young girls are worth a lot in terms of product."

His boss was playing devil's advocate, which he was used to, but that didn't make him back down.

"She was worried for their safety. Wanted to know they were being taken care of."

"Gotta keep track of the product."

"Waters," Midas growled.

The team leader held his hands up in surrender. "I'm trying to remind you that ignoring a worst-case scenario does a disservice to you. What happens if you become invested in her and she turns out to be a trafficker herself?"

Biting his lip, Midas felt his heart plummet, and a greater fear took hold. "Or she could be a victim."

"Yes, that's true." Waters leaned forward. "I already ran the fingerprint scan, and nothing came up. No criminal record, no attachment to government jobs, no military. She's a ghost right now. Demon ran DNA, but that came up blank as well. For all we know, she could be working with the Salieri."

"Highly unlikely given her gender."

"Probably, but it's not like they might not see her as a valuable tool. Remember what Cherry said from her debrief after St. Lucia. The Salieri have found new uses for the nonbreeding females. A woman showing up at the compound would be much less suspect if trying to get close to the children."

"She's not working for them. Her first concern was the children," he reiterated. "She didn't even ask who I was, or where she was, or what was wrong with her."

"Wouldn't that be the case if she were part of their operation? Remember—they were willing to fight to the death to keep us out of there."

Midas shook his head. "No. I don't believe it, and I won't ever believe it. There was genuine concern in her attitude." He cleared his throat. "Speaking of that, I'd like to take the kids to visit her. I think it might go a long way in easing her fears. Maybe even help her recovery along."

Waters considered his request, looking as if he were about to refuse.

"Boss, she's alone, hurting, and frightened. All she can remember is something to do with a nursery rhyme. How would you like to be alone and bedbound in that situation? Maybe protection is unnecessary, but between the amnesia and the state she showed up to Mythos in, I'm not betting against it. We believed the soldiers were guarding those last few children and desperately wanted to keep anyone from them. What value do the children really have to them? None, unless they're being used in the mines, and we shut that shit down.

"But an adult female? There might be information locked away inside of her that's dangerous to them. Amnesia is a tricky thing. It can last only briefly, or it can hold on forever, especially if the information is traumatic enough, and it can reverse itself in pieces or completely. I'm with you in that she's connected to the Salieri, just not in the way you're thinking, so my guess is those men weren't interested in the kids. My suspicion is they wanted her. There has to be a reason for that. And until we know for sure who, or what, they were after, I'm not leaving her unprotected, even inside our walls."

Waters smiled, his expression almost proud. "Agreed. I think your impulses are spot on."

He couldn't help but be shocked into temporary silence. When he finally managed to gather his words, he asked, "What the fuck? Why did we go through all of that nonsense about her being part of the Salieri?" Then it dawned on him. His conversation earlier with Nemo. "Were you testing my responses?"

Shifting in his chair, the team leader had the grace to look guilty. "I wouldn't call it 'testing.' I'd call it 'gauging your skills to look past emotions.' Since your brother left us, you've changed."

Midas made to protest, but Waters cut him off.

"That's not a bad thing, Midas. It's like a breakup. You're still working through his leaving. But before he left, your first priority was always Nemo. Now, he's not."

"If my brother needed me, he'd still take precedence," Midas warned.

"I wouldn't expect anything else. Family loyalty is important, and you were lucky that the two of you were a package deal. But now you're in the field more. Your responsibilities are increasing, and you've grown into a leadership role. This most recent project proves to me that I'd be more than comfortable leaving you in charge."

"So it's true. You're grooming me for your job."

Waters grimaced. "Someone let the cat out of the bag?"

Midas considered what to say. "More like the dog."

"Ah… Well, it's not really a secret. I think everyone but you knew God and I were watching you specifically."

"Steel or TB won't be pissed?"

"TB would not be a good choice, and he knows it. Steel? I think he welcomes it. He's always preferred the shadows. I've been watching. You've grown into it. It's increased your duties a bit, which concerns me, but it's also sped up a lot of intel on projects because you're there on scene and able to act quicker." He took his pen and made another note on his pad of paper. "I'll approve the visits with the girls as long as they don't set back her recovery or upset her in any way. You're right. I think it would be good for her. Maybe she or the girls will say something that gives us some hint as to who she is or where she's from. Sometimes people don't know that they know something, so the littlest random detail can be helpful. When?"

"She has a checkup with Demon on the ankle tomorrow. We're hoping she's able to move to crutches for short distances. That's going to take a lot out of her. Day after tomorrow?"

"I trust your judgment."

"Thanks." Midas rose and went to the door. Before exiting, he turned. "We could do a movie night or something. You and Kubrick. Nemo and Gem. The four older girls, at least."

"I trust your instincts."

As he exited, Midas realized the entire conversation had gone only about a third of how he'd predicted. He needed a workout to relieve some tension. Then he would return to his apartment for a shower and something to eat. He'd spent the last several nights in the upright armchair in the room, catching catnaps or working. Tonight, he'd move the recliner into her room for when he sat with her, but he'd force himself to sleep in his room. Then at least he could lie back and get some actual sleep.

6

JANUARY 24, 2024

Mouse

When Midas had left the room, she had felt an edge of panic. Every time she'd woken, he'd been there. He felt familiar. Safe. She didn't think she'd felt safe in a long time. Other than the woman they called Medusa, who came to help her to the bathroom and back, and the doctor named Demon, he'd been the only one here. His brother didn't seem like he was dangerous, but he was unfamiliar. It made her nervous.

She was also frightened because she hadn't seen the girls. The only thing she had were assurances that they were cared for and safe. She wished she could see them for herself.

Nemo stood in the doorway with two bowls in his hands. "You like sherbet, Miss Mouse?"

Inside her head, there was a click. A corner piece of a puzzle being laid down on the table of her brain. It startled her heart, causing it to race. Her nickname from the girls! It wasn't her real name, but it was something.

As if knowing why she looked so stunned, he admitted, "Shakira told us that's what they called you."

She nodded.

He handed her the bowl with a wink. Holy moly, the man was good-looking to start with, but he was downright gorgeous when he smiled. She preferred the softness in Midas' eyes and his larger build, but she could admit to herself that all the tattoos and piercings would make a lot of heads turn.

"Just don't tell Mr. Grumpy," he confided. "I'm not sure it's on the approved food list, and it certainly isn't a very healthy replacement for a typical meal, nor is it eight ounces of liquids unless it's melted. But I'm not exactly known for following directions well. I thought if your throat was still sore, it might make you feel better. It's just orange flavored, but I didn't know what you liked, and I figured this was safe. If you prefer something else, Flame has a freezer full of ice cream upstairs."

She shook her head and smiled at him in thanks. At least the pounding in her head was dimming, and the nausea from moving it was easing.

Nemo sat down in the chair his brother had been sitting in. He also had what looked like a sundae cup in his hand. The dog's ears perked, and her head went up. With a soft chuff, she hopped off the bed and went to sit in front of her handler. "*Goeie meisie,*" he said with a smile. Setting his bowl on the table next to the bed, he ripped the cover off the doggy sundae cup and held it at mouth level for her. Instantly, the dog's snout was in the cup.

A huge sneeze broke the silence in the room. Ice cream was all over the tip of her nose. "Eat it, don't snort it, you goofball." He smiled at her indulgently while she tried again, much daintier this time.

She smiled.

"You've got a very pretty smile, Miss Mouse. Glad to see it. Midas taking care of you okay?"

She nodded.

"You feeling okay? In pain?"

She shrugged.

"You need anything?"

She shook her head.

"Don't talk much, do you?"

She shook her head again, gesturing to her throat with a frown.

"Rest is best then. That's okay. I can talk enough for both of us."

She looked up into his grinning face and couldn't help but give a small smile back. He really was gorgeous, but her brain flashed to the dark-haired, dark-eyed brawny man who'd sat in the same chair a short while earlier. That man? He made her heart rate speed up, which was a little uncomfortable since she knew next to nothing about him.

Nemo's voice broke into her thoughts. "I bet you have questions."

She swallowed, her throat feeling like it was folding in on itself. He must have seen the flash of pain on her face from the dry swallow because he gestured to the sherbet. "Try it. Let's see if it helps."

While she took spoonfuls of the icy treat, he left the room, then came back a few moments later with a notepad and a pen. He held them to her. "Don't talk. Write."

She took another spoonful of sherbet, then traded it for the items in his hand.

The girls?

He grabbed his bowl of sherbet and moved to the other side of the bed so he could sit on its edge and read what she wrote. Looking up at her, he smiled. In between bites, he spoke. "Safe. Doing well. Paris is with one of my co-workers. His girlfriend just had a baby not too long ago so figured she'd be best off there. Waters, Midas' team leader, and his girlfriend have Liliana and Catalina, and my other half, Gem, and I are watching Shakira and Ona. We're trying to let them be little kids without worry right now. Watching movies. Eating lots of fast food and junk food. Stories. They love Scheherazade." He nodded over to the dog. "She's especially fond of the baby."

He shifted the conversation. "The girls have asked about you. We promised them you were okay, but you needed to rest before they could see you."

Don't want them to see me like this.

He nodded. "We figured. Didn't want to scare them. You're pretty banged up, but the good news is, you're already looking better."

What will happen to them now?

"Honestly? I don't know. We haven't made any decisions yet because we wanted to talk to you. Midas said you don't remember much."

Looking down at the paper in her hand, she shook her head sadly.

"It's okay, Miss Mouse. It will come back. You just have to try not to press. My brother's the smarter one when it comes to psychology stuff, but I remember him saying once that the harder you try at something, the worse it makes it sometimes. Try to just let it come to you, okay? There's no pressure. You and the girls will be taken care of in the meantime."

Separated?

She knew her face likely showed her desperation that they wouldn't be pulled away from each other, but the reality was, they likely would be.

"Not now. My bosses, the ones who run the school where you were, aren't likely to do that, especially after what happened. They know that would be traumatic for all of you. You're safe here. No one can get to you."

Told us that in Cairo.

"Well, I can guarantee you're safe here. You're not even in Africa anymore. The men who attacked the school have no idea you're here."

Where's here?

"Los Angeles. You're at a place called Tribe. My brother lives and works here. He can explain it to you more later."

There was a soft knock on the door, and both looked up to see Midas standing there, looking unsure. "Everything okay?"

Nemo stood. "Yeah. We were just chatting about the girls and what happens next. Reassuring her that she and the girls are safe and not being separated."

He glanced at her. "Do you need anything?"

She shook her head. The pad of paper lay loosely in her lap, the pen on top of it. She was incredibly tired all of a sudden.

"I should go check on the kids. Make sure they haven't duct-taped Gem to the ceiling."

She smiled sleepily. The girls were a rambunctious group. She had no doubt they'd run the woman ragged.

"If my brother doesn't treat you nicely, you let me know," Nemo told her. "I'll come rescue you."

"Get out of here." Midas cuffed his brother good-naturedly on the shoulder, then put him in a headlock and mock-fought with him.

"I'm going if you'll let go of me, you *doos.*"

Midas gave him a shove out the door. "I'll text you later."

With a wave to her and a soft whistle to the dog, man and beast were gone. She heard him shut what she assumed was the main apartment door behind him.

Midas noticed the ice cream dishes on the bedside table. "I see he brought you a healthy dinner," he teased. Picking up the bowls, he looked down at her. "Are you hungry? Would you like some actual dinner?"

She shook her head.

"You look tired. You should rest." He picked up the pad of paper and pen, placing them on the bedside table. "I'll just be across the hall." He reached into his pocket and pulled out a simple phone. "It only works on internal numbers, but if you need me, speed-dial five. Don't hesitate to call."

Touched at his kindness and how he looked out for her, she smiled as she settled back. Her eyes closed, and within seconds, she was asleep.

7

JANUARY 26, 2024

Midas

"Knock, knock!" His soft rap on the door accompanied the words. He peeked in the partially open door to see that Mouse was sitting up in bed, propped against her massive number of pillows. She looked infinitely better than she had the day they'd brought her to Tribe. The bruises were beginning to yellow, and she was much more alert and moving around more on her own, thanks to being approved for crutches for very short distances, and that had massively improved her attitude. Another couple of days and she'd be able to move independently once Demon put a walking boot on her foot to keep her sprained ankle stable, and the bruising would go down.

Her head turned, and he felt his heart stutter at the smile she gave him, bruises and all. "Good morning, Mouse. How are you feeling?"

She opened her mouth, and a raspy "Better" came out.

"Is it okay for me to come in?"

She nodded and pushed herself up further in the bed.

"Did you sleep well?"

She grabbed the notepad and pen on the bedside table and wrote her response.

Weird dreams but slept okay. You?

"Slept okay." He sat on the edge of the bed, his laptop tucked under his arm. "Anything you want to talk about?"

She scribbled on her notepad.

Don't really remember much. Just a backpack. An empty room with a table. Felt scared, but

She crossed out the "but."

In a hurry.

"Hmm. Not much to go on. Maybe something will come to you later." He reached over to the bedside table for her water and handed it to her. "Drink more. It will help. I know you can't really talk, and I'm sorry to do it, but I need to ask you a few questions. Are you up to it?"

He watched her suck in her bottom lip in worry, but she nodded. Quickly, she scribbled a question of her own on the paper in front of her.

How are the girls?

Smiling, he met her concerned gaze. "They're good. Some nightmares, but that's to be expected. That's one of the things I need to ask you about. Do you know anything about that? We don't know anything about their histories, so we weren't sure if they were related to the attack or something else."

He watched her eyes get glassy, then she took a deep breath before she began to write.

Very brave during attack. They weren't in good shape when they came to the compound. Starved. Beaten.

"We thought maybe that was the case," he said quietly. "I'm sorry they went through that. Any idea who hurt them?"

Their father was abusive for as long as Shakira could remember. She said their mother was raped and murdered in front of them the day they were taken away from their home.

"Fucking Salieri," he breathed out. "Seems to be a pattern for them. What about the other children? Do you know anything about them? Where they came from?"

She frowned.

All I really know is that they can't go back to their families. The twins were brought to us a few weeks ago by a pretty blonde girl. British. Curly hair. Lots of piercings and tattoos.

"That's Gem. My brother's girlfriend."

The other children were there when I arrived.

"And when was that?"

I'm not sure. June or July, I think. I don't really remember much about when I first arrived. Everything's hazy. Sister said I was dazed and hurt.

"So, no memory of your name or where you came from. None of it came back in the months you were there?"

I don't think so. I remember things from when I was at the compound but nothing before. It's like I was born as a full-grown adult the day I arrived there.

He could tell that was causing her the beginnings of panic. Laying a hand on hers holding the notepad, he tried to soothe her. "It's okay. We'll figure it out. I'm pretty good with computers. In a day or two, I'll take your picture and run it through my facial recognition software. I have an AI assistant named Nova, and she can search a lot of databases. It's almost impossible to be somewhere without a picture these days."

He gave her hand a squeeze. "This next part? It's a little harder. I need you to write down everything you remember from your time at the compound. And then, if you have any impressions or memories pop up about before then, or the attack itself. Even if you're not sure they're real memories. Anything at all. The smallest thing can be helpful. Can you do that for me?"

She glanced to her right, looking out the window into the buildings across the street. The windows were tinted—she could see out, but no one could see in. He gave her time to process his request.

It was several minutes before she whispered her reply, "Yes."

Somehow, the fact that she'd spoken her agreement instead of writing down her answer, or simply nodding, seemed significant.

"Thank you," he told her. With another squeeze to her hand, he stood. "I know it's going to be difficult to relive some of that. You're incredibly brave for doing it." He smiled. "I'll leave you to it. If you need a break, take it. I'll go grab you some breakfast."

He'd returned fifteen minutes later to find her hard at work, scratching away on the notepad. She didn't even look up when he set down a bowl of oatmeal, brown sugar on top, some milk, and a cup of peaches. He'd tried to come up with foods that would be easy to swallow but still get her a quality meal. Hopefully, in a day or two, she'd be able to eat more substantially.

An hour later, he'd peeked in to find her still hard at work, only this time she was frowning at the page, her pen stilled, as if she was thinking of something. Remembering? Trying to figure out how to say what she was remembering? He didn't want to interrupt, so he went back to working on his laptop at the breakfast bar in the kitchen.

Struggling not to hover, he forced himself to wait for another hour to pass before he checked on her again. This time, he found her asleep, leaning back against the pillows, the notepad in her lap, the pen loose in her hand. As quietly and as gently as possible, he slipped the pen out and placed it on the bedside table, then picked up the notepad and her breakfast dishes, noting with surprise that she'd eaten everything he'd given her.

Sitting down with the notepad, he began to read what she'd written. She'd remembered a few things that precipitated the attack, and with each sentence, it became more and more convincing that the attack had nothing to do with the children.

He hit a button on his watch, sending out a text. Within a few minutes, a series of beeps lit up the face. A tap to the screen brought up Nemo on the video call.

"Yes?"

"The compound has video feed, correct?"

"Should. Not really my area, but I can find out. What's up?"

"I had Miss Mouse write me out everything she could remember from her time at the compound. I want access to all the footage while she was there."

Raising an eyebrow, Nemo's smirk suggested his brother had nonprofessional curiosity going on. "Stalking is a crime in any country, bro."

Rolling his eyes and sighing, Midas didn't bother to waste the energy to flip his brother off. "I'm serious, *doos*. Two and two are multiplying to four thousand. I don't know what Waters has told you, but I'm more and more convinced this attack had nothing to do with the girls. I think it was about her. I need to be able to see whatever's been going on there. As a professional courtesy, I'm asking for the footage. You know I can hack in and get it."

"Relax, Mighty Midas. I'll get you the footage. It might take a couple of hours though. Cerberus is mid-flight to go blow some more shit up, and the computers are his baby. All the damage at the compound, that footage might be minimal."

"I'm more concerned about her and the months leading up to it. If he can get me her arrival to start with, I can wait on the rest."

"Got it. Watch your inbox." With that, Nemo shut down the link.

A tap to his computer screen brought up his AI. "Nova, I'm going to be feeding you some handwritten pages from Miss Mouse. Store, email a copy to Waters, and copy the team at large, including Cherry, God, and Mythos. Then, begin analysis of the events laid out to see if you can project a timeline for dates and times mentioned." Using his portable scanner, he fed each page in and directed them to Nova.

"Priority level?"

Knowing that time might be limited, he said, "Level one. Level three for all other projects."

If what he suspected was true, time was of the essence.

8

JANUARY 26, 2024

Midas

THE CHIME ON MIDAS' APARTMENT DOOR WENT OFF. FLIPPING the screen to his security camera, he saw that it was Waters. He pushed back from the breakfast bar and went to answer the door. "Figured you'd be here quickly."

Closing the door behind his boss, Midas followed him into the kitchen area, where Midas returned to his original seat while Waters stood across from him, arms locked and leaning on the countertop.

Midas told him, "I took a copy of her picture from when we did intake, figuring it couldn't wait until after reading her statement. I started with Cyclopes. If he doesn't find anything, I'll snap another photo tomorrow and have Nova start over with a more complex set of searches. Maybe we'll get lucky."

"Good. How is she?"

"Took her around two hours to write everything down. She's been sleeping since. Guessing it was emotionally exhausting."

Waters grunted. "Next steps?"

"I had Nemo forward me what video surveillance he could from the compound. Right now, I just have the day she arrived. Cerberus is working on compiling everything after that date. Should have it by tomorrow, and I can set up some parameters. I'll have Nova work on it. It'll take me way too long to go through it all by myself. He also gave me what he could from the day of the attack, but it's sketchy. Too much damage at the early onset, and it's in bits and pieces. He's trying to see if he can clean it up, but it's not looking real good."

He turned the laptop so that both he and Waters could see the footage from the day she arrived. "It was actually July first that she showed up at the gates."

They watched in silence as she came limping into the frame from the east. When she arrived at the gate, she looked around, pressed the speaker button there, spoke to someone a moment later, then collapsed. Two guards came running from somewhere close by, opened the gate, and took her inside.

"I'm working on trying to backtrack her movements to see if I can figure out a more definitive path that she took to the gates. If I'm really lucky, I might get a point of origin."

"Doubtful. Anything of interest to the east of there?"

"Not really. The school is on the outermost edge of the city, so there are some buildings to the west and south, but after you reach the compound walls, everything to the east is river, and everything to the north is field." He switched from the footage to stills, showing Waters the layout. "The side of the compound runs along the river for just under a mile. The compound itself doesn't share any wall space with anything, but there is a road along the south wall that eventually leads to a public access pier. Across the road, there's a market, a clothing shop, and a hole-in-the-wall restaurant. Most of the businesses are to the south, and it gets more urban as you go past each block. We were pinned down three blocks south and west of the school until Cerberus' diversion. Locals were scared out of their frickin' minds when we came through. I'm still amazed the local law enforcement didn't get involved."

"I'm guessing they were paid off to look the other way. Anyway, Mythos has feelers out to the area to see if anyone saw or heard anything beforehand. A stranger—including a battered woman— should stand out. The question becomes whether or not anyone will speak about what they've seen. Any buildings in the area you noticed that might be suspect?"

"There's nothing that screams of a place that a woman would need to escape from, or a place that would likely hold trafficking victims. Then again, just about anywhere could be used these days if it's one or two people being hidden. The only place I see that would suggest a large-scale hiding place would be if she came from the boat landing. There's a storage facility there. I planned to dig and see if I could find security cameras on site that I could hack, but from what I can tell, it's a reputable local who owns it. Not very big, and it doesn't appear to have underground access. I put one of our traditional guys on poking into the owner and the space itself, as well as records of who has come and gone with a boat, specifically around that time period. Who knows how accurate the records will be. It's not manned twenty-four seven."

"Replay the footage," Waters ordered.

Midas shifted the screen back to the video. He put the short clip of her arrival at the gate on a loop, and they continued to watch the scene several times, up to when one of the guards carried her into what used to be the infirmary in the compound.

"Can you get closer?" Waters asked.

"I'd have to be accessing their system for that kind of control. What we're seeing here is a copy of the real-time footage the cameras picked up. If I try to blow the picture up on my end, it'll just go grainy."

Waters looked up at him. "Think they'll let you into their system to look deeper?"

Shrugging, he blew out a breath. "With Mythos, it's difficult to say. Our relationship with them, I figure, is about 25/75 as to what they allow us to see after Demon and Cherry's undercover work in St. Lucia. You'd think it would be the opposite, but for some reason, the more we work with them, the more they keep back. I can try and see what they say, but..." He flashed a look up at Waters. "You might have better luck getting it if you ask Medusa than if I ask someone. You two are on more equal footing."

Waters bit his lower lip. "Maybe I'll skip a step and have God ask."

"Do we have any clue who their big boss is yet?"

"No. If God knows, he's not saying. Same with Cherry. I'm guessing they know more than we do but have deemed it unnecessary to share."

After a few more loops of the footage, Waters asked, "So... what are our next steps?"

"More assessments of my abilities?" Midas griped.

"I'm pretty sure I know what you're going to say, but humor me. You know that tech is not my area of expertise."

Midas turned the laptop so that the screen was only in his view. "While I'm waiting for the rest of Cerberus' video footage, I've got Nova rerunning her fingerprints and DNA but through tighter nets. Once I have all that data, the hard work of combing through it begins. Maybe we catch a break and some things start coming back to our mystery lady."

"And...?" his team leader prompted.

"And I'm also using facial recognition on the Salieri grunts we managed to capture on film, see if we get any hits. We've got the one hostile TB and Steel managed to wrap up. TB's been working on him for whatever information he can get, and I've been running his photo, fingerprints, and DNA. We'll probably get hits there, but whether or not they give us any hard leads to follow, that's a whole other story."

The look on Waters' face suggested there was more to come forward with.

"And"—he placed exaggerated emphasis on the conjunction—"if

you're all bringing the kids up at dinner time, I'll be sure to be present and listening carefully to see if I pick up anything there. Nothing like pizza, ice cream, and Disney movies to loosen up a child's inhibitions."

Waters' eyebrows went up.

"And..." He dragged the word out even longer. "I'll keep questioning her."

"Excellent." His boss unlocked his arms and crossed to the door to exit.

Shaking his head, Midas closed up his laptop, tucked it under his arm, and headed back to the bedroom. His guest was sleeping, but her face was scrunched up like she was in pain, a soft whimper coming from her throat. Ditching the laptop in the chair, he moved to sit on the edge of the bed, his hand reaching for hers that was clutching the covers. The soft whimper turned into frantic eye movements beneath her closed lids, her head tossing back and forth on the pillow.

"Shh, *heuning meisie*. You're safe. Open those pretty eyes for me. I promise, you're safe."

Her dark lashes fluttered against her pale skin as she woke, her eyes darting everywhere in panic, yet unfocused.

"Shh, that's it. You're okay. Everything's okay."

She gave a soft cry of distress, ripped her hand from his, and threw herself into a sitting position, her arms clutching at him in fear. Startled at her reaction, it took a moment for him to return the hug, his arms enfolding her gently. He allowed one hand to curl up around her neck, his thumb brushing back and forth across the tendon as he crooned to her in Afrikaans. He knew the words wouldn't matter, but the tone of his voice and the whisper volume would go a long way to easing her distress.

When he felt her body begin to shake, he pressed the side of his jaw to her temple, his hushed voice spoken into her hair. After a few minutes, she quieted and stopped shaking, and her breathing returned to normal.

"Are you all right, *heuning meisie?*"

She nodded and pulled back to lie against the propped-up pillows.

"Bad dream?"

She nodded again. "Sorry," she whispered.

"Don't apologize. After what you went through, I'd be surprised if you didn't have nightmares. There's water here. Do you want some?"

When she nodded, he reached over to grab the bottle and cracked the seal for her. He handed it to her with the reminder, "Small sips. Don't want to upset your stomach."

She followed his instructions, and after three separate swallows of the liquid, she handed the bottle back to him.

"It's me who should apologize," he told her. "I'm likely the reason you had the nightmare. I asked you to dredge up a lot of stuff this morning, and I know it wasn't an easy thing to do."

"It reminded me of the fact that a lot of the past is missing," she replied.

Midas smiled. "Your voice is sounding better. That's good. Don't push it though."

Her smile was weak, but he could tell there was a little relief behind it as well. "Can you tell me what's going on?"

"A little bit. We're hoping you're going to be able to fill in the blanks, eventually."

Her smile dropped, as did her head.

His hand reached out to tip her chin up so that she was looking him in the eye. "Hey. It's okay. We'll figure it out together, all right?"

"Okay."

"So, let's see. Gem got a phone call that the school was under some kind of attack. They'd managed to pull out most of the staff and the students, but there was a teacher and five children left to extract. There was one guard still there, but he'd been injured, so they needed help extracting them. It took us four days to get to the country and work our way to you, but we managed to get in, find you and the girls in a classroom, and we brought you here to our home and offices."

"The guard?"

Midas shook his head. "He died, unfortunately. Last time we were able to speak to him, he knew he wasn't going to make it."

Her eyes were glassy, but she didn't cry. "I remember him. I didn't know him well, but he was great with the kids. He gave them piggyback rides all the time in the yard." She swallowed hard. "When those men chased us from the river, he got shot, but he still saved Ona. She got hit by a piece of the ceiling when it fell, and it knocked her to the floor. She was too stunned to move. If he hadn't swept her up, the wall would have crushed her when it went down a few seconds later. I knew he was hurt, but..." Her voice faltered.

"He protected you all to the end. He was a good man. I'm sorry, but the sister died as well."

"Yes, I knew. She was hit by that same wall. I was trying to get to her when I got hit with what felt like hundreds of pounds of rocks."

He smiled. "You did good hiding the girls in that cabinet. That thing was really sturdy. Barely a scratch on it despite the disaster in that room."

"Sturdy English oak from the eighteen hundreds is no joke," she commented. "How are they?"

"You'll be able to see for yourself in a little bit. Nemo and Gem are going to bring the girls up for a visit, and Waters and Kubrick are coming with the twins."

The smile she gave him lit up the room. "Thank you."

"Dramatic subject change. Do you want to talk about your dream?"

Her smile disappeared, and she turned her head toward the window. "I don't really remember anything. Impressions really."

"Impressions of what?"

Her eyes closed as if blocking out what was around her would help her remember. "There was a man and a woman. He wore glasses. He was smiling."

"Do you remember any sounds? Sometimes those are stronger in dreams."

"A phone ringing. Maybe?" She opened her eyes and turned to look at him. "I'm sorry. It's not helpful."

He smiled at her. "Maybe not that we can see right now, but a lot of times the things we dream are memories, or at least based off memories." He squeezed her hand. "Don't stress about it. Your brain will let things go when it's ready, and not before then."

"You sound like you know a lot about dreams."

Shrugging, he downplayed his knowledge. "I have a degree in psychology. You can't have that without spending time studying dreams. Even if Freud is being debunked on a regular basis nowadays, there's still a lot to study about what they are, how they work, and all that."

His doorbell chimed. With a tap to his watch, he saw who was there. After squeezing her hand again, he stood. "Medusa is here to help you get ready to see the girls. Let her know if you need something, and I'll make sure we get it for you."

With that, he left the room to let the Mythos team leader into the apartment.

9

JANUARY 26, 2024

Mouse

She heard their whispers and shuffling feet, along with Midas' encouragement, before she saw them. Finally, a small, dark-haired head poked its way through the cracked door. Shakira. There was another rustling noise, and a smaller child appeared beneath her, one hand clutching the doorknob. Sad brown eyes peered at her from the space between the door and the frame. Ona. Poor, sweet girl.

"Miss Mouse?" came the whispered voice.

"Shakira! Ona!" She held her arms out to them.

It was all the encouragement the girls needed. One moment, they were in the doorway, and the next, they were launching themselves into the bed, one in the crook of each arm, sobbing, heads buried into her body. The twins followed right behind until they were all piled together. She leaned down and clutched them tight, pressing a fervent kiss to each head.

Lifting her eyes, she noticed Midas had snuck into the room and put himself into the far corner to watch the reunion. He was smiling at how excited they were to see each other.

She watched him flash a look at a blond man in the doorway, who returned the smile with a nod. From behind him, a leggy blonde stood to the side, one hand on his arm. She was clearly happy to see the reunion as well, but there was something else in her gaze. It wasn't fear, but something like it. Was she worried that the woman holding the girls would hurt them?

Miss Mouse turned to Midas, tears falling. "Thank you."

He nodded. "This is my boss, Waters, and his girlfriend, Kubrick. They've been watching over Liliana and Catalina."

"Thank you," she told them as well.

"It's been our pleasure," Waters told her. He turned his head to Kubrick, rotating his arm up and over her shoulders to pull her into him. A kiss to the side of her head was clearly meant to be supportive.

"Miss Mouse! Miss Mouse!" Shakira's head poked up, and she lifted her arm. "Look! Look!"

Shakira proudly held up her cast. Demon had let her pick the color, which turned out to be neon pink. On the cast were the signatures of all the Tribe members and the Mythos members. She very specifically pointed out each signature and read the messages and names they wrote, as well as making sure to point out the little pictures some of them had drawn, like Nemo's fish and Medusa's snake.

"Wow! You must feel pretty special, huh?" she asked Shakira.

"My favorite is Nemo. Did you know he's named after the movie fish? He's got *two* broken fins!"

She looked at Midas, a question in her eyes.

"He can purposely dislocate both his shoulders. Don't ask."

"He didn't show her, did he?"

He laughed. "No. Not that she didn't try to make him."

Suddenly, there was hollering from the living room. "Who wants pizza?"

Shakira shrieked, "Me!" and took off running, with Ona close on her heels.

Catalina looked up at her, eyes wide and begging, even though the child was hesitant to leave her side. With a kiss to the girl's forehead, she whispered, "Go on, sweetheart. It's okay."

The little girl put a hand to her face, then turned toward Waters and Kubrick, her arms in the "up" position. "All right, baby girl. Pepperoni time," Waters said as he reached for her, immediately wrapping herself around him like a monkey in a tree, her head to his shoulder. He headed out to the hallway, Kubrick rubbing the child's back as they passed. The blonde cast a quick glance at her, smiled tentatively, and then held out her hand to Liliana, who went without a whimper.

When they left the room, Midas remained leaning against the wall, studying her. "You okay?" he asked.

She nodded, wiping the tears from her eyes with the backs of her hands. "That was really nice what they did for Shakira. She hasn't had much to be happy about, and she definitely looked happy. They all did."

"They have cause for celebration because they're happy to see you're okay. Been asking for you almost nonstop."

"But they're also happy with them."

Midas nodded. "Yeah, the twins attached to Waters and Kubrick pretty quickly. It goes both ways." He walked to the edge of the bed, his thumb reaching out to wipe away a last tear. "What's wrong?"

"It's just good to see them."

"They're cute kids."

"They're adjusting okay?" This was her biggest concern. Bumps and bruises healed. Mental and emotional wounds ran deeper, and without the proper care, they might never heal.

"Seem to be. Physically, they're all in good shape. Injuries are taken care of, and luckily, they're all relatively minor. Catalina's still having some nightmares, so we're working on getting a therapist for her."

Relief coursed through her. These people truly did have the girls' best interests at heart.

"You hungry?" he asked. "I don't know if you're ready for pizza, but I've got some other options available in case."

"I'm not sure I can walk out there," she admitted. "I'm aching quite a bit today."

"No worries. I've got ya." He pulled the covers back, then slipped an arm underneath her knees and the other behind her back. Surprised at how smoothly he lifted her, she threw her arms around his neck with a gasp. He winked at her. "Just consider me your own personal transportation source." Before she knew it, he was striding out of the room with her in his arms.

Out in the living room, there were squeals of excitement from the girls, barks from Scheherazade and another dog that looked just like her, only younger, and a general hubbub as the four adults in the room talked to each other. The television was sitting on the home screen of a streaming service. Nemo was setting out pizza boxes on the breakfast bar, Kubrick was diving into the refrigerator, and Waters was pulling glasses out of the cupboards, one arm still holding tight to Catalina.

Gem was pulling napkins and paper plates out of the kitchen cupboards and placing them at the start of the pizza box line. The tiny woman glanced at her, eyes twinkling, and a smile breaking across her face. "Hi, Miss Mouse."

Midas took her into the living room and tucked her into the lounge portion of his sofa. His voice broke through the noise. "That's Gem. You remember her?"

"I didn't know her name until you told me, but yes. She was usually the one who brought the children to us."

Once he had her settled, making sure her ankle was elevated and she had a pillow behind her back, he leaned over her, one hand on the arm of the couch. "Want to try pizza, or do you want something blander?"

"Plain cheese, maybe?"

"Catalina will be thrilled she doesn't have to fight you for the pepperoni."

"How often have you been feeding them pizza?" she asked in semi-horror.

"Don't ask. They're picky." He chuckled as he walked back into the kitchen to get her some food.

Suddenly, there was a small body burrowing into her side. She looked down to find Ona curling up to her. "She's not hurting you, is she?"

She looked up to see Kubrick standing next to her, two plates in her hand.

"She's fine. It's the ankle that's the issue now."

With a smile, the woman sat down. "C'mon, Ona. Time to eat. You can cuddle when you're finished."

The child raised a hand to touch Mouse's face. A tiny smile turned her lips upward, then she clambered down to sit at the coffee table. Kubrick had cut the child's pizza into small pieces she could pick up with her fingers, and her heart swelled with happiness at watching how excited the little girl was.

By the end of the movie, bellies full, the girls were passed out on the sofa—Ona curled into her side, Liliana with her head in Kubrick's lap, and Catalina passed out in Waters' lap. Shakira was the only one still awake, lying on the floor on her stomach, side by side with Midas, watching the movie. Even the six adults were basically comatose on the furniture and floor, with Scheherazade using Gem's butt as a pillow, and Ali, one of her two pups, sleeping belly up and drooling on the other side of Shakira.

Waters was the first to get up. "Guess we need to get these girls to bed," he whispered.

Kubrick stretched with a moan. "You hate to move and wake them up, but I also hate how my back feels when I finally can move."

"I'll give you a back rub later," her other half murmured.

Kubrick winked at Miss Mouse. "Magic hands," she mouthed.

Mouse smiled and gave a wave goodnight to the sleepy child

whose head lay on Kubrick's shoulder. A tiny little hand let go of the film director and gave two flashes of open and closed fists before the other snaked around Kubrick's neck, and her eyes went closed. She looked so natural there. So comfortable. It made her heart warm to see the child trusting in someone. The younger dog followed them out the door.

"We're going to head out too," Nemo announced quietly. "Mouse looks almost as done in as the kiddos." He stepped to Mouse's side and gently lifted Ona so that she sat on his hip. "Come on, girls. Time to let your teacher get some rest and for you to go to bed."

Shakira sat up and exchanged some sort of complicated hand-shake, fist-bump combination with Midas, then came up to Mouse to hug her good night. Gem held out a hand to the girl, and Nemo slung an arm around the woman's shoulders as the tattooed couple and their dog followed the other two out the door Midas had opened for them.

She watched as he returned to the living space and began collecting the detritus of a movie night. "You seemed really at ease with the chaos. The invasion of friends. The dog. The kids."

"Yeah, I don't mind it. When we hang out together, it's generally here in my space. Like a holiday family gathering with this new bunch." He smiled. "I love kids, which helps. This is the first time we've ever had kids at Tribe. It's been fun."

Something about children tickled her synapses, but the thought wouldn't come. Was it connected to the dream she'd had earlier? Did she have a child or a younger sibling and didn't know about it? That thought pained her. What if some poor child was abandoned some-where and she couldn't recall because of her amnesia? Somehow, she thought she'd "know" if there was a child, but then again, she didn't even know her own name, which seemed even more basic.

"Thank you again," she told him.

"Anything to see your smile, *heuning meisie*." He dumped the garbage, then put the now-cooled pizza boxes into the refrigerator. "Do you need something more to drink?"

"Just some water. I think I have meds coming up."

Midas brought her a bottle of water, opening it as he crossed to the couch. Then he pulled a small pill container out of his pocket and dumped the contents into her hand.

Frowning, she threw the pills into her mouth and took a swig of water to wash them down. "You always carry my meds around?"

Apparently, talking while taking her meds was a bad idea because a pill got stuck and caused her to start coughing. Midas gave her a few taps on the back as she tried to dislodge the pill. When it finally came back up, she took another swig of water. Well, that wasn't embarrassing at all.

"You okay now?" he asked.

She nodded.

"Tired? You want to go back to bed?"

"If you want to go to bed, I'll go in for the night. Otherwise, I'd kind of like to sit up a bit yet."

He waved her off. "I'm going to be up for a while. Don't sleep much. Too much work to do. You mind if I work out here with you?"

"No, not at all."

"'Kay. I'm going to go grab my laptop. I'll just be a minute. Don't move."

When Midas returned, he sat down on the opposite end of the sectional and opened his laptop.

"What exactly do you do?" she asked.

"Me? Or who I work for?"

"Both, I guess."

He shifted, his eyes traveling down to his computer screen, and his fingers began typing. "I'm the IT guy. Tribe, whom I work for, we're in... acquisitions." The slight pause before the final word made it clear he wasn't going to share the real purpose behind their work, which made sense given they'd come into a firefight that wasn't theirs to rescue strangers.

"Sorry. I shouldn't have pried."

He wrinkled his nose and shook his head. "It's okay. We just don't really talk about our jobs since we work in the shadows."

"I understand."

He stopped typing and looked up. "Why do they equate you with Snow White?"

"Excuse me? Oh, you mean the girls." She looked down and threaded the fringe ends of the blanket tucked around her legs. "I guess the first time they saw me, I was singing, like a Disney princess wandering in the woods." Her eyes went wide as she looked at Midas. "I just remembered that. Why did I just remember that?"

"I tried to ask the question nonchalantly. Out of context, so that your brain was relaxed. Sometimes when we think too hard or try too hard to do something, the brain refuses to cooperate."

"Nemo said that too. So you're not going to ask me my name again?"

He shook his head. "No. It hurts you when I ask you that."

She looked down at the blanket again. "How do you know that?"

"Your face scrunches up, and you put pressure on the bridge of your nose. Looks like you're trying to relieve a sinus headache. I don't like the thought of causing you pain. You have to feel alienated enough."

"I remember the children. Not... linearly? I mean, I remember bits and pieces of my time at the school, but nothing seems connected."

"Could be a byproduct of the hard hit to the head you took. The brain is a funny thing. It shuts down what it doesn't need in order to heal itself. You have to be prepared that things might come back in a flash like that. Unprompted even. It will probably be disconcerting, but not harmful."

Biting her lip, she paused. "Will it all come back?"

"I wish I could say 'yes,' but it's possible some things won't. Or if they do, it could be a very long time. Another woman we rescued years ago, when she was debriefing, had a memory surface from twenty-four years ago. Hadn't thought about it in all that time. We see that a lot, actually. I've also known people who have never recovered periods of their lives."

"Why does it hurt me, do you think, when you ask me my name? It shouldn't do that, right?"

"Honestly, I'm not sure. I wouldn't have thought so. Perhaps there's something psychosomatic going on? Like a physically painful moment that centers somehow on your name?"

"Psychology and you're the IT guy?"

"Yep. Feast or famine behind the computers. Sometimes you have a lot of time on your hands, waiting for something to happen. Filled some of that downtime with the degree. Did it all online."

"Guess it helps when you're trying to question people. You know how to approach them."

Midas closed his computer but let it sit on his lap. "Yes, it does. But I'm here because I want to be. Any of the guys could trade off and babysit you. I volunteered."

"Gathering 'research' on amnesia victims?"

"No, although that is a bonus I shouldn't overlook."

"Then why?"

He traced a South African flag sticker on the lid of his computer. "Do you remember anything from when we pulled you out of the school?"

"Not really." Just the vision of an angel in camouflage, but she didn't give voice to that.

"Since I pulled you out of the building, I guess I feel some responsibility for you. But if I'm one hundred percent honest? It was your eyes. I felt this... pull toward you. They opened for a few seconds in the helicopter, and I gotta admit. They're beautiful."

She felt herself blushing. "It's odd. When I look in the mirror, sometimes I get a glimpse of someone else. Like, it's me, but it's not me."

"Maybe your mother? A sibling? Someone with the same eye color who's related to you, I'll bet. Could even be a memory of a picture of yourself from when you were younger."

"Maybe," she agreed.

Thoughtful, she rolled onto her side and snagged the remote from the edge of the coffee table. Of course, her blanket got all twisted, and her foot came off its elevated perch. Midas came over to retuck her in and help her put her foot back in place.

"Put on whatever you like. It won't bother me." He returned to his seat, opened the computer, and began working again.

She searched through the streaming services until she found what she wanted. What seemed like only moments later, she felt herself being scooped up from the couch and carried somewhere. Midas. She must have fallen asleep during the movie, and he was carrying her back to bed.

He set her down and covered her with the blankets. The light was already off, but she heard him speak quietly into the wall monitor, and behind her eyelids, she saw the darkness lighten slightly. He'd put the bedside lamp on low for her. Lord, this man was sweet. She nestled further into the bedding, and before she drifted back into sleep, she felt his lips barely touch her temple.

"Sweet dreams, *heuning meisie.*"

JANUARY 27, 2024

Midas

"How's she doing? Kids weren't too much?" Waters asked.

"No. She woke up this morning the most positive I've seen her, so I think it really was the best thing for her and them."

"Anything new from her locked-up brain?"

He hesitated but realized there really wasn't any sense in hiding the answer. "She hasn't remembered anything new since yesterday. With each question I ask that she can't answer, she withdraws more, getting quieter and quieter, which is a little concerning, given she was already silent much of the time. She feels guilty about not being able to answer."

Waters flashed a look at the telescreen where their boss' voicebox sat. Six years and they still had never seen their boss. Waters looked back at Midas. "It's been eight days, Midas, and we're no further ahead. God broke another tooth in his anxiety. Cherry had to hide his suckers again," Waters said.

"I found another supplier," their boss grumbled.

The team was sitting in the conference room, joined by Mythos, who were hanging around to see what shook loose from Mouse and the kids they'd rescued.

"I can't make her remember anything. I've gotten lucky on a few random, unexpected questions, but it's tiny stuff. Her nickname. She likes oranges. She's really good at math. That's about it."

"I get that, Midas, but I also agree with him. Is there anything you can pull out of your 'voodoo practices' to maybe jog something loose?"

"It's not voodoo, fuckwitch. It's hypnosis. I could try, but there's no telling if it will work. I also have no idea if it will cause her pain. Steel spoke up from the far end of the table. "She's still getting headaches when you ask her questions?"

"Sometimes," Midas admitted. "Not every question. Seems like the more I ask about her name or distant past, the worse it is. Something at the school? I either get information, or she can't remember."

Medusa and Loki shared a look, seeming to have a conversation without talking.

Midas narrowed his eyes at the silent communication. "What?" he asked them.

"It's possible," Medusa replied, "that there's a blocker in there."

"You mean like someone programmed her?"

With a shrug, Medusa hoisted herself up onto the credenza she had been propped against and sat cross-legged. She pushed her tinted glasses up onto the top of her head and squinted. Medusa had a rare eye condition that had removed basically all pigment from her irises. While she could still see perfectly fine, she was extremely light sensitive and suffered from severe migraines, even with the eye protection. Out of respect, Waters immediately leaned forward and hit the button on the room controls—a starfish-like apparatus in the center of the table—and dimmed the lights.

"Is that even a real thing?" Steel asked. "I thought that was just spy movie stuff."

Now it was TB and Midas' turn to share a look.

"I can't do it. But PsyOps could when I was in the Israeli Army," TB said.

"*Mierda!*" Steel whispered.

Midas understood where the man was coming from. The idea of planting ideas into someone's head was always a concern. Entertainer hypnotists admitted that even the smallest suggestions could stick with someone long after they were set free of their hypnosis state. He had even seen where people would seem to "fail" at becoming hypnotized while on stage, and then the suggestions would manifest much later. Messing with anyone's brain, taking away their free will, was dangerous.

"Are we talking brainwashing?" Waters asked.

"No," TB answered. "What we're talking about is much more invasive. Imagine you were in this room, but when you went to the door to exit, it was bricked up."

Midas continued the thread. "Only, in this case, it would be more like an electric fence. Every time you're asked a question where the answer lies on the other side of that fence, you get a shock."

"How do you make that happen?" Waters asked.

Midas answered, "Association. Ask her specific questions, and when she goes to answer, deliver a pain stimulus. You could even set the level of pain based on what questions were asked."

"Jesus Christ," Waters whispered.

"People act like it's science fiction, but it's a simple Pavlovian response. Pain delivery wouldn't even have to be high tech. She experiences headaches and eye pain. An extremely bright light flashed in wide open eyes, then connect that light to a poke with a sharp object, or what have you. Maybe a more severe form of pain, depending on the information you want blocked."

"She has no memory of anything at all before the school, and damn little from when she was there. That's a lot of time to erase."

TB spoke up again. "Well, they could have done a blanket suggestion. Say... tell her anything from her life prior to today."

"But it wouldn't hold as much strength," Midas told him. "That barrier could fall down, metaphorically, at any time. If you wanted to do it right, you'd have to isolate most everything in her life."

"Wouldn't that take a long time?" Demon asked.

Midas nodded. "Yes. A very long time. Especially if you were going to do it right."

Puzzled, Waters drummed his fingers on the table. "How long are we talking?"

"If I were going to hazard a guess? Pains me to say it, but it would probably require several years."

Someone in the room whistled.

God barked out, "Brain damage?"

A nod from Midas. "Possibly. The longer you tamper with a brain, it's possible. It's a fragile organ. Physically, brains don't regenerate tissue, so once something is lost, it's lost. If she were beaten and sustained head injuries, or drugs were administered as part of the process, or if oxygen deprivation were part of the programming, that could happen."

"Would we be able to tell if any of that has occurred?"

Demon piped up, "Not without full MRI and CT scans. From what Midas has reported, she's not showing any motor or cognitive skill loss other than not being able to remember anything, so my guess would be no."

Waters turned to Midas. "Do you think she'd let us run the scans?"

"Probably," he answered. "She seems genuinely as frustrated by the memory loss for us as she is for herself. I think if we told her it might help us get to the bottom of things, she'd jump at the chance."

"Okay, then that's first. Let's see what we can see. Midas, coordinate a time with Demon to run the scans."

There was a giant crunch over the speakers. One of the contraband caramel apple suckers. "What if there's no sign of brain damage?" God asked. "What next? We can't just be sitting here on our asses. According to our Dr. Freud here, she could keep those memories locked in there for months. Years. Forever. We need information sooner rather than later, and if this is Salieri connected, as we suspect, we needed it eight days ago."

"Once we have the scans," Midas said, "I'll have a better idea how to proceed. If there is damage, we'll have to see where and what that might affect. If there isn't, we can proceed with hypnosis, but at my discretion. If it appears to give her physical pain, I won't continue."

"Hmph," was the only response from over the speaker. Somehow, even his voice wave communicated irritation.

Waters moved on. "All right. Next item. Where are we with locating our on-the-run Salieri from St. Lucia? Do we have anything on Zion Norton, Andres, and General Howard?"

"All accounts with Nimbus Corporation have been closed off to Zion Norton based on a board vote, and a new CEO was named," Midas informed them. "He's got five kids, three of whom are girls, and he's married to his college girlfriend, so there's no way he's dirty. Three board members disappeared without a word. I've left their financials open to see if I can trace them for Mythos to go after. No one has touched anything yet, but Nova will let me know if they do. Money attached to Andres is open for the same reasons. I figure he might be less savvy about what we can and can't see on the computer. There was a hit on General Howard's accounts, but it bounced so many times, I lost it. TB suggested he might be getting help on the dark web. We're extending the protocols there."

"No locations though?" Waters asked.

"Other than the last Howard ping, which I'm sure is not where he is, no," Midas grumbled.

"We didn't expect it would be easy."

"What about that other kid we reached out to?" TB asked. "Howard's foster kid or whatever he was."

God came over the line. "Victim of a home invasion the day after we called and was in a coma. Died this morning. Isn't that coincidental?" The sarcasm was more than evident.

Midas piped up, "Howard hadn't reached out to him, either, since St. Lucia."

"I didn't really expect him to since they haven't spoken in years, but continue to monitor his phone, emails, and socials, just in case the general is unaware and tries to contact him."

Midas said, "We're also not sure if the trio is together or if they've separated. My bet is they separated. Andres most likely went with Zion, but of course, we can't be sure of that."

Waters tapped the file folder in his hand against his leg. "Any ideas where they've headed?"

Clicking on his screen, Midas brought up a world map on the telescreen. Several spots had flashing red and yellow dots. "Most likely locations of where we might find these guys, or that they'd travel to at some point. Zion has a home in Italy, as well as an apartment in New York City and a flat in London. I also looked into locations he frequents often. The rest are mostly places he goes for client meetings—military bases, cargo companies."

"Fuckin' Sallum again," TB grumbled. "That's where you guys found the coffins they were using for transporting the women, isn't it?"

With a sigh, Waters threw the folder down on the conference room table, then ran his hands over his scalp-cropped hair. He turned back to Midas. "Do we have people out watching the blinking locations?"

Loki, the Nordic member of the Mythos trio, spoke up. "We've got some of our contractors on it. They've been told to be extra careful since we don't know if Zion had photo surveillance of them like he had on all of you."

"What are the green lights?" Steel asked.

"Those are for Howard."

"And the white solid lights?"

"Locations we've checked and burned."

"Literally," Loki added. "When your traditional teams cleared them, Cerberus went in and worked his magic. Those locations are useless to anyone but scavengers now." He held up a hand to Waters' opening mouth. "Before you ask, yes, inhabitants either disappeared with the properties or are in our custody waiting for... 'clearance.' Can't afford to leave any Salieri or connections behind."

"And what if they're innocent?" Midas asked.

Gilgamesh, the dark-haired Mythos member, grunted. "Salieri don't work like that. So far, everyone we've found at these properties has been connected." He looked to Loki and Medusa before focusing back on Waters. "Unfortunately, one of them was tied to two of your new residents."

Waters' face tightened. "Liliana and Catalina," he guessed.

"Yes," Loki confirmed. "They're true orphans now. Father was a shipping line owner out of Barcelona. Recent 'acquisition' to the membership."

The skin around Waters' mouth tightened as he pursed his lips. "No family at all for them?"

"Not that we'd trust."

The team leader worked his mouth as if considering asking a question but held it back. Then his face went blank.

Through the sound of crunching candy, God asked, "Is the shipping line still operational?"

"No," Gilgamesh said. "We took that baby down immediately. 'Domestic Terrorist Attack' was the official report. We've got the records for Midas to comb through when he has time. See if we can't backtrack through them for some leads. In the process, we found a shipment headed for Dubai. We've got the kids at another one of our locations."

TB swore under his breath. "Are we going to be able to stop these guys? They're fucking everywhere."

"Where there's money to be made, there will always be douchebags," Steel reminded him. "If what Cherry gave us from her little escapade is even half true, we could be running these assholes down our entire lives and beyond. Full-time fucking occupation."

"Hence why Mythos was created," Medusa remarked.

"Yeah, but there're only six of you. Well, seven with Nerdbrain."

"Hey," Nemo complained good-naturedly. He sailed a paper airplane in the shape of a stealth bomber at the interrogator's head.

TB batted it away. "We're talking thousands... tens of thousands of these people," TB said.

Medusa smiled. "Aww. It's cute that you think there are only the seven of us. For all you know, there could be tens of thousands of us."

With a snort and a roll of his eyes, he blew her off. "Not likely. I'm surprised there are even seven of you."

"You'll never know, will you?" she teased.

"Okay," God interrupted. "So we've got financials closed down or under watch on our three principals, surveillance on their potential locations, and possible leads on a new branch of Salieri business to look into. We also need to relocate our guests because they can't stay here forever. What's our line on that?"

"For now, they're fine. They've adjusted well to us, and I hate to up and move them so soon."

"I agree with Waters," Nemo added. "No discussion has taken place on where to take them. TB and Flame have the baby since she's so close in age to Axel. Gem and I are good babysitting Shakira and Ona. It's like being ten all over. I may never sleep outside a blanket fort again."

Midas buried his face in his computer screen and rolled his eyes. Leave it to his brother to see this as an opportunity to play around. His twin would probably never grow up and be Peter Pan all his life.

"But we won't be here forever," Medusa warned. "A decision will have to be made, and soon. You'll all be needed to work projects. We'll need to place them before we can do that."

"Let's all get back to work," God groused. "Midas and Demon have some convincing to do, and hopefully that gets us some answers we didn't have before."

11

JANUARY 28, 2024

Midas

DEMON TURNED ON THE VIEW BOX, THEN TURNED OFF THE lights. Mouse sat on the exam bed, her posture ramrod straight, nervousness vibrating through her. Midas stood next to her, holding her hand.

"I don't see any signs of brain damage," Demon confirmed.

The relief on Mouse's face was readily apparent, her eyes closing, her breath escaping on a loud exhale. Midas gave her hand a gentle squeeze. "It's all good. Now we know."

Demon leaned against the waist-high cabinet in the infirmary, his arms locked on the top behind him. He stared at Midas. Message received.

He put all his focus on her. "Mouse, there's one more thing."

"What?" she asked. Panic flooded her face.

"Relax, *heuning meisie*. It's just... We'd like to try something. A little experiment to see if we can access your memories another way."

"How?"

"Hypnosis."

Her eyes widened, and he watched her swallow slowly. "Is it safe?"

"I promise I'm not going to make you cluck like a chicken," he joked.

Her smile was weak, but it lightened her tension a little further.

"I won't lie. I am going to poke at things that don't want to come out, so there's always some risk, but it's minimal. I've done it before and haven't had any issues." He swung around to the foot of the exam table and took hold of her other hand as well. He made sure her eyes were fixed on him before speaking again. "I can't promise you won't feel ill during or after. You know how sick some questions leave you feeling. I'm hoping because you'll be in a state of semiconsciousness, it won't hurt. If at any time you show signs of pain, I'll bring you out. Immediately. You have my word."

Her eyes searched his. A cough came from behind them. Demon. Shit. He'd forgotten the man was there.

The medic crossed to the door as he spoke. "I'll let you two talk." He gently closed the door behind him.

During all of this, his gaze hadn't wavered from Mouse's, nor had hers from him. There was a tension in the air between them. A tension that hadn't been there before. He'd been feeling that pull to her get stronger with each day he'd been taking care of her, and he finally had to admit he didn't want that tension to be one-sided. Unfortunately, given her situation, he wasn't sure exactly how to proceed.

"Midas?" Mouse's voice reflected the question in her face. "What is it? Just tell me. It's worse not knowing."

"We think that someone might have placed what a layman would call a mind block in your neural pathways. Your body doesn't show any sign of chronic trauma, like physical damage or excessive drug exposure—things that might render you unable to remember. That means that someone would have had extensive, private access to you.

That they used psychological conditioning on you so you wouldn't remember things. Putting you under hypnosis might allow us to get at some of those missing memories, particularly the ones at the school, as well as letting me know what we're up against in getting at the rest. But I'm not going to lie. It could be painful in more ways than physical."

"You'll be the one doing it?"

"Yes." One hand, still holding hers, raised to trail a finger down the side of her face. "I'll take care of you, *heuning meisie*. I promise. I wouldn't hurt you for anything."

"Okay."

"Just okay?" He searched her face for any hint of hesitancy, then smiled when he found none. "Okay. I'm proud of you. You're being very brave."

"I don't feel brave. I feel terrified. What if I don't like what you find? What if I'm a terrible person? What if it's bad?"

"Search your heart. Do you feel like a bad person?"

She shook her head.

"Then if we find something 'bad,' it's not going to be something you did. Your brain might not remember specifics, but it's not going to change who you are at your core. Your brain will always remember that much, all right? And if whatever we find is hurtful to you, I will make sure to help you through it afterward."

She had an odd look on her face.

"What is it, *heuning meisie*?"

"Cinnamon roll," she whispered.

"What?" Midas asked. "Did you say 'cinnamon roll'?"

"Yes." Her gaze met his. "I was thinking about you." She blushed as she realized how that sounded. "How sweet you are to me. How comforting. And then I remembered a story I read, about a motorcycle club. The hero was everything you didn't expect someone like that to be."

"What kind of book?" His voice had taken on a slightly lower register, and his finger brushed her cheek again, like he was trying to coax the information out of her.

"It was a romance." She could feel her face heating further. "There's a certain kind of main character. He's sweet. Thoughtful. But still an alpha male when it comes to protecting his girl. Like he'd burn down the world to save her." She frowned. "Why do I remember that, of all things?"

He felt a frisson of heat pass through him and over to her. "Sometimes, little things come back first. The brain found it easy to let go of it because it wasn't significant at the moment. Or maybe it was. You said you were thinking about me and how I've been with you. Maybe there's something in that book that connects specifically to something I've done with you."

"That could be a lot of things," she teased. "You carry me around so I don't screw up my ankle. You let me stay in your apartment rather than by myself in a strange place. You made sure I got to see the girls…" She trailed off. "It had something to do with girls. Kidnapped girls," she whispered. "But it's gone." Her pulse began to race, and she felt a sweat break out through her skin. A sudden pain behind her eye caused her to wince and pinch her skin above her eyebrow, massaging it as if that would make the stabbing feeling go away. "Why can't I remember?"

She felt his arms go around her, pulling her tight to his chest, one hand cradling her head and laying it against his heart. "Shh, shh, shh," he soothed. "Don't push it. Let it come when it wants to come. You'll just make yourself sick over this."

His hand brushed up and down her spine, his touch light. He didn't say anything.

"Another trait," she whispered. "I just remembered that I don't speak unless I have to, and that I prefer people who are the same way. People who talk for the sake of talking make me anxious."

Lips pressed to the top of her head. Today was a day for revelations of all kinds, apparently. "That's good, Mouse. Real good. Each little piece we get helps form a picture. We never know what will be significant and what won't be."

"Remembering that book might be though. Is it possible to figure out which one?"

"I bet there're a lot of books, even romances, with motorcycles and plots of kidnapped girls, but yes, we can set up a search and ask the computer to populate a list. Once we have that, I can show it to you. Maybe a title will jump out, maybe it won't. But it's one more piece of you either way, yeah? If nothing else, it will give you a TBR a million miles long," he teased.

She wrapped her arms around him, returning his embrace, and buried her face in the center of his chest. "I just feel helpless. Useless. It's frightening to not know who you are. Where you've been. What you've done. Thank you for helping me. You could have just turned me loose, but you didn't. Most people would have considered their job done once they pulled me out of that building."

"You're not a job, Mouse. Not to me. You're a person. I would help you no matter the circumstances."

They stayed like that for a few minutes longer, his mind whirling with what-ifs.

"Let's get you upstairs for a rest. I'll make the arrangements for the hypnosis."

"Tonight?" There was a squeak in her voice.

"We can wait until tomorrow if it would make you feel better," he offered.

Her forehead rolled back and forth on his chest. "No. Anticipation might make it worse. Let's get it over with."

His arms squeezed her just a little tighter. "So brave," he whispered.

12

JANUARY 28, 2024

Mouse

"Look into my eyes and breathe with me, Mouse." His voice was low and covered her like the softest blanket. His lips upturned at the corners as she gave him her trust and followed his instructions. "In through your nose on the count of four." He inhaled deeply, counting each beat, and she followed. "Out through your mouth on a count of four." He exhaled as he counted, and again she followed.

They'd chosen to do the hypnosis in Midas' apartment, a place that felt safe and comfortable. Demon was the only one present other than her and Midas, although she knew the others were watching a video feed. He told her he wanted the medic nearby in case she became ill.

Midas held out his hands, palms up. "Place your hands in mine." His hands were warm beneath her ice-cold ones. "Keep breathing with me." She never broke his gaze, and subconsciously, she felt herself sink into the warmth of all things Midas.

"Close your eyes, Mouse." Her eyes drifted closed. Her breathing remained in the pattern Midas had established.

"Can you see anything?"

"No."

"Okay, that's good. I want you to imagine you're in a pitch-black, empty room. You're safe, even though you can't see anything. In a minute, I'm going to ask you to walk forward. There's nothing in the room for you to bump into or trip over. With each step, the room around you is going to lighten just a little bit. The tenth step will put you exactly in front of a sink with a faucet. There's no need to temper your stride. Just walk straight at your normal pace. Count your steps with me. One. Two. Three..."

His voice became tinny, like it came out of an earbud. And just as promised, with each step she visualized and counted with him, the space around her got lighter.

"Ten."

She stopped, and before her was a white sink with a stainless steel faucet.

"You're doing great, Mouse. I want you to reach up and put your hand on the faucet. Turn it on, but so that there's just a trickle of water emerging."

She followed his instructions. Drops of water came from the faucet at a slow but steady drip. The sound echoed in the empty, imaginary room.

"All right, Mouse. Go ahead and open up the faucet a little more, until the water is a very thin, steady stream."

She saw her hand reach for it again and gently turned the spigot so that a small amount flowed from its opening. "The water is running."

"Excellent. Every time you increase the flow of the water, I want you to picture the pipe that's coming from the wall. The water is your past. The pipe goes from the past on the other side of the wall, which is a storage space for your memories, to today on this side. Follow the pipe in your mind. When you come out the other side of the wall, tell me what you see."

Mouse felt herself split into two, the second version of herself starting to shrink to a size that would fit into the mouth of the faucet. Her second self crawled into the pipe and began to walk into the water's flow. She felt the water rushing over her feet as she walked, and in front of her, a light appeared. Her second self slipped from the faucet mouth at the other side, then immediately grew in size. But, instead of her normal height, she seemed to only be about four feet tall. She could feel her present self scrunch up her nose in confusion.

Midas' voice sounded in her head again. "Remember. You are in control of everything that happens from this point forward. If at any time this gets to be too much, return to the faucet, go back through the pipe, turn off the water, and back up ten steps. When you're back in the dark, then you can open your eyes, and you'll be here with us. Okay?"

She nodded.

"Words, Mouse." She shivered. That phrase was a command despite its low volume. A command she could never deny.

"Yes, Midas."

"Good girl."

She smiled at his praise.

"Okay, Mouse, what do you see?"

"It's a kitchen. I'm pretty sure it's an apartment because there's no wall, and I can see into a living room. But something's weird."

"You're safe. I'm here. What do you mean by 'weird'?"

"My body. It feels short." She looked down at herself. "I have black shoes on, but they're scuffed. Well-worn. I'm wearing light-blue jeans with a patch on the thigh. A rainbow. There's a beaded bracelet on my wrist. The colors are also in rainbow order. And then beads that are hearts. They have letters on them. A, M, and Y."

"What about what's around you?"

"There's a man sitting at the kitchen table. He's calling me over to sit next to him."

"What does he look like?"

"In his forties, maybe, but on the young side. Brown hair, but there's gray along the sides. Just a touch of it. He has a beard, but it's close to his face and nicely shaped. He wears glasses. He has a sweatshirt on, but I can't read whatever it says. The table edge and his arm are blocking it."

"Go sit with him, Mouse. Is there anything on the table?"

"Books. A chemistry textbook. A notebook with what looks like classroom notes, some in one handwriting, some in another. I think one must be mine and the other must be his. He starts walking me through the notes. It's some sort of chemical equation. There's a handout of a periodic table. A calculator. A backpack. There are some sort of sticks and balls of different colors. Model pieces. He's having me build something with them." She paused. "Covalent bonds."

"Is there anyone else there?"

"A woman. She's drying dishes and watching. She's smiling at us."

"What else do you see?"

"The furniture and appliances look old but nice. Like we don't have money, but we're not poor. There are papers on the refrigerator, but I can't read them." She stopped and scrunched her nose again. "There's a calendar on the wall."

"Can you read the month? The year? Can you tell what day it is?"

She felt a pounding start in her head, like a bass drum far in the distance, belting a steady beat.

"The calendar says 2010. May. There's nothing on the page that says what day it is."

The pounding of the drum was getting louder, the speed of the beat gathering quickly.

"My head hurts, Midas."

She felt a squeeze to her hands. "Okay, Mouse, listen carefully. I want you to go back to the sink, go back through the pipe. Can you do that?"

"Midas—"

"Relax, sweetheart. Walk to the pipe. Go back through."

She felt ill. The drum was so loud, it sounded as if it were right behind her, and the beats were so close together, she knew that very soon it would just be one loud noise. She felt her second self shrinking, scrambling to get back into the pipe. She slipped, and her body washed toward the other end of the connection with startling speed, hurtling through the mouth of the faucet.

She grew to normal size and merged with her other half.

"Turn off the faucet slowly, Mouse. You're safe now."

She reached for the faucet and turned the spigot off.

"It's off."

"Close your eyes and back up slowly ten steps. Count with me. When we get to ten, open your eyes. I'm right here."

She heard herself counting with Midas. The farther she got from the sink, the colder she became until she was shaking violently.

"Ten." Her body pitched forward, but Midas caught her. "I'm here, Mouse. I've got you."

Midas was always there to catch her. She felt herself being lifted into strong arms, a soft sweater underneath her cheek. She clutched at it, knowing she was probably clawing the cashmere, but she couldn't get close enough to him. The closer she was, the less pounding in her brain. She didn't know how she knew that would be true, just that it would be.

A hushed, deep voice—not Midas'—said, "Let's wrap her in this." Almost immediately, she felt her body exchange from Midas to another. Before she could do more than moan in protest, she felt sherpa fleece engulf her, cocooning her, and then she was back in Midas' arms. She burrowed down as far as she could go, the pounding easing in volume and pace.

"You did great, Mouse. Rest now."

She felt soft lips on her forehead. Midas reassuring her.

There was a brief snick of a door opening and closing, and then stone silence.

She felt Midas shift, and then there was a bottle at her lips. "Drink, sweetheart. Just a few sips." The cool water touched her lips and slid down her throat. "Sleep now. I'll be right here." In the distance, she thought she heard him say, "So proud, *heuning meisie.* So brave."

The last part came so quietly, she wasn't sure she heard him right. She snuggled back into Midas' arms and felt herself drift off.

13

JANUARY 28, 2024

Midas

He just held her. What else could he do?

She was compassionate. Beautiful.

But it was her bravery that got to him. So fucking brave. Her absolute willingness to give of herself despite the fear she so clearly felt. To do what she did today, to let him open her mind and ask her to walk around in the past, he wasn't sure he could do it himself. And it had been painful. He could see it, he could hear it, and worst of all, he could feel it. His heart had actually hurt.

He heard the beeps of his door code and the soft opening of the door. He saw Waters out of the corner of his eye. "She asleep?"

Midas nodded. "She'll probably be out for a while. Give me a second." He stood with her in his arms and carried her to her bedroom. After tucking her in, he went back to the living room.

Waters sat on the edge of the armchair, his forearms leaning on his thighs, his hands gripping each other between his knees. "What do you think?"

Midas sat on the couch. "I'm not sure what to think, to be honest. It was clearly a memory. Based on the calendar, the way she described being dressed, and the textbook material, she would probably have been a sophomore or junior in high school. That puts her somewhere between twenty-eight and thirty years old."

"Does that help us at all?"

"Search parameters are way too broad but not impossible. It does give us a range of time to search, which narrows that piece, but it's still a huge time frame. It's going to take time, and God's not very patient. If I had a city or some sort of landmark through a window, it would make it infinitely easier."

"The beads on the bracelet."

Midas nodded. "Could be her name. Possibly initials. The odds of locating her that way? They're astronomical."

"But you could search the census database. Populate a list, then compare against data from a rough band of years around her age. That helps limit as well."

"Still a large number. It will take time."

"Understood." He held up his wrist, showing him the yarn threads he wore and flipped his wrist to show him the letters weaved into the portion under it. "I got this from a boy in Afghanistan. The unit played soccer with him, and he made this for me. It's a friendship bracelet. The three letters are initials. His initials."

"So the letters on her wrist could be a friend's initials."

"Exactly. Or..." He hesitated. "It's also possible the Y is for a maiden name."

Midas winced. He hoped that wasn't the case.

"There were no photos of anyone in the missing person's databases that matched with facial recognition, but I'll search again, as well as passports highlighting those initials. If we get nothing, I'll go back and hit with just the first two letters and leave the last one open-ended. Makes an even more insurmountable task, but we've got to try."

"Agreed. Maybe try going backward too. Given how total this brain block is, I'm assuming she's probably been missing for a while. If she were an adult at the time of her disappearance, she might have gone undetected. We've seen how easy it is with Flame's situation for people to go missing with no one reporting it. A couple of those women... people just assumed they picked up and left. Adults are allowed to do that, and the police don't often dig deep or for long because other, more important cases come up."

"Like kids. I've got a de-aging program," he said. "I could run her photo through that. It's not one hundred percent accurate, but we might be able to get a close approximation of what she looked like when she was younger and compare it against missing and abducted children."

"Do it." Waters paused for a moment. "The people she described are most likely her parents, or at the very least, guardians. The home sounded positive. If she had gone missing as a child, they would have reported it. Maybe we'll get lucky. This brain block. Can you break it?"

"Probably with time. The level of pain she's in when pushed suggests unnatural causes. Blunt force would be inadvisable. If she's been tampered with, depending on why, forcing my way in could trigger a protocol. I'm not sure what it would do to her. I refuse to destroy her, even accidentally. I'm good at what I do. I can find what we need without her, but it will take time. And before you say it, I know: we don't have time."

"No, we don't."

"Waters—" He stopped when he felt the scrutiny of his boss. "What's that look on your face for?"

His boss seemed to be contemplating whether or not to say something.

"Can we talk in private?"

Midas looked around. "This is pretty private, bro."

"Hallway. She'll be okay in there for a couple minutes. We'll just be outside the door."

Midas felt himself frown, but the tone of his boss' voice was weird. He followed Waters through the door, and they stopped just outside it.

"I'm worried," Waters said, his voice low.

"You're worried?" Midas matched his level. "About what?"

"You're attached to this woman. You're hyperfocused on her after less than two weeks. That's not you."

"What the hell, Waters?"

"I'm just trying to look out for you."

Midas sighed. "This is unreal."

Waters leaned against the wall. "Look. If it were anyone else on our team, I wouldn't even bat an eye. How you're responding to her, though, is so out of character. You obsess over Nemo, rubber squishy cats, NikNaks, and terabytes, not women. Hell, I've never seen you with a woman in the entire time I've known you, and that includes when I was researching you. So am I surprised at your reaction to her? Yes."

"Please tell me that this is not the hot office gossip?"

"Seriously? Of course it is. You should know better since you've run the betting pools in this office from day one. It's *all* the guys are talking about, and now they've actually dragged Mythos into the nonsense. Everyone's got a theory as to why you've been as celibate as a saint."

"Fabulous. What's yours?"

"You've been the direct opposite of your brother. I just assumed you were extra discreet because of his habits. But now? I don't think it's just discreet. I'm betting there hasn't been a woman in your life. At all."

Midas shrugged. He was silent for a few minutes as he gathered his thoughts. He knew Waters would wait in silence to let him process his ideas and put them together.

"Part of it might have been a reaction to Nemo. You know our history. When our dad took off, somehow, I became responsible for him. I spent most of my younger years rescuing him from shit, including his hookups, and it probably put me off from the whole idea. It made it all seem cheap, I guess. When Gem came along and he got ten times worse than a normal guy? I knew it was related to her, but I figured he'd fuck it out of his system.

"We were busy making a living. Surviving. Then we came to Tribe, and he got worse the second time around after he ran into her again. I realized I didn't want the kind of pain he seemed to be experiencing. I mean, how do you fall for someone that completely in just a couple of hours? I'd certainly never met anyone who gave me even a tenth of that feeling.

"This job doesn't particularly lend itself to getting involved with women. Especially mine, since I didn't often get to leave the sacred halls of Tribe to do it, and God pretty much kept me chained to my desk. Then, all of a sudden, you guys start dropping like flies." When he continued, he was even more soft-spoken than normal. "From the moment those girls told us there was another person in that building, I knew something was coming. It was almost like that feeling you get when shit's about to go sideways. But not quite the fear portion of it. Just... anticipation."

Waters nodded. "I get it. She's a beautiful woman. But we know nothing about her, Midas. I'm just looking out for you because you're acting in a way that none of us have ever seen you act, and I'm being protective, I guess."

Midas opened his mouth to speak, but Waters cut him off.

"I'm not doubting that what you feel is real. Fuck knows, I took one look at Kubrick and I was a goner. But this is not the same situation. I had my fair share of hookups and fucking around, so I know the difference between what's real and what isn't. I hope she's everything she seems to be, but we know so little about her, and I don't want to see you get burned because she turns out to be something other than how we see her or watch your heart break because she has a past that she needs to go back to."

"Thanks for caring, Waters. Really. Unfortunately, I think it's too late to worry about whether or not my heart gets broken. I've never felt this way about anyone. Never even knew it was possible. I may not know the finer details about her, but I know the important things.

"She loves those kids to the point that they are always her first concern. She'd do anything to make sure they're able to grow up safe and happy.

"And I know she's the bravest person I've ever met. The trust she has in me? In us? Despite whatever has happened to her—and by no means do I think we're done with the ugliness of her past—she picks up and keeps moving forward, no matter what anyone throws at her.

"Waters, I can no more hold back how I feel about her than I can stop the world from turning. But," he emphasized, "I know the risk I'm running, and I've worked hard to keep from letting her know. She doesn't need that pressure. It's not fair to her." He blew all the air out of his lungs. "So if it goes bad, then it goes bad, and I'll have to pick up what she leaves behind and figure out how to move on."

"There's nothing better than having a woman who's capable of being that strong. Kubrick, Flame, Gem, and Cherry? They're special women. I hope it all works out for you. I think she'd fit in well with them and be very good for you." He moved off the wall, ready to walk down the hall. "Take care of her. One way or the other, I know we'll get what we need."

When Waters pressed his code into the elevator, he turned and delivered his final message. "When you find that strength in a woman, you gotta run to her. Don't question it. Don't second-guess it. Don't try to resist. All it ends up being is time wasted." And with that parting wisdom, he was gone.

In that moment, he knew he'd do anything to protect this woman, whether it was from whatever was in her past, an unknown enemy, or even his own tribe. He'd suspected she was his, but now it was inevitable. As Nemo had once told him about Gem, her or no one else ever.

14

JANUARY 29, 2024

Mouse

She awoke disoriented by dreams she'd had during the night. Dreams that were disturbing, not because they were violent or harmful to her, but because they were full and complete.

They also were from when she was much younger, and she guessed the hypnosis session yesterday was what had prompted them. Unsure what to make of what she'd dreamt, she knew she had to tell Midas, as she was certain they were actual memories. But one of the things she remembered edged out all the others, even though it was probably in the middle of the pack in terms of significance.

A name.

She had a name.

Anastasiya.

The profoundness of having an identity again, even if it was just a label rather than a history, was not lost on her.

She supposed the girls would always call her by the nickname, but Midas? Would he still use the nickname, or would he call her by her given name now? She tried to imagine what it would sound like as he said it. Would it just roll off his tongue naturally, friend to friend? Or would it hold warmth like she'd felt in the infirmary? Would hearing her real name coming from his lips create the same low, bubbling heat his gentle touch had? Would it cause her blood to warm into a comfortable bath, adding an extra layer of security to what he already provided her? Or would it boil in a frenzy, making her burn for more?

She shivered at the thought.

The clock said it was just after eleven a.m. She'd slept almost fifteen hours. Swinging her legs over the side of the bed, her head spun slightly. The drums were no longer pounding, but the lingering of her headache still remained. Standing, she made sure the boot Demon had put on her foot the day before was secure.

Her head swam again briefly. Before she went to find Midas, she ducked into the bathroom to splash some water on her face. In a drawer, she found some over-the-counter painkillers, which she took to try and dull the throbbing behind her eye.

As she came back into the room, Scheherazade yawned, a high-pitched whine emitting as her jaw hit its largest gap. She scratched the dog's head. "When did you get here, girl?"

The dog gave a soft chuff, then stood, stretching like a typical dog—front legs out front, butt up in the air, and as far back as she could get it—then hopped off the bed, nosed the door open further, and trotted out to the living space.

Following on the dog's heels, her eye struck on her backpack on the shelf of the open closet. She bit her lip. It had blipped through her dream several times, and bits and pieces of memories floated back to her again. Hastily, she grabbed it, put it over her shoulders, and left the room.

Arriving in the main room, she found the Tribe team and Nemo sitting around Midas' living room, talking in low voices as if they'd been trying to avoid waking her. Her eyes were automatically drawn toward Midas, where he leaned against the breakfast bar, shoveling an orange chip into his mouth. Several bags of the chips—"NikNaks," the bag said—were present around the room, each of the Tribe men appearing to have their own. As if he, too, were tuned in to her presence, he looked up to see her standing tentatively just inside the hallway shadows.

He stood up. "Mouse, what is it?"

The men all turned to look at her, their eyes gentle. She wondered if they could see how she felt. Out of place, lost, a touch of fear. But why? Even though she barely knew them, other than general knowledge, she should know by now that none of them would ever hurt her.

"Can I come in? You sound busy."

He smiled. "Never too busy for you, *heuning meisie*. Come over here." He held out his hand to her as she came into the room, which suddenly seemed much smaller since she had to skirt all the bodies sitting on, standing around, or leaning on the available surfaces.

Nemo got up from his spot on the couch so that Midas could help her get situated. "Whatcha got there?"

"My backpack. I had weird dreams, and when I was leaving the room, I saw it. It triggered some of the pieces of my dream to come forward."

The men exchanged glances around the room.

"What did you remember?"

She pulled the empty backpack off her shoulder and laid it in her lap. Waters snorted, and she looked at him quizzically. "Sorry," he apologized. "Kubrick carries a Backpack of Death on her at all times. I was just thinking I've never seen hers empty."

Mouse smiled shyly. "Yeah, at the movie night, she mentioned to Gem that she took out the candy dish on Cherry's desk the other day. Candy went everywhere."

He groaned. "That means I'm going to owe Cherry a new crystal dish. Damn. That woman of mine is getting such a spanking later."

"TMI, dude," TB said with a snort.

"Seriously? You're going to get on me about mentioning spanking someone?"

"Never mind," TB grumbled.

"Back to the backpack, Mouse," Midas redirected. "What does it have to do with your dream?"

"I dreamt I was young again. I don't know if it was real or imagined, but I saw the same couple I saw last night when you hypnotized me. Anyway, we were sitting around a kitchen table. They were my parents. Mom was in the kitchen, and Dad was helping me with my science homework."

As she began to unzip the main zipper, the men glanced around at each other again. When the zipper was completely undone, she turned the bag inside out and laid it flat on the coffee table. She stared at the backpack.

"In the dream, my backpack was hanging off the chair next to me, and that's what made me think of it. I remembered that my dad had an envelope that he gave me that I was to carry with me at all times, without fail, in case of emergency. I was never, ever, ever to go anywhere without it. I remember carrying the envelope in my backpack."

"I hate to tell you this, Mouse, but that backpack is clearly as empty as a church on Friday night," TB said.

"And it's unlikely that, if it is a real memory, that this would be the same backpack," Midas reminded her.

"I know, Midas," she acknowledged. "But what if I switched backpacks and knew I still had to carry that envelope? Wouldn't I have switched it into the new one?"

"Possibly, but there's nothing here."

"I remember him telling me it was so important that I keep it, but it was even more important that no one else even knew it existed because it would keep me safe. So I stitched it inside the layers of the backpack."

Everyone looked closer at the insides of it, but nothing seemed out of place.

"Sweetheart, you're clearly seeing more than we are."

"Wait, wait, wait," Demon halted them. "Mouse, may I?" He gestured at the backpack.

She nodded. Demon knelt and reached across the table and began to inspect the seam where the straps attached toward the bottom. "Well, I'll be damned," he whispered. Reaching into his cargo pocket, he retrieved a switchblade. With a series of gentle tugs, he snapped three seemingly invisible threads of what looked like a natural seam. Once he had a large enough hole, he dug the tip of the knife into the aperture he made, then gave a quick wrench. The ripping of the nylon material showed an empty space.

Like a light bulb went on, his eyes gleamed, and he pursed his lips. "You're one smart mouse," he told her. Then he took the knife again and began to snap more threads until another pocket inside the opening appeared. From inside it, he pulled out a small white envelope the size of a party invitation, making sure to only touch the very tip of a pointed corner. It was wrinkled, beat up, and it had a name on it.

Anastasiya.

"A name," Midas murmured to himself. "The A on the friendship bracelet."

"Yes," she said quietly. "That's my name."

She couldn't read the look on his face. Did it mean something to him? Did he think it was fitting for her? Pretty? In the long run, it didn't matter. Her name was her name, no matter what he felt about it. But somehow, it did matter to her.

"Do you know what's in this envelope, Mouse?" he asked.

She breathed in deeply, then let out the air in an emphatic rush. "Instructions. I think."

"Instructions?" TB repeated. "Interesting choice of words." He glanced around the room.

She nodded. "I remembered some other things too."

Midas crouched down in front of her, taking her hands in his. They felt warm and reassuring. "Let's go slow and recap some things, okay?" She nodded. "You're sure the adults are your parents?"

"Yes."

"Do you remember their names?"

"No, but I remember that my father was a high school chemistry teacher. My mother was a foreign language teacher."

"What language did she teach?"

"I don't remember."

He smoothed his hand up and down her back to calm her. "Nothing to worry about. Just questions, sweetheart. Did you have any siblings?"

"No, it was just the three of us. At least, that's all I remember living in that apartment."

"Can you describe the apartment?"

She proceeded to describe everything she had told him about when under hypnosis. TB halted her. "Hang on, Mouse. Midas, could this just be recall of last night?"

"I don't think so, TB. Some of the details she's giving weren't in the original description. Her name. Details of the adults."

"Maybe she didn't tell you."

"No, it doesn't work that way. If I don't ask for something, the subject can't recall it. She's giving me things I didn't ask for earlier. These are real memories."

"Shit," someone muttered.

Mouse looked around at the men. "I'm sorry. I didn't know. Honest! I didn't remember any of this until today."

Midas stood, swept her up off the couch, then sat in her seat. He gathered her close, tucking her head under his chin, and held her tight. "Mouse, no one's angry. The brain is a funky computer. I told you. It holds onto information for long periods of time, but it has a tendency to store away things it thinks it might not need for a while, and it puts them in some pretty locked-down, tight drawers. Never know when those drawers are going to unlock themselves. What else do you remember?"

"There was a phone call while we were at the table. I had a test the next day on covalent bonds that my father was helping me with. Mom answered the phone. She was very quiet when she first started speaking. Then she called my dad over. He left me working on a new problem, something I was struggling with, and he crossed over to her. They argued in whispers. Then he took the phone from her. He spoke quietly, but I don't think it was the only phone call like that."

"Do you remember what he said?" Waters asked, speaking up for the first time.

Mouse shook her head. "No, it was too quiet. But he looked nervous, even though he was trying not to. And my mother was pretending to wash dishes. Her back was to me, but her shoulders were up around her ears. Like she was tense or in pain."

"Mouse." Midas tilted her chin and looked into her eyes. His hands framed her face, and he smiled at her. "I do *not* care what the answer is to this question. You hear me? I'm only asking so that I know what we are dealing with here. Okay?"

She nodded, but she felt panic boiling in her stomach, creating nausea. She tried to hold it down, but he must have seen panic flaring in her eyes. "Stay with me." He kissed her forehead and whispered against it, "You've been so brave, but I need you to be brave just a little longer, *heuning meisie,* so that we can get this straightened out for you and keep you safe." He moved his lips and returned his head to a somewhat normal distance from her face. "Is it possible that you were born outside of the US?"

Frowning, she shook her head. "My English is accent-free. I suppose it's possible if they brought me to the States before I could talk, but I think they had been teachers here longer than my age."

"No worries," he assured her. "Can we open the envelope?"

She nodded.

Stepping up to the coffee table, Waters pulled a pair of latex gloves out of one of his many pockets. He held his hand out to Demon, who turned over his open knife, and then he gently slid the knife's edge under the flap to separate it from the envelope without ripping. He dumped the contents onto the coffee table.

A quarter.

Three one-hundred-dollar bills.

A slip of paper with "Sterling House" written on it.

A small silver charm for a necklace or bracelet of a dancing bear.

Everyone stared at the items in confusion. TB asked, "How are these meant to be instructions for anything?"

Midas replied, "You'd have to know the context. I'm guessing that back then, Mouse would have understood what they meant or how they went together." He looked up at her. "Any idea what these are?"

"Not a clue," she admitted.

Waters spoke up. "Midas. We need you to go in again."

He huffed in frustration. "Not today. It's too soon. Maybe tomorrow, if she agrees."

Clutching his sweater, she nodded vehemently. "I want to, Midas. You need this information for the girls, and I need to know for myself. Let's do it now."

"No. You're not even recovered from yesterday. I won't risk it. Maybe tomorrow. I'd feel better if it was the day after, at least. Besides, it will give me time to do some searching. With names and more details now, I might be able to find your parents and contact them. I'd prefer not to go rooting around in your brain again unless it's absolutely necessary."

She watched everyone flash looks around the room at each other. She also felt their frustration, even if they understood Midas' concern. Or if they didn't understand, they respected him enough not to voice their opinions out loud in front of her.

JANUARY 31, 2024

Midas

She was jumpy. Tense. Ever since the hypnosis session and the outpouring of memories, her smile had remained hidden behind sad, frightened eyes. He'd felt even more compelled to solve this mystery for not just Tribe but for his beautiful honey girl who lived behind an iron door from her previous life.

So he spent most of the night and most of the next day searching for anything about her parents. He had more details that narrowed the search, and knowing their professions had been a huge help. He'd found out plenty, and the picture he was beginning to put together? Unfortunately, it was one he didn't like.

However, that was for another day. He'd gone to Waters and told him she needed another day of recovery. She needed fresh air and something fun and mindless. He had just the thing. Waters heard him out, and while Midas could tell he wanted to say no, he gave him permission for the outing he proposed.

Tomorrow, he would hypnotize her again, and they would see what else they might find.

When he asked Nemo and Gem about his idea, they were one hundred percent on board.

After breakfast, he broached the outing. "What do you say we get out of here for a bit today?" Midas asked.

"Where?"

"Thought we could take the girls, go get some food. It's a bit cool, but we can bundle up. Figured you'd be missing them, and maybe they'll help you relax a bit."

She laughed softly. "Are you talking about the same girls you brought home with me? Because there's no relaxing with them. They're a lot."

"I don't mind," he assured her. "Nemo and Gem are coming along. We thought we could take them to the Santa Monica Pier. They have a Ferris wheel, a carousel, and a roller coaster. The latter might be a bit much for them, but they might enjoy the others. And there are tons of food carts—hot dogs, burgers, treats." He lowered his head and chuckled. "We can get them all sugared up before we send them home with their babysitters."

This time, she giggled, and he felt the tension about her loosen slightly. That had been his intention, so he was pleased it had worked.

Her expression grew wistful. "It won't be dangerous for you? I thought you all didn't like to be out in the open."

Shrugging, he stood straight, then headed to his closet by the door to the hallway. "It should be fine for a few hours. Not like we go there regularly, and the kids will help us blend in." He pulled a couple of hooded sweatshirts and a leather jacket out of the closet. "You and Kubrick are about the same size. She's probably got a jacket you can borrow."

Two hours later, Midas, Mouse, Nemo, Gem, and four of the children filled up two Tribe vehicles and headed to the Santa Monica Pier. Midas purchased wristbands for everyone so they could ride whatever they wanted, as many times as they wanted. He wasn't sure how they would respond to all the sights, sounds, and smells, as he didn't know if they'd ever seen anything like this before in their lives. Eyes wide, heads whipping back and forth, they were clearly overwhelmed.

Hoping to ease them into the fun, he made their first stop the carousel.

The music was loud inside the building, especially since the space was uncrowded due to the cool weather, and the adults had to coax the girls onto the platform. After helping the children onto the horses, Nemo and Gem each had one of the twins in front of them, Shakira sat on her own horse, and Mouse had Ona, leaving Midas on his own horse next to Mouse while they rode.

As the music played and the carousel turned round and round, he watched the quiet and tension slip away from Mouse. He looked over to her, her head tipped back in laughter as Ona screamed in glee, clapping her hands to the music. She glanced back at him, her eyes sparkling, and he felt himself grinning like crazy. He looked behind him to his twin, and Nemo was staring directly at him, a twinkle in his eye. A single head nod and a tilt in Mouse's direction was his version of approval.

Yeah, as expected, his brother knew him all too well. And if Waters and Nemo knew how he felt about her, that meant everyone else did too. The team members were worse gossips than old men sitting around a checkerboard in a sleepy, small town.

"Again!" Ona shrieked as the carousel slowed to a stop.

"Again?" Midas said in fake surprise. "I don't know. Are you sure?" He winked at Mouse. "Aren't you dizzy?"

"No!" the girls chorused. "Again!" They began to chant over and over, and all four adults were laughing at their excitement.

With a swirling gesture of his finger to the operator, the ride began again.

After three rides on the carousel, they made their way to the arcade. Nemo was in a dance-off with Shakira on some obnoxiously loud dance video game, while the rest of the adults taught the others how to play a bowling game. After collecting all the tickets they won and the cheap prizes, the men headed to the ring toss to try to win stuffed animals for all the girls. Since they seemed comfortable sharing everything, though, they opted to trade up their individual prizes for a ridiculously large dragon that made Catalina's eyes grow big with wonder. Once it was down from its hook and on the ground, she hugged the giant purple beast, giggling merrily as Midas teased the top of her head with the tip of its big floppy tongue.

One trip to the taco and hot dog truck each, the four adults and four children sat at a brightly painted picnic table, enjoying the absolutely terrible-for-them food. The girls seemed to be most intrigued by the hot dogs, especially since Ona was concerned that they were made from actual dogs. Nemo reassured her multiple times that they weren't. Apparently, Scheherazade's absence had made Ona extra fearful that she was, in fact, the victim of her lunch, so Midas made Cherry text him a picture of the dog sitting at her feet in the lobby of Tribe.

The girls refused to go on the roller coaster, and the Ferris wheel was only achieved with promises of cotton candy, something they'd never seen before. Midas envisioned a lot of stickiness to be washed off when they got back to Tribe headquarters, and a weird wave seemed to ripple through his body. Gentle and warm, it began a slow rise from the soles of his feet. When it reached his chest, he automatically took a deep breath, his lungs expanding to what felt like twice their normal size, and his heart as well. Finally, it ebbed upward to his brain, and upon reaching it, the roots of his close-cropped hair felt electrified.

An image of him and Mouse, readying the girls for bed. Washing faces, brushing teeth, pajamas, and story time. Sleepy heads on shoulders under fairy lights, teddy bears in the crooks of arms, goodnight kisses, mumbled goodnights, and gentle snuffles as the girls burrowed into their blankets and pillows. Completing that image was a glance over their sleeping forms to a honey-eyed woman with a soft smile on her face.

Whoa. He had to shake his head subtly to try and make the image go away, but it didn't work. Then again, it didn't help that the honey-eyed girl was across from him in the Ferris wheel carriage, Shakira at her side, their heads in profile as they looked out over the pier from their high perch. At his side, Ona was tucked into him, kneeling on the seat and looking out at the sights below, her arms wrapped like a python around his neck. In turn, he banded his arm around her waist, keeping her safe, although her fear at their height above the ground kept her from moving.

Mouse's attention on Shakira, looking where the girl was pointing and chatting with her so softly Midas couldn't hear her, gave him a chance to study the woman he'd rescued. He felt a pang in his chest. Not a painful one, but it did ache. He realized quickly that he wanted this. Normalcy with her. He couldn't explain it. He just knew.

Unfortunately for him, normalcy meant hiding in plain sight. He could never offer a woman a marriage in the traditional sense.

A family? Possibly. But he saw what that was doing to his teammate, TB, and it saddened him. The man would never be able to publicly be recognized as Axel's father because he was a wanted man, and suddenly reappearing from the grave would make Axel, Flame, and TB vulnerable. He'd have to go on the run with his family, living in secret, most likely completely off the grid, which was no life for them. While it would allow him all the privileges of a father, Axel would never know the total freedom of being an everyday little boy. It was a no-win situation.

How could he possibly offer a woman anything? Logically, he knew his reaction was partially based on fear. After all, Waters, TB, Nemo, and Demon had connected with amazing women and were making it work, despite the challenges, but he couldn't see how he could make it work.

Again, he knew that thought was irrational, based on his fear of opening up to someone with that awkward truth about himself and compounded by the feeling like he had nothing to offer someone. They were legally declared dead, which meant they owned nothing of their own because Tribe provided everything they wanted or needed without question.

TB had money hidden away from his days on the dark web as The Collector, but none of the others did. Everything they might have once had was gone, surrendered to their families upon their "deaths," or to whatever their wills laid out at the time. They literally came to Tribe with the clothes on their backs. The only thing left from their pasts was a house once owned by Waters' family that they had turned into a safe house, but it now stood empty since they'd used it to house Kubrick briefly two years ago.

Since they knew nothing concrete about Mouse's past as an adult yet, who's to say she didn't have a beautiful life in her past that she'd left behind and could be returned to? A job, friends, a family who loved her, or a partner or spouse to share her life with. Children even. There were just too many variables that came with her, and until he knew for sure, a future together wasn't even worth thinking about.

And once they did know the truth? Even if she turned out to be free. Even if she miraculously returned his growing feelings for her. How could he possibly bind her to a life of isolation with him, never getting the chance to do all the things she might have once dreamed of?

He couldn't. It wasn't in him. At his heart, Midas was a protector. He'd watched over his mother until her death, forced to be the man of the house when their father left them. He'd defended his brother, no matter what trouble he got into, until Nemo left to be with the woman he'd loved these past seven years. He'd devoted his life to being the interference that kept his teammates safe, and would do so until the day he died. So no, he had no room in his life for Mouse, even if it were possible. He was destined to be on his own.

"You look like you're thinking hard."

Mouse's voice, pitched low, interrupted the sad path of his thoughts. He must have looked confused because she emitted a soft laugh. "They're asleep. I don't want to wake them until we have to."

He looked between the two girls and realized they had, in fact, drifted off at their sides. He nodded. "This was good for them though. You all needed fresh air."

Damn. Shakira looked completely relaxed, with Mouse's arm around the girl and leaning against her torso. Glancing down, he realized that Ona was still kneeling on the bench, but she'd laid her head on his shoulder, her sweet face burrowed into the crook between his shoulder and his neck. Soft, warm breaths puffed against his skin in a steady rhythm.

"She likes you," Mouse observed.

"My shoulders make a nice pillow."

Her expression grew wistful. "Do you want kids?"

How did he answer that question? It was sticky. "When I was younger, I always wanted a big family. It was just Nemo and me in my family, and given how our childhood was, now I'm glad it wasn't more. Mom could barely make ends meet as it was."

"But now you seem stable."

"Definitely. However, for years, we didn't really believe we could have relationships and work this job. It's like the military, only ten times worse. Most women wouldn't understand our being gone at the spur of the moment, or for long periods of time, or even sometimes what our jobs ask of us. The last two years have been an adjustment for everyone as we've started to see that we can balance both. As for families, yeah, I still want one. Would love a large one."

The carriage stopped just short of the top of the wheel, and Midas looked down to see that they were loading a child in a wheelchair onto the ride as it spun in a slow, constant motion. The sun was just beginning to set over the horizon, so they sat together enjoying the extra time with the view and the girls. He noticed that Mouse's face had gone pensive in those silent moments, and he wondered what she was thinking about. It didn't look good, or else she was working through something.

"What about you? Do you want a family of your own?"

There was a wistfulness to her reply. "I loved working at the compound with the girls. They were the highlight of every day. Watching their joy as they learned to read, write, add and subtract, sing, paint... whatever. Shakira and Ona had been denied those things as girls in their culture, at least other than the rudiments of knowledge, but every time one of them discovered something new? There was a rush inside me, knowing that I'd helped them gain that. That I'd helped them become one microstep closer to free girls on their way to becoming independent, confident women."

"Sounds like you would make a great teacher. Maybe you were one before your amnesia took hold. Like your parents before you. But it doesn't really answer the question about wanting a family."

She looked down at Shakira's head, her hand smoothing the flyaway strands from the girl's braid. Despite the smile of affection on her lips, her body held a tension that bespoke pain.

"I feel as if I want one, but there's something in me that says, for some reason, I won't get to have that." She kissed the top of Shakira's head, then looked out over the side of the car at the ocean's horizon. "I have a name now, and some vague details about my childhood, but I don't even know who I am. Silly, I suppose, to feel so defeated that I'm denying myself a future that holds what I want. I mean, who's to say I don't have a family out there, waiting for me to come home? I found myself worrying the other day about whether I'd somehow stranded a child or a sibling when I disappeared."

A pang hit him. She didn't sound very happy about the fact that there might be someone out there, waiting and hoping for her return. For himself, he also felt a touch of sadness. It was something he and

Waters had talked about. He chose to ignore the pain and the idea for now. She could just as easily not have a man or a family in her life. No sense borrowing trouble.

"You seem to really love the kids though."

"I do. When I woke up here, they were the first thing I thought of. I think Shakira and Ona must have been the ones I looked over the most."

"They do seem bonded with you. Not that the other children don't like you, because when I asked if they wanted to see you, all of them lit up like Christmas lights."

She smiled. "That's nice to know. I'd hate to wake up and find out that no one cared if I was gone."

Again, her face had a look to it he couldn't quite describe. He was willing to bet she was feeling terribly lonely. There were no obvious reports of her as a missing person, which suggested nobody was, in fact, looking for her. He also hadn't found any reports from the years surrounding when they thought she'd gone missing, which was even sadder. How could someone not report a missing little girl? Even a school would file a report with social services if she stopped showing up. It was beginning to look more and more like she really was alone. Completely and utterly alone.

The ride started up again, cresting the top and beginning its slow descent. When they reached the bottom in about fifteen minutes, they'd have to disembark.

Mouse still looked out of sorts. He whispered, "Hey. You okay?"

Slow to answer, she returned her gaze to his. "Yeah. No. I don't know," she admitted. "I have questions, but... not here. I don't want the girls to overhear."

"Got it. We need to get them up anyway."

Waking up the girls was amusing, and he found their grumpiness cute. Their grumbles and whining would probably get frustrating eventually, but he found himself wondering how long that would take. How would Mouse respond to it?

Covertly, he watched her with them. Their crabbiness didn't

seem to bother her in the least. She soothed Shakira by stroking her hair and encouraging her to wake up, using the promised cotton candy treat as a motivator. He smiled when that seemed to wake her up instantaneously.

Ona, however, refused to wake up fully, so he cuddled her close, putting the child on his hip. Her thumb went into her mouth, and her eyes fluttered closed. Warmth radiated outward from his chest. He needed to be careful, or these girls would make him want something he couldn't have. When the time came, and they and Mouse left Tribe to go off to the Mythos property they would be transferred to, it would hurt if he was attached.

When they caught up with Nemo and Gem, both had children on their backs for piggyback rides. The warm feeling increased and pulsed out again over his body. It was all so domesticated, and seeing the couple with the children painted a picture of a family life that he desperately wanted, not just for himself, but for his brother. Heaven knew their own childhood, while it hadn't been bad, had certainly been lacking.

Nemo rescued the oversized dragon from the Ferris wheel operator. As predicted, by the time they'd returned to Tribe, all the children were sticky, with pink and blue dye smudged all over their faces. Everyone was going to need a bath.

Nemo handed Waters the dragon with a wink and a grin. "He's all yours, big guy."

"Great," Waters deadpanned. "Ali will probably tear him apart within two minutes of getting him in the door."

He wasn't wrong. Scheherazade's offspring was a holy terror on toys.

Then their boss looked at the girls and groaned. "You got them all sugared up, didn't you?"

Nemo chuckled. "Yep, and I have no regrets." He clapped their team leader on the shoulder. "Enjoy bath time and trying to get them to bed. My work here is done."

"Turnabout is fair play, di—jerk," he corrected himself.

Kubrick came out of Waters' office, and the smile that appeared when she saw the twins lit up her whole face.

"Looks like your aunts and uncles gave you a good time today."

Gem handed over Liliana to Kubrick, along with a plastic bag with the pink fairy floss packed airtight inside. "She's the least sticky."

Kubrick laughed, then pressed a cheek to the child's head. "Thanks for taking them today. Wish I could have gone along but had to finish up my editing."

Midas waved her off. "Happy to do it."

Waters held out his hand to Catalina, and she grabbed it eagerly, giggling as he swung her up into his other arm, juggling her and the giant stuffed dragon with ease. He looked at Midas. "We'll see you tomorrow?"

The question wasn't really about him showing up for work. It was about getting another session of hypnosis out of Mouse. Inwardly, he sighed. Both he and Mouse were tired, but he'd have to broach the subject tonight, and it sounded like she was worrying about something. He hated to subject her to another walk through her brain, but he recognized it couldn't be helped.

The two couples and the girls headed to the elevator, along with the new houseguest, whom Catalina announced they'd named Drago. Once the elevator light showed they were on the third floor, Midas pushed the button to recall the carriage.

He looked at Mouse. Her skin had some color to it from being outside, making her appear a little healthier, but the dark smudges under her eyes showed that she had probably done a little too much today. "You look done in." He brushed a lock of hair back that had escaped the clip she used to hold it today. "When we get upstairs, you should take a shower or a warm bath, relax a bit. I'll get us some dinner, then we can talk, okay?"

She nodded. "Sounds great."

An hour later, stir-fry made and eaten and the kitchen cleaned, Midas had Mouse situated on his couch, tucked under a blanket. He dimmed the lights and sat on the far end of the sectional. As much as he wanted to be sitting next to her, curling her into his side, he knew that wasn't a good idea.

He frowned. "How's your ankle? You probably shouldn't have been on it all afternoon."

"Honestly, it's throbbing, but it was worth it. I promise to rest it tomorrow."

"I'll be making sure of that. No walking tomorrow. If you need to move around, I'll carry you."

"You're going to get sick of doing that."

"Nah. Makes me feel all alpha male."

She bit her lip and looked down at her hands in her lap. "Can I ask you something?"

"Anything."

"I have a name now, but you all still call me Mouse." She looked at him. "Why?"

"All of us, our clients, everyone, have a nickname. It's for safety, primarily. That way, if we talk about you publicly, or if someone would happen to overhear us talking or get into our emails, whatever, they don't know who you are."

"Oh."

"Do you want us to call you by your name? I mean, technically, you're not a client. You're a guest."

"Mouse is what I've been for so long... Well, as long as I can remember," she half joked, then blushed. "I like how it sounds when you say it. Something about the accent."

"You like my accent?"

She nodded. "It's unique. Not one I've heard a lot. At first, I didn't know where you were from. It makes you... special. Not that you aren't anyway," she rushed to say. Her blush went deeper. "And it makes me feel like I belong somewhere. Anastasiya is too exotic for me."

"I don't know about that. I think you're pretty special, yourself. Have since I met you."

The air in the room felt a little heavier to him, as if the pressure was changing. Not in a discomforting way. More like how a security system made someone feel safe. Yeah. Definitely. She made him feel safe to be himself.

They sat in the quiet for a few moments before she spoke again. "I need to go under again. I need to know. There's something... It feels like something is pushing against my skull. Something trying to find a weak point so it can come out. Something important."

"Are you sure you're recovered enough? You're looking pretty ragged yet, and I don't want to make it worse."

"Are you saying I look like shit?" she teased weakly.

"Never," he assured her. "But you've been through a lot. It would be a lie if I said you didn't look exhausted. We can wait another day or two if it's too much."

"While that's tempting, that pushing feeling makes me feel like whatever it is that wants to come out is important. I know you need it now, but it also feels like I need it now. Like—" She sighed. "Like I'm in danger."

16

JANUARY 31, 2024

Midas

HER PROCLAMATION SURPRISED HIM. WHAT THE HELL HAD they stirred up, forcing her to go through hypnosis? The brain was an intuitive organ and often knew things without making them readily apparent to its owner. It was why he never did hypnosis unless it was the bad guys who weren't leaving the subterranean levels of Tribe. Even then, he always had a momentary twinge of guilt, not that those fuckwitches ever deserved his concern.

She clutched her arms as if she were cold, her teeth began to chatter, and she whimpered. Keeping his distance was impossible. This was fear. Something inside her head had been tripped in the space of a few seconds. Comfort and security were needed to keep her from spiraling into shock. The fact that she hadn't broken down before now was miraculous to him. So fucking brave!

Burying his concerns, he moved to her side, picked her up, then slid them back into her spot and tucked her into his lap. The blanket had slid to the floor, so he reached down to grab it and covered her again. Then, with one hand, he cradled her head with his palm, pulling it down to his shoulder like Ona had cuddled into him earlier today. His other arm banded around her on the outside of the blanket, and he murmured to her quietly in Afrikaans, hoping his low volume and gentle tone would comfort her. He knew she wouldn't understand any of it except for his endearment of *"heuning meisie,"* but it was the best thing he could think of to do.

It was as if the gates of hell opened and unleashed everything horrible into the world. The first sob burst out of her like a demon trying to flee her soul, and then it was like she couldn't stop. It was killing him.

He spoke out into the room. "Nova, call Nemo. SOS, level two."

The AI repeated his instruction through the speaker on his watch. He had never been so glad he'd kept his brother connected in the Tribe protocols. He was still mad. Still hurt. But the man was his twin, and despite their recent struggles, he knew Nemo would drop everything to come to him, no matter the time, no matter the level of emergency. Luckily, his apartment from his time with Tribe was on the same floor.

Seconds later, he heard the keypad outside his door being accessed. After the eighth number, there was a click, and the door swung open with Nemo's push. "Midas?"

"Living room."

Nemo came down the short foyer. Midas could tell that Mouse's sobbing was distressing to him as well. "What do you need me to do? Do we need Gem?" his brother asked.

Midas stood. "No. Just hold her a minute."

As soon as he tried to hand Mouse to his brother, her sobs got louder, and she threw her arms around his neck in a stranglehold to prevent him from handing her over.

"Heuning meisie, it's just for a moment. Please. I'll take you right back."

If anything, she clutched him harder.

"Okay, okay, I won't pass you over." He looked in concern at his brother, clueless and in a bit of a panic at how to help her. "Shit," he muttered. "Okay, let's do this a little differently. Go in my bathroom. There are scissors in the top right drawer. I need you to cut me out of my shirt."

"Huh?" Nemo looked puzzled.

"She needs skin. Touch. I've read about how it decreases stress and anxiety for some people."

Without another word, Nemo moved with purpose to get the scissors. When he returned, he moved behind his brother. He pulled the long-sleeved T-shirt free of Midas' jeans, then slit it up the center hem to the neck. He then cut each sleeve from bottom to top and was able to pull it free of his brother's body with a gentle tug, even from where Mouse was plastered tightly to him.

Midas reclined on the sofa, Mouse on the inside between him and the back, making sure to tuck her to his chest, head beneath his chin, her hands on his pectorals, his arms around her mid-back to hold her tight.

Nemo grabbed the blanket and put it over both of them. As soon as she was resituated in her cocoon, the sobs became quieter, but Midas could still feel her tears hitting his bare chest and sliding down his side. After a few minutes, her breathing seemed to even out. He wasn't sure if she was asleep, but at least she wasn't crying anymore.

"Do you know what brought it on? She looked so happy today."

"She got quiet while we were riding the wheel, and I think she got into her head, pushing herself to remember things. Maybe something about today triggered a memory under the surface? I don't know. We started talking after dinner, and she confessed it felt like something was pushing at the barrier, like it was fighting to get out. Whatever it was scared her." He looked from her head, where it lay on him, to his brother. "She said it felt like danger."

Digesting this new information, Nemo's face took on its contemplative look, one that people didn't see a lot.

"I'd be lying if I said I didn't have reservations about hypnotizing her again. I'm worried about what will come out." He sighed and pressed a kiss to the top of her hairline. "Unfortunately, I don't see any other way out right now."

Nemo nodded. "You need anything else? Want me to hang out a bit?"

"No, I think we're good for now. I just wasn't prepared for her to lose herself like that."

"Okay. Call me if you need something or if you want Gem to pop over. She could bring the girls if you think that might help."

Nemo turned to leave.

"Hey! Sawyer!" he whisper-yelled.

His twin turned back to him.

"Thanks. I mean it. And I'm sorry that I've been such a dick. It's... I know I'm not alone. I've got the team, but it's not the same. It's been a difficult adjustment to not be needed anymore."

Nemo gave a nod to the sleeping woman. "Is that what this is with her? She needs you? Because if it is, that's not fair to her. I see how she looks at you. If this is just filling a void for you, she's going to get hurt."

With a shake of his head, Midas denied it. "Maybe at first. Now I've gotten to know her, and it's something else."

"Then don't hold it back. Gem did that, and we were separated for years that we could have had together. Maybe it wasn't our time then, but I wish she hadn't run."

"I just worry that she has a life somewhere that will keep her from me, you know? Until I know she's free, I've got to keep myself apart, at least somewhat."

"That the only thing holding you back?" Nemo asked.

"What do you mean?" He knew very well what his brother meant, but he wasn't going to admit it.

"Dude. Come on. It's not like I forgot everything about you. I know you were a monk up until I left, and I also know there hasn't been anyone since then either. You're not reluctant because you've never had sex, right? Like, you're not afraid of it?" His eyes got a little wider. "You're not, like, damaged physically, are you?"

"*Doos*," Midas said. "No, I'm not damaged. Everything works fine. As for afraid? Fuck no. Just haven't found anyone worth it."

"Until now."

"Yeah. Until now."

17

FEBRUARY 1, 2024

Mouse

He held his hands out to her, an encouraging smile on his face. "Ready?"

The flutterings of panic began in Anastasiya's stomach, clutching and clawing at her throat to escape through her mouth. She closed her eyes, took a deep breath in, slowly breathed out, then reopened her eyes to gaze back at Midas. Seeing his calm demeanor caused the panic to slowly recede. She nodded and put her hands on top of his upturned palms. "I'm ready."

They were in the apartment again, as was Demon, and both teams were watching from the conference room again. This time, Midas had an earpiece in so that he could hear them if they had a question they wanted him to ask her. It was unnerving, but she understood why it was necessary.

Yesterday had been wonderful. While she knew he was a good

man, she'd been able to see him in an all-new light. The girls adored him; he had a wonderful relationship with his brother and his brother's girlfriend, and he'd been incredibly attentive to her.

And then when they got back to his apartment, it all went to shit. She didn't understand exactly what had caused her to break down so completely. She'd confessed that she felt like she was in danger, and then her entire body had gone cold. Colder than she'd ever been in her life. Immediately after that, the floodgates opened, and all she could do was sob in terror while Midas held her. She hadn't even known what she was terrified about. The next thing she remembered was waking up in her bed, her head in Midas' lap, with Midas sitting against the headboard, reading something on his computer. He didn't leave her all night.

She would admit to everyone that she was scared of what she might learn, but his presence made her feel as secure as she could be. He would always watch out for her.

"So brave, *heuning meisie*," he whispered so only she could hear. Slowly, he reached up to tap his earpiece and unmuted the microphone on his watch so everyone would be able to hear him. "All right. Look into my eyes and breathe with me, Mouse. Same thing as last time. Breathe with me, in through your nose on a count of five, out through your mouth on a count of five."

The counting of the breaths and the instructions for "in" and "out" faded into the blackness behind her eyes. Since she knew what to expect, it was much less terrifying this time.

"Remember, you're safe in the empty room. You're going to walk forward, one step for each number I count. There's nothing in the room for you to bump into or trip over. Imagine yourself walking at a normal pace, and with each step, the room around you is going to lighten just a little bit. When I reach 'ten,' you'll be back in front of the sink."

He began to count, his voice echoing slightly in her mind as she walked.

"Ten. Are you in front of the sink?"

"Yes."

"Excellent. All right, you know what to do. Turn on the water to a trickle."

She saw her hand reach out to the faucet and turn it. In her impatience to figure out who she was and what was going on, she accidentally opened the faucet too wide. The water burst forth from the pipe in a violent stream. Her panic began to well up again. She whimpered.

"The water!"

"Turn the water back, *heuning meisie*. Slowly."

"It's cold."

"What is?"

"The room. So cold."

There was a pause. The silence felt oppressive. Tense. Debilitating. A fog began to gather along the floor at ankle height, and soon she couldn't see the floor at all. A thick tendril began to rise out of the undulating mist at her feet. She heard a menacing hiss, and then slowly it began to wind itself tightly around her legs, curling around her body like a snake. It felt evil. While she could see through it, sometimes partially, sometimes fully, the holes never stayed open for long, and it continued to work its way up her body.

"*Heuning meisie*, what's going on?"

His voice stayed even, but she knew he was concerned. He always cared about how she was feeling. What she was thinking.

"It's going to smother me!" The panic was blooming. Despite it being mist, and even though, in the back of her mind, she knew it wasn't real, she was paralyzed. She needed out of this room. She needed Midas. It was too much.

"What's going to smother you?"

"There's a fog pouring into the room. Help me, Midas! I can't move. It's winding around me, and soon I won't be able to move at all."

There was another pause, and she choked back a sob. The mist was just below her waist, coiling around and around her, her arms locked in place as if chained to her hips. Was it able to sense her anxiety? It seemed like the tendril began to curl faster, its grip squeezing further. Her arms were now bound to her sides, and she could feel her lungs being restricted by the pressure. As the tendril made its final loop around her shoulders, it extended, stretching thin, and rose in front of her, its rounded tip bent back toward her face, as if looking her in the eyes.

Controlling. Malevolent. Sadistic.

"Midas!"

"Mouse, I want you to listen carefully. Listen for my footfalls. There will be ten of them. I'm coming to you."

She knew that wasn't possible. He couldn't suddenly appear in this state of semiconsciousness as a real person, but it felt reassuring to know he was going to help her, or try to, by having her project himself into the imaginary chamber.

Footfalls. Slow. Measured. She turned her head in the imaginary room, the only movement allowed by the smoke, and saw him walking toward her. He was dressed in the gear he'd been wearing the day he rescued her. She hadn't had much time to register it in detail, but to her, it looked the same. She'd thought of him as her rescuer, an angel in desert camouflage. A part of her brain registered that it made sense he would appear to her this way in her moments of fear.

The tip of the tendril in front of her began to roar in agony, its jaws unhinged like a cobra ready to strike. It was mad. It was afraid. Midas' presence, even if just in her mind, was powerful enough to threaten it from completing its task of engulfing her and swallowing her whole. At the same time, the mist along the floor began to roll back to wherever it had come from, sucking the winding bindings from around her, and it sounded like hundreds of souls wailing in agony at being sent back to hell. Its intent was no longer to hurt her but to escape him.

When Midas appeared completely at her side, the snakelike smoke immediately loosened and retracted with lightning speed into the last of the mass, then, with a whoosh, disappeared into the seams of the floor along the wall. Sobs broke free in relief.

"Mouse?" The voice was searching, and his spectral hand rested on her shoulder. "I need you to slow your breathing. In through your nose—one, two, three, four, five. Out through your mouth—one, two, three, four, five."

They went through several cycles. She lost track of how many. Finally, she felt a shudder pass through her and then calm.

"You're safe now. I'm here. Do you want to go back? Your choice, *heuning meisie*. No one will force you to go further."

"No, I need to go forward. I can't live scared like this anymore. I need to know."

"Okay. Go slowly. At any time it becomes too much, then you start backing up and return the way you came. Tell me, then I'll count you back out. All right?"

"Don't leave me," she begged.

"I won't. I will go with you, but remember that I can't see what you see, so you're going to have to verbalize it for me."

"Okay." She felt herself nod, then she reached for the faucet and opened the spout again so that this time the water truly was a trickle.

"Good girl. What did I tell you about the water?"

"The water is my past. The pipe goes from my past, where my memories are, to now."

"Excellent."

Deep breath. "I'm going into the pipe."

"Take my hand."

Her spectral hand took hold of his.

"Lead me through, *heuning meisie*."

Again, she felt herself become two people—spectral Mouse on one side of the wall, and memory Mouse on the other. With each step, her head began to hurt as she traversed the pipe. Her hand squeezed Midas' harder, and she felt herself wince at the pain, but she kept going.

This time, when she reached the other side, things had changed. She wasn't at the table, and the apartment was decorated in shadows. Turning her head, she saw the darkened hallway, and under the closed door on her left, she could see that the lights were on. Muted voices traveled on the air, but she couldn't make out what they said.

"I'm back in the apartment, but it's not the same day. I don't know how much later in time it is."

"You said there was a calendar on the wall the last time you were here. Can you see it?"

Her head turned, but it felt sluggish and heavy, like someone was trying to restrict her movement but didn't have quite enough strength to stop her. "2010. September. There's a date circled. I can't read the number, but it looks like a Wednesday."

"Okay, good job. What else do you see?"

"Silhouettes of furniture. The walls. One is brighter because the moonlight is coming through the window. I can see the hallway that goes to the bedrooms. I hear voices coming from behind a closed door."

"I want you to carefully walk toward the door where the voices are coming from. Can you do that?"

"Yes."

One hand still held onto Midas, the other trailed along the dark hallway. When she reached the door, she saw a shadow crouched outside of it. It was the girl she'd seen last time, except this time, she could see her face. "There's a girl here. She's crouched on the other side of the doorway. She's trying to hear what the voices are saying."

"Does she look familiar?"

Mouse nodded. "I'm pretty sure it's me, but as a teen."

Spectral Midas gave her hand a squeeze.

She put her ear to the door. "The voices are the man and the woman from last time, but they're hushed."

"Reach for the doorknob. Turn it and push the door open. They can't see you."

Her hand shook as she reached for the knob to do as Midas wanted. When she went to push it open, it stuck. "It won't open."

"Your brain is resisting. Can you push harder? Don't hurt yourself opening it."

She put more force behind the push. The door seemed to give way slightly, but it stayed closed. She put her shoulder to it, but it wouldn't budge. "It won't open." She heard the frustration in her voice and felt helplessness sweep over her.

There was a pause before Midas spoke again. "Can you reach the top of the doorframe?"

Frowning, she stretched on her tiptoes. "My fingertips can just reach."

"Good. Concentrate. Stretch just a little bit further. When you can get the pads of your fingers over the edge, run your hands along it. Doors that lock usually have a key on the outside of the room, kept there in case of emergency. It won't look like a normal key. More like a bent nail."

Concentrating on extending her spectral hand, she felt it go an inch further. She swept her fingers along the frame. At the far edge, she found the key. "I've got it."

"Well done, sweetheart. Now. Insert the key into the lock. Open the door."

In slow motion, her hand with the key went to the lock. It didn't want to fit smoothly inside, but she managed to wiggle it into place. Seated in the mechanism, she turned the key. This time, with strong pressure, she turned the knob and pushed the door at the same time. The door creaked, and the hinges screamed, but it opened.

"I'm in," she told him.

"You're being incredibly brave. So proud of you. What do you see?"

"It's a bedroom. There's a bedside lamp on. It's the only light in the room." Turning her head to the right, she saw the woman from her last visit to this place. "The woman is sitting on the bed against the headboard, her knees pulled up to her chest. She looks afraid. She's crying."

"What else?"

"The man. He's sitting at the foot of the bed. He looks... scared, maybe?"

"You said you heard voices. Are they talking?"

"Yes, but I can't understand them. It's another language."

FEBRUARY 1, 2024

Midas

"Do you know what language it is?"

"Da."

"Irish, Northern England, Scotland, or Wales, maybe?" He heard Gem ask Demon.

"Then why wouldn't he be speaking English?" Demon replied.

Midas heard their whispers and frowned. "Your father is there?"

"*Da, i moya mama tozhe.*"

Medusa's voice came over the line. "She's saying, 'Yes, and so is my mother.' It's Russian."

Waters told someone, "Get God on the line. He needs to hear this."

Midas put his attention back on Mouse. "Can you hear me, *heuning meisie?*"

"Yes."

"Good. Can you tell me what they're saying?"

"*Nam nikogda ne sledovalo syuda prikhodit.*"

Medusa translated. "We never should have come here."

Waters asked, "Medusa, you speak Russian?"

"Enough," she admitted.

"Keep translating," he ordered. "Steel, are we recording?"

"Yeah. Midas set it up before we started."

Midas urged Mouse to continue. "You're doing so good, *heuning meisie*. Just repeat what they say. Don't worry about describing anything. We'll sort out who said what later."

As Mouse spoke, Medusa translated.

"We shouldn't have fallen in love. We shouldn't have had a child."

"We shouldn't have done a lot of things. Now we're paying the price."

"Lev, what are we going to do?"

Midas whispered over the line, "Lev Yurichenkov. That's her father. I found their names last night."

"I don't know."

"I'm frightened, Lev."

"I know, Talia. I'm sorry."

Midas whispered again, "Talia Yurichenkov. That's her mother."

"Talia, you must listen to me. They're going to come for me. They're going to question me. I will do everything I can to protect you both, but you need to leave. Take Stazy. Follow our plan."

"No, Lev!"

"You must, Talia. I can only stall them for so long. I will leave in the morning. Pack a bag for yourself and Anastasiya. Make sure she has her backpack. Get to your first stop, pick up the next packet, and follow the instructions. I will come to you as soon as I can."

Waters asked, "What does that mean, 'next packet'?"

"If I had to guess? Exit contacts," Gilgamesh replied.

Steel shook his head in amazement. "*Jesuchristo*, Waters. Spies? Is that what this is? She's the child of fucking Russian spies? I thought the KGB was dead."

TB offered, "It dissolved in 1991, but don't fool yourselves. It's just divided into 'sanctioned' departments. They would no more give up their security organization than we would dissolve Homeland or the alphabet agencies."

Loki grunted. "He's right. Call them whatever you want, the major players in global relations all have their spies."

"*Heuning meisie*, are they saying anything else?"

"I... I can't." He watched her wince and duck her head in pain. "It hurts."

"Okay, we're done. I want you to turn and walk out of the room. Put the key in your pocket and do not close the door. That's very important, Mouse. Do not close the door. Walk down the hallway to the kitchen. Get in front of the sink and come back through the pipe."

Mouse began whimpering. "The drumming has started again."

"It'll be okay, but you have to keep coming back the way you came, sweetheart. Don't rush. Just normal speed."

A few seconds later, the whimpering seemed to let up.

"Are you through the pipe?"

"Yes, I'm back in the empty room."

"Okay. Listen to me. I do not want you to shut off the water. I want you to slow it to the least amount of drip you can, but not all the way off. Then turn back the way you came and walk back to me. Ten steps. When you get to the tenth, you'll open your eyes, and you'll be back here with me."

He counted her back to consciousness, and she opened her eyes. Her eyes were wide with fear. She hung her head, fingers rubbing her temples. "What the hell is going on?"

That was the million-dollar question, wasn't it? Midas had his suspicions, but he needed to check some things out before speaking, both to her and the team.

Demon had crossed over to crouch down in front of her. After shining his penlight in her eyes, he placed a pressure cuff around her wrist to check her oxygen, pulse, and blood pressure. The machine beeped, and after looking at Midas, he said, "BP and pulse are elevated. Oxygen is low. By the looks of it, she has a monster headache. She needs rest."

Midas nodded, and as he stood, he swung her up into his arms. "I'm putting her to bed. I need to check some things. Can someone sit with her?"

"You onto something?" Waters asked.

"Might be. And I don't know how long it will take me to dig around, but I need access to some things in my office. Old files. I need uninterrupted time, and if I'm with her, I'm going to get distracted."

"I'll sit with her," Medusa offered.

"Make it happen," Waters agreed. "Midas, let us know when you have something. Get your girl situated and get to work."

This was not good, and he still felt like the hammer hadn't completely fallen. But if what he suspected was true, she was going to need to be completely rested for what lay ahead, mentally and physically. This woman could not catch a break.

19

FEBRUARY 3, 2024

Mouse

She stood in the doorway for several minutes, watching his fingers fly across the keyboards, squinting at the monitors, and muttering in Afrikaans to himself. Disturbing him was the last thing she wanted to do, but he'd been gone a long time, and she needed the feeling of safety he created for her.

"Midas?"

She bit her lip as he looked up from his monitors, his brain clearly trying to catch up, his eyes with dark smudges under them.

"Mouse." His voice finally caught up to her presence.

"Medusa brought me down. Is that okay?"

"Yeah. Yeah, it's fine. Come in. How are you feeling?"

"Tired," she admitted. "She said I slept for over twelve hours after the session."

He glanced at his watch, then removed his black horn-rimmed

glasses and rubbed the bridge of his nose. "I'm sorry. I guess I got in the zone and didn't realize how long it had been."

She may have been sleeping for over twelve, but he'd been gone for over twenty-four. Apparently, no one else thought anything of his working that long because they hadn't seemed concerned when she'd asked about it. "Can you take a break? I'm guessing you haven't eaten anything except NikNaks and lemon-lime sugar water, judging by the state of your desk."

With a grimace, he began to clear off the empty bags and bottles from his desktop. "Yeah. That happens when I get working on something." He glanced up at her again. "I wish I could take a break, but I've got another hour or so of work, I think. You're welcome to hang out if you want, although it gets pretty cold in here due to keeping the computers cool."

The reminder of the temperature brought on a shiver. In response, he tapped out a message on his watch. "Have a seat on the couch. I've got a blanket coming."

She nodded, making herself comfortable on the leather couch he had along the opposite wall. Medusa appeared moments later with a blanket, which she handed over to him, then left. Carefully, he tucked her in. "I'll try to make this as quick as possible, then we'll go get something to eat, yeah?"

"Don't rush on my account. Do what you need to do. Everyone seems to be working on stuff, so I didn't want to interfere."

"But you were getting lonely," he surmised.

With a shrug and a small smile, she replied, "A little. It was weird being on my own after you were with me twenty-four seven." She gave him a wave with her hand. "Shoo. Back to work."

"You got it." Immediately, he dove back into his screens, glasses once more perched on his nose.

Feeling sleepy again, she lay down and covertly studied him from beneath half-closed lids. His focus was absolute, and she found herself wishing that his focus was back on her as it had been when she'd been recovering. At least, while she was awake. The muttering began again, and his brow furrowed as his eyes peered intently at the screens in front of him. Just as she was drifting off into another nap, she briefly heard a voice over his monitors, but he'd swiftly put in earbuds, and it cut off the sound.

When she woke, the room lighting was dimmed so that only the glowing of his monitors' blue screens reflected onto the walls, and the lights on the servers behind them blinked. She sat up, the blanket falling into her lap as she stretched, and she looked to her left at the monitor that held all the security cameras. She could see almost every part of Tribe from here, including where the two teams were sitting in the conference room, talking. Whatever the conversation was, it looked intense because no one was smiling, most were sitting ramrod straight, and their gazes were directed to something off-screen as Midas typed. A telescreen, maybe?

Suddenly, Midas looked at his watch, which had lit up. A notification? A text? Whatever it was, she had a feeling she didn't have much time. There was something she needed to do. Not wanted. No, it was a driving force inside her. An imperative.

Her head turned back to the abandoned monitors. Without thinking, she stood and walked around the desk to face the screens. Something was pulling her in their direction. She looked down at the chair for a few seconds, then sat down tentatively in it. She must have jogged the table just slightly because all the screens woke up. Every monitor had a login screen appear. Knowing Midas, those passwords would be long and convoluted. Shit. It wasn't likely that she'd be able to get beyond the screens.

She stopped, her hands hovering over the keyboard. What the hell? Why did she need to access Midas' computers?

A female voice came through the speakers. "Can I help you, Miss Mouse?"

"Ex-excuse me?" Her heart began to beat triple-time.

"I was wondering if you needed something since you'd moved behind the computer desk."

The AI, Nova. Of course he'd have her monitoring the room, possibly even monitoring her.

She needed to tell Midas about what had just happened, but a pain sliced through the lower portion of her forehead. Drums began pounding lightly, and a flash of light appeared behind her closed eyes. Instantly, she began to wonder if she could keep her movements a secret, and the pain decreased. However, the AI knew where she'd been, so she didn't think it would look good if she said nothing, and the AI reported her actions. Best to tell him right away before Nova could. Hopefully, he wouldn't be angry, and he'd be able to figure out what was going on with her.

"No, thank you, Nova. I... I'm not even really sure why I'm sitting here."

Her eyes flashed up to the monitors, and she saw that Medusa was leaving the conference room. To come get her? Had the AI already notified him, and he was sending Medusa to find out what she was doing? This was all such a mess. She was so confused.

Knowing there was nothing she could do to make the monitors go to sleep, she scurried out from behind the desk and out into the hall, hoping that if Medusa was on her way to collect her, she could head the woman off before reaching the office. Sure enough, as soon as she turned toward the elevator, there was a ding signifying the carriage had arrived, and the doors opened to reveal the Mythos member.

"Good, you're up. Midas sent me to come get you and bring you downstairs. He's got some information."

"Oh, okay." Dammit. She needed to be cool and not telegraph to Medusa that anything was wrong. Whatever had happened regarding the computers was not something she wanted to share with anyone but Midas. While he might get mad, even distrust her going forward, he would never hurt her. She didn't think Medusa would have the same self-restrictions.

Silence coated the elevator like a weighted blanket. It made her skin itch, and she scratched at her forearms to ease the feeling. She should have known that the other woman wouldn't miss her tension.

"You okay, Mouse?"

"No. Yes. Why?"

"You seem unsure about how you're doing."

"If you were me, how would you be feeling right now?"

Medusa shrugged. "Confused. Disoriented. Angry. Hungry."

"Huh?" Of all the things the woman could have said, "hungry" didn't even make Mouse's list of guesses.

"Stress eating. Whenever I'm feeling out of sorts, I have this need to eat everything in sight. Can't imagine what would happen if I smoked weed and then encountered a stressor. You've had more stress than anyone I know of lately. Figured maybe being female, you'd be like me."

"I am nothing like you."

With a muted chuckle, Medusa pursed her lips and tilted her head. "Probably a good thing. I don't have a lot of positive attributes."

"What the heck does that mean?"

"I drink too much. I sleep too little. I don't follow orders or communicate well. And I've heard a rumor that I have a perpetual bad attitude."

"Well, when you put it like that..."

"See? It's a good thing."

There was a short pause before Mouse spoke. "Maybe those are downsides, but I actually wish I were more like you. I think you're pretty badass."

The door opened on the second floor, and the two women stepped out. Medusa stopped in the middle of the foyer in front of Cherry's desk, her eyebrow raised. "You want to be a badass?" There was no smile on her face, but Mouse thought for sure she saw a twinkle in the woman's eyes.

"Maybe not as badass as you," she mumbled. Her voice returned to its normal volume. "But I definitely wish I were stronger. I feel... helpless. Dependent. Everything is so... vague or completely unknown, and it's making me jittery. I feel like something's about to happen, and that I'm totally unprepared for whatever that is."

The head tilt was back from Medusa as she stared at Mouse. She resisted the urge to back up or shrink in on herself, not wanting to seem any more vulnerable than she already felt.

"What would make you feel more prepared?"

Shaking her head, Mouse raised her arms in a gesture of helplessness, then let them fall back to her sides. "Not a clue. The only time I really feel safe is when I'm with Midas." Heat flared in her face. "The rest of the time, I constantly feel like I'm waiting for something to come around a blind corner. Sometimes when I wake up, it's almost like something's looming over me."

"Hmm. Maybe we can change that. I can't pass on my bad attitude, but maybe I can make you feel a bit more badass by teaching you some ways to protect yourself. Knowing how to defend yourself can ease a lot of anxiety. Makes you feel you can handle things, and if you practice enough, it becomes second nature, so if you ever need it and adrenaline kicks in, your body knows what to do without really telling it. After Midas briefs us, if that's something you want to do, let me know. I'll do what I can."

"Why?" The question was out of her mouth before she could really think about it. "Not that I'm refusing, because I'm not. But I'm curious why you would offer to help me? I don't exactly get warm, fuzzy feelings from your team. Sometimes I even feel like you all think I'm the enemy."

"It's not that, exactly," Medusa said. "Mythos—and by Mythos I mean, Loki, Gilgamesh, and I—are pretty deeply scarred. Our trust factor is next to nil. It would be less than nil if that were physically possible. All three of us have serious baggage, and it's caused us to be very skimpy on providing trust to people because so often they have secrets. There are too many unknowns with you. Unknowns that I think Midas has managed to work through, which is what he wants to talk about right now. Until the three of us are unanimous in our lack of distrust, you don't get any. Harsh, but true, and it's saved our lives more often than not.

"Tribe is probably more accepting because they know that Midas is fond of you. Waters trusts his judgment, and he has spidey senses, according to his teammates, and he's generally a good judge of character. That helps your case, but we never let other people dictate anything for us. We have to experience it on our own terms to accept someone. Jury's still out on you."

"If that's the case, then why offer to help me?"

An emotion crossed Medusa's face so quickly, Mouse wasn't even sure she'd seen it, and then it was an impenetrable mask again. "I don't like when my gender feels helpless. Too many times, women are taken advantage of, like by these Salieri fucks, and that will not go down with me. And while having men to back us up is nice, every woman should be able to depend on, as well as defend, herself as much as possible. My experience has been that women are still too conditioned to wait for others to help them out in a tight spot. We're better, but not anywhere close to what I think we should be."

With that, Medusa turned and began walking toward the conference room. "Come on, let's see what your cyber geek has to say."

20

FEBRUARY 3, 2024

Mouse

ENTERING THE CONFERENCE ROOM, A HUNDRED SPARROWS swooped and screeched as they attacked her insides. The urge to run swept through her at the turn of all heads in her direction, and when Waters hit the security button on the starfish controller on the table, the sudden change in lighting, along with the thunk of the door locks, caused her to physically recoil into Medusa, who stood behind her.

Run! Hide!

The immediate panic caused her to whirl around one hundred eighty degrees, making her head spin and creating a loss of balance. The woman grasped her upper arms to steady her.

A body behind her rose from its chair, sandwiching her.

Trapped!

A keening sound spread throughout the room, and it was as if she were looking down upon the action there. It took a few seconds to realize that the noise was coming from her, indistinct but obviously pained and fearful.

Two hands dropped lightly onto her shoulders from behind, and instant security like a waterfall flowed throughout her body. The woman in front of her moved her hands from her upper arms to her forearms. A gentle pressure to the skin. A face before her that held no malice. No threat. A simple nod of reassurance before she stepped away to perch cross-legged on top of the credenza.

"Mouse?"

The quiet question sent another cascade of calm over her surface, reinforcing the previous wave. She took a shaky breath. Midas. He was here. He would help her. Her safety net to catch her from free fall.

She turned toward him, prepared to burrow into his broad chest, when out of the corner of her eye, she noticed there were three photos on the screen on the far end of the room. It took her brain a moment to catch up and a gasp to escape her lips.

When she could breathe again, as if drawn by a magnet, her feet took her to the screen. Her fingertips raised up to trace the woman's face. "*Mat'?*" A tear escaped as that same hand covered the man's face. "*Otets?*"

Subconsciously, she registered Medusa's husky translation. "Confirmation. Mother. Father."

Her head turned and registered the picture of a young girl, looking exactly like the one she had seen in her hypnosis sessions. While she had suspected that the child was her, it was another thing to have the reality in front of her.

"Mouse. Is that you next to the man?"

It was Midas' melodious voice, a tinge of concern behind it.

Opening her mouth to answer, words wouldn't come. Nausea overwhelmed her. She could feel the bile bubbling in her stomach, the muscles pushing it through her esophagus, and she knew that at any second it would boil over into her mouth and spew out of her.

Her lungs constricted, the same as when she'd been in the empty room being squeezed by the mist-snake. The drums pounded again, louder with each beat, and pain lanced through her head.

Midas' voice cut through all of it, like a scalpel. "Stay with me, Mouse. These are conditioned responses. Fight them. Answer the question, and the things you're feeling will recede. You can do it. I know it hurts, but I'm right here. You're safe. No one here will hurt you."

She turned her head to look at the screen. At the school picture of an adolescent girl with a shy smile but a mischievous twinkle in her eye. Her mouth opened, then closed. Frustrated, she looked at Midas, her mouth once again opened and closed. The words wouldn't come, dammit!

The hands holding her left her shoulders, and she wanted to cry out at the rejection. Before she could, his warm hands were back, stroking the sides of her face from the top of her head to her jawline. He stepped closer, the toes of his shoes touching hers. His forehead met hers, and he lined up the tip of his nose to hers as he murmured to her in Afrikaans, the only words she understood being *"heuning meisie."* Honey girl.

Of their own volition, her hands reached for his shirt, pulling it from his waistband, and her palms crept underneath until she could lay them flat on his chest to feel his heartbeat. Her breathing began to fall in line with his. Slow, even breaths in and out as he exaggerated his inhales and exhales to guide her. Almost immediately, she felt herself even out. The bile receded, along with the panic. The drums didn't disappear, but they quieted, and the same with the pain behind her eyes. Midas was here. She was safe.

"That's it, *heuning meisie.* Touch me all you want. Breathe with me. You're safe. Take your time."

It was several minutes before she felt like she was back in control of herself. When she pulled back from Midas, there was nothing but concern in his eyes.

"I'm sorry," she whispered.

She started to pull her hands out from under his shirt, realizing what that must look like in front of the others. Lordy, she was so embarrassed. However, he dropped his hands and placed them over hers through the material.

His voice was barely above a whisper, his words meant only for her ears. "Nothing to be sorry about. You've been through a lot, and I wish I could say that's all over, but I don't think it is. If you need to ground yourself, I will always be your anchor, okay? And whatever you need me to provide so you can do that, I will. No need to be embarrassed."

She sneaked a glance at the others in the room, but no one was looking their way. They were all discussing papers in front of them with each other or making notes. The fact that she'd basically ripped his clothing apart to get to his bare skin hadn't even fazed them. Or if it had, they'd shifted their attention to give her and Midas what privacy they could in the confined space.

The tension in her hands ebbed away, and he let go, only so he could smooth her hair down the sides of her head and caress her face. "Is that you, Mouse? On the screen?"

She nodded.

"And when you went to answer me, the pain started, didn't it?"

Again, she nodded.

He kissed her forehead, one hand trailing down her arm. When his fingers touched hers, he took her by the hand and led her to an empty chair next to him at the head of the table.

After he sat her down, Demon appeared with a bottle of water and a chocolate bar. "Eat that. It will help with the shock. Drink the water. When we're done here, Midas will make sure you get some more rest."

Everyone came out of the conversations they were in and focused on Midas, who now sat behind the table. When he spoke, it was directly to her. "After the hypnosis session, I did some digging. Do you remember what you saw and told me about?"

"Yes, I think so. I was back in the apartment, and I overheard my parents having an argument. My mother was afraid, and my father was trying to calm her. They were speaking another language."

"Russian," Medusa supplied. "You were speaking it while hypnotized."

Surprise flooded her. "I don't speak Russian."

Midas squeezed the hand she had clenched in a fist on top of the table. "I promise, you were speaking Russian. You wouldn't have been able to repeat it if you couldn't speak it already. And it was fluent with the proper cadences and intonations, so somewhere in your past, you knew how to speak it. You also gave me their names. Do you remember them?"

"Lev and Talia."

"Yes. So, while you were sleeping, I went to work. Now that I had three first names, I was able to triangulate more easily. Still took a little bit, but I found those three pictures in the New York City school system. Lev, Talia, and Anastasiya Yurichenkov.

"From there, I typed in 'Sterling Arms' and found a pay-by-the-week hotel in a rundown area of the city." He put a picture of the outside on the screen, and then a few interior shots of the lobby, a hallway, and the inside of one of the rooms people could see online. "Does this look familiar to you?"

"No. That's not the apartment I saw."

"I didn't think it would be but thought I'd ask. I hacked into their security system, such as it is, and this place is a haven of gang activity, drugs, and crime. You don't even want to know how many of these people are on the sexual predator list."

"Why the hell would her dad be so insistent she carry that envelope and have the name of that place in there?" TB growled. "Certainly not safe for anyone, let alone a woman, and particularly a child."

Midas ignored the question. "Your father called you 'Stazy.' Does that sound familiar?"

The moment the nickname was out of his mouth, her body froze. Split-second scenes flashed in front of her of the days following the argument she'd overheard. She zipped from scene to scene so fast, the time between the moments created a blurred wormhole effect, erasing the less-important moments. The experience was so disorienting, she felt herself pitching forward as her head spun due to the nausea and pain.

FEBRUARY 3, 2024

Midas

It happened so fast, Midas was late in grabbing her before she hit the floor. Every chair around the table was pushed back in panic, each person ducking under or around the table to see how to help her.

Medusa moved the fastest, launching herself from the credenza over the open space, and sprawled on her stomach across the table, reaching down to try and reach her before any of the men had even bent over. "Mouse!" she shouted.

Someone's hands touched her. They were large. Strong. Cold. Unfamiliar.

"Don't touch her!" Medusa snarled. Immediately, the hands retracted. "Midas!"

He reached for her, gently extracting her from under the table and into his arms. "Mouse? I've got you, *heuning meisie*. Wake up. Come back to me."

He sat on the floor, her body supported by one arm and draped over his lap. With his free hand, he brushed back strands of her hair and continued to croon softly to her.

It was several minutes before she woke, and she was slow to be completely aware of what was around her. "My head hurts," she whispered.

"Nova," Midas spoke out, "dim the conference room lights fifty percent."

"Dimming lights," she replied.

Demon approached from the other side of the table and knelt at his side. He handed Midas the bottle of water, which he cracked open for her, and the candy bar. "Is she cold?" the medic asked.

Midas put the backs of his fingers to her cheek. "Yes."

"Nemo, grab me a blanket," Demon ordered. "There's always one in the cubby behind Cherry's desk."

"On it."

Demon looked to Midas. "Okay to touch her?"

Weakly, a voice said, "*She* says it's fine for you to touch her."

Looking down at the woman in Midas' lap, the medic's mouth curved up into a smile. "My apologies, Mouse. I promise I would have asked you next, but your knight in shining armor is a bit overprotective when it comes to you. I didn't want him taking out his gloves, slapping my face, and challenging me to a duel if I touched you without asking him." He winked at her. "May I touch you?"

"Understood. Yes," she replied.

Demon pulled his penlight out of a pocket and examined her eyes. "Pupils look okay." He took hold of her hand and turned it over to feel her pulse. "Pulse is a little rapid. How is your heart rate? Beating too fast? Feel erratic? Sluggish?"

"It was out of control for a bit. It feels better now."

He turned his gaze to Midas and nodded, then stood up and went back to his seat.

By then, Nemo was back with the blanket. Midas stood, settling Mouse on her feet so he could drape the blanket around her shoulders, then helped her sit. He put the water bottle into her hands and opened the chocolate bar to break it into pieces for her. Midas watched as Scheherazade came to comfort her, ears down, chin on Mouse's thigh, eyes sad.

Everyone else returned to their spots. Medusa, still lying across the table, asked quietly, "You good, Mouse?"

"Yes. Thanks."

With a nod, Medusa slid off the table, hopping back up on the credenza.

Waters flashed him a look, and he felt himself scowl in warning. However, the man wasn't their team leader because he shied away from crabby team members. "I hate to do this, but we really need to talk, Mouse. We need as much information as we can get, as fast as we can, and as much as Midas will bitch at me for pushing, we don't have time."

"She doesn't remember anything, Waters," TB reminded him. "Two hypnosis sessions and a million questions aren't going to make all the memories come back."

"Actually," Midas interrupted, "I think they are starting to come back, aren't they, Mouse?"

Fingering the corner of the candy bar wrapper in front of her, she nodded. "When I came in and saw the pictures, there was a crashing noise in my head. Like bricks were falling. The drums I heard were louder, and it seemed like everything around me got brighter. Suddenly... I can't explain it, but suddenly everything crashed back into my brain at once. I couldn't breathe. My heart felt like it was going to explode."

Midas nodded. "When you left the apartment during your hypnosis, I had you leave the bedroom door open, and I had you take the key so that the door couldn't be locked. Or, if somehow it closed and locked again, you had the key 'on you.' Then, when you came through the pipe, I had you leave the faucet open enough to drip water. Psychological metaphors. I left the channels open so that the information was free to pass to you. I wasn't sure it would work.

Obviously, it did."

Loki grunted from his spot leaning against the floor-to-ceiling windows. "So you were right. A brain block. Someone purposefully fucked with her head."

"As sure as I can be. The psychosomatic reactions—loud noises, bright lights, severe temperature shifts—all meant to induce pain anytime she tries to remember anything about her past. There's information inside her that someone does not want to come out."

Drumming his fingers on the tabletop, Waters stared at their only link to the events at the Mythos compound. Midas knew he was divided. They were stuck, and Mouse was their only resource, but the man also didn't want to hurt her. It was a difficult spot to be in.

"What's happened?" Mouse asked. "Something's changed, or you wouldn't be trying to figure out how hard to push me."

Midas cleared his throat. "Yeah. We've got some unanswered questions, and then we've found some things that don't make sense. We're hoping you can fill in the blanks."

He shut his laptop and put all his attention on the woman next to him. While she was likely the only one with the information they needed, he would not push her to the point that she suffered. To prevent that, he needed to catalog her responses, both verbal and physical. If she showed any signs of distress, he would notice and be able to shut down questioning.

He flipped over a photograph he'd had beside his laptop and slid it closer to her. While she was studying it, he pulled his chair from the head of the table and faced her directly. His finger tapped it. "Do you know her?"

Her hand reached for the photograph and picked it up. "I think... Ayla? I think her name was Ayla."

"How did you know her?"

There was a brief pause. "Yes, Ayla. We shared a room together. She helped teach the children."

"When was the last time you remember seeing her?"

When she continued to stare at the woman's picture, which he'd found the day before, he plucked the photograph from her fingertips when she appeared to frown in pain. He turned her chair so that they were face-to-face, knees-to-knees, and took her hands in his. They were freezing cold, so he began to rub warmth into them. "Don't force it. You'll make yourself ill."

"But you need to know."

"Your health is more important."

"Something happened to her, didn't it? Something bad?"

"We found her body while we were making our way to the compound. The group she fled with showed up yesterday at a Mythos safe house. When that group was ambushed, the men chasing were only concerned with her."

Her face turned back to the picture, sadness behind her eyes. "I honestly didn't know much about her," she explained. "No one there was particularly interested in sharing their history because none of it was good, and I couldn't remember my past, so there was nothing to tell. We focused on the day-to-day. The first time we saw Ona smile after arriving at the compound. The baby's milestones. Things like that."

The quality of her voice had changed. Even when talking about painful things, there'd been a core of strength behind her words. A sense of self. The woman speaking to him now had none of that. She sounded... defeated.

Gently, he turned her face so that their gazes meshed. "*Heuning meisie*, I'm sorry to push you, but it's better to get this out and over with. I promise you, I will not leave your side. You are safe, and no matter what, I'll help you through, okay?"

Her eyes gazed flatly into his, as if she were giving up. She nodded at him, but it was as if the answers she was going to give him could no longer be avoided and would seal her fate to something negative.

With a squeeze to her hands, his eyes never leaving hers, he asked Demon to get her some tea from the break room. "I'll make sure it has lots of sugar," the medic replied. Obviously, he still saw signs of shock as well.

"Mouse, the guard who brought the group in, the group she had been with, said that they were very single-minded in their pursuit of her. There were chances to snatch up children that got separated, opportunities for other women to be taken hostage, but they ignored them to pursue her specifically. Are you sure there was nothing she said or did to suggest someone might be looking for her?"

"No. Nothing. I mean, I suppose it's possible that I just don't remember."

"But you remember other things about her?"

"Yes. So, no, there's nothing she did or said to suggest that." She bit her lip and flashed another look at the photograph. "There is something you should know though."

"What's that?"

"It was supposed to be me with that group. We switched places at the last minute. Ona hid, and we couldn't find her. Ayla knew she wouldn't come out for anyone but me, so she said she would go with the group, and I could stay and look for Ona."

Waters' voice joined their private conversation. "Superficially, she could be described the same as you. Tall, light-brown hair, brown eyes."

Her head turned toward Waters. "You think those men were sent to collect me from the compound and thought she was me. Then, when they realized they had the wrong woman, they killed her and returned to attack the compound."

Midas noted that what she said were statements, not questions. She was putting the pieces together, just as they had.

"Yes."

Her gaze darted back to Midas. "I don't understand what's so special about me."

"Shh," he soothed. "It's okay. Just because you've remembered some things doesn't mean you know what's behind the actions of others. But all evidence is pointing to you being their target, not the children, so someone's worried you're going to remember something, or maybe say something that, even if you don't know it's important, leads us to them, and they clearly don't want that.

"There's more. You've been through a lot already, but after your session the other day, we were able to make some educated guesses on what was going on back then. After digging around, I was able to confirm some things, but mostly, we have more questions. Now you're starting to remember things. I'm fairly certain that a lot of what's going on with you now—the memory loss, the people looking for you—is connected somehow to what's in your past. That means that things could get a whole lot worse, and you need to be prepared for that."

He raised her hands to his lips, brushing her knuckles with their caress. "We have questions. You have answers. Somewhere between these two things is the truth we need. However, your physical and mental health are my first concern, and I will make my teammates wait if going further right now is going to hurt you in any way. Make no mistake, I'm not going to stop pursuing the information they want, but I will force the process to slow down if that's what you need."

"It's okay. I trust you. You always make me feel safe, so I know that even if everything is awful, you'll make it better if you can."

Her words, and the obvious honesty behind them, made it feel like the sun had broken through a lifetime of cloud cover. He hadn't realized how cold and dreary his life had been until this moment. This woman's life had been turned upside down in every way possible. She had every reason to be terrified, and she wanted so badly to give in to the exhaustion, yet she still felt safe with him. She shouldn't trust anyone or anything, but she trusted him. Could there be anyone more perfect?

"So fucking brave," he whispered. A little louder, he assured her, "You need to take a break, you let me know. A few minutes, an hour, until tomorrow. Whatever it is, you tell me, and that's what we'll do."

She nodded. One more time, her eyes were drawn to the photos of her and her parents on the screen at the foot of the table. "I have to ask one question."

"What's your question?"

Her eyes turned to his again. "My parents. They spoke Russian. They were getting secret phone calls. They were scared. They were spies, weren't they?" She blushed. "Sounds crazy, doesn't it?"

Looks were exchanged all around the room. Either she'd remembered much more since the hypnosis session, or she was very intuitive. Probably both.

"Melodramatic, crazy, sensational, whatever you want to call it, that's what we think, yes. Because I had three first names, it was easy for me to find your family. Your last name, birthday, last known address, where you went to school. So the basics you know already.

"Then I looked at their jobs. Add to that the phone call they were trying to keep secret from you, the conversation they didn't want you to overhear, and the fact that they'd planned ahead for an escape route, hopefully for the whole family, but definitely for you. Then I looked at the time when this occurred. From there, I traced their lives backward, and based on what I found, I believe they were far more than just individual spies."

Frowning, she asked, "What do you mean?"

"I believe your parents were part of a sleeper cell. You were born on Easter in 1993. Your mother was hired as a foreign language teacher in 1989 for the New York City schools. Every two years, she moved to a new school. Some sort of language exchange program they had where the languages offered changed every couple years. Your father was hired at the school where she worked in 1990.

"That part was likely planned—designed as a way for them to meet appropriately, create a cover. In this case, a relationship where they would get married and wait for the call to do whatever it was they were supposed to do. Their skills to do whatever they were trained to do somehow worked together. Maybe eventually, they hooked up with other people. Friends they 'made' during their time there. Together, they formed a cell of people who had a job to do when they were activated.

"I think they fell in love for real. Maybe since no call came, they figured they were safe. They had a beautiful little girl and went about their lives. Then the call finally came. Maybe someone in the group turned them in. Maybe they refused to comply with their directives."

"There are other options too," Medusa interjected. "Maybe the Russian alphabet soup discovered two of their operatives had broken protocols, and they were calling them home. Maybe someone checked on them and wanted to see how badly they were compromised. We'll probably never know why they called, but from what you overheard, it's probably one of those three options."

Mouse looked between the two operatives. "So they broke the rules and were going to be questioned to make sure they were still usable."

Medusa was never one to sugarcoat things. "Yes. I'm a glass-half-empty kind of gal, and I'd be willing to bet they planned to find out what type of damage control was needed before erasing all of you. It's what I'd do. I'd call them in, saying I just wanted to talk. No trouble. A marriage in name, that would be okay. Probably part of the assignment."

"But wouldn't a child cement the relationship?" Steel asked.

"Yes, but if feelings become involved, whether it's a significant other, or a spouse, or a child, now there's something else between you and the homeland's mission. Something worth protecting instead of worth dying for."

The room was silent again.

After a few moments, Mouse said, "So I'm the child of Russian spies intent on harming people in this country."

The admonishment came out of Midas' mouth quickly. "Hey. You are not responsible for their actions. Stop what you're thinking right now."

"Even if I'm not responsible for them, I'm a product of them."

"So?" Nemo spoke up from across the table. "Midas and I are the product of a piece of shit who left his wife and sons when things got tough. Doesn't mean we'll leave the people important to us. Why would you assume that you're going to be destructive because your parents' intentions were subversive? Did they teach you to hate your country? Did they want you to do things that were harmful to others?"

"No." She rubbed her forehead. "I don't remember anything like that. Even if that's true, though, they're missing, probably dead, because of me. Because I was born, they're gone." The last part was a whisper, and her eyes were now wide with panic and pain. "No matter what they did, or planned to do, they were good to me. They couldn't have been all bad, right?"

Medusa spoke up from her perch. "Mouse, you listen, and you listen well. You are not at fault. You didn't ask to be born. And they could have given you up for adoption or even aborted you if they hadn't wanted you. Harsh but true. So knock that shit right out of your head. Based on the fact that they had plans on how to get you to safety if something went wrong means they intended to choose you over their assignment. That makes them good people."

"But how do you know they didn't complete their assignment?"

"They're not here anymore, are they? I'm guessing that right after that phone call is when your parents had that fight you listened in on, yes?"

Mouse nodded. "They sent me to my room. I didn't know what was going on, so I tried to listen at the door."

Medusa nodded and looked at Waters. "So typical protocol in these situations is a 'friendly' contact. 'Hey, we haven't forgotten about you. We'd like to debrief on how things are going.' Maybe they even said they had new instructions to give them. However, Lev was already suspicious that the call wasn't everything it seemed, so either he figured out they were being watched, or more likely, they mentioned they knew about Anastasiya as a way to keep him honest."

"Why didn't they just take off?" Steel asked.

Gilgamesh, quiet up until this point, chimed in. "The three of them taking off together actually increases the danger for all of them. Slows them down and makes them easier to spot. It's possible that their handlers might even expect them to run. If he reports in, he diverts attention. Then, at some point, she enacts their plan. She goes one way with Mouse, he goes another. Protective strategy. Worst-case scenario, he sacrifices himself so that they have time to get away. Best-case scenario, if he's able to, he knows the plan. He'll catch up."

"But if they knew where they were," Waters began, "why wouldn't they just come and get them? Save themselves the hassle if they run."

Medusa replied, "Why chase if you don't have to, you mean? It's a loyalty test. Part of how they determine just how damaged their assets are. Lev would have known that. He'd make some excuse. She wasn't feeling well, or whatever. He'll go back home and get her. Blah, blah, blah. In the meantime, Talia should have taken their emergency bag and gone. Used the exit contact she had. But for some reason, she didn't."

"Oh my god," Mouse muttered.

Midas turned to her. "What is it?"

"She didn't go because of me. I remember her saying we had to run an errand she forgot about."

"Mouse," he admonished. "Remember, none of this is your fault." He brushed back her hair from her forehead. "You're remembering something else? What?"

"It was the next day. She said the errand was important. I didn't want to go because there was a dance at school that night. I'd never been to one, and the whole grade was so excited that we finally got to have one. It was a big deal at our school.

"She got upset when I complained. Angry. Mom never got angry, so it scared me, and I kept arguing with her. She grabbed my back-pack and went to my room, started throwing things into it haphazardly. I ran after her, begging her to explain what was going on, but she wouldn't. She was frantic. Almost manic. She grabbed me. Bruised me. Asked if I had my envelope. I said yes, it was in my backpack. She reminded me again to never lose it. That it might save my life. That was the point I remember being terrified.

"After that, she went into the kitchen and started unscrewing an air duct vent. It was one I'd always complained wasn't working very well. In the summer, I refused to go into the kitchen if I could avoid it because it was always so much hotter in there, and no matter how many times they said the manager had been there to look at it, it never seemed to get fixed. She pulled a bag out of it. I guess they lied so that no one found the bag, and that's what was blocking the airflow."

He squeezed Mouse's hands, his thumbs brushing back and forth across the backs. "Go ahead. Stop when you need to."

She took a big breath in, then let it out. "She sent me to school, like normal. I debated staying after, just to spite her, but I couldn't do it. I'd never been a disobedient child, and I wasn't about to start with this, especially since I knew my parents had fought. I didn't want to add to their worry.

"So after school, I headed home. It was a bit of a walk, but I hated taking the bus, so by the time I got home, it was rush hour. New York City was awful then, like L.A. Considering what I know now, I think she planned for that. Maybe so we'd have the cover of the crowd? Easier to lose whoever was following us? What I don't think she planned on was that it also worked against us, and we got separated at the subway station in the crush of people."

Midas gave her hands another squeeze. These memories had to be brutal, and he wished there was something he could do to prevent her from having to go through them. He had a sense the worst was yet to come.

"I got on the subway. I wasn't sure what else to do. After a while, I realized I'd been on the train so long that it was getting back to where I started, so I got off there, hoping Mom was waiting, but she wasn't there. I waited on the platform for about an hour. By then, it was getting late, and the subway was starting to be a dangerous place for anyone, especially someone my age alone, so I went back home. Maybe she'd be there waiting.

"When I got about a block from the apartment, I knew something was really wrong. There was a car parked out front. A fancy black one with diplomatic plates. Two men were standing by it in suits, but they didn't look like men who should be wearing suits. They looked more like bodybuilders. I waited around the corner, watching. Finally, two more men came out, and they had my mom between them. I wanted to run to her, but something kept me from doing it."

"That probably saved your life, Mouse," Medusa said.

Mouse glanced at her. "I know that now." She looked down at her lap. "That was the last time I saw my mom, and I never saw my father again either. I was on my own." She sniffled and wiped away the tears that had started. "I realized it probably wasn't safe to go into the apartment. Maybe there'd be someone waiting for me, and I somehow knew I didn't want to get into a car like my mom did."

"Smart move," Waters murmured.

"I stayed in the alley that night, trying to think about what to do. I waited all day. I was so hungry, but I didn't want to leave. I was worried I'd miss them when they showed up, but eventually, after two days, I realized they weren't going to. I had no idea what to do. I had no money on me. The clothes I had on and a few items my mom had thrown in my backpack. No books, no reminders of home, no way to even make a phone call, not that there was anyone to call. We didn't have friends, and I'd never been allowed over to my school friends' homes, so I didn't know where anyone lived. Looking back, that should have been a clue, but I never knew another way, so I never questioned it."

"You're doing great, *heuning meisie*. I'm sorry you're having to talk so much, but the more we can learn, the better off we are. What happened next?"

"No, I understand. It's okay." She gathered herself and sat up straight.

While he was happy to see her returning to herself, he found he didn't like her pulling away.

"I knew I needed to get away. Do something. I was just a kid, so it wasn't like I could really get a job. If I went back to school, people would question me, and I had no answers. None that wouldn't make me sound crazy or put me into social services, anyway.

"I went to the bus terminal, washed up a bit in the bathroom, and changed clothes. My feet just sort of took me there. Might have half-assed thought I could stow away and get somewhere else? For some reason, I took the envelope out of my backpack and put it in my pants pocket. I have no idea what told me to do that except that my father told me always to protect it."

"You're lucky you did," TB said. "That backpack would have been long gone, probably trashed before you even left the station."

"That's where it all went wrong, didn't it?" Medusa asked. "Those are the memories that just came back, aren't they?"

Mouse nodded and started crying, silently this time.

Inside, Midas knew this was not going to be good. In preparation, he dropped her hands, scooped her out of her chair, and brought her onto his lap. He didn't care they were in the conference room and in front of his teammates and Mythos. She was going to need a safety net, and if he was hers, then that's what she got.

"A woman came up to me and started talking. She said she could see I was on my own and wondered if I needed help. I was so scared. I wanted my mom and dad, and she seemed so nice. I know now I shouldn't have talked to her, but at the time..."

"Shhh," Midas soothed, kissing her temple. "You were a child, sweetheart. No one can blame you. There's nothing to be blamed for. Adults are supposed to help kids. You're supposed to be able to trust them."

Someone handed Mouse tissues, which she used to wipe her eyes and nose, then crumpled and uncrumpled them continuously as she finished her story.

"She offered me a place to stay for the night while I waited for the morning bus. Foolishly, I said yes. She took me to a house on the edge of the city, gave me something to drink, and then took me to a spare room. It was small and old but not nasty. I was so tired. I lay down and fell asleep. When I woke up, I had no idea where I was. It wasn't where I'd fallen asleep. I felt so heavy. My head hurt. It was dim, and I couldn't see anyone because there were curtains, like hospital partitions, up. But I could hear people moving around. There were groans and grunts and squeaking. People were speaking, but it sounded like a foreign language. I couldn't really tell."

"A portable brothel. Like in Zimbabwe," Gem said. She'd observed those herself when she broke into a diamond mining facility posing as a sex worker.

"Fucking animals," TB whispered. He, more than anyone, had unresolved issues regarding sex traffickers because of what happened to his partner, Flame, and an incident in his history where he'd rescued a young girl in a very similar situation. The situation that had earned him his nickname of Total Bastard.

"I heard the woman's voice, from the bus station, and she said my name. Something told me to hide the envelope, so I found a ripped seam in the mattress I was on and shoved it inside the ticking. Just in time, too, because someone entered the partitioned area, came up to the bed I was lying on, and then I felt a poke in my arm. Whatever they gave me acted fast, and everything went hazy. I could just make out people standing at the foot of my bed. Their voices floated in and out. They were talking about money and getting something cleaned up. Next thing I knew, I was being yanked out of bed. I was stripped, thrown into a shower, and then re-dressed. They pulled me back to my room, and then they handcuffed me to the bed. This time, I was given something to swallow: some sort of pill. I was so out of it. I could feel what was happening, but I was too tired to fight, and all the colors in the room started to change. Nothing seemed solid."

More swear words came under muttered breaths. She heard a thud, as if someone had thrown something into the wall. She hung her head, her hair covering her eyes in shame. "A man came into the room. He was talking, but I was so drugged, I couldn't understand him. I felt all warm and floaty. And then..." She swallowed. "Well, you know. Apparently, being so young and a virgin was worth a great deal of money to them.

"I'm so sorry, Midas. It's not much information. I've no idea where I was, so that doesn't help you. I don't even know how long I was there. They kept me pretty drugged up so that I wouldn't fight. There were times I was allowed to be sober. I guess when some of the men wanted someone to fight them. But by then, I was so broken, it didn't matter. I didn't fight."

A hand fell on Midas' shoulder, and he looked up to see Waters. He mouthed, "Take care of her." Then he pointed at his watch as if to say "Text me," and he silently gathered everyone up, and they let themselves out.

Nemo had signaled Scheherazade, but for the first time ever, she disobeyed a command. Instead, she looked directly into Mouse's eyes. Mouse put out her hand to stroke the dog's ears, and Scheherazade bunted her hand, causing the woman to smile. The dog seemed to understand, gave Mouse's hand a soft lick, then walked over to Nemo. Together, man and dog headed to the door.

Medusa was the only one to remain, eyes glittering in anger. In a fluid motion, she propelled herself off the credenza and rounded Midas to settle in a crouch in front of Mouse. Her voice was quiet, but it was filled with righteous anger. "I've got you, Mouse. We've all got you. Never, ever doubt that. Even if Midas hadn't already claimed you as tribe to his team, they would have done it as a family. Mythos claims you now as well." She rose and locked eyes with him. Midas knew what she was saying.

Find those fuckers and kill every one of them.

No mercy.

He nodded. On silent feet, Medusa left the room, leaving them in the dim lighting to sit and rest. Time passed. He just held her. What else could he do? How did you fix years of sexual abuse and pain? How could he help her? One thing was certain. He needed to show her she had survived, that she'd stepped back out into the light. Remade herself. She was no longer a victim. The only way he could figure to do that was to get her talking again, but this time about how she got out and what came after. There were still unanswered questions, and he wasn't sure if the blocker in her brain had come from then, or after, with someone else. That thought made his blood run cold.

"Remember. Not your fault." He kissed the side of her head, leaving his lips there. It was a miracle she would even let him touch her, give her these gentle kisses. She was so fucking brave. So fucking trusting, even after the last time she had trusted someone, it had almost destroyed her. "Something changed, didn't it?"

"I'm tired, Midas. I don't want to talk about this anymore. Not today."

"Trust me, sweetheart."

It was a long time before she spoke.

"One day, the visitors stopped. Days passed. No drugs. No visits. While I was thankful that had stopped, it was hell as the drugs cleared my system. Someone brought me food and water each day, but they said nothing. Didn't even look at me.

"Then one day, I was taken to the showers. That water felt so heavenly. It was just a temporary respite though. After I cleaned up, I was given some clothes, similar to what prisoners wear, but softer. Nothing with laces or buttons. I was taken to another part of the building and put into a room of my own, but it was little more than a bed and four walls. Not even a window.

"Then the trips to the lab started. They strapped me into this chair, showed me lots of terrible pictures, played lots of really loud music and sounds. They talked to me, but I couldn't make a lot of it out. I'd just go away in my head. All the time, I was watched by this man. He looked like he was in the military because he wore some kind of uniform, but he never spoke to me, and I only ever saw him through the big picture window into some sort of control room. Endless days in the lab. Endless pain."

She shuddered.

"Then suddenly, I was in Egypt at the orphanage gates. I had no idea how I got there. I don't know if I got away or if they let me go, but I must have been somewhat aware, as I had a backpack, and somehow, through all that time, that stupid envelope was still with me. However, everything was just gone from my head. The people at the compound kept me isolated for a while, but then they must have felt I was safe because they allowed me to be around the children, where I helped in the school. They moved me to a room with Ayla. Then the compound was attacked, and you all showed up."

"You're safe now. I promise, Mouse, we will never harm you. Never put you through what you've been put through. Tribe and Mythos? We work against stuff like what you've been through. We've rescued trafficking victims. People who've been kidnapped." He was silent for a minute. "You might talk with Flame. That's TB's other half. She was a victim of sex trafficking. Slightly different situation, but if anyone would understand what you're going through, she would. It might help to know you're not alone."

"Maybe. Not yet."

He nodded.

"Midas?"

"Yeah, *heuning meisie?*"

"I'm glad you found me."

He kissed the top of her head. "Me too."

22

FEBRUARY 3, 2024

Mouse

THEY'D SAT IN THE CONFERENCE ROOM IN SILENCE UNTIL darkness fell. She had to be causing his limbs to go numb, but she couldn't seem to find the energy to move, and he didn't seem to be in any great hurry to move either. She wished she could stay here with him forever.

His watch beeped twice, but he ignored it. Didn't even twitch. A few minutes later, it beeped twice again. He still didn't move. Eventually, he got several sets of double pips in a row, somehow managing to sound annoyed even though they were just beeps. With a sigh, he let go of her and flipped his wrist to look at his watch.

A quiet word flew out of his mouth, which she guessed was a swear word in Afrikaans.

"You need to go?" she asked, not looking at him.

"Yeah. TB did some searching. Nova's pissed off because he's trying to access her since I'm 'tied up.'"

She tensed. In all the excitement, she'd never told Midas about the computer situation earlier. If Nova was upset about TB trying to access her, it was probably only minutes before she mentioned Mouse trying to access her. That news needed to come from her.

"Midas? I need to tell you something."

"What? Another memory?"

"No. Something happened earlier."

"Earlier when?"

She sat up from where she leaned against his chest so she could look him in the eye when she confessed. "When I woke up, and you weren't in your office, I was really out of it. It took me a minute to remember where I was, and then—"

"And then?"

"I found myself in front of your computers. I was going to try and look at them, I think."

Now it was his turn to tense up.

"I didn't touch anything, but there was this compulsion to try and break into your computers. I don't know how I would have. I don't really have any experience with computers, but it was scary. If Nova hadn't interrupted me, I'm not sure what would have happened."

His face was a blank mask. What was he thinking? He didn't look angry. He didn't look anything. It was as if all emotions had been erased from his person.

"I'm sorry," she whispered. "I knew I had to tell you. Figured it was connected to whatever was going on. I understand if I can't go back to the apartment with you and you need to lock me up somewhere."

"Excuse me?"

"Well, I could be dangerous. Somebody's messed with me, right? It makes no sense why I would need to access your computers. No one would know that I would be rescued by your team, or that I'd come here once I was rescued, but clearly there's something they, whoever they are, want me to do."

He lifted her off his lap and put her back in her chair. He opened his laptop and began typing in a flurry. Then he opened a channel to Nova. "Nova, I need video of my office from when I left at fifteen hundred to when Mouse left. Sound and visual, please."

"Copy that, Midas," she replied. Seconds later, she was back. "Video has been sent to your email."

She huddled in the chair, her legs pulled up tight to her chest, watching as he plugged earbuds into his ears and viewed the video. His eyes were as intense on the monitor as they had been when looking at her minutes earlier. Every so often, his thumb dragged across the trackpad as if reversing the footage.

Speaking into his watch, he put out an all-call to the team members, requesting them to come back to the conference room. Then he returned to watching the video. He said nothing to her. The only thing he did was blindly reach out his left hand to her. The gentle squeeze when she lay her palm in his, and the brushing of his thumb back and forth, gave her hope that things weren't as bad as she thought they were.

One by one, Tribe and Mythos members drifted back into the room. Nemo was the last to arrive. "Gem's watching the girls. What's up?"

Waters pressed the red button on the starfish. There was a ding, and he hit the green button, bringing God over the line. "Go ahead, Midas."

The video footage popped onto the telescreen at the foot of the table, frozen, showing a sleeping Mouse on the couch. "I just found out about this. And before anyone goes apeshit, Mouse told me about it herself."

While everyone watched the video, his hand never left hers, but he still didn't look at her. Like the others, he watched. With quick keystrokes, he shrunk the video to half the size of the screen and brought up another. This one was from the camera of the computer she had been sitting directly in front of.

"Look at her eyes," Medusa said.

The room had been dim when she'd awoken earlier, but even she saw what Medusa had noticed. Her pupils were slits, barely present. In the darkened room, they should have been open more to let in what light was present so that she could see. Even though the computer screen reflected light back at her, it shouldn't have been enough to allow the pupils to close like that.

"That's not normal," Demon commented.

"Psychosomatic reaction," Midas told them. "The body is remembering what it's conditioned to." He stopped the video footage a few seconds later when it was clear that she'd come out of whatever trancelike mode she'd been in and returned to herself, realizing where she was. The emotions were clear on her face. Surprise. Confusion. Fear. They'd been genuine, but would these people think so?

TB looked around the table. "Is everyone thinking what I'm thinking?"

God's voice came over the speaker. "Salieri plant confirmed."

The anger radiated throughout the room, which scared her more than Midas' withdrawal earlier at her confession. "You've mentioned that name before. Who is Salieri?" she asked meekly.

Midas finally turned his face to hers. "You've never heard the name Salieri before?"

"No." Even she heard the hesitancy of her answer, and a mild throbbing began behind her eyes. She reached up to rub her forehead.

"She's in pain," Loki noted. "That suggests yes, she has."

Midas' eyes were watching her closely. "I think she's being honest. At least, on the surface. Maybe there's something stuck deeper in there that will come out later. Right now, it means nothing."

"Midas, I—"

"Shh. It's all right. Just breathe, okay?"

"Okay."

He turned back to the table, his focus on the starfish controller in the center of it. "God, we're talking about long-term psychological control here."

"She can't be left to wander at large," their boss said.

"She's not going to be locked up either," Midas growled. "It's not her fault."

"No, it's not, but that doesn't mean she won't attempt to follow through on whatever she's been programmed for. We can't risk it."

"We can keep someone with her at all times," Gilgamesh suggested. "We're clearly not going anywhere for a while. Not until we get this figured out. There're enough of us around, and obviously Midas is going to have things to research, so it can't be him."

The panic welled up again. Whether it was at the compulsion inside her to do... whatever she was supposed to do, or whether it was at being separated from Midas, or being watched like a hawk twenty-four seven, she didn't know. But there was a scrabbling of claws coming up from her stomach, into her throat, and trying to escape through her mouth in a flurry of keening and whining. She barely registered when her body pitched itself into the corner of the room behind her, face to the wall, arms over her head, tucked as tightly into a ball as she could. Cold. So cold. The drums were back. Lights flashed behind her eyes. Her body began to rock.

A voice began to break through the noises, quieting them. Warm hands brushing over her head, a soft blanket being draped around her. Then nothingness.

23

FEBRUARY 4, 2024

Midas

Standing in front of TB's apartment door, Midas took a deep breath and blew it out before he pushed the doorbell. This could backfire in his face. It meant dredging up some potentially painful memories. Who was he kidding? Potentially? They couldn't be anything but painful. What the hell was he doing?

Too late. The door opened to TB standing in the foyer, Scheherazade's second puppy, Jasmine, pushing at him to get to Midas.

He grunted. "Wondered how long it would take you to stop by. Medusa won. She's gonna end up worse than Steel if we keep letting her into the betting pool. Come on in, if Jasmine will allow it." The giant turned and left Midas in the doorway, assuming he'd follow.

"You were betting on me?"

"Yep. How fast you'd stop by and talk to Flame about you and Mouse. Need a beer?"

"Yeah."

Midas walked into the apartment, making sure to give Jasmine pets and that the door closed tightly behind him before entering the main living area. He marveled at how different the place looked from before Axel was born. Prior to then, the apartment had been so stark that even when TB had been single, it always looked like no one lived there. He had never invited people in, preferring to spend most of his time in the gym or the armory. Flame still owned her home in the suburbs, where he spent most of his off hours, but since they were hosting Paris temporarily, he had asked Flame to stay here with Axel so the baby was in proximity to the other girls from the compound.

Now? The apartment looked like a day care had erupted. There was a playpen in the middle of the room, along with a bouncy chair on wheels and a swing. Stuffed toys were everywhere, and he watched as TB bent over four times on his path to the refrigerator, picking up teething rings, a pacifier, a block with a K on it, and a vinyl book. Without blinking an eye, he set the items in a bin by the sink and continued to get two beers.

"Should have texted you first. Sorry to stop by unannounced," Midas apologized.

TB popped the tops on the beers and handed one over. With a wave of his hand, he gestured to the living room with the one holding the beer bottle. "Like I said, we were expecting you at some point, and you weren't interrupting anything."

Jasmine brought a squeaky toy to Midas. He took it from her and looked at it carefully. "How do you tell if it's a dog toy or a kids' toy?"

"Fuck if I know," TB said. "Right now, it's all interchangeable in my eyes. She licks them to death anyway, so if it's a kids' toy, a little dog spit isn't going to hurt them. Axel and the dog were one thing. Now that Paris has entered the mix, it's chaos central."

Midas grinned. "Admit it. You love it."

TB gave a genuine smile. "Yeah. I do. Wouldn't trade it for anything."

"You don't worry about if something happens to you?"

"I worry about that every damn day, but I still wouldn't trade this. I know you all would take care of them. Especially the new one."

"Holy shit. She's pregnant again?"

TB laughed. "No. I'm not risking her being that sick again." He took a long pull from his beer. "We just talked to Loki. We're adopting Paris."

Well. That was unexpected. "Wow."

"Figured it's a good choice. She wants more kids but doesn't want to be ill like she was with Axel, and I certainly don't want that either. Paris is close enough in age to Axel that it'll be good for them."

"You gonna be able to handle it? I know you're concerned about how that's going to work for you all as Axel gets older. You, umm... need me to start moving anything around from your accounts?"

TB shook his head. "No. We've talked about it. We're not going anywhere, but thanks. We'll figure it out as it comes."

"Does anyone else know?"

"Waters does, which means God does, which means Cherry probably knows. Not sure if she'll spill it to Demon or not, but probably. I'm sure Flame will share it with the girls soon, so it'll be common knowledge by dinner time, I'm guessing." He took another pull from his beer, then stood. "You didn't come here to talk to me though. I'll hustle her along," he said.

"Hustle who along?" a soft voice said from the hallway.

TB walked over to Flame and kissed her forehead. "Thought you were having difficulty getting the rugrats to sleep." He looked down at Paris in her arms, his large hand reaching out to take hold of the baby's tiny fist. A gentle smile took over his face. "Apparently, I was only half wrong."

"Like a freakin' kewpie doll. Lay her down, her eyes pop right open. Not unhappy, just doesn't want to sleep."

Without ceremony, she walked over to Midas and handed the baby to him. "See if you can work your voodoo."

"It's not voodoo," Midas grumbled.

"Call it what you want. Every time I see you with one of the girls, they're asleep."

TB whispered, "That's because he's b-o-r-i-n-g."

"Who are you spelling it for?" Midas said with a laugh. "I know the word boring. So does Flame. Paris won't understand it yet."

The man shrugged and returned to his chair. Flame sat on the other side of Midas and smoothed down Paris' tuft of hair atop her head. "So, can I assume you've come to talk to me about Mouse?"

Midas swallowed hard.

"Need me to leave?" TB asked.

"No." Midas shook his head. "I probably could use your take as well." He sighed. "Okay. I don't think it's any secret that I've developed feelings for Mouse. I think she has feelings for me too. Or at least, she's fond of me."

"Fond of you?" TB snorted.

"Hush," Flame chastised. "Go on," she said to Midas. "I don't think debating that is what you came here for."

He shifted his gaze to Flame. "I don't want to upset you, but... I don't know where else to go for advice. This is uncharted waters for me." He snuck a glance at TB, who simply sat, stone-faced, then he flicked his eyes back to Flame.

Shifting sideways on the couch, Flame leaned her elbow on the backrest, her head in her palm. "I'm guessing she's got some things in her past similar to mine?"

Midas nodded.

"Right. So, first things first. *You* could never upset me. I'll probably never be completely free of my past, but that's exactly what it is. My past. Thanks to all of you, I'll never have to worry about Gendry again. The things he did? Those will never go away, but I think about them less every day. That's why you're here, right? To get a sense of how Mouse is doing because of the similarities between us?"

Midas nodded. "I'd... like to pursue something with her, but I'm worried that she won't respond to me that way. What she's been through? I know I'm sharing something that's hers to tell, but I'm really stuck. Between the trafficking and losing her memories? It's hard to believe she'd want to be with anyone. At least... not... *that* way. But I look at you and TB, and I look at the lifestyle you lead with the BDSM community, and I can't help but have hope that it's possible. I just don't know how to get us to that point. I mean, not the BDSM part. That's not for me. Just... a relationship."

"You mean one with sex."

He blushed, looking down at the baby in his arms. It was safer to look at her with Flame being so blunt.

She reached over and touched his shoulder. "Midas, if there's one thing I've learned from TB, it's to spell things out exactly so that there are no misunderstandings. In the BDSM world, you have to be to-a-fault honest. I don't mean to embarrass you."

"I'm not embarrassed. Not really. Just not used to talking about this stuff. This is completely different than joking around with the guys, or you in our DMs when we're talking about your books, or even about giving my opinion on your shopping choices."

TB groaned.

Midas gave a small smile. "Dude. You've benefited from it, and you know it."

"Please don't remind me."

Flame shushed TB again. "I get it, Midas. This is personal, and it means a great deal to you. Let me ask you this, and it's relevant to what I just said. Have you thought about just asking her?"

Midas glanced over at TB. He offered, "She's not wrong."

"I'm not supposed to know somehow?"

TB started laughing full on. "Such an innocent. Are you kidding? You've watched the four of us fumble around trying to figure out our women. Demon was the only one who had a clue how Cherry felt, and that's because they had some sort of weird agreement they were going to ignore their feelings. Yet we all knew they weren't, even when they were denying how they felt."

"We girls weren't much better," Flame admitted. "The point is, putting yourself out there like that is going to be scary, no matter how it happens. Asking directly is like ripping off duct tape. Quick. Possibly painful. Definitely leaves a mark, especially if the other person says no. Trust me on this. I don't know exactly what she's been through, but I get the sense she's very unlikely to give you many signals, and highly unlikely to say something first. As for the sex part, you'll probably have to work your way slowly to that."

"I wondered if I shouldn't let her lead that," he offered. "When she's ready, she'll let me know."

Flame and TB exchanged a look.

"How did you two get through it?" Midas shook his head. "Sorry. Inappropriate question."

Flame giggled. "No, it wasn't. Even if it was, it's what you came here to ask, wasn't it?"

"Well, yeah."

"Well, it was TB, so..." She looked over at him with a smile. "He just sort of took over. I wasn't left with much of a choice."

"You always had a choice," the man growled.

She threw a pillow at him. "You know what I mean."

TB caught the pillow, put it behind him, and leaned his forearms on his knees. "The point is, each situation is different. You never really know unless someone comes straight out and tells you how they feel. It's terrifying. Trust me. Before I took over"—he rolled his eyes—"I had no clue what I was doing with Flame. Hell, there are still days I'm not sure. We just throw it out there and know that the other will be honest. We negotiate limits and all that beforehand. Vanilla couples? They could learn a thing or two from the kink community."

Flame cautioned him. "Unfortunately, I don't think that TB's method would work with Mouse though. She's in a different place than I was. It sounds like her trauma is a bit more complex, and I'm guessing there hasn't been any time to process it. So my advice? Put it all on the line for her. Be honest, be firm, but expect slow progress. Reassure her that no matter how honest she is, it doesn't damage the friendship you have, even if you have to take a few steps backward.

Encourage her to talk about what happened to her, if she can remember things, but remind her that it changes nothing about how you feel about her or what you want from your relationship."

TB interrupted. "Make her actually say yes or no to things. Nodding is not an option. If there's any hesitation, ask her to talk through the thoughts in her head. It's not necessarily a no or a hard limit. She just might need time to think. You could even use the traffic light system for BDSM if you think that would help. More relationships could probably use that," he grumbled.

Flame nodded. "We even use it for nonsexual things, like with the kids. If TB or I do something we're concerned about, or that we want to stop, the colors will keep the kids, once they're older and know words, from understanding that we're disagreeing about something. But back to Mouse. You can assure her that she can ask for what she wants. But otherwise, if she's okay with it, then you're always going to come right out and ask first. That's a good choice, especially in the first days as you navigate the changes between how you are now and what you want to become. If anything is too much, she needs to be honest and tell you. Maybe you end up retreating a bit, but it doesn't mean forever." She bit her lip, concern across her face. "Did any of this help?" Flame asked.

"Yes and no. I think maybe I'm just nervous? I don't... have a lot of experience with women. I'm not my brother, who's never been nervous about a thing in his life."

Flame started laughing so hard, she put her arms around her stomach and leaned over her lap. When she finally composed herself, she wiped the tears from her eyes that had leaked out. "Is that what you really believe? He's always been all confidence on the outside, all hot mess on the inside. When it came to Gem, he knew less about what he was doing than all of you put together, mostly because he didn't have her around to figure it out."

He sat silently for a few moments, looking at the baby in front of him. In his mind, for the first time, he wanted this for himself. He wanted a family again. He wanted it with Mouse, but they needed to solve the riddle of her and the Salieri. When that was over, maybe he... no, they could have that together.

He leaned over to kiss Flame's cheek, then handed a sleeping Paris back to her. "Thanks. I have a lot to think about. I appreciate you letting me bother you about stuff that's really not my business."

"Any time, Midas. You know that." She took off with the baby down the hall toward the nursery.

TB walked Midas to the door, but before he could leave, his teammate grabbed him by the arm. "Whatever you decide, don't suddenly treat her like she's broken. You've been really good at that. Reassuring her how brave she's being. She needs that. So if you suddenly change gears and treat her too delicately, like she's fragile, she'll read that in a heartbeat, and it will cause her to withdraw. I made that mistake with Flame. I could have lost the best thing in my life if I had continued on that path.

"Yes, Mouse is shy and unsure. Yes, she's scared, and who wouldn't be? But she's a fighter, like Flame, which you already know. It's a different kind of strength, and sometimes I think it's a far better kind than Medusa or the other women have."

"You're a bit biased, dude," Midas joked.

"Maybe. But that woman went through a hell no woman should go through. Same for Mouse. Neither of them gave up. Ever. They may not see it that way, but it's true. I've a feeling shit is going to get a lot worse than it has, and I don't need Waters' spidey senses to feel it, so protect that in her. She needs you."

With a hesitant nod, Midas gave TB a punch to the shoulder and headed to the elevator. He had mysteries to solve, and while he was doing that, he needed to think about what TB and Flame suggested.

24

FEBRUARY 4, 2024

Mouse

SHE WOKE UP IN HER BEDROOM. CLEARLY, SHE'D BEEN ASLEEP for a long while again. The smell of coffee drifted down the hall.

After showering and changing into comfortable clothes, she walked down the short hallway to find Medusa sitting at the breakfast bar, reading a book.

"You my babysitter today?" Mouse asked sadly.

"Yup. Volunteered even."

Medusa was a puzzle. Mouse had the impression that the woman didn't normally speak much, and that Gem and the men were nonplussed by the fact that the enigmatic logistics expert of Mythos seemed to have adopted Mouse. She didn't exactly give off maternal vibes.

"Want some coffee?" the woman asked.

"No, thanks." She went to the refrigerator and grabbed a bottle of water from inside it. As she closed the door, a thought popped into her head. Something she had been too tired to ask about yesterday. She turned and leaned against the refrigerator. "Midas never answered me yesterday. Who, or what, are the Salieri?"

Medusa pursed her lips in thought, then seemed to come to some sort of decision. Sliding a bookmark to save her spot, she shut the book. "You probably deserve the answer to that question, and I'm sure Midas won't volunteer that information until he's ordered to or he absolutely has to. Not because he doesn't trust you. He does. It's more that you've been hit with a lot the past couple of weeks. He doesn't want to add to that."

Mouse picked at the corner of the label on the water bottle she'd yet to open. "He's a good man."

"One of the truly good ones," Medusa admitted. "He's in love with you. Don't hurt him."

The voice held more than an edge of warning to it. In fact, she'd bet there was a threat tucked away in there as well.

"I don't know about that. Fond of me, maybe."

"No. Hands down, in love. Makes no sense, and he knows it because it shouldn't happen that fast, especially when you're still such an unknown entity, but... he is. However, I get the sense that the Tribe men fall fast and hard, especially since they've learned to grab onto good things when they see them." Medusa's head tilted to the side, a gesture she often did when thinking about asking a question. "What about you? How do you feel about him?"

"What does any of this have to do with this Salieri group?" Mouse deflected. Or tried to.

"Answer the question first."

The water bottle became even more interesting to her as her brain raced. How to answer the question?

"He makes me feel safe."

"Are you attracted to him?"

She felt the heat rush to her face.

"I'll take that as a yes," Medusa said.

"Who wouldn't be?"

There was a soft chuckle from the breakfast bar. "You're not spilling any secrets, Mouse. I was pretty sure you were, and I think everyone knows something's afoot. He claimed you as tribe, and these men don't do that lightly."

"What does that even mean?"

Medusa pushed her book off to the side, then leaned on her forearms on the breakfast bar, her fingers threaded together in front of her. "For these guys, 'tribe' means family. They don't have any... well, except for Midas and Nemo. They came as a package deal to the corporation. Otherwise, all the men were erased. They have no spouses, no siblings, no parents. Nothing.

"When they were picked for this job, it was because they had certain skills that were the best of the best, but also because they had a certain temperament. They click together. They love each other like family, even though no blood ties bind them to each other. They would do anything for each other, including die so that the other could live. When they started adding women to the equation? That bond became even stronger. Midas has selected you as 'his.'"

"What if I didn't want him?"

Now Medusa laughed full out. "'Who wouldn't,' I think is what you said earlier?" Her tone became softer. "He didn't choose lightly, Mouse. These guys have rescued plenty of women over the years who they've sent on their merry way, and I'm sure more than a few of those women would have loved to have grabbed on to any one of them. He wants you, and it's okay to want him for yourself."

She walked around the breakfast bar and sat opposite Medusa. "So, the Salieri?"

"Bear with me for a minute while I give you some quick backstory. You know what Tribe does—mercenaries for hire. Mythos, whom I work for, along with Loki and Gilgamesh, is different. We don't work for anyone other than ourselves. Our whole mission is to wipe out the Salieri. All three of us have connections to people who were taken by this organization. You're familiar with the mafia?"

Mouse nodded.

"Think of the Salieri in the same way, except their reach is global. They're an organized crime family that has been around for a very, very long time. Since before the time of Christ. There was a man who called himself by that name. Salieri. He selected seven men whom he trusted without fail and called them the Worthy. After creating a manifesto, he sent the Worthy out, one to each continent, to set up a home and follow the tenets of his beliefs. The short version of how this affects us today is that they have very specific rules about women, and they've resorted to sex trafficking to obtain brides for breeding."

"I'm guessing this doesn't work out well for the women?"

"No, it doesn't. The Salieri only allow for sons. Female children, up until recently, were killed, as were all immediate female family members upon members' initiation into the membership. Once a woman gave a member a son, she was killed as well."

"That's horrible!"

"Yes, it is. Mythos and Tribe came together almost two years ago when TB's partner was being stalked and kidnapped by a low-level member. You can ask her for details if you want. She's pretty open about it, and her situation prior to meeting TB is not too far from your own. She could be someone you'd benefit from talking to."

"Midas said the same thing. I'm not ready yet. Maybe someday."

"When, and if, you want to. No one's going to pressure you, although don't be surprised if at some point she offers to tell you herself."

There was silence that stretched long past comfort.

"Ask me, Mouse. I can see a question spinning behind your eyes."

"Those men. In Egypt. They weren't after the children. They were after me. Why?"

"That's a really good question," Medusa admitted. "We don't know. Could be a variety of things. We were running with the option that you somehow escaped wherever you were and found your way to that compound. Whoever was controlling your actions is desperate to keep the information inside your head from leaking out. However, your confession yesterday clued us in that it was far more than that. You were a tool for another purpose."

"Midas' computers."

"It seems far-fetched, but it's really not. We got the closest to the Salieri we've ever been last year. They've known about Tribe for a long time, and they have an axe to grind. Some of their members are very unhappy with Waters, and there are some connections to Cherry that are uncomfortable for her. Namely, her uncle is one of their members. It's a long story. My guess is that they were already programming you and decided you'd be a good option to dangle before Tribe."

"They did this brain-block thing, programmed me to go to the compound, then they raided it, knowing that Mythos would call in Tribe for help. Make it look good, that Tribe had rescued me and the girls, then they bring us back here, and my programming kicks in to help them get inside."

"Knew you were bright. However, it sounds like your programming wasn't a complete success, and you were released without them knowing that. Explains why Midas was able to break through that block. You may have felt like you were giving in, but inside you is a will to survive, and you've been fighting that block. Otherwise, you would have proceeded with your attempt to get into the computers yesterday, and you never would have told Midas about it."

"They're going to come for me, aren't they? They're not going to be able to leave me in peace."

Medusa reached across the breakfast bar and grabbed hold of her wrists. "No, Mouse. They're going to keep coming. And to be honest? They may succeed. These guys are good, and they'll protect you with their lives, but the Salieri have always played the long game. They'll never give up, even if they seem like they have." The woman paused. "Do you still want to learn how to protect yourself?"

"I think it's more a need rather than a want now, wouldn't you say?" Mouse pointed out.

"I agree. So I have one question. Why do you want me to teach you? I would have thought Midas would be the more obvious person."

"I just... I wish... well, the guys all seem to respect you so much, and I see how they look at you, and I see how they look at me, like I'm fragile."

"Midas doesn't look at you like you're fragile."

"No," she admitted. "He's the exception. I know the guys don't mean to do it, but it's there. And, frankly, you seem like the best person to go to who will help me without being too careful with me, even if you scare the shit out of me."

"Sweetheart, I'm an assassin. If I didn't scare you, I'd worry something was wrong with you."

"It's not that, even. I mean, it probably should make me nervous that you could kill me and leave no trace, even though everyone knows we're alone in Midas' apartment together."

Medusa chuffed a laugh.

"I don't have aspirations to be like you. Whenever the guys talk about Kubrick, especially Midas, it's like they're all in love with her kick-ass self. No one thinks twice about letting Gem out loose in the world, doing dangerous things. Same with Cherry. Even Flame is looked at like this paragon of strength. I just want to be... I don't know... I guess I don't like them seeing me as weak."

"You're not weak, Mouse. You're a survivor."

"I don't feel like a survivor."

"In a world of fight, flight, or freeze, you're a fight person."

"I don't understand."

Her companion shook her head with a smile. "I didn't think you would, but you'll come to it eventually."

"So what do I do in the meantime?"

"You keep fighting." Medusa got off the stool and came around the breakfast bar. "Come on. I've got an idea, but we need to talk to Midas first so he doesn't lose his shit completely."

25

FEBRUARY 4, 2024

Midas

"Nova, I don't give a shit how difficult it is. Find me some damn video camera footage."

He wasn't really pissed at Nova. He was pissed at Nemo. The *doos* had just visited his office, flung a box at him, saluted, and walked away, whistling. Shaking his head in confusion, Midas looked down to see that it was a box of condoms. A hundred forty-four pack.

Holy hell, horseshoes, and hand grenades! How much sex did Nemo think he was going to have? Maybe have. Fuck. He'd still be a virgin when he was forty at this rate. Not that it mattered. She wasn't ready for him to pursue that yet, so he would be patient. Given her past, he had to admit he'd be surprised if she would ever be ready.

So here he was, irritated as fuck, taking out his frustrations on an AI.

"Midas, you know I wish to give you everything you ask for, but this is not as easy as it normally is. Even for me. The use of video surveillance was not nearly as prevalent when Miss Mouse was a child, and even where it exists, many companies did not archive the footage on servers or make it accessible online. And if they did keep the footage, it would likely be on VHS cassette, gathering dust in a basement somewhere."

"VHS? Christ, can it get any more primitive?"

"As a matter of fact, the precursor to VHS technology was referred to as Beta—"

"Ignore that question, Nova. It was rhetorical."

"Very well, Midas."

"Just keep searching."

A soft knock came at his door, and there was a slight sense of déjà vu when he looked up to see Mouse standing in his doorway. He felt the smile break out on his face. "*Heuning meisie.* Good morning. What do you need, sweetheart? Not that you need a reason to come see me," he quickly added.

She walked a few steps in the door, followed by Medusa, who perched her ass cheek on the corner of his desk. She grabbed a rubber cat from his collection, the things he used for stress balls when he was working on a problem, and began tossing it from hand to hand.

Shyly, he watched as Mouse glanced at the warrior woman who'd been on guard duty today, and he felt his pulse kick up a notch. She looked so unsure of herself, and he stood up from behind his monitors and came around the desk to her. He held out his hand to her, which she took, and he could feel the tremor in it. "You look nervous. What's wrong?"

"Medusa and I were talking."

She watched as the two women exchanged a look. No words, just blank faces, but they were clearly understanding whatever each other was thinking. The pairing of the two was so odd, but he wasn't going to question it. While he trusted any of the men and women he worked with to protect her, he sensed Medusa would do so the most fiercely, after himself.

Midas turned his attention back to her. "What about?"

He noticed that she turned her head so she could see Medusa's face.

"Mouse, ask him," the woman said.

"They're coming for me. Aren't they?"

His eyes bounced to Medusa, who shrugged. "She figured it out on her own. She knows enough to understand who the Salieri are and what we believe is her connection to them."

He stared at the woman for a second, his gaze boring into hers behind her tinted glasses. "Nova, take down the lighting fifty percent."

"Unnecessary, but thanks," Medusa said.

Turning back to Mouse, he pulled her face up so he could look her in the eyes. His hand smoothed her hair down the sides of her head before he framed her face. "Mouse," he started, "I really don't want you worrying about that. You're protected here. We've got you. No one's going to get to you."

"Just say it," she whispered.

Midas waited a moment, then simply said, "Yes."

She swallowed nervously. "And they're going to try and take me, aren't they?"

"They'll try," Midas said.

Her body stiffened in his hold.

"You can't possibly protect me every minute of every day."

"If I can't, someone else will be with you at all times."

"So I'm a prisoner. Again."

"No, Mouse—"

"Whether it's for my protection or not, I'm still being kept inside Tribe's walls. I'm being guarded all the time. It's still a form of imprisonment." Her hands raised and rested on top of his. "I need you to allow me some freedom. I don't need to leave the building," she rushed to assure him. "But I do need to know how to protect myself because I can't stay inside these walls forever. I want Medusa to teach me how to protect myself."

He felt himself rear back in fear and concern.

"I mean, not with a knife or anything, but what to do if they catch me. How I could get out of some situations, like being tied to a chair or thrown in a trunk. Or how to fight back without hurting myself. Just knowing a few things would at least make me feel a little better. I may not use any of it, but knowing it would help, I think."

"Mouse, I'm telling you right now that—"

"Midas." Medusa's voice went tight. "You can't promise her what you want to promise her. You know they'll bide their time. You know that at some point, someone will get complacent, and she will become vulnerable. It's also very possible she could be taken. She's right. You can't keep her locked inside forever, but we can give her some tools to protect herself."

He hissed at Medusa. "She doesn't need to know this stuff."

Mouse moved a hand from on top of his and laid it against his cheek. "But I do, Midas."

Emotions rocketed through his body, primarily fear. Even though he knew it was good for all women to know how to protect themselves, she shouldn't need to have to know it. She should always be safe.

She continued to try and convince him. "I can't hide in the shadows all the time. You all need to work, and you can't do that well if someone is always looking after me. I need to feel like I can take care of myself if something goes wrong."

Medusa told him, "I will gladly teach her anything she wants to know. I will, no matter what, but I wanted to tell you so that you were aware of what we were doing."

Midas felt his jaw working and his teeth grinding to keep from saying something.

Medusa chuckled. "You're going to need God's dentist if you keep that up. She's fine. I've got her, and I've got you." She emphasized the last word, which Mouse didn't understand but figured it was some sort of team talk.

"Fine," he let out through clenched teeth. "I appreciate the warning. I'm not happy about it, but simply because my stupid alpha-male self feels like she shouldn't have to learn." He turned his lips in toward Mouse's palm. "Be careful. Take it slow and don't overdo it."

She smiled. "Got it."

Medusa strode out of the room with Mouse in tow. When she hit the threshold, Midas called out, "Mouse!"

She turned to look at him.

"I promise. We will do our best to keep you safe."

"I know, Midas, and I trust you all. But, just in case... I need this." Then she continued down the hall to catch up to Medusa.

26

FEBRUARY 4, 2024

Midas

"Midas! SOS, level three!"

Midas jumped up from his seat and was out the door toward the elevator. The voice was Medusa's, and it was panicked.

Medusa never panicked.

"Where are you?"

"The gym."

Midas stopped dead in the lobby, and by then Waters, TB, and Steel had also rushed out of their offices, sliding weapons into the backs of their pants or into holsters.

"What the fuck?" TB looked at Midas.

Medusa came back on the line. "I need Demon. And Midas? I've no idea where she is."

The three men made for the stairwell, taking the steps three at a time and exiting onto the third floor where Tribe Corporation housed its training facilities. There was a gym, complete with a boxing ring, mats for hand-to-hand sparring, a climbing wall, and basically every-thing you could want to physically prepare yourself for a job like the men did. They also had other training facilities in the subbasements that were more specific to weapons and simulations.

When Midas and the three men found Medusa, she was sitting on the floor, her back to the wall, cradling her arm between her torso and her knees. She was also going to have one hell of a black eye in an hour or so.

"What the hell happened?"

Midas could feel panic seeping in and rising mightily. How the hell did someone get inside Tribe? Nothing was foolproof, but his security measures were top of the line, and he tested them vigorously and often. No way was he leaving the safety of his teammates and their women to chance. If Medusa was in this broken state, though, someone had gotten in anyway because she was a total badass.

"Who got in here? Where is she?"

Demon appeared in the doorway and began immediate triage on Medusa's arm. "Spiral fracture. How the hell did that happen?"

"Stop freaking out, Midas." She winced as she admonished him. "Nobody got in here."

"What do you mean, 'Nobody got in here'? You've got a broken arm, and Mouse is missing."

"I had her in the chair."

It was then that Midas noted the wooden straight-backed chair tipped over on the floor.

"I was teaching her how to make space inside of knots. I figured that was the best place to start. Chances are that she'd be tied up if she were captured, so if she can make sure there's at least room in the ligatures, she maintains circulation, and it's not so difficult when she gets cut free and needs to move fast. I should have known something was wrong because she got twitchy, big time, when we did the ropes around her wrists and ankles, and it got worse when I put a rope around her chest. She started to hyperventilate. I foolishly assumed it was just nerves at being tied up."

"Christ, don't go slow or anything with tying her up now," TB admonished.

"Relax, TB. I talked her through it, and she calmed down. I went through how to make the space while being tied up, and she did well. I untied everything, asked her to review what I taught her, she repeated back, then I retied her, and she repeated it again. She did great. So then I put the flex cuffs on, and as soon as that zip tie made the ratchet noise, she sprang at me. Her tied-up wrists grabbed my hands, she shouldered me in the eye socket, twisted my arm, and broke her cuffs. Next thing I know, I'm on the floor looking at the ceiling." Medusa looked at Midas. "She changed. It was like someone flipped a switch, and she became..."

"Someone else."

"Yeah. Someone else. How did you know?"

"I saw it the other night. Fuck! We all did when we watched her sitting at my computers on the video footage. It's why I was so angry. Not because of what she'd tried to do, but because not only has she been programmed, but I figured whenever her programming took over, it might cause a psychotic break." He whirled around to talk to Waters. "We really need to find her. There's no telling what she might do in this state."

Nemo flew into the room at full speed. "Found her! I had Nova search for her while I was heading up here."

"Shit," Midas whispered. "I should have done that first thing."

"Where is she?"

"Nova has her on sublevel three."

Everyone stopped what they were doing and looked at Midas. Nobody breathed.

Waters' low voice came through. "I'm sorry, I thought I heard you say sublevel three."

"You did."

Demon started helping Medusa up off the floor, her wrist already in a loose splint until he could get her to the infirmary.

"That's the armory," TB needlessly pointed out.

"Yes, I am aware," Waters snarked.

Demon grumbled, "If you don't mind, I need to get this set so she can fly that monstrosity she calls a baby bird. Call me if you need me."

Demon and Medusa left the room, while Midas started for the armory, TB hot on his heels. Waters was already pulling up footage on the monitor on the gym wall, his voice shouting commands at Nova for what he wanted.

Midas tapped his watch to keep him in touch with Waters and the rest of the team. "Heading down the north stairs to sublevel three."

"I've got her on screen," Waters informed him. They heard a whistle over the speaker. "Fuckin' Frankenstein," he murmured.

"What are you seeing? Is she still there?" Midas asked.

"Oh yeah. She's still there. And you wouldn't believe me if I told you either. Watch yourself. She's armed."

Midas and TB stood just outside the doorway from the stairwell to the armory floor. Midas ordered, "Stun only. You go low. I'll go high."

TB reached for his hip holster, removed the stun gun, and charged it. Angrily, he whispered, "What are you going to use? Harsh language?"

Midas whispered back, "No weapon for me. No idea what's going on. I doubt she'd actually shoot at me, but if she does, I still don't want you to shoot her with a real gun."

"Pussy-whipped," TB breathed out.

"And you're not, Sultan of Spank?"

"Whatever. You call it."

"On three."

Midas counted down on his fingers. *Three. Two. One. Go!*

Fingers tight around the handle of the stun gun, TB took position as Midas depressed the door handle and pulled it open. Both looked into a quiet, empty space. She was nowhere in immediate sight. What was disconcerting was that all the lights were on in the armory, the door was open, and there were pieces of weapons on one of the tables in the middle of the room. Silently, slowly, the two men entered the room and stood next to what used to be Nemo's workspace. On the table, a rifle lay in pieces, as if someone had dismantled it to clean it, then got interrupted.

Midas glanced down the hallway and saw that the lights were on in the shooting range. Midas cocked his head to the left, and both walked down the hall, TB leading with the stun gun aimed in front of them. The shooting range was silent as a tomb, but they saw that a target had been set up, used, and then brought up to the galley.

Neither were prepared for what they saw.

Mouse was standing in the galley in front of the used target, arms loose at her sides. The gun and ammunition she had brought into the stall were on the table in front of her, and she had taken three steps back from the table, clearly out of range of snatching up the weapon. With his weapon still trained on her, TB stood off to her back and to the side as Midas approached her. She didn't appear to hear or see them. She just stood. Lost in space, it seemed, like when he'd seen her sitting in front of his bank of computers.

"Mouse?" he said softly. She didn't answer.

"Anastasiya?" he asked a little louder. Still no response.

"*Heuning meisie*, where are you?" He reached out a hand to touch her cheek.

"Midas," TB growled.

Fingers touched frozen skin. "She's cold." He tapped his watch. "Demon, I need you."

"I'm a little busy at the moment." There was mumbling in the background, then a sigh. "On my way."

TB kept the stun gun trained on Mouse's shoulders while Midas stepped tighter into her circle. His outside arm reached for the gun on the table. When he picked it up, he noticed that it was empty of bullets. TB circled around and took it from him, sliding the weapon into yet another of his cargo pockets.

"Status, Midas," Waters barked out over the comms.

"She's in some sort of... I don't know... stasis state. She's not responding to us. Almost like a robot awaiting orders."

TB made a hissing sound. "Midas. Look at the target."

Midas turned his head to see what his teammate was referring to. He exhaled. "Fuck Frankenstein, the wolfman, and the mummy."

As they looked at the target, there was certainly cause for alarm. Ten perfect shots. Nine to the heart. One to the forehead, right between the eyes.

In the silence, Mouse just kept standing there, her eyes frozen straight ahead. He stroked the backs of his fingers down her cheek. "Mouse, it's Midas. Come back to me, *heuning meisie*. I know you're in there. Come back."

He heard Waters talking, but he paid no attention to what he was saying. All that mattered right now was that he somehow brought her back to reality. He couldn't lose her. Not now.

Demon came through the shooting gallery door. "Will she let you touch her?"

"Yes. But she's not responding. She's not even blinking."

"Shock?" TB asked.

Demon shook his head. "Can you get a pulse on her? Or do you want me to do it?"

Midas was gratified that Demon asked to touch her before doing so, but now was not the time to go alpha on everyone over her. "You do it. She's so far gone, I don't think it will register."

Demon snuck over to her other side and took her pulse. His lips pursed. Then he took out a penlight and flashed it into one eye, then the other, then back to the first. The pupils remained like pinpoints.

"That's not normal," Midas commented.

"Nope," Demon agreed. "Even if she were catatonic, the pupils should dilate and adjust with light changes."

"Why is she so cold?"

"It's not shock. This isn't physical. I don't know what this is, but I would suggest getting her out of here. Can you move her, or is her body locked?"

Midas reached for her arm and attempted to manipulate it. It went docilely around his shoulder and neck, where he placed it. "Her body is totally movable."

"All right. Let's get her down to the infirmary, but I don't know that there's much I can do for her. We're just going to have to wait for her to come out of whatever this is."

Midas didn't voice his concern, but he knew the others would know what he was thinking. What if she never came out of it?

27

FEBRUARY 5, 2024

Midas

IT WAS THE WEE HOURS OF THE MORNING, AND HE WAS CURLED around Mouse in a hospital bed. Her eyes were closed, and she lay on her back, but her breathing was so slow and deep that she appeared dead. The dark lashes of her closed eyes against the pallor of her skin didn't help that appearance at all.

Waters wandered into the infirmary and sat down in a chair next to the bed. When he spoke, it was just above a whisper. "How is she?"

"No change."

Minutes passed before Waters spoke again.

"Any clue what happened?"

"Nothing confirmed."

"But you have an idea."

"An idea."

"Did her protocol get triggered?"

"I don't think so because even though she armed herself, she didn't do anything beyond shoot at the target. Medusa said she was twitchy when she used the rope, but the zip ties did something to her, and she seemed to change personality. Not a normal trigger but possible."

"So what are you thinking?"

"I've nothing to prove it, but I think her two sides, the programmed and the unprogrammed, are testing each other." He smoothed the hair back. "She's still so cold. I don't know what to do."

"Nothing you can do, brother. Just be there. She'll wake up at some point. Just be there when she does."

Midas snorted. "You're not going to make one of the other guys sit here and make me go upstairs to get sleep, and all that crap?"

"Nope, wouldn't dare. One, I know you wouldn't go. Two, this is a little bit different than the traditional hospital visit. If she woke up and you weren't here this time around, I'm not sure how she'd react."

"I love her, Waters," Midas confessed.

"I know." He smiled. "It's all over your face every time you look at her. It's the same way I look at Kubrick. Or so I've been told."

The woman in question moved slightly in his arms. Was she waking up?

"Mouse?" he whispered. "*Heuning meisie?*"

"Midas?" Her voice was groggy, swimming up from the depths of her subconscious. "Where am I?"

"You're in the infirmary."

Her movements were still sluggish, but they had slightly more fight to them, as if she didn't realize that what was tethering her to the bed were Midas' arms.

"Shh, relax. It's just me. You're not restrained. I've just got my arms around you."

She settled, but he could tell by the expression on Waters' face that he was concerned about her awareness.

"Hi, Mouse," he said softly. "How are you feeling?"

"Waters?"

"Yeah, it's me. You okay? Thirsty? Cold?"

"Thirsty."

"I'll get you some water. Hang tight."

Waters rose and went to the sink, his back turned to the couple to give them a tiny measure of privacy. Mouse shifted, and Midas helped her turn to face him.

"What happened?"

He worked to keep his face neutral so he didn't scare her. "You don't remember?" Midas asked.

She shook her head. Her eyes never left his, but he could sense her thinking.

Waters returned to the bedside, handing over a covered cup with a straw. Together, he and Midas helped her sit up so they could raise the bed as she drank.

Finally, she spoke. "I remember coming to your office with Medusa. She was going to teach me some ways to protect myself. In case I was taken again."

"Yes, that's right," Midas confirmed.

"We went to the gym. She explained to me how it was important to create tension in my hands and feet if someone was going to tie me to something. That way, there'd be looseness in the knots so I could maybe work free when no one was around."

"Good. Anything else?"

"We practiced that a couple of times. Then she tried it again, but with zip ties." She paused, a look of horror crossing her face, and she darted her gaze between Midas and Waters. "I hurt Medusa."

"You remember hurting her? What did you do?"

She scrunched up in the bed, creating less of her body to be exposed. "I didn't want to hurt her. I heard the zip ties, and it was like I couldn't control what my body was doing. It was weird. Like I split in two, similar to what happened during hypnosis, and part of me was pulled back from the other part. Or maybe the other part moved forward. I don't know. I hit her in the face." She winced. "I used my shoulder and drove it into her eye."

Waters looked at Midas. "Self-hypnosis?"

"I don't think so." Midas contemplated for a moment. "She actually formed two distinct selves, like I thought." He refocused on Mouse. "What happened then?"

She sucked in her lips behind her teeth, her eyes twitching left, then right, as she tried to picture the event in her head. "I twisted her wrists. I heard something snap."

"Anything else?"

"I think I, ummm... I threw her over my shoulder, and she hit the ground on her back? That doesn't seem right, but that's what I see in my head."

"Then what did you do?"

"I left. I needed to get something. I didn't have a choice. I had to get to a gun. I needed to protect myself." She looked at Midas. "I think my father taught me."

He could tell the memory hit hard, like it propelled itself through the air and struck her in the middle of her forehead because she actually recoiled.

She hung her head, speaking in a whisper. "He taught me all about guns. How to load one and unload one. How to shoot it. How to take it apart. How to clean it." Her eyes started to fill with tears. "Why would I need to do any of that?"

"Okay, so you needed to find a gun. What did you do then?"

"I went to the elevator and pushed the button for the armory. I remembered you telling me what was on the different levels of the building."

"And what did you do?"

"I went in, I looked around, and I needed to remember if I could still do all those things Dad taught me. So I took one of the guns and stripped it down as fast as I could, then put it back together. Then I took it apart again and laid it all out on the table in order. Whenever you touch a gun, you clean it." She startled and looked at Midas. "How do I know that?"

"Don't worry about that for right now."

She burrowed into him in her usual position.
He looked at Waters. "This has to stop."
"I'm open to suggestions, Midas," the team leader responded.
"We start with Egypt. See what's left of the compound."
"I'll get Medusa to ready the jet."

28

FEBRUARY 7, 2024

Mouse

Since they were under lockdown and had four rambunctious little girls who had been living on pizza, they decided to make tacos instead. Flame was watching her son and the baby. Kubrick was teaching one twin how to wash and pull apart the lettuce, then shred it, while Cherry had the other twin shredding cheese. Gem was teaching Shakira how to dice tomatoes. Meanwhile, Mouse and Ona were setting the table. They had Midas' stereo set to an eighties playlist, and the girls were having a blast.

Throughout the meal, Mouse participated in conversation with the girls, but it felt forced. She was missing Midas, especially given what had caused him to leave for Egypt. He said no one was mad and that they were going to the compound to try and resolve why she was having these blackouts. Even Medusa had visited her to reassure her that there were no hard feelings and that she still had Mythos' support. However, she couldn't help feeling raw and exposed.

It had only been two days, but he'd become such a fixture in her day, even when he was downstairs working, that she found it difficult to concentrate now that he wasn't there. She wondered what they were doing. If they'd found anything. If they had run into trouble and hoped they were safe. It wasn't until after the meal and the girls were camped out in the living room playing video games on Midas' giant television screen that she found herself sitting at the dining room table with the women.

"You miss him, don't you?"

Mouse shook herself out of her daydreaming when she realized that Kubrick was talking to her. "Excuse me?"

"You miss Midas. You've been quiet all afternoon."

"It's weird, him not being here, but he needs to work. I can't interrupt that."

"Doesn't mean you don't miss him," Gem said. "Hell, I'm with Nemo twenty-four seven since we work together, and I feel his absence, even though there are days when I want to stab him like a voodoo doll."

"Me too," Cherry admitted. "Then again, Demon and I are still 'new' as a couple, so it makes sense."

"Honeymoon phase," Flame simpered. "Gawd, I love it. All those 'sexy' times whenever you want, wherever you want. Having a baby does force one to be more creative," she admitted.

"Even so, are any of us out of the honeymoon phase, really?" Kubrick asked. "These guys are like over-sexed book boyfriends. In the best possible way, of course."

There was a pause. She hoped that meant the conversation was going to shift directions, especially since it didn't apply to her and Midas.

Did she want it to? A part of her knew she'd love to have a relationship with Midas, and she'd all but admitted it to Medusa, who seemed to believe that he also had feelings for her. He hadn't said it outright, but then again, things around them didn't really lend themselves to romance right now.

Was it even smart to be thinking in that direction? While her more recent memories were coming back in a slow, consistent trickle, just like the faucet Midas had instructed her to leave on in her hypnosis space, there were still issues. She'd been writing down those snatches of her past when they came so they didn't drift away like wisps of smoke after a fire.

The most important one was positive. There hadn't been a man in her life. Not a romantic partner anyway, so she wasn't creating any sort of love triangle.

But one that might kill any hope of a relationship with Midas was the memory of visits to see the doctor at the compound when she arrived. They'd treated her immediate injuries. They'd examined her regarding her amnesia and come up with nothing physically wrong with her, suggesting that her loss of memory was due to trauma.

In the rest of her tests, however, they'd discovered that she'd undergone major trauma at some point, and her uterus was damaged. It was so bad, it was doubtful she'd ever be able to have children. The reason why they'd likely never know. It could have been any number of reasons. An illness of some kind. Damage from the abuse she'd suffered, sexually or physically. It wasn't like she could ask anyone about it, and there were no records to find since it had been done, most likely, by one of her captors.

The pain in her chest grew by the hour. Midas wanted a family. He might be fond of her. He might want her. He might even grow to love her. But she would never be able to give him the family he told her he wanted, and so that meant it would be best for him if she held back her feelings.

Unfortunately, that seemed to make her long for him even more.

"So, Mouse?" Kubrick circled back to her original question. The blonde's chin was resting on the palm of her hand, which was propped on the dining room table. "I didn't forget what I asked. We're dying to know."

Mouse surveyed the four women, all focused on her, not threateningly, but definitely intensely. She cautioned herself repeatedly not to cave into the fantasy, but it was so hard. "Well... I mean... yeah, I guess."

"You guess?" Cherry asked. One eyebrow was arched over a gray eye, a soft smirk on her perfectly painted lips.

"Don't let them push you, Mouse," Flame said. "The girl gang has a tendency to share way too much information with each other. You haven't been a part of us that long. It will get easier with time. Even then, if you don't ever want to share, it's okay."

A part of them? She'd never be a part of them. She and Midas were over before they'd even gotten started.Losing the women? That, too, made her sad.

"Yeah, you need to be careful, or you may end up in one of her books," Gem said with a snort.

"Hey!" Flame interjected. "You should be flattered. That was my highest-selling book yet. Besides," the author grumbled, "it's not like anyone knew I based all the sexy scenes on you and Nemo."

"No, just all of you. And the guys. Nemo is still getting harassed about the taxi scene."

"Do you have any clue how hard it was to recreate that in the 1880s? They didn't exactly have cars back then."

There was a series of giggles at that point. "So hot," Cherry agreed.

"I'm sorry, I'm confused," Mouse said.

"Oh, you don't know!" Kubrick leaned forward, as if telling a naughty piece of gossip. "Flame writes romance novels. Smokin' hot historicals. All shifters. You have to be careful what you tell her. Any sexy stuff is fair game for a scene in her books. Just telling her is open permission, so beware. Midas has got to have his copies of her books somewhere. He's her sprint timer and her alpha reader, the lucky fuckwitch. She goes by Sylvan Jones."

"Midas reads romance novels?" she asked incredulously.

The girls exchanged a look. "Well," Flame began, "I'm pretty sure all the guys have read my books, or at least most of them. It's partially a joke, and partially in support. Plus, they love to harass TB about the sex scenes. You know. Tease him about helping me with my research. But Midas, I think, just likes them."

"Cyber spy thrillers, I would have guessed. Even books for research. Not steamy romances."

The girls exchanged another look.

"I'd like to read one of your books, Flame."

"Oh goodie! New opinions. If you love it, I want to hear all about it. If you hate it, pretend you never read it! Lemme think. Which one would be the best start?" she asked Kubrick.

"Well, I wouldn't start with *Nature of the Beast*. Might want to work up to that one," Kubrick told her.

"And definitely not *Inhuman Restraint*," Cherry warned.

"Yeah, that's not a good one for first-timers," Flame admitted.

"What about the one Medusa was reading? *Shift Happens*, I think it was called."

The table went quiet, looks of shock all around. "Did you say 'Medusa'?"

"Yeah. The morning after I had my blackout, she was sitting at the counter, there. Reading it. Was about three-quarters of the way through it."

"Holy shit!" Flame squeaked. "Medusa's reading my books?" The author's face was as red as her nickname, and she looked like she was on the verge of a panic attack.

"Wow. You swore. That means you're upset." Cherry giggled. "Think she's read the one where the female main character is based on her?"

"Oh god, I hope not. Think she'll recognize herself?"

"The reference to the eyes will probably give it away," Cherry suggested.

Flame shuddered. "I refuse to think about it." She put her attention back on Mouse. "*Shift Happens* would be okay to start, but I think *Wild First Love* might be best. Cinnamon roll and all the green flags. Virgin hero. Perfect." The women froze again. "Oops," Flame offered again. "I just can't seem to stop sticking my foot in it."

With a frown, Mouse looked at her. "Why? What's wrong with what you said?"

The women looked at each other, uncomfortable.

"Oh!" Understanding kicked her hard enough that her brain suffered whiplash. "Really?" she whispered.

Kubrick shifted in her seat. "I mean, we don't know for sure, but... we're pretty sure." She looked at Gem.

"Don't look at me," the curly-haired woman exclaimed. "Nemo tells me a lot, but not that kind of stuff, and definitely not that about his brother for sure."

"It doesn't matter, does it?" Flame asked.

"No, why would it? I mean, it's not like we're involved, and it wouldn't even come up," Mouse replied.

Kubrick snorted, then schooled her facial features. "Sorry. My mind goes places only a twelve-year-old boy's goes. Sweetie, if you think that boy isn't interested, you're blind. He's had eyes for nothing except his computers and Nova until you came along. I don't even think he uses his computers to watch porn. In fact, I was starting to think he was asexual. Other than his weird habit of keeping track of my swear words, he's shown zero interest in anything female, or male for that matter, in the entire time I've known him. Even Waters commented on his interest in you, and he's closemouthed about the guys' personal lives."

"Is that what the whiteboard is about? What are the numbers?" Mouse asked.

"Yeah. He keeps a list of my creative swear words on his board, apparently. The numbers are bets. The guys have a terrible habit of betting on anything and everything. Midas was always in charge of the money end. Anyway. Back on topic. Sooo... Are you interested in Midas?"

It seemed ridiculous to try and hide her feelings, and she felt like maybe these women could help. It wasn't as if she had any experience with relationships, either, although she clearly didn't have the virgin status they thought Midas had.

"I definitely miss him," she said shyly. "I'd have to be blind not to be attracted to him. And I'd be stupid to turn away from someone who seems to be so..." She waved her hand, trying to come up with the word.

Each of the women offered up an option.

"Sweet?" Kubrick.

"Protective?" Flame.

"Giving?" Cherry.

"Loyal?" Gem.

"I think I was going for 'attentive,' but yes, he's all of those things and more."

"When he comes back, are you going to tell him?" Gem asked.

"I couldn't!" Mouse said with a gasp.

"Why the hell not?" Kubrick asked. "Seems to me the man needs a little push."

"I hate to say it, but I have to agree," Cherry added. "Given your history, he's probably paranoid about moving too quickly. Worried you won't respond well. Because that man is definitely interested."

Mouse made a noncommittal noise. Certainly, the women wouldn't encourage a relationship if she couldn't give him something he wanted. Something he deserved.

The youngest girl chose that moment to voice her unhappiness with something the other girls were doing, and everyone except Cherry and Mouse scrambled to go resolve whatever the issue was.

Her hopes that the subject had been abandoned were dashed when Cherry began speaking. "Mouse, he really does care for you. No lie. I've never seen him like this in all the time I've known him. Not only that, I vetted each and every one of them, so other than Nemo, I know his history better than anyone. I highly doubt we're wrong about anything we've said this afternoon. Don't let him hide behind his fears of rushing you."

Maybe she could dissuade them by claiming fear? "I've never been in a relationship, Cherry. A lot has happened to me, and I'm awfully damaged. Not only that, but I'd probably suck at it. Too many fears and insecurities."

"We all have our moments of suckage when it comes to relationships, trust me. Each of us here has our own closet full of insecurities. I mean, look at the hotness we've all hooked up with. But think of it this way. If what we suspect is true, Midas hasn't been in a relationship either. You'll figure it out together."

She looked behind her at the chaos in the living room, then back at Mouse. "The only real thing to be concerned about at this point is if you can handle his being invisible ninety-nine percent of the time. I don't know how Kubrick handles it, to be honest. Her job is high visibility, and she can never claim Waters publicly. The rest of us, it's easy because we're already pretty isolated.

"I won't lie to you. It will be difficult at times. He won't be able to tell you anything about what he does. They often disappear at the drop of a hat, and you'll never know when he's coming back. Because of the danger the Salieri represent, we've taken on a new policy of complete radio silence, so they don't text or call. There's nothing between the time they leave and the time they get back. I'm the only link the women have to what's going on since I'm the guys' handler, but I'm forbidden to tell them anything."

"Then you know what I've been through more than they do, and you know that my experience has been anything but romantic. I wouldn't know the first thing about how to respond to him that way."

"No. So maybe that makes it the perfect match." She patted Mouse's hand. "Find Midas' stash of Flame's books. Read one, and the important parts are pretty much the same from book to book." She winked. "The fun parts have patterns to them, but that's where the creativity comes in."

29

FEBRUARY 8, 2024

Midas

He hated Egypt. Not because of the people or anything like that, but because the city made everyone itchy. Tribe had history with the country since Waters had been captured and tortured here, and since the man's sister had died here. They'd been too late to save her, but they'd pulled their team leader out of a complete hellhole, which they now knew had ties to the Salieri. All the more reason to hate the place.

Now he hated it even more because the compound had turned up nothing. Nada. Zilch. Every shred of paper, every photo, every computer, all of it had been removed in the time they had been back in the States. Mythos was being completely tight-lipped on the missing items, which he hoped meant they had been there and removed all traces of the staff and girls who'd been housed there. Unfortunately, the fact that they let Tribe go on a wild-goose chase to look for things they knew weren't there didn't sit right. That meant the Salieri now had whatever had been there.

Loki had been circumspect about the situation. "We kept very few real records here. Intake papers on the health of the girls when they came to us. Records of their educational progress. Adoption logs of when girls left us, but no names, locations, etc. Everything else was uploaded to secure servers, and when confirmed that it had been received on the other end, destroyed on this end. Standard operating procedure."

"But you don't know that," Waters had confirmed.

"No, but likely. I'll have Cerberus check into it and see when the last transmissions went through."

Midas entered the half-destroyed room Mouse had shared with Ayla. The room appeared to be exactly as the women had left it that morning. Some clothes in drawers. A few novels. Other than that, nothing personal existed, but then again, it didn't sound like they'd had anything personal to store. He'd thought briefly about bringing the clothes that appeared to be Mouse's, then decided to leave them behind. None of it seemed like it had been something she'd be attached to, and he guessed she wouldn't want to remember much of her time here, other than the girls, so he left it all where it was. If she wanted replacements of the books, he'd get them for her, and Tribe had already bought her clothing and necessities.

The Tribe and Mythos teams, without Gem, stood in the main room of the schoolhouse where they had rescued Mouse and the girls. They were hot, tired, and frustrated. Only Medusa appeared calm and unmoved, as always, sitting atop a desk she'd turned right-side up.

"Well, I'm open to suggestions," Waters said.

No one spoke.

"I hate going back with nothing," Midas grumbled.

"But you don't have nothing, do you?"

All heads turned to Medusa.

"Serious, Golden One?" She huffed out her disgust. "You tried it the easy way, but in reality, it's the worst way. You're trying to work backward rather than forward. Loki told you. Mythos doesn't keep any records of note on-site at the compounds. Other than tracing back video footage Cerberus got you, you've got nothing. She doesn't know how long she wandered, or where she came from. All we can guess is that she was either turned loose, in which case you've got an issue with whether or not she's going to carry through her programming—"

"Which she still might," Gilgamesh dropped in.

"Or," she continued, "that she broke out of somewhere. It's not like whoever was holding her is going to file a missing persons report."

"And, again," Gilgamesh said, "she might still carry out her programming."

Midas frowned and chose not to deal with the programming piece of the puzzle, although he knew it would always be a concern. "So you want me to work from what we've been able to find from her youth, twenty years ago." He really didn't want to go this route. It would be incredibly painful for her, probably trigger numerous panic attacks, induce night terrors, and traumatize her even worse.

"Only way through is forward," she advised.

"Fuck," he breathed out.

Waters looked to him for answers. "What do you want to do?"

Midas shook his head, frustrated. Medusa was right. They had to work forward.

"We know hers and her parents' names. I have the address of their last known workplaces and their apartment. We have the name on the piece of paper in her envelope. It's a long shot, but we could trace some of her steps—possibly—forward.

"Might not get us too far, but if there's archival footage at the bus station, maybe I can find her and that woman on it. Facial recognition, if she's in a system somewhere, and without too many changes to her face, I might be able to trace her. It's a real long shot," he warned. "I'm good, but it was a long time ago. That video footage will be even more primitive, and who knows what condition it's in."He looked around the room. "Guess our next stop is New York City and the Sterling Arms."

"We'll have to go home first," Waters told him. "We'll need that envelope. And her. You gonna be able to handle that?"

Having Mouse out and about in public, where it would be much easier for the Salieri to target and snatch her? Yeah, that was a big no. "Probably not. Don't know what other choice we have though."

No one spoke, but like Midas, they really didn't want to put Mouse through this either. If a trip to New York City couldn't resolve some of the mystery, their work became a whole lot harder.

The ride to the private airstrip was quiet and contemplative. Midas closed his eyes and lay his head against the door, but even through his closed lids, he felt eyes on him periodically. Wondering if he was going to crack? While parts of him felt like he was splintering to the point where one wrong word, one wrong touch, one wrong result would cause him to shatter, he couldn't allow it. It would be so easy to give in to the rage and frustration, but Mouse needed him to be brave for her. To see this through at her side.

He was the last to get out of the truck and head toward the jet where Janus, their replacement pilot, waited for them. Medusa probably could have flown the bird even with her broken arm, but Loki put his foot down, threatening to tie her up and duct-tape her to a seat if she even got near the cockpit. She'd grudgingly behaved, but she did promise—not threaten—to kick him in the balls the next time they sparred if he didn't let her at least copilot to New York. Wisely, he agreed.

As he made his way to the plane, Nemo stepped up beside him. "We can protect her, bro," his twin assured him. "There are enough of us. We can make sure two of us are right beside her at all times. No exceptions. She's tribe."

Midas nodded. She was it. She belonged to him, whether she wanted to or not. He already knew it was her or no one else, just as his brother had known that if Gem walked away, there would never be another woman in the playboy's life. So whether she wanted him or not, he would always be hers.

30

FEBRUARY 10, 2024

Midas

OVERALL, IT HAD BEEN FOUR DAYS AWAY. FOUR LONG, wearying, fretful days away from Mouse. It was the first time they'd been apart. They'd taken extra precautions and not contacted home the entire time they'd been gone, so he hadn't been able to check on her. He'd done nothing but worry. Had she slept okay? Had she eaten? Had she had nightmares or more blackouts? Nova hadn't let them know that anything was wrong, but he didn't trust it.

Fuck, he'd missed her. He'd been able to shut her out while they were working, at least most of the time in any way other than a clinical one, but all the way home, she was all he could think about. Had she missed him? Every time she grew a little stronger, it seemed like another hit came and took her back a few steps. She was brave though. So fucking brave. Every time she got hit, she regrouped. She pushed forward. It was that strength that kept drawing him back to his little mouse.

Arriving back in Escondido on the private airstrip they used, he was slow about gathering up his things, his thoughts centered on how to handle all these inflamed emotions. Every day they grew stronger, and he'd yet to say anything to her. The time was coming when he didn't think he could hold it back anymore. What if she didn't feel the same?

By the time they'd arrived back in the underground parking garage, he still didn't have any clue or answers. He'd been so lost in thought, he hadn't realized the others were long gone. The only sounds left were the muted, typical hustle and bustle of Los Angeles. When he slithered out through the door with his gear, TB was waiting for him in the empty elevator carriage, leaning against the back wall.

The door closed behind them, then descended to the armory.

"Got a text when I turned my phone back on. Flame wants to see you before the formal triumphant return."

Seriously? He was tired. He wanted a shower. He wanted to sleep.

He wanted to hold Mouse and reassure himself she was okay.

TB must have read his incredulity at her request. "She said it couldn't wait, and the minute you got back, you needed to talk to her."

He nodded his thanks and stayed behind when TB left the elevator, watching the numbers as he ascended to TB's floor. What did Flame want?

She let him in the door. "Welcome back. We'll be downstairs to greet you all formally, but this couldn't wait. Some discussion occurred while you were gone, and, well... I'm interfering where I shouldn't, but I just can't let this go by."

Instantly, he was on alert. "What's wrong? Something with Mouse?"

"Yes, about her. I don't know that anything's wrong, per se. But I needed to tell you that we pushed her a little bit about her feelings for you. Normally, I wouldn't interfere, but given our conversation before you left, I thought the intel might help you out."

He set his bag down on the floor of the entryway. "What happened?"

"You were worried about how to proceed with her. I know you didn't say anything before you left. You need to. She definitely has feelings for you, but she's feeling unworthy. Like she has nothing to offer you. She's concerned her past interferes with a relationship with you."

Fuck. Why did he wait? She was already unsure, and then he left. Four days of no contact, she probably thought she didn't mean anything to him. "Did she say that?"

"No, not those words, but it wasn't difficult for me to piece together because a lot of her worries seemed to be like mine with TB." She reached out and touched his forearm. "Tell her, Midas. Tell her as soon as you see her. You're patient. You'll be good for her. You'll give her the space and time she needs, when she needs it, to figure things out.

"Right about now, I'm guessing she's missing you so much she's going to be ready to take it to the next step. I think she was ready before you left, but then you needed to leave immediately. That wouldn't have been the right time. Being with you, then you leaving so quickly, would have made her extremely vulnerable. But now that you're back, I think she'll be very happy to welcome you home."

"It's too soon."

"Too soon for what? To tell her you love her? I think we let the cat out of the bag on that one while you were gone."

"Even if I told her, and even if she feels something toward me, the rest of a relationship is a long time off."

"You mean sex?" She shrugged. "Maybe, but don't you think that's for her to decide? Are you ready?"

"What kind of question is that?" he asked, puzzled.

"Well, you don't strike me as a one-night guy, like the others were. And if you've waited this long, I imagine it needs to mean something pretty important to have waited as long as you have."

He stood there, stunned. How the hell did she know?

"Oh, come on, Midas. We talk a lot about my books, and it didn't take me very long to figure out you wear your virgin status like some sort of merit badge to prove you're not like your brother. Well, he's not that way anymore, but you're still holding onto that. Trust me. It's not like you're going to have sex and become him. Doesn't work that way. I mean, sex is good, but it's not going to turn you into a manslut."

Still, he said nothing. He wasn't sure how to respond, or if her comments even required a response.

"It's not a big deal, you know. I mean, having waited. I think it's pretty sweet, actually. She's a lucky woman to have you all to herself from the first time to the last time."

"Does everybody know? I mean, Nemo does. Waters does."

"I don't think it's a secret. I seriously doubt it's discussed. Much." She blushed. "And these guys? They don't care. It's not their business. But a word of caution regarding Mouse. No one knows how they'll respond after abuse like she's been through. I imagine some women are never ready for a physical relationship. However, she doesn't strike me as one of those. There's something in the eyes, in the confidence level. She's shy, but she's a fighter. She'll want normalcy, and she wants it with you. I think she'll respond quickly to the idea. Yes, she'll go backward at times. Most men wouldn't be very patient with that, or even try to understand, but you will. And I don't know that anyone else is as good for you as she will be."

He thought about what Flame had said. After a few moments, he nodded and gave her a soft smile. He leaned down and kissed her on the cheek. "Thanks. I'll go clean up and then head to her."

"I'll make sure she's in the lobby. You need to have your first offi-cial triumphant return." She smiled, her eyes a little glassy. "I'm happy for you, Midas. We love her already."

31

FEBRUARY 10, 2024

Mouse

WHEN THE TEAMS RETURNED TO TRIBE, THEIR FIRST STOP WAS always the armory to unpack the gear, then they went to the gym to shower and change to be presentable for the women. Flame had begun a tradition where the women were all downstairs in the lobby when their men returned. Mouse wasn't sure she should be there with them, but they wouldn't let her stay in the apartment, and she found herself being dragged by Cherry out the door and down with them to the lobby.

TB was first out of the elevator, and he unerringly shifted left, as if his Flame radar told him exactly where she'd be standing. His personal bag hit the floor with a clunk, then his hands were framing her face, his mouth swooping down on hers. The kiss was fast but thorough, and then he was checking in on both of the babies she held, kissing the head of the little girl, then grabbing Axel and lifting him up high. The boy shrieked and giggled all at the same time, and as TB brought him down to chest level, he began to babble at his daddy as if to tell him everything that happened while he was gone.

Waters went to greet Liliana and Catalina, crouching down to chuck them under the chin. Both girls moved to hug him tightly, one on each side, and Mouse watched as he kissed each girl on the cheek. His eyes flew up to Kubrick, who was standing back near Cherry's desk, and he nodded to her with a whispered "Yes," and a huge smile on his face. With one more squeeze to each of the girls, he stood up. "Pizza and princesses in a little bit, okay? I need to talk to Kubrick for a few minutes. Go with Nemo and Gem, yeah?"

The girls nodded, then watched him beeline straight for Kubrick, pick her up, throw her over his shoulder, and go straight to his office.

Ona got a very concerned look on her face. "She in trouble?" she asked Shakira.

Shakira giggled. "I don't think so. I think he's going to kiss her."

Ona appeared satisfied with that answer.

Nemo was next, hands in his pockets, a huge grin on his face as he sauntered up to Gem.

"What's wrong with your face?" she asked. "Your mouth looks swollen."

He opened his mouth and stuck out his tongue, an already unwrapped condom stuck to it. She laughed and plucked it off the muscle.

"Sorry. Not black licorice," he apologized.

"*Doos*," she teased. "Not in front of the girls."

"It'll have to wait, anyway. Somehow, I drew the babysitting straw."

They stood forehead to forehead, nose to nose, his hands on her waist and hers on his shoulders.

Demon was the last one in the carriage. He was leaning against the back wall, hands propped up on the gold rail, keeping his arms locked, his eyes laser-focused on Cherry over the tops of his sunglasses. Mouse heard an audible gasp from Cherry and a murmured "BAMF mode." With a crook of his finger in a "come here" gesture, she was in the elevator and in his embrace before the door had closed behind her.

Nemo had one twin in one arm and Ona in the other, while Gem had the other twin in her arms and Shakira by the hand. He looked at Mouse. "Don't worry. He's on his way. He was told to come to the lobby instead of going to the apartment."

When the newly emptied elevator appeared, Nemo, Gem, TB, Flame, and all the kids got on. Nemo mouthed, "Wait for him," and then they were gone.

She felt silly waiting in the empty lobby, but she watched the elevator climb to TB's floor, then the brothers' floor. It sat there for a long time. She was just getting ready to give up when she saw the numbers above the door start to count down. She held her breath as it reached the third floor, where the gym was, and she expelled it when it started again and came to the second floor. Was it him? Butterflies began to swarm in her stomach.

Before the doors had completely opened, he was through them and on the tile floor. She may have decided that she should hold back, but it was like her heart refused to listen to her brain's logical reasoning. Mouse didn't hesitate and leapt into his arms. He didn't seem to mind, though, because he reached under her ass to pull her higher and wrap her legs around his waist. His hug was just as tight.

"Mouse," he whispered into her ear. "I missed you."

"Missed you more," she whispered back.

He pulled back, and she saw him cataloging that she was all in one piece. "Everything good while I was gone?"

"Yes. Other than the apartment was too quiet."

"No blackouts?"

"No. The girls took very good care of me."

"Good. No nightmares?"

"No." She blushed. "I might have slept in your bed while you were gone though. Think that helped."

His eyes got wide at her admission, then a lazy grin crossed his face. "Gotta admit, I like the sound of that, as well as the visual."

They stood in silence. Well, Midas stood. She clung to him like a vine on the side of a building. Should she try to get down? She didn't want to. Was he uncomfortable? Was she too heavy? He didn't seem like either was true. He was well-muscled, but she was tall, and that could be more uncomfortable than being too heavy.

"I don't want to get down. I don't want to let go," she admitted.

"I don't want you to get down or let go either," he replied. "Mouse…" He started and stopped. She could see him debating something. It was in his eyes. So unsure.

"Mouse, I can't do this anymore."

"Midas? What's wrong?" Oh god? Had everyone read him wrong? He'd just said he didn't want her to get down or let go, but he looked pained at what he was about to say.

"I've been trying to come up with a way to tell you something. Wanted to tell you before we left, but the timing seemed wrong. Now I worry I should have anyway. I'm not good with words. Always been a little bit awkward with that. I don't have the charisma of the other guys, especially my chick-magnet brother. Tried to come up with a pretty, romantic speech, but"—he blew out a breath—"none of it sounded right. So I'm just going to say it. I can't pretend that I don't have feelings for you, and I'm hoping that the greeting I just got means you feel at least partially the same way."

Her hand stroked the side of his face. She felt her eyes begin to tear up. "You mean that? Even knowing my past? You still want me?"

"Mouse, even if you chose that history, I'd still want you. I know it's not what you would have chosen for yourself, but it's part of what makes you a strong woman. You've fought every step of the way. Even when you were taken again, you still fought. If you hadn't, I wouldn't have been able to break through that block so easily."

The butterflies had quieted, but they still flitted around. "I don't need flowery words, Midas. I just need you. All of you."

"Can you handle being the other half of a deadman? I can never walk alongside you in public. Not in the truest sense. You deserve a life out and about after all these years. To do and see all the things that were taken from you. I can never give you that. All I can give you is the freedom to do those things and hope you come back to me. But if you do, I promise you, no one will love you more than me."

"I don't want to go away, Midas. I want to stay here with you. We have no idea what's to come with me. I could be hunted for the rest of my life. I could continue to have blackouts. I could hurt someone again. Look at what I did to Medusa, without even knowing I could do those things. I don't think my babysitting detail is going to lift anytime soon." She stopped, fear causing her voice to tremble.

"No. Probably not. But you'll be protected, even if it means we have to protect you the rest of your life."

"I don't think I could function in the real world like a normal person."

Midas brushed her hair back from her face and behind her ears. "*Heuning meisie*, you could never be normal, and it has nothing to do with what's trapped in your head."

"You're always building me up, Midas."

"Kash."

She looked at him, confused. "I'm sorry? What does money have to do with this?"

He laughed. "Nothing, sweetheart. It's my real name. With a *K*."

"Oh." She thought for a moment. "Why are you telling me that? I thought none of you had real names anymore?"

"Officially, we don't. But I'd prefer if you called me by my real name."

"Why?"

"Let me answer that with a question. May I kiss you, Mouse?"

She stilled in his arms, her hand on his cheek, searching for answers. The sincerity she saw inside his dark-brown eyes shone clearly. It made her heart want to burst from her chest like a flurry of birds escaping into the sky. This was what Midas did for her. He made her want things that she felt only he could give her. The power to soar and be free yet still feel sheltered and loved. Never smothered. Never shackled. He gave her the power to choose what she wanted, whether it was what flavor of ice cream they had at night, or whether he could hold her, and now whether or not he could kiss her. Always her choice.

She should tell him about the issue surrounding his desire for a family. She should. It wasn't fair to go forward when she couldn't give him something so important. But he was here, and he wanted her, and she wanted this with him. Even if it ended up they couldn't be forever, and she had to let him go to find someone who could give him what he deserved, she'd take what she could for now.

"Yes, with one condition. If you return the gesture and call me Ana."

"Ana," he whispered. He smiled. "I like that."

Midas raised a hand to lay it over hers on his face, and he turned his head just enough to kiss her palm. Then he gently took her hand in his and brought it down to his chest, just above his heart, and held it there. Slowly, he moved toward her lips, giving her more than enough time to back out of her decision if she wanted to.

She watched his every move with intensity, but she didn't stop him. And when his lips were but a breath away from hers, she heard him breathe her name again, causing her eyes to flutter closed in preparation for his kiss.

The first gentle touch of his lips to hers had her melting in his arms. Firm but sweet, his lips touched and retreated, touched and retreated, then touched hers one more time, lingering a moment before pulling back. He smiled. "That's why I want you to call me by my name. When I hold you, when I kiss you, and maybe someday when you let me love you the way you should be loved, I want to hear my name on those lips. Who I am, not my role at Tribe. You see me as the man I was. The man I still am, just hidden underneath this job that I hold. I want you with *me*."

She smoothed a wrinkle out of his T-shirt. "I'd like that, Kash. We can go slow, right?"

"Your pace, sweetheart. Always your choice. But... is it okay if I don't put you down? I'm not ready to let go of you just yet."

She answered by burying herself in the space between his neck and shoulder, breathing him in. "Don't ever let me go, Kash."

She felt the stutter in his breathing, knowing he understood the meaning behind her words. She thought he was about to say something else because he inhaled deeply, but then he changed his mind, turned, entered his code on the elevator keypad, and was inside it before the door was barely open.

When they got upstairs and he'd keyed in his door code, she thought he'd put her down on the ground, but he didn't. He continued to the back of the apartment, dropped his bag off his shoulder just inside his bedroom door, and then gently unwound her from his body, sliding her to the floor. He didn't move away but instead curled his hands beneath her hair and around the back of her neck so he could tilt her head to the side and seam his lips to hers. Again, the touch was soft and brief, but there was no doubt in her mind that he enjoyed kissing her.

His hands brushed from the top of her head, across her shoulders, down her arms, to where he laced their fingers together at their sides. "I'm glad you were waiting downstairs."

"I wasn't going to, but the women claimed it's tradition. I worried you would think it too forward. Like I was assuming something about us that wasn't true, but they insisted."

"I've never had anyone here waiting for me. I don't think I could be without it now."

"As long as you want me, I'll be there every time you come home," she assured him.

His hands gripped hers tighter at their sides, and he brought them up, resting them together on his chest. This time, when his lips dipped to meet hers, she parted hers slightly, signaling he was free to take the kiss further. Instead of sweeping inside at her voiceless invitation, he was true to his word, making sure things were always her choice.

"Yes? It's okay to kiss you deeper?"

"Yes," she whispered. "Please do."

She thought maybe he'd crash into her with force and speed, but instead, he moved slowly and with purpose, as if he wanted to savor each second of the experience. Rather than let go of her hands, he held them pinned to his chest, and he used his nose to brush against her jawline to tilt her head further back. When his lips finally touched hers, they were offset so that he could encase her lower lip between his and gently suck it, then let go and pulled back just enough to ease his tongue out to swipe against her flesh to ease the tension he'd put there.

Eyes on hers, he stepped what felt impossibly closer, bringing his mouth to hers again, this time subjecting her top lip to the same treatment. Only, instead of pulling away after swiping his tongue across her this time, he slid it between her lips to trace the opening, featherlight. She felt as if he were breathing into her, giving her air, then pulling it from her mouth and feeding his own lungs with her breath. It was heartbreakingly sweet and romantic all at the same time, and she never wanted him to stop.

After several exchanges of the soft touches of his lips against hers, his tongue learning the opening of her mouth, he pulled back to look her in the eye. "I don't want to stop. I want to lay you down in this bed where we'll have plenty of room to spread out, but won't because we'll be too wrapped up in each other to notice there's room to move around."

Holy crap! Her breaths became shaky, and she could feel the tremble spread throughout her body. "And you said you couldn't find the right words. Those are pretty good ones."

He smiled. "Maybe Flame's books are rubbing off on me a little bit."

"Oh lord, I hope so."

His head kicked back in surprise, and she felt her face heat up.

"Oh my god, I said that out loud." She couldn't help but laugh. "I'm sorry, I—"

It was then that he moved in with force. It wasn't a violent clash of tongues and teeth, but he pulled her hands over his shoulders, encouraging her to wrap around his neck, then he wrapped his arms around her waist and carried her back to the kitchen. Then he let her go and took a step back.

When she opened her mouth to protest, he pointed a finger at her. "No. You? Dangerous territory right now. I'm going to write my report now so that I've got no distractions later. You're going to go order some dinner. I'm guessing you haven't eaten yet today, or if you have, it's been junk. Especially if you've been hanging out with Kubrick.

"When I'm done, we'll have dinner. I'm going to be a good boy and not touch you until after, when we're curled up on my couch, not watching whatever movie you put on because we're going to be too busy, like we're two teenagers making out. Maybe you'll let me get to second base by the end of the night, but even if you don't, I'm gonna have a helluva lotta fun trying to get there." He leaned over, kissed her lips hard and fast, then pulled back, turned her around, and gave her butt a soft swat. "Go. I'll be out in less than an hour."

Turning swiftly, he headed back toward his room, muttering to himself. She couldn't hear what he was saying, mostly because she was sure he was speaking in Afrikaans, but she turned from the door with a smile on her face because it felt good to have driven him to distraction.

32

FEBRUARY 10, 2024

Mouse

"WHAT ARE WE HAVING?"

She yelped, jumping what felt like at least a foot in the air but was really just a jerk of her body. She'd just reached up to get a couple of glasses out of the cupboard, and he'd totally scared the crap out of her. He really needed to announce himself before he entered a room.

Hand to her pounding heart, she turned toward Midas to chew him out for sneaking up on her, but the words got stuck in her throat when she caught sight of him. Oh yeah. Announcement definitely needed. A trumpet fanfare. A herald with one of those long, rolled-up scrolls that took an hour to read, spelling out all his accomplishments and detailing every totally delicious characteristic of him. Even that might not be long enough to prepare for his arrival if he showed up like this.

He'd changed clothes. His feet were bare, he had on some sort of athletic pants, and holy wow... he was shirtless. He smelled like rain. He was shirtless. Had she thought that one already? Didn't matter. It was worthy of being mentioned twice.

"Sorry!" He was backed up against the breakfast bar, hands raised in a gesture of surrender. "I didn't think."

She shook her head, but she wasn't sure it was communicating the correct message. "Shirt."

He frowned. "Huh?"

"Shirt." She pointed at his chest.

He looked down, then back at her, the confusion rampant on his face. "I'm not wearing one."

"Exactly. Go put one on." She whirled around to face the cupboards, her entire body feeling like it was on fire.

A soft chuckle sounded, and she knew if she turned around, he'd be right behind her. Not close enough to make her feel caged in but close enough that it would be nearly impossible not to touch him if she moved.

"Are you laughing at me?" she asked.

"Maybe a little." His hands settled on her shoulders and turned her into him. "It's not the first time you've seen me without a shirt."

"No, but apparently the previous times I was a little out of it."

His hands grabbed hers and placed them flat on his chest. "Relax, Ana. It's just me. Same guy I was with a shirt on. If it will make you more comfortable, I'll go put one on."

"No, no," she rushed to get out. "You just got back from what I'm sure was an uncomfortable trip. You should be comfortable now that you're home."

"Ana." He tipped her chin up so she'd look him in the eye. "I don't want to make you uncomfortable. A shirt is not going to make me uncomfortable."

His watch beeped, signaling their food was downstairs in the lobby. "Well, now I will put one on. Don't want to make whoever's watching the desk uncomfortable." He grinned and stepped away, grabbing a zip-up hoodie that was over the back of one of his dining room chairs. As he was going out the door, he slipped on a pair of sneakers, and as he zipped up the hoodie, he grabbed the neck near the hood and brought it up to his nose.

Drat. It was the one she'd been wearing while he was gone. It had his smell all over it, and it had made her feel less lonely at night.

He turned to her, his eyes blazing. "You were wearing my hoodie?"

"Yeah. Sorry."

He crossed back to her and pulled her into his arms. It was his turn to bury his head into her neck, although his mouth rested just below her ear. "Never be sorry. Wear all my shit. I like the smell of us together." After a quick kiss, he pulled back and headed toward the door again. "Go put something else of mine on." His head turned. "As little of it as possible. I'll go slow, but I want easy access whenever you're ready."

With that, he was out the door.

"Holy shit," she whispered to the empty room. Trying not to think too hard, she went to his room and opened drawers until she found what she wanted.

33

FEBRUARY 10, 2024

Midas

When he returned a few minutes later, he came to a dead stop in his foyer. Yeah, his blood was boiling even hotter than the Thai food in his hand, which he set out on the breakfast bar when he remembered how to move again. She'd put on another zip-up hoodie for his favorite rugby team. From wearing it himself, he knew it was well-loved, meaning it had thinned and softened from the hundreds of washings over the years.

It wasn't that it was overly revealing. He'd actually seen her in less, although it had been early on when she first arrived, and she wasn't awake very often. Then, however, he'd been helping Demon with her medical checks, and he hadn't really paid attention out of respect for her. The hoodie covered her about the same as the night-shirt Kubrick had bought for her when she first arrived and had nothing to wear other than what she'd been found in. He couldn't help but wonder what she was wearing underneath, but he'd probably get a sense if she bent over for something or sat on a chair. If her expression was anything to go by, she was nervous about her choice, but as far as he was concerned, it was spot on.

"Looks way better on you," he murmured in her ear.

She blushed beet red, then hopped up onto one of the breakfast barstools, and he noticed she was careful to pull the hemline under her ass as she did. Didn't necessarily mean anything, but still. Wondering made him especially glad he'd chosen to unpack the food containers on the other side of the bar from her so she didn't see how good his dick thought it looked. Guess he was eating standing up, because sitting down with the hard-on he was working was not going to happen.

Dinner was mostly silent, he assumed because they were both occupied with his comments from before he went downstairs. He hoped it was anticipatory on her end, although he guessed that she wouldn't have followed his instructions if she wasn't on board. It was important to him that she get all the things she'd missed as far as dating went. It would probably make them both more comfortable.

After dinner, she seemed to be dragging out the cleanup process. He let it go for a short while, disappearing into the bedroom briefly to make sure everything there was ready by turning on the television and setting it to the home screen so she could pick something for them to watch. Maybe. He smiled a little bit and sent out a plea to the universe that they saw next to nothing of whatever she picked. Figuring she'd had more than enough time to settle her nerves, he cruised through the apartment, shutting all the drapes and lowering the lighting in the living room. When he returned to the kitchen, he realized she was stalling for real, so he took the cloth out of her hand that she was wiping down the counters with, placed it over the faucet, and scooped her up into his arms to take her into the bedroom.

He laid her down on his king-size bed, one he was especially glad he'd exchanged the original one for when he'd taken residence, and then handed her the remote. "Relax, *heuning meisie*. I had planned on giving you the high school boyfriend, making-out-on-the-couch experience, but then I thought that might be too constricting. Just a change of setting, not a change of plan." He nodded at the remote. "Pick something. Anything. Doesn't matter what."

He felt her eyes on him, a bit like a timid rabbit watching a wolf in the distance, as he kicked off his shoes, then unzipped the hoodie he'd been wearing. As soon as the zipper cleared the tab at the bottom and he began to peel it off his shoulders, she switched her view to the television and pulled up a show. He half lay down next to her, facing her, and leaned on his bottom elbow to prevent her from feeling caged in. The couch would have had him halfway on top of her, and he worried that might be a trigger for her. He was going to work to avoid every pitfall he could.

Music started in the background. He wasn't really paying all that much attention at first because he was trying to read her expression. But when he saw the twinkle in her eye and a smile at the corners of her mouth that she couldn't quite suppress, he knew she was up to something. A voice came on in the background, and he groaned good-naturedly. "Seriously? A documentary on sperm whales? Have you been taking lessons from Kubrick's ten-year-old boy alter ego?"

The laugh escaped her then in full force, and it was completely worth it to see her like this. She had a beautiful smile that lit up her whole face, and it was one he didn't see very often. In fact, the last time he remembered seeing it was at the Santa Monica Pier while riding the carousel with the girls.

She was laughing so hard, she let out a snort. "You should see your face. So worth it."

"Whoever named that beast should be shot. What were they thinking?"

She shrugged. "Another person with a ten-year-old boy alter ego?"

"I lied. It does matter what it is." He grabbed the remote out of her hand and rolled onto his back to change the selection. Cruising through the channels, he picked his music app, then lowered the volume to just barely able to be heard. He tossed the remote on the nightstand next to the bed, then turned back to her and resumed his original position.

They lay facing one another, simply gazing into each other's eyes. He raised his hand to brush back her hair to fall behind her head, threading his fingers through it from root to tips, most of the silky strands slipping free before he reached the ends. "If at any time you feel panicked or trapped, you let me know. Nothing happens that you don't want, okay? You want to just lie here and talk, that's what we do. You want more, I'm down for most anything, but I don't want to have sex tonight."

She squinted at him. "That could encompass a lot of things. Define 'sex' so that we're on the same page."

"Nothing that requires a condom. If I had my way, we'd be a ways away from that. At least a week." He waited a moment, purposefully letting her see in his expression that he was teasing.

When she caught on, she giggled. "So restrained."

"I just don't want to rush you. We've got all the time in the world because I'm not going anywhere. I don't want this to be unpleasant for you, and I don't want to trigger any unhappy emotions."

"I want this, Kash. I want to be yours. If something's too much, I'll say so."

Nodding, he continued to run his fingers through her hair. "So, slow. Step by step. I want you to have all the build-up experiences in a relationship that you never got to have, and—" He stopped. Blew out a big breath. "And I want those too. I didn't date when I was younger because by the time that age rolled around, our father had up and left, leaving my mother, who had no education beyond secondary school, in dead-end jobs trying to keep us fed, clothed, and the utilities on. She wasn't always successful, so I went to work to help out.

"I was also busy trying to keep Nemo out of trouble. He was a lothario, even back then, and if I wasn't rescuing him from his sexual escapades, I was keeping him from getting into fights or bailing him out of jail. Sometimes it felt like all of my wages went to that. There wasn't time for girls, and then... it just sort of continued into my adult life."

"So what you're saying is, you've never been with anyone."

He paused. He wasn't ashamed of being a virgin, even at his age. He'd never really felt the urge to get involved, short or long term, with anyone until Ana. One thing he'd always appreciated about Nemo was that his brother had never given him grief over it or made fun of him. Sometimes he wondered if Nemo hadn't been a little jealous, especially once he met Gem. However, he wondered if it would matter to Ana. She'd had shit experience with sex, so he wasn't concerned about it being a comparison thing. He just wanted to make sure that he turned it into a positive experience for her.

"Nope. You'll be the first, and if I have my way, the last. My only."

There was a look in her eyes where Midas could tell she'd gone inside her head for some reason. He wasn't sure what he'd said that caused the look, and he was about to back off from his plans until she spoke.

"Can we pretend it's the same for me?" she asked.

"What you experienced wasn't a relationship, and while it may have been sex by the technical definition, it doesn't count. As far as I'm concerned, it is true."

He shifted to get himself closer to her, one arm sliding underneath her, the other curving around her waist, his hands meeting in the middle of her back, one above the other. His thumbs brushed back and forth against her spine through the material of the sweatshirt.

A light tickling sensation fluttered above the waist of his pants, and he realized it was the pads of her fingers brushing across his skin. The touch was soft, as if she were afraid to touch him at all, even though he'd held her against his bare chest several times when she'd suffered panic attacks. Then, she'd been mostly unaware, her subconscious finding comfort in his warmth until the attack subsided and she fell into sleep. Now, she was completely aware of him and tentative about touching him.

With ease, he pulled her close, then rolled himself under her. "Sit up," he said.

She was being careful not to settle on him anywhere uncomfortable, which he appreciated, but he sensed some of the carefulness was actually assessing his emotional comfort with what she was doing.

Once she was astride him, looking down, he grabbed the pillow underneath his head and bunched it up to provide a little bit more of an angle so he could look up at her without straining. "Go ahead," he encouraged. "Touch me all you want. Trust me, I won't mind."

He let her explore, keeping his hands on her hips to steady her, and his eyes on her face to watch her reactions as she mapped out the dips and curves of his muscles, as well as the scars and marks left behind from previous projects. Her fingers stuttered over a purple streak, about two inches long, cheese grater in texture, along his side. Her eyes questioned him.

"Bullet graze from a cartel soldier."

They slid up his chest to his shoulder, easing the pressure of her touch as she passed over a bruise about the size of a softball, the center blue and purple in color, the edges beginning to turn green.

"Broke down a stubborn door at the compound."

Her fingers dragged down his arm to a jagged scar all the way up the inside of his forearm.

"Piece of steel embedded when a building blew up."

Finally, she stroked a thin, white scarline along the side of his face.

"Blown out window put a chunk of glass in my face."

She lowered the upper half of her body to kiss the scar.

It would take no effort at all on his part to turn his face into her kiss and take her mouth with his, but he held back. This was about her. What she was capable of right now. He warred with himself over following Flame and TB's advice or to completely back off and let her set the pace. His impulse to give her the control felt like the right thing to do. But what if she never pushed further because she worried too much about her reactions? Or worse, his? He'd wait as long as it took, but would they be wasting precious time they could have together?

She began to sit back up, but he stopped her by lightly grabbing her elbows. "Don't. Unless you're feeling trapped."

"I never feel trapped with you. Only safe. Protected."

"Good. That's how you should feel."

One hand brushed her hair back behind her ear, then curled around the back of her skull, his palm applying gentle pressure to bring her down to him. The closer she got, the more rapid his heartbeat, until it felt like he'd implode. When their lips touched, his body went up in flames. He meant to go slow. He really did. He blamed it on her.

Mouse apparently didn't want slow, or else she was feeling their connection with the same intensity. By opening her mouth to his, she stole his breath away as she welcomed him into the fire, and the flames burned away any hope of letting her set the pace. His brain was misfiring, unable to perform its normal logical processes, and all he could do was feel. The softness of her lips seamed against his. The power behind the press of her mouth. The wetness as their tongues chased one another. Never once did it feel awkward or clumsy. It was as if they'd been doing this their whole lives.

Without thought, his hand slipped from her hip to her lower back, fingers splayed to keep her grounded above him. The hand threaded through her hair palmed the back of her skull to help support her neck as he rolled her onto her side. Ensuring her head rested on her pillow, his bottom leg inserted his thigh between both of hers, her bare skin underneath. He could feel her heat already.

He was reluctant to stop their mating tongues, but he needed more of her. Needed to taste her skin. He broke away from her for just a split second, and she protested with the sweetest "No" on her breath, but he didn't leave her wanting. He left a line of kisses from her swollen lips to her jawline, then down her neck to her beating pulse. He rested there for several seconds, his lips pressed to the throbbing beat, then opened his mouth to allow his tongue to sneak out and lick the erratic pounding in her throat.

"I know, *heuning meisie*. Relax. I'm here. I'm not going anywhere, and I'm not stopping unless you tell me to."

His mouth pressed to her pulse again, then continued down to the hollow in her throat and the small expanse of her chest he could see above the zipper. After applying several chaste kisses to her skin, he raised his head to gauge her reactions. While she clearly wanted his touch, he wanted to make sure there was no fear mixed in with her need.

Her eyes were half open, her gaze riveted on him. Her tongue swept between her lips as if moistening them after being exposed to dry winds and heat and no water. Hands framed his face, and blunt nails lightly depressed into his skin to keep him from moving.

One hand still on her back, the other drew down her body, moving from her shoulder to her hands, threading their fingers together briefly, giving her a squeeze of reassurance. Then he let go as his hands reached the hemline of the sweatshirt she wore, which had pulled up from completely covering her. Part of him wanted to glance down, to see how much of her was peeking out from beneath his clothes, but he kept his eyes on hers. There'd be time to look his fill eventually. Instead, over and over, his fingertips brushed back and forth along the top of her leg, and his knee pushed a little bit further up to her core. Heat blazed hotter against his thigh.

"I don't want to upset you, but I need to tell you something else before I go any further. And if you want me to stop after I tell you, I will."

"Okay."

He could see confusion and a little bit of trepidation on her face. While she was still pliant in his embrace, she had to be worrying about what he was going to say. His hand gripped her thigh, pulling it snug over his. Already he could feel her arousal dripping onto his pant leg, no doubt leaving a wet spot. He didn't care. It felt good to know that, at least right now, her body was responding to him.

"I had a talk with TB and Flame a few days ago. About you. More about her, really. I needed advice on how to move us forward, or if that was even possible. The last thing I ever want to do is bring you discomfort or panic. I thought that maybe talking to Flame about her experiences would help me understand what pitfalls I might hit. She reminded me that all survivors are different. That there's no magic formula for when they're ready, or if they're ready, to experience a physical relationship.

"I definitely want that with you. I think you do too. I want all the choices to be yours, but she suggested that I come out and tell you bluntly how I was feeling. She also recognized that I shouldn't expect to know what you wanted, and she said that one way to combat worry would be to always say things straight out so there were no misunderstandings. Like what she and TB do when they negotiate scenes. It still gives you all the choices, like I want you to have, but also might leave you less reluctant to push for what you want.

"My impulse was to let you run everything. To tell me when you were ready to kiss me or touch me. To sleep in my bed. To have sex with me. But she said that might be overwhelming, given the circumstances. That was how TB brought their relationship alive. I'm not a Dominant like him, never will be. However, I want you to set the limits of what you want or don't want. Is that what you want? Do you want me to wait for you to give me direction? Or do you want me to move at what I think is a good pace and negotiate as we go?"

Her fingertips relaxed against his head and traced the shells of his ears, her eyes turning slightly glassy.

Uh-oh. He'd upset her. "Are you mad that I spoke to them? It's okay if you are. I just... I didn't want to fuck this up, and I didn't know who else to ask."

"No, I'm not mad. I think this is exactly why I'm so attracted to you. You always seem to do the right thing, even when you're unsure. The fact that you'd be that concerned about scaring me or making me unhappy that you'd put yourself in that uncomfortable position—and I know it couldn't have been easy to talk to them about this—tells me that you'd move mountains for me."

"I would, Ana. I'd climb them, go around, through, under... I'd blow them all out of the way for you. I'll happily hold your hand and surmount them with you. All you have to do is ask. So, do you want me to make the decisions regarding our physical relationship, and you say yes or no? Or do you want to lead?"

"You decide, and I'll say yes or no," she replied.

No hesitation. One hurdle cleared. All he could feel was relief. He'd chosen correctly.

"So let's see how that goes then. Ana, can I pull this zipper down a little? Can I touch you underneath? Just your breasts."

She nodded.

"No nodding. Yes or no. I need the words."

"Yes, but..." She shuddered. "No pinching, pulling, slapping, or biting. Pain is a no-go."

"Thank you for telling me. I would never want to hurt you in any way."

He also didn't want to take his hands off her skin, even to unzip the hoodie she wore. It was like a compulsion to keep his skin against hers at every possible contact point. Instead of taking three seconds to reach up and unzip the jacket partway, he leaned over toward the zipper tab and grabbed it with his teeth.

Since he didn't want to startle her with rapid movements, he had intended to be firm but go slow. That way, she had time to stop him if she needed to. However, he realized what he was doing was making her hotter, so he purposefully dragged the zipper down slower than he would have to drag out the anticipation. Being on his side rather than over her, it was a little awkward, but he made it work.

He stopped when the zipper was three-quarters of the way down her front, the natural weight of the garment along with her position making a deep vee of cleavage so he could see her creamy skin. His gaze locked briefly on the side swells of her breasts, the material catching on her nipples, leaving the tops and outer edges covered. His breath caught. Somehow, this was way sexier than seeing her completely bare.

Turning his eyes up to hers, his breathing stopped yet again at the hunger in her expression. "Still good, Ana?"

"Kash, please," she whimpered.

"Please what?" He was certain she was begging him to touch her, uncertain emotionally of what to say, but he was going to hold to the plan. If he made her tell him specifically what she wanted, how she was feeling, what she didn't want, then he couldn't make mistakes with her. Or at least, not big ones, he hoped.

"Please touch me."

"Mouth or hands?"

"Both."

"My pleasure, *heuning meisie*. And hopefully yours."

He didn't hesitate. Hesitation might communicate he was unsure, or that the action he was about to complete was undesirable to him, and he never wanted her to doubt anything with him ever again. Dipping his head toward her, he allowed his mouth to nuzzle into the hollow of her throat, kissing, nibbling, and licking a path down her skin until he rested at the top of the valley between her breasts. Lips not leaving her flesh, his jaw brushed aside the material covering the top of the swell, his tongue slipped between his lips to lick the areola, flicked once across the nipple that was already distended, and then he blew a breath across the wet surface.

She gasped, her nails denting the surface of his skull where they gripped him, but he didn't care. He took the bite of pain in celebration. His choices were good, and it spurred him to continue on.

Without breaking contact, his hand slipped beneath the hem of the hoodie where it rested at the top of her thighs, smoothing over her bare hip. She wasn't wearing anything under his hoodie, and he felt his dick grow tighter. He'd been hard ever since he first saw her in it when he came upstairs, but he'd been doing his best to ignore it. Now, knowing that she'd come to him wearing next to nothing, there was no holding back his reaction. After keeping his hand on her hip for a moment, as if to register that, yes, he really was touching uncovered flesh, he continued to slide his hand up her stomach to curve around the underside of her breast. He gently curled his hand around the globe, the perfect handful to allow him to support the weight and brush his thumbs over her nipples. With each brush, he felt her breathe in a little deeper.

He raised his mouth from her skin, shifting carefully to bring it so close to hers, they could share their breaths. "Put your arms around my neck and kiss me, Ana."

Her eyes flickered open to stare into his, then languidly she moved to do as he asked. When her lips touched his, his heart clenched. Shy, maybe, but not afraid. Like her decision, her lips met his with quiet assurance, and after she'd given him a lingering kiss once... twice... she carefully nipped his lower lip to request permission to enter, which he immediately granted.

He allowed her to explore again, the tip of her tongue tracing the upper and lower swells, then flicking shyly inside to make contact with his tongue. As soon as he felt her do that, the hand not holding onto her breast cupped the side of her face, and he deepened the kiss. His body rolled slightly more over her, but he was careful not to cage her in, unsure of how that might make her feel. Much as he knew he'd be gentle with her, he didn't want to run the risk of triggering a bad memory, even if it was more sensation than fact.

He applied pressure more firmly, tangled his tongue with hers, learned her flavors, and drowned in the taste of her. He was completely lost, and all they'd done was kiss and some light petting. He focused on the slight movements of her body, the sweet sounds she was making, and the feel of her warmth against his. He felt completely lost in time to anything but the feel of her beneath his body, mouth, and hands.

It had been no small amount of time trading kisses, one hand still curved around her breast, stroking the tip, when a featherlight touch along his shoulders caught his attention. She'd moved her hands to slide over his skin, the pads of her fingers flowing over the ridges of bone and muscle to connect with him.

Pulling back from her mouth was painful, but he only went so far that he could bring his forehead and nose to hers, soaking in her touch. With each pass, her touch became heavier, as if she gained confidence in his enjoyment of it. Eventually, her hands were smoothing down over his arms and to his sides, since he was still caressing her beneath the sweatshirt. Then her light touches began again, learning him from a new angle.

"My skin feels like it's on fire," she whispered. "I don't know if it's me, or if it's your body heat, or if it's my body going haywire from your touch."

"Is it a good burn?" he asked. "The kind where you feel alive? Where every nerve is tingling and you feel like you could fly?"

"Exactly like that."

He kissed her cheek, then down below her ear, nuzzling into the space between her neck and shoulder, the reverse of the pose she so often formed with him. "I feel it too," he admitted.

The muted music was the only sound around them as their hands stroked each other's skin and their mouths met over and over again. No rush to get further than where they were. No pressure to do more than what they were doing. Just happy to be together where they were.

Some time later, he decided to make one smaller push. This felt good for her, but it could feel better, and he thought the sooner he took away the unknowingness, the better. "Ana?"

"Hmm?" she murmured as she kissed his neck.

"Look at me."

Her face had a flushed appearance, and her eyes were bright with arousal. He felt the dampness between her thighs pressed against his leg, even through the material between them, so he knew she was still aroused, but that didn't mean she was ready for more.

"I want to give you an orgasm. Is it okay for me to touch your clit?"

He felt the slightest of inhales from her, a minuscule hesitancy before she answered. For him, that meant no, she wasn't ready for that. He removed his hand from her breast and used both hands to frame her face. "It's okay. We don't have to. I just want to make what we do feel good. That's all. But if you're not ready yet, you're not ready yet."

"No, it's fine. Really," she assured him. "I just... I guess part of me is still surprised you want a physical relationship with me based on my past. It's hard to let go of that. Feeling ashamed, even though, deep down, I know it's not my fault. Not something I chose. I'm actually more than okay with you touching me wherever you want. And I want to have you give me new memories. The ones I have are mostly connected to pain and fear, yet distorted. Blurry even. Sometimes I hope those memories never come back."

"Then we'll drown those out, if and when they ever show up. I'll promise to love you so well, make you feel so good, that the only important memories will be wonderful ones." His mouth gently met hers. "I meant what I said earlier," he confirmed. "I'm not making love to you tonight. But I'm all kinds of good with touching you all over and making you feel better than you've ever felt before. Dying to do that, actually."

"Make me feel good, Kash."

He kissed her one more time, then slid one arm around her under her neck, pulling her tight to him. His other hand swept down the front of her body, catching on the zipper of the hoodie that was still a quarter closed, dragging it apart the rest of the way, allowing the material to open completely. Rather than immediately reach down between her legs, he brushed his hand back and forth across her abdomen, allowing her to get used to his touch on this portion of her body.

When he felt she had gentled enough, that her pulse, breath, and heart were elevated but not to the point where she might hyperventilate, he moved to slide his free hand down to her mound, the flesh smooth and silky against his fingertips. Again, he stopped, letting her get used to his touch.

Slowly, he slid his fingers between her lower lips, caressing back and forth along the flesh. When he was sure she was comfortable, he began kissing her again, their mouths seaming together, tongues playing and exploring. Reaching the top of her labia, he used his middle finger to drag across her clit with just enough weight to cause her to gasp, sucking his air into her lungs.

With each circle he traced around the nub, he applied more pressure until he felt her raising her hips and grinding against his touch. Pulling back from her and resting on his elbow, he watched her soak in his attention. Her eyes were closed, her cheeks flushed, and the sweatshirt fell off her shoulders and to the sides of her body, exposing her breasts to the cooler air in the room.

He continued his strokes, watching her respond to his touch, her breaths becoming pants of need. She began mewling in his arms, inarticulate pleas of want. He couldn't wait until she was ready for him to slide his fingers inside her, to taste her, to plunge inside her, and show her just how much he loved her and her body. For now, though, his little mouse needed to come, and he was not about to leave her wanting.

His touch went a bit firmer, a bit faster, and he felt her entire body tighten against him, her mound pressing hard against his hand, and then she was crying out as the pleasure rushed through her. He continued to work her through the spasms, whispering against her hairline in Afrikaans—how beautiful she was, how she was so brave for letting him touch her, how lucky he was for her to let him pleasure her.

When she hissed and pulled her hips away, he realized she was feeling oversensitive. He eased down with his touch until she lay still beneath him, her eyes closed, her head turned to the opposite direction. He smiled. She was beautiful in this state. With his hand, he drew circles on the skin of her inner thigh, reveling in the fact that they were here. She'd come so pretty for him, caught up in the emotions and pleasure of the moment, just as he'd known she could.

Time to settle her in. He sat her up, whimpering in protest that she wanted to go to sleep, and he smiled. She sounded like the girls had after the day of being at the pier, all grumbly and grouchy but in a cute way. Gently, he helped her slide into one of his T-shirts. Much as he would have liked to have her naked in his bed, he didn't want her to wake up in the morning and panic about what they'd done.

After getting her resettled, he placed a kiss to her temple, slid out of the bed, went into the bathroom, and wet a washcloth with warm water. He returned to her side, gently pushing her legs a little wider, sweeping the soft cloth over her skin, careful to clean up all evidence of her orgasm. She didn't even stir. He dared a kiss to the top of her thigh, then slid off again to take care of the washcloth.

Returning to the bed, he snuggled up next to her, and she automatically curled into his chest, warm puffs of breath against his skin. He had to admit, his cock was uncomfortable, still fully hard from their playtime, but he figured if it was still an issue in the morning, he could take care of it in the shower. He wasn't concerned. Based on what had just happened, she'd want to do that again soon.

34

FEBRUARY 11, 2024

Mouse

"Little mouse," a deep, breathy voice whispered. The whisper was followed by a kiss to the shell of her ear, its warm caress light and tender. She shifted in her sleep, trying to burrow into the pillow and the heat behind her. There was a light chuckle, and the voice grew arms that turned her onto her back, then hips and legs that slid between hers. "Wake up, little mouse," the voice cajoled, hands now sliding up her arms, over her shoulders, up her neck, the fingers threading through her hair. "Much as I'd love to wake you up the way I put you to sleep, we have to get up."

Groaning, she reached up and pulled him down on top of her, burrowing into his chest, his muscles smooth, strong, and warm. "Five more minutes."

His chuckle vibrated through her body since they were touching from hip to feet, the bulk of his weight propped on his forearms on either side of her. "Sorry, *heuning meisie*, we have to get up."

She felt his warmth disappear, the sheet pulled back, and her body raised into the air, his arms around her. Somehow, he stood her on her feet next to the shower, started the water, and then stood her against the glass wall on the outside as the water warmed. After kissing her fully awake, he slipped off the T-shirt he'd put on her before going to bed and put her under the spray. Another quick kiss and he was out the bathroom door, whistling.

She didn't think she'd slept so well in a long time. There had been patches of good sleep while here with Midas, but she still had bad dreams occasionally. At least they weren't full night terrors. Last night though? He'd been by her side all night, his arms around her, and there'd been no bad dream. Would that happen every night? Probably not. Was it the terrific orgasm that tired her out so much she passed out? Yeah, that combined with the safety of his arms was more likely the cause.

Just another reason on the list of why she loved Midas.

Holy crap. She loved him.

This was not good. Her brain wandered back to her dilemma over a relationship with him. Kids. Family. Her damaged womb standing in the way of making that happen. What was she going to do?

She should have told him yesterday in the hallway. Yes, it would have ruined the moment, and yes, it would have broken her heart to watch him pull away, but at least he would have known before getting physically involved with her. Last night was wonderful. It had been so freeing to forget everything and just let themselves be together.

In the morning awakening, however, she knew she needed to tell him before this went any further. The guilt over allowing him to get as invested with her as she already was made the rock in her stomach turn into a boulder. She had to confess. He was going to be so disappointed. Not angry. Midas didn't seem to be the type to get moved to anger often. She was about to hurt him in a way she'd never wanted to.

When she came out of the shower, she wrapped herself in a towel and walked into Midas' bedroom, resolved to get dressed and face him with her confession immediately. However, her eye caught sight of the rumpled sheets, and she found herself forgetting about the intended discussion, distracted by the memories of last night. As she remembered their make-out session, her hand drifted across her front, the palm cradling her opposite breast, giving it a gentle squeeze, as if to remind her of his touch. Soft. Sure. Arousing. It took effort, but she managed to suffocate the moan she wanted to let loose. This was going to be so painful. He'd made her feel so good—

All of a sudden, her stomach did a little roll, like someone had dropped a rock into it and stirred up the acid with the suddenness. Another roll, bigger this time, and she felt nausea bubbling up. All kinds of crazy thoughts jumped through her brain to the most logical conclusion as to why someone who claimed to have no experience with women would be able to make her feel like she had. He'd. Lied.

"Inexperienced, my ass," she murmured. "He knew exactly how to make me come undone."

She whirled out of the bedroom and into hers across the hall, searching for clean clothes. She heard the popping of a stitch as she yanked a ribbed tank top over her head, then jerked each leg of her jeans up her body. She probably destroyed the neck of the sweater that she yanked off the hanger in her closet, but she couldn't find it in her to care. She shoved her feet into her flats and stormed out the door.

The nerve of the man! He didn't have to lie to her to get her to feel comfortable.

In her own bathroom, she yanked the comb through her hair, muttering to herself about how disappointed she was. With each stroke of the comb, however, she calmed down another notch. He wasn't that kind of guy. He genuinely cared for her. She was positive about that. Yes, she struggled with his wanting her physically, and she probably would for a long time, but Midas would never purposefully hurt her, and he knew lying would, so it seemed impossible that he would do it. However, she could see him distorting the truth if he felt it was what she needed because that's what Midas did. He wanted to help people.

After putting her hair into a messy bun on top of her head, her panic and temper had receded some but not completely. They had talked last night about being one hundred percent honest about their physical relationship, which extended to the rest of it. He'd said she could tell him anything, and he wouldn't get mad. That she controlled the yeses and nos. Did he really mean it? People often said things they didn't mean, even if they weren't lying outright. Her parents, for example. The only way to know if he was truly being honest about this was to ask him. Bluntly. No misunderstandings.

She went out to the kitchen, following the smell of pancakes and coffee. Stopping just short of the breakfast bar, she watched him in silence. While he was wearing a shirt this time, it didn't help because it was molded to his body like it was tailor-made for him. "So unfair," she muttered.

"What's unfair?" he asked.

Oops. His back was to her, but he obviously had the hearing of an animal if he heard her over the coffee maker, the running water in the sink, and the griddle sizzling.

He shut off the sink, unplugged the griddle, and brought her a plate of pancakes. He'd already set out fresh strawberries, bananas, syrup, and butter, as well as juice for her, since he knew she didn't drink coffee.

"How do you eat like this and look like that?" She gestured with a wave of her hand from the pancakes to a sweep of his physique.

He looked down at himself, confused. "Ah. The shirt. That's what you were muttering about." He grinned at her. "Glad to know you're enjoying the view."

"Ugh. You're impossible." She put some fruit on her pancakes, making sure to pour the juice from the cup onto them since she didn't use syrup or butter. As she was cutting into the fluffy circles, she looked at him under her lashes. "However, it is unfair that you look that good. It's distracting." She stabbed the piece of pancake, making sure there was a strawberry on it, and popped it into her mouth.

"Sorry, *heuning meisie*. First one I grabbed. I usually use this for sparring with TB because he cheats and grabs clothing in the ring when we go hand-to-hand. I learned quickly not to wear a loose shirt, or he can choke me out with it by grabbing the back of the neck."

Rolling her eyes, she continued to chew her food, readying another forkful to shove into her mouth after she asked her next question. "I thought you said you weren't experienced?" In went the forkful of food.

He frowned. "With what?"

Holding her hand up in front of her mouth, she said, "Women."

Midas stopped, the coffee mug halfway to his lips. "I'm not."

She shook her head at him, then focused her gaze on the food in front of her. "You seemed to know an awful lot, based on last night."

He restarted the coffee on its way to his mouth, took a healthy swig, and swallowed as he set the mug down. "Are you talking about your orgasm?"

She nodded.

He crossed his arms in front of him, then leaned on them to talk to her. "Believe me, no one was more surprised than me at the success of that. While I'm not ignorant of the technicalities, what I know, I know from reading."

"Reading."

"Yeah." He shrugged. "You know what Flame does for a living. At first, I read a few of her books because we were gathering information on her. The bonus was the shit we were able to give TB since he was so head over heart for her." He shrugged. "She writes pretty good stories as well as sexy stuff. Reading one led to another, so I just kept reading them. Learned a lot about what to do from that." He blushed. "Glad to know it paid off."

Could she believe that? Romance novels were fiction. Yes, the basics were accurate, but you didn't become an ace at technique from just reading. Her disbelief must have shown on her face because he reached over the table to take hold of the hand that wasn't holding her fork.

"Hey, what's going on in that pretty head of yours?"

"So you didn't understate your experience? I thought maybe you'd under-exaggerated to help make me feel more at ease."

"Absolutely not. We agreed on total honesty, didn't we? Well, other than parts of my job that I can't tell you about, but total honesty everywhere else."

Total honesty. Right. That secret she was holding back caused the churning in her stomach to return. Now would not be a good time to come clean, based on this conversation.

He stood up from his stool and came around the breakfast bar. "Let me guess. You woke up, and you started to second-guess."

Unable to restrain herself, she reached for him, slipped her arms around his waist, and placed her cheek on his chest. Inhaling deeply, she took in the soothing rainfall smell that always clung to him. "I panicked. As I got ready after my shower, I started to calm down. Think more rationally. I knew I should just ask you straight out."

He returned the hug, pressing a kiss to the top of her head. "Don't apologize, sweetheart. Not to me. There are going to be these moments where you have doubts. Maybe even where you withdraw from the physical side. I'll never be upset. We'll get through it together, okay? And I promise, I will never lie to you. Ever. Just like I know you would never lie to me. Thank you for trusting me enough to ask before jumping to conclusions."

Right. She'd never lie to him. Lord, she needed to tell him, and she opened her mouth to do it, but before she could get the words out of her dry-as-the-desert mouth, he dropped a kiss to the top of her head and pulled away. "Eat your breakfast. I hate to throw this at you this way, but... I need you to pack a bag. We'll probably be gone a couple of days. Not really sure."

Babies and families went out of her head in a flash. "Gone? Where?"

"Since we struck out in Egypt, we're left with one other location. New York City."

She simply stared, her heart rate increasing. No. She didn't want to go back there. A headache bloomed, and she felt herself start to break out in a cold sweat. "Why?" she whispered. Then she realized why. "The envelope. You want to follow the clues to see if they will lead you anywhere."

"Yes. We have the first clue, so we're going to go there and see what turns up."

"The chances of anyone who knows anything still being there after all this time are really low."

He sighed. "I know, but it's the best we've got right now."

"I'm scared, Kash."

He returned to her, stepped between her legs, and hugged her close, swaying back and forth slightly. "I know. I'd think you were foolish if you weren't. And I'm not going to lie, I'm scared too. But we need to do something, and this is the best course of action right now."

"Is it safe?"

"I'll be with you every second. If, for some reason, I can't be, two of the others will be. They won't leave your side for a moment."

"Okay." Her voice was small and unsure. Despite her fear, her heart trusted Midas completely.

"C'mon. Eat your breakfast, pack your bag, and then we'll be off. It'll be okay. Whatever happens, we'll handle it together. Yeah?"

"Together."

35

FEBRUARY 11, 2024

Mouse

Within an hour, they were on their way to Escondido to catch the jet and then on their way to New York. Cherry, Gem, Flame, and Kubrick were put on lockdown with the girls at Tribe until the team returned.

The men were spread out along the plane, while Medusa and Janus were in the cockpit. Mouse busied herself with a copy of Flame's recommended book. The author hadn't known Midas when she wrote it, since it was one of her earliest books, but it felt like she'd written him as the hero. Tall. Broad. Dark-brown eyes. Protective. Sweet. That meant that every time she read a scene with the hero in it, she pictured him. Of course, the heroine had light-brown hair and golden eyes. Well. They were golden when she shifted, but still. It was as if Flame had predicted her and Midas years before they met.

At one point, Midas gave a soft laugh. She thought he'd been sleeping, but apparently, he'd been watching her as she read and caught her blushing at a sexy part.

He leaned in to read what was making her overheat. He whispered in her ear, "Tonight. When we're alone? We'll do whatever that was."

A squeak escaped her mouth, and she slammed the book shut, her eyes glued on the seatback in front of her.

He chuckled and threaded his fingers through hers, his arm on the armrest between them, hers lying atop his. The gesture let her know he wasn't making fun of her. "That'll keep your mind off of worrying about being in New York."

"Aren't you supposed to be napping?" she asked. Yeah. Redirect the conversation. That would get her out of this embarrassing moment.

"Nice try, little mouse," he teased.

She stared down at their hands. The gesture was so Midas-like. A total metaphor for how he cared for her. He entwined himself into her life, then cushioned her. A refusal to let her go or cause her discomfort. She fell a little bit deeper in love with him, and she admitted to herself that it was useless to resist. He would always be a part of her, ruining her for anyone else.

He did manage to nap for an hour or so, never letting go of her hand, even in his sleep. When he woke up, she was still buried in Flame's book, but she marked her place and put it in her bag beneath the seat in front of her. "Waters said when you woke that he wanted to meet quickly," she told him.

"Figured he would." He turned his head to look toward the back of the plane, where voices were slightly raised. "Better go before they break out into a real war. Sounds like they're playing Risk, and it never ends well."

Sure enough, there was a game board out in front of the men, and it appeared they were playing with partners. When Midas moaned, she looked at him quizzically.

"They're playing partners. *Star Wars* version."

"That's a bad thing?"

"It is with these partners. The universe may implode."

She looked at the table. Loki and Gilgamesh, TB and Nemo, Steel and Demon, and Waters and Medusa. The latter team was clearly winning because nearly all the pieces on the board were theirs. The team leader was smirking. Medusa was sitting back in her chair, eyes closed. Meanwhile, the various partner groups argued about how to break the two Sith Lords they'd named Emperor Fuck-witch and Darth Maleficent.

When the group realized Midas and Mouse had materialized, Nemo quickly swiped up all the game pieces into the box with an "Oops! How did that happen?" and a cheeky grin. The players made room for the couple to sit. From his pants pocket, Midas drew out the envelope they had found in her backpack and handed it to her.

"Your show, Mouse."

She reopened the envelope and pulled out the contents—a quarter, the money, the charm, and the slip of paper. They were laid out in front of her in a straight line, along with the envelope. Midas covered the hand closest to him with his own, lending her support.

The team leader put all his focus on her. "I don't suppose that anything has come to you about these items?"

"No," she replied. "Nothing."

"Well, I figured that was the case, or you probably would have told us, but just thought I'd confirm. Since I was right, I'd like to try a little experiment," Waters said. "I want Midas to hypnotize you again, but this time, I want to see if he can put you back to the moment you saw your mom being taken. Instead of following the events that happened, though, I'm hoping he can be suggestive enough to have you find the envelope and see if your young self knows what to do with it."

Midas frowned. "Hypnosis doesn't work like that. It has to have actually happened for her to recall it."

"But wouldn't she have a clue as to what the contents mean?" TB asked. "Maybe she didn't think of it right then, but she'd understand the significance, and she should be able to recall that."

"I don't know. I've never done that before. It could be an epic fail."

"But it might work," Waters said. "What do you think, Mouse?"

She flashed a look at Midas. "You'll pull me out if it goes bad?"

He squeezed her hand and nodded. "Always."

Blowing out a breath, she agreed. "I'm willing to try."

Steel reached out to the controller on the center of the table and dimmed the lights in the cabin. She turned herself slightly so she could look at Midas. After another squeeze to her hand, he began walking her through the process. Closed her eyes. Imagined the dark room. Went through the faucet into the apartment, which this time was empty, except for her.

"Exit the apartment, Mouse, and leave the door open. No one will go inside while you're gone. I want you to walk down to the street corner where you saw the men who took away your mom. When you get there, tell me what you see."

Entering the corridor, the space seemed to elongate and become blurry around the walls. She passed the elevator she'd always hated taking, afraid that it would get stuck with her in it, and started down the five flights of stairs to the lobby. Once there, she looked around, seeing the mailboxes and the front desk where the manager sat during business hours.

She passed through the revolving front door and looked at the roadway in front of her. "The curb is open. The men in the suits and the car aren't here."

"Go ahead to the street corner. When you get there, I want you to look at the traffic light. Tell me when you get there."

The blurriness factor of the street became worse, the sounds muffled, as if they were underwater, and everything seemed to slow to half speed. Finally, she found herself at the corner. "I'm there."

"Excellent. What color is the traffic light?"

"Red."

"Okay. I want you to stay put, your back to the apartment building entrance. When the light turns green, I want you to try and remember as much detail about yourself that day as you can. What you were wearing. The weight of your backpack. When the light turns yellow, let yourself remember how you were feeling. If you can, what thoughts you were having. Then, when the light turns back to red, I want you to turn around and see what you saw that day."

She watched the traffic light and followed his instructions. When it turned red again, she turned, and her perspective seemed to change. She felt shorter. Her brain buzzed with all the irritation she'd felt that day at her mother. Her longing to go to the dance that night. And then she saw them.

"There are two men. Both are wearing gray suits, gray shirts, black ties. They're very tall. Broad-shouldered, like bouncers. They have short hair that's cut like they're in the military, and they're wearing sunglasses. They have curly cords coming out of their ears. Like old-fashioned phone cords."

"Do you recognize the men? Have you ever seen them, before or since then?"

"No."

"Describe the car for me."

"Black. Four doors. Big."

"And the license plate? Can you read it?"

She strained her eyes. It wasn't clear, so she took a couple of steps closer. "It's dark blue with white letters. D, zero-zero-two, four-zero-six-one." Her breath caught in the back of her throat, and she clutched her chest. "There are two men bringing my mother out of the apartment building. She's not struggling, but I can tell she doesn't want to get in the car. She's crying."

"Go in the alley, Mouse. You said you hid there after your mom was taken. Go now."

Her feet felt rooted to the spot as she watched the men hustle her into the car and drive away. Every part of her body hurt. Where were they going? Why was she crying? Where was her father? She didn't know what to do.

"I know no one can see you, but your heart rate is getting too fast. Use the alley like the black room to calm down."

The soft yet commanding tone made her do as he asked. "It's nasty here."

"I know, sweetheart. Just for a little bit, okay? Now. I know this isn't what you did that day, but I want you to think about your backpack and the envelope. Think about the contents. Your father told you to carry this with you everywhere, all the time. He must have thought you'd know what to do. So I want you to think about the items and see if you can tell me what to do with them."

She concentrated. "Dad loved puzzles. Treasure hunts. The strip of paper is the first step. I need to go there. I don't know what the other pieces will do. I'll figure out what to do when I get there." The alley started to darken until it was pitch black, and she opened her eyes. She was back in the plane at the table, everyone looking at her. "What happened? Did you bring me out?"

"No," Midas said. "You just opened your eyes, and here you are. Do you feel okay? Headache? Anything?"

She shook her head. "Why didn't I have to go back the way I came?"

"I'm not sure. My guess is because there's nothing left for you there. Your brain knows that, and it closed all the doors." Midas looked at Waters. "I won't be able to put her under again, and she won't be able to return there. We've got everything we can get."

Waters nodded. "We're about to land. When we hit the tarmac, we'll go to the hotel and check in. We'll stagger our departures and arrivals. You'll go first. At eighteen hundred, we'll meet at the Sterling Arms. Steel, Nemo, and Medusa will cover the building from outside. TB is going to get there early and see if he can secure a room for rent, a place for us to meet. Demon and I will follow you and make sure no one's watching. Loki and Gilgamesh will follow us as a countermeasure. When you get to the lobby, let's see what we can see."

36

FEBRUARY 11, 2024

Mouse

At six p.m., Mouse and Midas were standing in the lobby of the Sterling Arms. She shivered, despite the ski coat Kubrick had loaned her for the trip. New York was warmer than usual—almost forty degrees—but her skin was crawling, and she felt a sheen of grime settling on it, despite touching nothing. The lobby wasn't at optimum cleanliness, but given the clientele they saw coming in and out, she wasn't surprised.

Loki and Gilgamesh were stationed outside, watching the building from ground level. Steel and Medusa were up on the roof of an abandoned building across the street, watching through the scopes of their rifles. Nemo had taken up a position at the back entrance.

"All right, Mouse," Midas began. "What does your gut tell you to do?"

She looked at the envelope contents that she'd taken out and placed in her hand. Considering them, she put the quarter in her pocket, folded the money into a quarter of its size, and hid it in her hand. That left her with the bear charm. Looking up, she noticed the desk worker behind the bars protecting him from patrons was watching her closely. On the wall behind him was a vintage poster for a Russian circus that had passed through the city in the late nineties. Centered in the picture was a dancing bear wearing a tutu. Her feet propelled her to the desk, where she put the bear charm into the shallow metal dish beneath the bars, allowing the man to pick it up.

He looked at her closely, then turned and went to his safe. After opening it, he placed the item inside and removed a key on a plastic placard. Back at the window, he said to her, "Two hundred for the week." His accent was Russian.

She glanced at Midas, then back at the desk worker. "What if I need it just for the night?" she asked.

"Only by the week."

Another glance at Midas had him nodding at her.

As discreetly as she could, she peeled off two of the hundred-dollar bills from her stash. The man pulled the money to his side of the bars, put it into a locked drawer, and then slid the key to her through the dish.

"Thank you."

He grunted and went back to his newspaper.

The key had the number three-ten on it. Midas took it from her hand, then steered her to the stairs of the six-floor walk-up. She was glad that he didn't want to take the ancient-looking elevator, even if it did mean climbing three floors. As a child, she'd been used to the five-floor walk-up of her home, but now, as an adult, by the middle of the second landing, she was flagging. Midas, however, wasn't even winded.

She had an odd, creepy feeling as they traversed the stairs and then the hallway to the assigned room. Like she was being watched. She didn't say anything to Midas, and she probably should have. But she figured they were being watched by everyone they could see as they made their way to the room, as well as people behind the doors looking through their peepholes, or even those who cracked their doors open at the sound of footfalls on the wooden floor.

Outside the door, Midas sent a quick text to let the others know where they should meet, then used the key to open the door and usher them inside. While they waited for Waters, Demon, and TB to arrive, Midas did a quick look in the bathroom to ensure there were no unwanted visitors, and she looked around the room. He was back by her side in less than thirty seconds.

It was a depressing sight. It smelled musty, with a lingering hint of sadness and desperation. This was not a place people came to start a life. It was where lives ended.

The space was a single room with dingy walls that hadn't been washed or painted, likely since the building opened. There was water damage in multiple spots on the ceiling, and black stains along the floorboards that looked suspiciously like mold. The windows were so grimy you couldn't see through them, and they appeared to be painted over so that they couldn't be opened. The management was probably afraid people would jump from them if able to raise the panes.

There was a rickety kitchen table that looked like it was from the fifties with its chipped top and rusty metal edges, and two chairs, one of which looked to have one leg that was shorter than the others. In the corner, a dormitory-size bed sat with no linens. The mattress had several large stains on it that she had no desire to know what they were. The only other thing was a string of cabinets above a counter with a hotplate on it, the cord frayed, a sink that probably ran brown water out of it, and a small refrigerator that made more noise than someone talking. No way was she opening it. She was sure there was something dead in there. A science experiment at the very least.

A knock came at the door, and Midas backed off to look through the peephole. He opened the door, and his three team members slunk through the doorway quickly, taking up spots around the room.

"I spent time in a jungle prison better than this," TB grumbled.

Demon looked at him from behind his sunglasses. "That's news."

"Well, I wasn't there very long. I was pretty motivated to get out of there."

Midas came back to Mouse's side, taking hold of her hand. "It's clear you were supposed to come here." He looked at his team. "She showed the desk worker the charm. He knew exactly what it was and gave her the key to this room. It was stored in the safe, like it was waiting for someone."

"I noticed the poster in his office," Waters said. "Good catch, Mouse." He looked around the kitchen area, running a finger along the countertop, the pad coming away caked with dust. "Anything she was supposed to come here for, or someone she was supposed to meet, has to be long gone by now," Waters said.

"Muggy as hell in here. I can hear the air running, but it must be super fucked up," TB observed.

"Air flow," she whispered.

"What's wrong, Mouse?" Waters asked.

"The air flow in my parents' apartment. It was terrible in the kitchen, remember?"

She walked around the space, finding only one vent that should have been pumping air into the room. While she had no delusions that it worked well in any of the units, the flow definitely wasn't coming out correctly. Studying the vent, she noticed the four screws, but all had been painted over.

Her brain kicked into gear, and she went to the kitchen table, dragging one of the chairs directly under the vent. She dug in her pocket for the quarter she'd been given, then hopped up onto the chair. Hands shaking, she put the quarter's edge into the groove of the first screw and worked to try and turn it. It wouldn't budge.

"Let me, *heuning meisie*," Midas cut in.

He reached for her and lifted her down onto the floor. When he stepped up onto the chair, it groaned under his weight, but miraculously, it held. From one of his many pockets, he removed a screwdriver tool that extended to a variety of lengths. After finding the right size head and the proper length to easily remove the screws, he depressed the button and began to extract them.

"Gem's little tool has made the rounds," Waters said. "I'm guessing Nemo gave all of us one for Christmas."

The tool made short work of the screws, and when the vent was removed... nothing. Midas clicked a button on the screwdriver and switched the screw head to the flashlight function. "There's something back a bit. Frickin' need Steel or Gem."

"I'm the littlest of us here. Let me," she offered.

Midas jumped down from the chair, dusting himself off from the paint chips and detritus from the air vent. He helped her onto the chair, then boosted her up by the hips so she could wiggle partway into the vent. "Got it!"

Midas pulled her out of the duct and placed her down on the floor next to him. In her hands was a very old duffle bag. One corner had been chewed on by mice, and likely there was a nest inside, but otherwise, it was simply dusty. She set it on the table and unzipped the top. Inside were some basic items. Some granola bars wrapped in a plastic bag, totally inedible by now. Toiletries that had dried up. Some clothes for a teenager. The bulk of the bag, however, was filled with banded stacks of money.

"Well," Waters said, "you might have been able to get farther away with this, but you'd still have been on your own."

Demon whipped a knife out of a leather sheath along his leg and handed it to Mouse. "Go on. I bet there's an envelope in there somewhere."

Immediately, she attacked the inside seams, and sure enough, there was an envelope inside a pocket that was inside another pocket.

"Fucking brilliant, Demon," TB congratulated him.

"Not just another pretty face," Demon reminded him.

TB rolled his eyes, then everyone turned to look at the envelope Mouse held.

"Go ahead. Open it," Midas told her.

The seal popped easily due to being left alone for so long. Inside, there was a postcard that featured the Lincoln Memorial, a bus locker key, and a name on a slip of paper. Elliott Howard.

A chorus of expletives was muttered.

She looked around the room.

Waters stared at the envelope's contents.

Demon growled, his eyes glaring at Mouse as if she were suddenly poison.

TB said nothing, but his eyes bored into hers.

She didn't understand. Why did they look angry with her?

Midas put an arm around her shoulders, pulling her tight to his side. The men didn't seem to change stances or attitudes. "Midas?" She put her arms around his waist and buried her face into his chest. Panic rose. Oily. Slick. Nauseating.

"Fuck, guys, stand down! She's going to have a panic attack. This is not the time or the place for that." He paused. "She's tribe," he reminded them.

Demon swore, then stormed to the door, yanked it open, and jerked it shut behind him as he exited. TB seemed to deflate slightly, and Waters' face went to regret.

"You can't say you weren't pissed off, Midas," TB said.

"Yes, I can because I wasn't," he disagreed. "I used my head. I remembered a few things. This bag is from around 2010, not recently. She was a child at the time. She wouldn't have known. Besides all that, she's a female. Howard would have been more a danger to her than a haven."

"Then why send her to him?" TB argued.

"I don't know. All we know is that he was a member of the Salieri at that time, and that, somehow, he was a refuge point for the family if they had to flee. You're right. It doesn't make sense, but it doesn't mean she had any knowledge of him personally, or even that her parents did for sure. A lot of times, exit contacts are strangers. You know that. Both of you."

Waters' jaw worked before he gave orders. "TB, grab Steel. See if you can locate Demon and get him back to the hotel." He waited for the man to leave the room. He sighed and rubbed the back of his neck, his body tight with tension. "Midas, take Mouse back to the hotel. She doesn't go out of your sight."

"She's not the enemy."

"I didn't say she was. I'll be honest, this is far too coincidental for me, and now my spidey senses are off the charts. Protect her. Do not leave her for any reason. I'll put someone on guard duty in the hallway, but neither of you leave the room. If one of us comes knocking on your door, make us give you the entrance code. If any of us sends out the distress code, you grab her and get the fuck out, you hear me? You know what to do."

She watched Midas give him a nod, and his arms hugged her tighter.

Waters flashed her a look. "They'll come around, Mouse. This Howard guy? We've been looking for him for a while. He's responsible for attacks on several of our women, and in case you haven't noticed, we're a little overprotective."

"That protection should encompass her, asshat!"

The hazel eyes of the team leader flashed angrily at Midas. "Again. I didn't say it didn't. You knew that a Salieri connection was possible from the start, and you know that's going to affect Demon and TB the most. So calm the fuck down! Do what I told you to do. I'll get together with the teams to talk this through, and we'll come find you after we have. We need to decide what our next move is."

"You're cutting me out?" Midas asked incredulously.

Mouse felt his pain at being ostracized from the team. All because of her. If he didn't regret her right now, he would as soon as he'd had a chance to process.

"Fuck you. You know that's not what this is if you'd stop and think for just two seconds. I need to calm those two Neanderthals down, and you puffing up like a goddamn ape, beating your chest over her, isn't going to help me do that. Now are you going to do what I asked, or am I going to have to shoot your ass so I can drag you back myself?"

Midas tucked her tightly behind him. "And Mouse?"

"Jesus Christ! No harm will come to her. You have my word, and you know that your team will protect her too. Go calm down."

With that, Waters closed up the bag with the envelope inside, put it over his shoulder, and left the room, slamming the door shut behind him. She began to shake in fear. Her thoughts started to crack, ready to fall apart with the slightest vibration. *Get out! Run! Run!* She didn't understand how or why, but her presence was unwanted by his team and possibly putting Midas in danger of losing everything important because of her.

A gentle shake brought her back to him. "Ana, look at me!"

In the space of her blanking out, Midas had grabbed her by the arms and was trying to get her to focus on him. Her teeth were chattering, but she was sweating. Her head hurt. Her eyes were watering. Her legs felt rubbery, and if he hadn't been holding onto her, she would have collapsed. She opened her mouth to deny him, but all that came out was a rush of unintelligible words even she didn't understand.

"Sweetheart! *Heuning meisie!* Stop! You're going to make yourself sick."

Suddenly, her hands were on warm flesh. He'd unzipped his jacket and untucked his Henley, shoving her hands beneath the material so she could touch his bare skin.

"I'll keep you safe. I promise. No one is going to hurt you. No one!"

She had no idea how long they stood there, only that it must have been a while because the room was basically pitch dark when she came out of her blackout. Midas was still there, still holding her, still crooning at her in Afrikaans as a way to comfort her.

"Midas?" Her voice cracked.

"There you are, *heuning meisie*." He tilted her chin up so she could see his face. "Let me see those pretty eyes."

"It's dark. You can't see them."

"Yes, I can, sweetheart." He pulled her tight again and pressed a kiss to the top of her head. "We need to go. This place is giving me the creeps, and besides that, it's not safe for you here. We'll go back to the hotel and hunker down. Order some room service. Watch some bad television. Waters will come find us when there's a plan. Come on."

"Will you tell me what's going on? I'm terrified. I don't know what you're all talking about, and I feel like I've done something wrong."

"No, you haven't done anything. We just... I'll explain, but not here. I want you out of here yesterday."

37

FEBRUARY 11, 2024

Midas

Midas hustled them down the street several blocks, then hailed a cab to take them back to the hotel. He hadn't seen their outside protectors, but he assumed that at least two of them were trailing them there.

His argument with his team leader was a knee-jerk reaction to the men's treatment of Mouse, just as their reaction to her had been. They'd been searching for Howard for months now, and everyone was getting twitchy over it. So seeing his name on that piece of paper where it should have no place being? He understood why it was a shock. It had shocked him, too, but that didn't mean that Mouse was knowingly connected to the Salieri. Had the men been thinking clearly, they would have known that themselves.

When he and Mouse arrived at the hotel, he made sure all the curtains were drawn and all the lights were on. His watch beeped at him, letting him know that Waters needed to talk. He gave her a hug and a kiss on the top of her head. "Go ahead and take a shower," he urged Mouse. "I can tell you feel like your skin is crawling."

"Yeah, it is." She peeked up at him. "Want to join me?"

Whoa. That was brave. She rarely asked for anything, but this was a pretty big something. He wasn't sure her request was a good one given the emotional hits from today, but there was no way he could tell her no. If he turned her down, even for a good reason, the first time she asked for something, she might see it as him not keeping his word. He refused to hurt her that way.

"If you're sure, I'd love to, but I need to do something first. I'll join you in a couple minutes, okay?"

She nodded with a shy smile and headed into the bathroom.

When he heard the water start up, he opened his laptop, encrypted the chat, and called Waters.

The man popped up on the screen.

"You've got two minutes, and then I'm heading in to take care of Mouse," Midas told him.

"I got everybody down off the ledge, although Demon's still got one foot on it. Be reasonable, Midas."

Midas schooled his face to show no emotion. He wasn't letting them get away with this. "No, you be reasonable, Waters. Would you have stood for that behavior if it had been Kubrick in that room?"

"No, but I would have understood that they needed time to process the information. Look, D's gonna react the way he's going to react. He'll calm down, but you know it takes him longer. He doesn't compartmentalize the way the rest of us do. Cut him a little bit of slack, okay?"

He ignored the request for flexibility. It was just time spent spinning his wheels when he could be doing real work on the problem. Or better yet, under the hot water with Mouse. "Do you have something important to tell me? Because if not, I have a shower to get to."

It took Waters a moment, and then he snapped himself into work mode. "Right. Okay, so we're thinking we take the next leg of the journey."

"We're gonna follow all the steps to whatever its eventual end is?"

"Seems the most prudent thing to do. Clearly, I don't expect to find Howard in DC, but Demon pointed out that Howard was in that area for a time because of the whole Cherry obsession years ago. We need to check out his home there. Mouse would have had to find him somewhere."

"What about the storm coming in?"

"Nova said it's going to hit us tomorrow in the early hours, so we're gonna hang out here until it blows over. Day after tomorrow, we should be back to normal and headed south." He cleared his throat. "Snow is going to be significant. Good chance to stay in and stay warm. Know what I mean?"

"Seriously? That's what you're gonna say to me right now?"

"What am I supposed to say? Jesus Christ! Is she okay?"

"No, she's not okay. Mouse is terrified now, and she's terrified of the wrong people because my team are being total shitheads. On top of that, we're stuck here because all we have is an envelope with clues to a stop on a trail that could go on forever. And now? Now I've got to tell her all this other shit, which will send her into the stratosphere of terror. Call me when you actually have something useful to say."

He disconnected the call. Staring at the black screen in front of him, he resisted the need to call his team leader back to apologize. In all of his years working at Tribe, he'd never lost his temper like he just had. He knew he was being a dick, but he couldn't seem to control it. What the hell was the matter with him?

Refusing to think about it, he started shedding clothes on the way to the bathroom, tossing them wherever he happened to be at the moment they cleared his body. When he entered the bathroom, Mouse was inside the steamed glass walls, rinsing herself. Pulling his pants and boxers down past his hips, he let them pool onto the floor and stepped directly into the shower, slipping his arms around her from behind, his head resting on her shoulder. Then he just stood there, which he realized was probably freaking her out more, but he needed to gain control of his anger, and he didn't know how else to do it.

"Is everything okay?" she finally asked.

He wanted to tell her yes, but he couldn't. He wasn't going to lie to her. "I'll be fine." Which he would be. At some point. Probably not today. Maybe not even tomorrow. But somewhere down the line, he'd get it together.

Slowly, she turned in his arms, the last vestiges of soap spreading to his skin when she put her palms on his chest. "What is it?"

Shaking his head, he kissed her forehead, closed his eyes, and took a big breath. "Later. Right now, I just want to hold you."

He turned her so that his back was taking the brunt of the water but also kept her tight to him so she didn't get cold. Her short nails scraped up and down his arms, and every few seconds, he felt her lips press a kiss against his chest.

"Why don't you have any tattoos?" she asked.

Huh? She was asking about tattoos? Of all the things she could be asking him about at this moment in time—What was the plan? Why were the guys so mad? Why wasn't his dick hard if they were naked in the shower together?—this is what she wanted to ask?

"You want to know why I don't have tattoos?"

"It just seemed odd to me. All the other guys do. Isn't it required of all alpha males?"

He pulled back his head and upper body, quickly realizing by the crinkles around her eyes that she was laughing inside, teasing him. He turned her so that she was back under the water, and he began threading his fingers through her wet hair. "Conditioner?"

"It's the leave-in kind. Don't dodge the question." She poked him in the chest. "No tattoos. Why?"

"Nemo has enough for both of us and then some."

"That's not a reason."

"I'm too beautiful to mark my perfect skin?"

She snorted. "Yes, but that's not why you don't have them. Everything's a choice with you, whether it's about you, the team, or me. So why?"

This woman was way too observant for her own good. It's probably why he'd been able to extract information from her so easily under hypnosis. She must always have been a naturally curious person.

He began soaping up his head, although there was very little there to wash since he kept it so short. "Tattoos make you recognizable. From the time I was old enough to get one, Nemo and I were already on the path to a life in crime. Knowing what I do about facial recognition and enhancing photos and video? I didn't want anyone to be able to recognize me, although I was mostly behind the computers. Nemo was pretty tatted up when we came to Tribe. He was concerned they'd make him laser some of them off. Especially the ones on his neck and hands. But he just always makes sure he's covered head to toe, even in the worst heat, and no one sees them."

"You were a criminal?"

The way she asked the question was... also not expected. She didn't sound repulsed. She didn't sound titillated at the prospect. It was more of a clarification question.

He squinted at her through the water, and soap ran into his eyes. When he hissed at the sting, she reached up with her clean hands to wipe away the worst of it, then guided him directly under the showerhead to wash out his eyes. When he was free of the burn, he pulled her back under the water to get her warm again.

"Yes, *heuning meisie*. I was a criminal. When our mother died, Nemo and I were left to fend for ourselves. We used my computer skills and his physical abilities and became international thieves for hire. We were damn good too. If Interpol got their hands on me, I'd never see the light of day."

"How did you end up with Tribe?"

He began to wash off the rest of his body, his equilibrium and energy starting to return, his anger and frustration washing down the drain with the grime from visiting the hotel. "Nemo and I had just pulled off a gold heist in Papua New Guinea. They have a reserve there equal to Fort Knox. Took some doing, but we managed to get in.

"On our way out of the country, we were caught at the airport and hustled off in a truck to what we thought was jail. Next thing we knew, we were waking up in some sort of solid steel cell. After a few days of no contact with anyone, the door opened, and we were whisked away to a room where our bags were waiting for us. Had a shower, got dressed, then were shoved into what looked like an inter-rogation room with another guy. Eventually, two more guys got brought in."

"Let me guess. Steel, TB, and Demon."

"Yep. Sad, sad circle of stupid we must have made." He laughed. "I don't know how long it was. Three? Four hours? That was when Waters came in and made us an offer we couldn't refuse. Work for Tribe or we'd be erased. Permanently. The only hitch was, we had to give up our real selves, and anyone, if there was anyone, had to be left behind. Officially, we'd be dead. Obviously, we all disbanded the circle of stupid and went to work for Tribe."

What the hell was he doing? He was naked. In the shower. With the woman he wanted to spend the rest of his life with, and he was talking about his job. Someone really needed to take away his man card.

Before he could convince her to leave the shower with him, he realized she wasn't there. Then two hands fluttered against his thighs, and he looked down to see Mouse on her knees in front of him.

"A-Ana?" he stuttered; he was so shocked. On reflex, he quickly reached up and reangled the showerhead so she wasn't the victim of the waterfall.

"Shh. You were in a dark place when you came in here, and now I've got you back with me. I want you to stay out of your head." Her shyness shone in her eyes, but she pushed through it to ask him her question. "Is it okay if I take you in my mouth?"

"Are you sure? This is a big jump from yesterday."

"I thought showering together was a big jump. Showering to blow job? Less of a jump. But I'd like to, if you want it."

"Sweetheart, I'd love for you— Fuck!"

His voice cut off on the invective because as soon as she'd heard the start of his agreement, she'd curled one hand around the base of his cock, which had woken up quickly when he'd seen her on her knees for him. Her other hand was gripping his thigh, and her tongue was licking up the underside like it was a spoon covered in melted ice cream and chocolate sauce. The tip of her tongue was pointed and leading the way; the rest was flat and dragging along the vein.

Rising taller on her knees when she reached the tip, she curled her lips around the head and tucked him tight inside her mouth, sucking hard and hollowing out her cheeks. He felt his knees start to give, so he quickly put his hands out to the shower walls to keep himself upright. She began to bob back and forth, never going farther than the middle of his cock.

"Goddamn, sweetheart. I had no idea." He hissed at the pleasure-pain from the pressure. "Can you go further?"

Her golden-brown eyes looked up at him through lashes beaded with water, her cheeks flushed, and as she drew back to the tip, she gave a gentle nod before plunging further down his shaft. "Holy shit!" He wanted to let his head roll back, but he wanted to watch her work his cock more.

She continued to slide her mouth up and down his dick, fast and light from tip to root, slow and tight from root to tip. When he finally felt his body catch up with what was going on, he was able to let go of one wall and allow that hand to drop to his side. "I'm going to put my hand alongside your mouth, sweetheart. Pull off or tap my thigh if you don't want me to."

In response, her hand reached for his, placed it on her cheek, and she stopped moving but continued to suck tightly around him. "Oh shit." He moaned, feeling his cock through her cheek, and he gave it a light tap. "Sassy girl. Expect payback." She giggled, and he grunted as her teeth accidentally—or did she do it on purpose?—scraped lightly along his shaft as she backed off.. By the look on her face? Oh yeah. She did it on purpose.

Afraid he was going to come in her mouth, he managed to pull out and step back. Two hands in her armpits, before she could even react, he had her lifted and against his chest. "Time for retribution, *heuning meisie.*"

One arm banded tight around her waist, he reached with the other to turn off the water, then shoved at the glass shower door and stepped out into the cooler air. He set her down on the mat, grabbed her a towel, and wrapped it around her body. "Stay put," he ordered. After grabbing his own towel and tying it around his waist, he swept her off her feet again, then put her over his shoulder.

She was laughing hysterically when they passed through the door, but he stopped short after two steps onto the carpet.

Her laughter stopped when she felt tension run through his body. "What's wrong?"

He just stood and stared.

"Kash, put me down. What's going on?"

He slid her down the front of his body, eyes still focused straight ahead. When she turned in the direction he was looking, he heard her gasp in surprise, then stayed frozen as she stepped forward to the table. "Who did this?"

Sitting on the table by the window, drapes closed, were plates, chopsticks, and tightly closed paper bags. She immediately dove into the bags and pulled out containers of soup and food, enough to feed five people. She looked up at Midas with a huge smile. "Do I still need to gain weight?" she said with a laugh.

"I didn't do this."

He walked over to the table and opened the last bag. When he found a bottle of Hibiki whiskey inside, he swore quietly. A lot of his mad from earlier faded away.

"Who did?"

"D. He loves Japanese food... and whiskey. This stuff can't be found everywhere, especially in this small bottle." He looked up at her. "He's apologizing for this afternoon."

"Oh," was all she said. She looked down at the food, the table, then the bottle, before returning to his face. "That was nice of him."

"He still needs to apologize and mean it," he grumbled.

"Don't worry about it right now, okay? I'm starving. Didn't realize I was so hungry."

His blank look turned to a shameless grin. He grabbed her around the waist from behind, lifting her off the ground with a playful roar. "I didn't just feed you enough, young lady?"

"You didn't let me finish, so no." Her laugh became infectious as he fake bit into her neck like an attacking animal. "Stop! Stop!" He knew she wasn't serious, but he set her down anyway and let go.

"Why did you stop?" she asked. "I knew you were only teasing. It was fun."

"I promised you that all the yeses and nos were yours. If you say 'stop,' then I stop. I have to go with the words and not what I think they mean. If I break that promise even once to you, then at another time, when it's more important, you might feel you can't trust me to keep my word."

Her hand went to her mouth, fingertips touching her lips. "I need to watch what I say."

"Don't blame yourself," he told her. "It's just how things need to be between us right now."

"So, if I said you should continue what you were doing?"

"Is that what you're saying?"

"Yes. You should continue what you were doing."

With a repeat of his fake roar, he reached out and grabbed her again, this time face-to-face, continuing his fake biting to the other side of her neck, then her shoulder, and her laughter started up again. After several feints and attacks to either side of her neck, he stopped to stare into her eyes, a huge smile on his face. "I love your laugh. When you truly let go with it? That's the best sound in the world."

After another growl and bite, he let her body slide down his to the floor. Their eyes were locked, their breathing elevated.

"Kash?"

"Yes, Ana?"

Her cheeks went beet red. "Can you go further?"

His hand rose up to caress her cheek. "How much further?"

"Will you put your mouth on me? Where you touched me last night? Like I did on you in the shower?"

"I thought you were starving." His voice sounded husky.

"I am. I mean, I was, but... I want something else now."

He swept her up into his arms. "Food can be reheated. Hang on tight."

38

FEBRUARY 11, 2024

Midas

"Does Waters have a plan?" she asked around a mouthful of chicken and rice.

He nodded, one finger on his lips as he finished the tamagoyaki he'd just popped into his mouth. "He wants to follow the clues to Washington, DC. Unfortunately, or fortunately, depending on how you look at it, there's a storm moving in, and we're stuck here until it breaks, probably the day after tomorrow."

It was an hour later, and they were sitting in the destruction they'd created of the bed, sheets pooled around them, the lights low, and devouring the food Demon had brought over. Mouse wasn't a fan of the sushi, but she dove into the soup and demolished the chicken dish he'd brought. He'd never realized how much energy orgasms drained from a person, and how much refueling they required. He made a note that the first time they made love, he'd better have a well-stocked refrigerator. And he was hiding all her clothes so that she had to eat wrapped up just in a sheet. Naked would be better, but the sheet looked pretty damn good on her.

"Hmm. Can't imagine what we'll find to do with the time."

"Hussy," he teased. "Well, I don't know what you're going to do, but I have work to do. I need to search out some more information on the name on your piece of paper. Elliott Howard."

"That's what set everybody off this afternoon, wasn't it?"

He nodded. "Have the Tribe women shared anything with you? About their situations?"

"Very little. I know Kubrick met Waters on her film set, and Flame was a victim of a drug dealer turned sex trafficker. Cherry works for Tribe, and Nemo used to, but now he works for Mythos and helps Gem bring children to safety. I think they're worried about saying too much."

"More like they know you've been through a metric ton of shit and are trying to spare you information overload."

"Are they allowed to tell me anything?"

"Technically? No. But since all their pasts seem to be weaving together in this Salieri shit, they know more than they probably should."

"Is it 'later' enough to explain to me what's going on?"

He shoved the empty food containers into a bag, set them on the floor, and then lay down on the bed. "Come here." He gestured for her to curl into his side. When she did, he pulled the comforter over them. One arm snaked around her shoulders so the hand could curl up around her head, and he could play with her hair. He kissed her hairline as she snuggled in, one hand and her cheek on his chest. "This might take a little bit, so let me work through it, and then you can ask questions.

"Two years ago, Kubrick showed up in our offices. Her brother sent her to us to find a consultant for a movie she was making about Navy SEALs. She really did need a consultant, but we figured out she was actually in more trouble than she knew, and it turned out her brother, another SEAL named Ka-Bar, had gone missing and wanted her under our protection. A bunch of shit went down on the movie set, Kubrick and Waters fell in love, and everything got set in motion for the women to come into our lives.

"Shortly after that, Kubrick introduced us to Flame. She had picked up a stalker, a drug dealer named Gendry, from her past. She ran away from him, came out here, and started her career as an author. We got involved protecting her, and it turns out that this guy, Gendry, was now hunting her down for a specific buyer. That buyer was General Elliott Howard. The stalker was trying to establish a logistics system for capturing and moving women through the sex trade in order to prove himself worthy of membership in the Salieri.

"Then, a few months later, Cherry and Gem nearly got themselves blown up in a street café. Turns out, the Salieri put out a hit on Cherry. She was helping extract Gem from a mess in South Africa, where she was gathering information on illegal diamond and gemstone mining, one of the ways the Salieri were funding their operations.

"For twenty years, Cherry's been pursuing leads on her father, who was kidnapped on the day of her high school graduation. Tribe is her baby. We finally got some significant leads in Africa with Gem, leading us to Cherry's uncle, a guy named Zion Norton, who was partners with her father in the aviation industry. She and Demon went down to his home in St. Lucia, where they ran into this guy, Felix Giudici, an Italian banker and high-ranking member of the Salieri. They also ran across General Elliott Howard of the US Army. Years before he tried to buy Flame, he had a fixation on Cherry. Has a thing for redheads, I guess. Anyway, the whole thing ended with Cherry being kidnapped by this ancient cult/crime organization."

Mouse had been silent the entire time he spoke. "That's..."

"Fucked up? No shit."

"Well, I guess I can understand why they all reacted like they did."

"You're far more forgiving than I am. How they acted is also fucked up. There's no way you would be working for the Salieri."

"Why not?"

He looked up at the ceiling, considering carefully what he was about to say. He wouldn't lie, but he had to admit he was nervous about how she would take the intent of the Salieri's mission. She already felt guilty for the things she'd done under the programming she'd been put through. If that mind fuckery had come from the Salieri, which was almost a certainty with Howard's name showing up, it could make her feel worse. It might cause a panic attack. It could trigger her. She might even devolve completely if her guilt became too great.

Best to just be clear and honest. He'd deal with the fallout, however it came. "The Salieri have very antiquated tenets. Do you know who Dionysus was?"

"He was a Greek god, right?"

"Yes. The Salieri believe in the Cult of Dionysus, but… they've warped the original tenets of that worship. Even in the times when the faithful of Dionysus were active, those outside the cult feared the members' rites and outlawed their practices. The Salieri believe that their divinity is found through male children and dominance, so they sacrifice their brides after they give them a son. Female offspring are also killed."

He turned his head to her. "Women are tools to them. Vessels. They're being taken from their homes, sometimes through kidnappings. Sometimes the women they take are born, married, or directly related to men who are welcomed into the membership. Part of the test of those men's devotion to the cause is to sacrifice all immediate family members who are female. Their wives might be allowed to exist, especially if they can be impregnated and give birth to a male child, but then once the child is born, they're destroyed. Daughters and sisters, if they're of childbearing age, might be sold to a member for breeding purposes, and then again, when a male child is born, they die. If a woman can't bear children, she's next to useless to them."

Her body was tense against him.

"I need you to breathe, Mouse."

After a long silence, she whispered, "That man. Elliott Howard. He was one of their members? He was going to hurt Cherry. Hurt Flame."

"Yes. He wanted them both as his bride to give him a son. We learned a lot of this from Cherry after she was kidnapped. Her uncle was also in the membership. In a warped way, when she was young, he tried to protect her. Then we stumbled into some Salieri business a few years ago, unknowingly, and it's what set this whole train of events in motion. When we rescued Cherry, we captured Giudici and a fellow conspirator, but we've been hunting Howard and Cherry's uncle, Zion Norton, ever since."

There was another pause. He could almost hear the wheels turning in her brain. "So your team thinks I'm a plant. That the Salieri programmed me and then turned me loose at that compound in Egypt, hoping I could get them information. Maybe even hurt one of you."

He turned over onto his side to look her in the eye. "It's not an option we can ignore. At first, I thought maybe you escaped on your own. While you clearly have some fighting skills, they're more defensive than offensive. Otherwise, you would have killed Medusa. I don't know that you necessarily have the demeanor, programming or not, because it's really, really difficult to change who a person is at their core. Nice people can't override their brains that much. In times of stress, can they do unthinkable things to survive? To save others? Sure. But those are temporary chemical boosters. They don't fundamentally change a person's wiring. It would be like..." He searched for an example. "It would be like rewiring TB so that he was a submissive instead of a Dominant. You can condition someone, but at their core, they're still the person they used to be.

"So, yes, I agree with my team that I think you were set loose on purpose. What that purpose is exactly, we don't know. We may never know. An educated guess on my part says that the Salieri know that since Mythos will call us in for help, it's a way for them to flush us out and pick us off one by one.

"They also want to collect their prize. You have blackout periods where you start one place, then suddenly you're somewhere else entirely. Those were probably times when your programming triggered you to contact them. Update them with information. I'm guessing you had one shortly before the attack ensued. You told them you'd be with the group of kids that Ayla ended up with, and they sent foot soldiers to collect you, their tool, so that we couldn't have access to you and learn anything about them from you.

"What they didn't know was that the two of you switched places, and because the two of you look superficially alike, especially to people who didn't know who you were to start with, they went after the wrong woman. Something must have clued them in when they finally caught her, so then all their attention focused back on the compound. Suddenly, they're fighting us, trying to find you. They're fighting Mythos as well, and they come up empty-handed.

"We thought they were after those kids. It wasn't until the Mythos guards, who had been with the larger group of children, told us how focused they were on getting to the teacher that we realized maybe the children were never the target. You were. And you were a means to get to us."

Her face filled with anger. "You should lock me up. I could still hurt you all. If I black out again, there's no telling what I'll do."

"Not. Happening." He leaned in and began kissing her. Soft, chaste touches to her lips. His free hand rested on her hip, his thumb brushing back and forth across her bare skin. Each caress of his mouth and his hand was intended to bring her back to him, much like she had distracted him in the shower. It took a while, but eventually she shuddered, her muscles losing their tension and allowing her to raise her hands to his chest.

"There you go, *heuning meisie*. Just be with me. It will all work itself out." He was just about to deepen the kiss and start another round of play when his watch beeped four pips. He chose to ignore it. A minute later, another four pips came through. Again, he ignored it. Another minute later, four more pips.

With a huge sigh, he pulled back from Mouse, who was looking all sleepy-eyed and ready for his attention. He really didn't want to talk to this man, but apparently, he was going to be insistent. He glanced at his watch and read the text.

"You've gotta be fucking kidding me," he muttered. He got out of bed and headed into the bathroom.

She clutched the sheet to her chest and sat up on one elbow. "What is it?"

He came back into the room, pulling his pants on, then rustled around in his pockets for his earbud case. Slipping one in his ear, he clicked a button on his watch and then zipped up while he waited for the other end of the line to pick up. "What do you want?"

"I want to talk to Mouse."

"Dude. Can it wait?"

"Did I interrupt something? What am I saying? Of course I did."

"Doesn't matter if you did or didn't, D. I still don't think it's a good idea for you to talk to her right now."

"I disagree," the medic said. "I think it's the perfect time. Just let me talk to her, and then I won't bother the two of you until we leave the day after tomorrow."

"Only if she agrees. If she says no, you're left with your dick out and swinging." He looked at Mouse. "It's Demon. He wants to talk to you. You up to it, or you want to wait?"

She was instantly awake and looking panicked. "Me?"

"You."

"Now?"

"Yeah. Now. His timing sucks." That was more for Demon than her.

She gestured down her body and whispered, "I can't talk to him like this. I'm not even dressed."

He didn't dare tell her that Demon heard that comment. The pickup on their watches was extensive. "Give us ten minutes." He severed the connection and popped the earbud from his ear.

He put his fists on the mattress and leaned over to kiss her nose. "Get dressed, let's hear him out, then we'll go back to bed."

Ten minutes later, there was a knock at the door. Gun pointed down at the floor at his side, safety off, Midas looked through the peephole to see Demon standing there.

"Code?"

Demon gave him the signal that he was alone and all was well. Midas opened the door, let the medic in, and didn't put the safety back on or holster his weapon until the door was locked behind the man. When he turned to face the room, he saw Demon and Mouse standing, staring at each other. The medic stood with his arms down at his sides, fists unclenched, deceptively calm. Mouse, on the other hand, had her arms crossed over her chest, her chin up, her face defensive.

He was about to cross past Demon to stand at her side when the man turned his head in profile. His eyes stayed on Mouse, but it stopped Midas in his tracks. "I'd like to talk to you. Alone."

"Fuck no," Midas said. "Have you lost your tiny Irish mind? I'm not leaving you alone with her."

"I just want to talk to her."

"I don't care if all you wanna do is look at her. I'm not leaving her alone with you."

He started to move in her direction, but when he came even with Demon, the man put out his arm and stopped him. "Ten minutes. That's all I'm asking. And if we finish early, I'll stay until you come back."

"Now you're talking not just crazy, you're talking insanity. Even if I left the room, I wouldn't leave the hallway outside this room."

His arm still outstretched and holding Midas back, Demon turned his head to Mouse. "She knows I'm not going to hurt her."

"You're right. She knows it because she knows I'm not leaving her alone."

"Midas!" His head snapped in her direction. "It's okay. Go. Take a walk. Come back in ten minutes. I'll be fine."

"Ana—"

"Kash. Go."

He wasn't sure if he should be mad or concerned. He didn't want to leave them alone. Not since his first days at Tribe had he not trusted one of the team. Their first project together had been one of the most harrowing, perhaps because they weren't used to working together yet, and it had driven them to trust each other quickly, even as jaded as they'd all been. To not trust Demon now felt alien. Unnatural. Wrong. Given his actions this afternoon, though, he couldn't help it. "I'm not leaving," he insisted.

"Kash. Please. Go. I'll be fine."

There was something about the way she said it. She was asking without asking, and once again, he needed to do as she wanted in order to keep his promises. He ground his teeth in frustration. He needed to trust Demon. More importantly, he needed to trust her.

"I'll be back in ten minutes. Not a second more." He swiped the key card off the side table and stormed out of the room.

39

FEBRUARY 11, 2024

Mouse

THE CLICK OF THE DOOR ECHOED IN HER BRAIN. SHE DOUBTED he was far away. In fact, she would be willing to bet he was standing right outside the door, waiting to bust in if she screamed bloody murder if Demon attacked her.

Despite Midas' reluctant exit from the room, she and Demon remained where they'd been standing from the moment he entered the room. The only sound she heard was the ticking of the heating unit behind her as it geared up to begin running again.

Abruptly, Demon moved in her direction, and she felt herself go completely rigid. She should have realized that he wasn't aiming for her because the angle of his body was to her right, but she was so paranoid right now, it didn't register. When he came up alongside her, then passed behind her, she was confused. What was he doing?

She heard the cracking of a seal, then the sound of liquid being poured into a glass. Refusing to turn, she concentrated on the continuing sounds behind her. The pouring stopped quickly, then started again. The pouring stopped again, then there was the sound of a cap being screwed back on, and the clunk of something being set on the table. Moments later, a glass came around the front of her, filled with a golden liquid. She looked down at the glass, then followed the arm it was attached to, up into the brilliant green eyes of the team's medic.

"Take it," he told her, his hand lifting higher to her.

Shakily, she took the glass he held, leaving it up in the air awkwardly. He didn't come back around to the front of her, but she did hear him moving. By the window, maybe? She remained standing where she was, lowering the glass to a more comfortable position, her other hand supporting it from underneath.

When he spoke, his voice was low and quiet, as if he, too, knew that Midas was standing outside the door, straining to hear what he had to say. "I love four things in this world. My surfing, my whiskey, which you have in your hand, my team, and my woman. I could give up the first two. I don't have to worry about the third because they can protect themselves. But Cherry? She's my everything. *A chuisle.*"

Mouse turned to him. "What does that mean?"

He shot the entire contents of his glass. "It translates to 'my pulse.'"

She didn't know where he was going with this, so she remained silent.

He refreshed his glass from the bottle on the table. "You never really know how good you have it until it's gone. It's a cliché, but it's true, like all clichés are. I had the perfect life for a long time. A family who loved me. A stellar education. A job I excelled at as a trauma surgeon at a premier hospital, and then one rogue wave set forth a chain reaction that changed the course of my life. I lost everything in the space of four months. My family. My job. My self-respect.

"Then Tribe found me and saved my life. Literally. I was one, maybe two days from going out on my surfboard and never coming back to shore. The day I met the men I work with? I had a family again. People I cared about. People worth sacrificing for. That's also the day I met her. *A chuisle.* My pulse. Some would call me overly poetic or dramatic, but until her? I don't think I ever truly understood what it meant to love someone so much that you'd die for them.

"I didn't realize it at first. I just thought she was someone who made me feel alive again." He stared down into the contents of his glass, as if it held all the answers. "From the moment Waters met Kubrick two years ago, all it took was seeing them together one time, and we were committed to protecting her. He didn't have to make her part of the tribe. Truth be told, we were all a little bit in love with her from the moment we met her. It was like she opened a door that God—our boss—had forbidden us to open. We didn't have to. She crashed through from the opposite side, and that door was forever destroyed.

"When Waters made her part of the tribe, she could have murdered someone"—she saw him huff in a silent laugh—"and we would have done whatever was needed to protect her and keep her from harm.

"Since then, three more women were added to the tribe. Flame, Gem, and Cherry. Three women that my brothers and I added to our lives, and it never crossed my mind to question their loyalty because I didn't question theirs. So when I claimed Cherry? Although technically, she was already part of the tribe because she worked there, it never occurred to me that someone would object. That she wouldn't be protected like the others. It just wasn't a question. Now there's you. Midas claimed you as his, and for the first time in my life, I forgot what being part of a tribe meant."

"Not surprising, given what little we know about me and what I'll do."

She saw her reflection, hazy in the window. He shifted his gaze from the snow that had started outside to her real person inside the room, and he took a swallow of the whiskey. Then he stared down into the liquid he swirled absently in the glass. "It's never been a spoken thing; we just did it. If we claimed someone as tribe, it didn't matter who they were, what they did, nothing. If they were tribe, then they were accepted without question. I forgot that today, and I'm sorry. You didn't deserve that."

"I'm a danger to the group. That includes Cherry. If someone were a danger to my other half, I think I'd be unapologetic to anyone who posed a threat to them."

"Maybe you are, maybe you aren't." He looked up at her. "But Midas loves you, and he believes in you. That means I should as well."

She chose to ignore the medic's statement about Midas loving her. "You don't even know me."

"I may not know *you*, but I know beyond the shadow of a doubt that you love Midas. It's in your eyes every time you look at him. I also know that any time something has come up with your past, if it has been potentially damaging to us, especially him, you're far more concerned with what it means to others rather than yourself. I know you love those girls. It's an integral part of every interaction with them. When we first brought you here, your first concern when you swam up out of unconsciousness was them, not yourself. Your devotion to others is part of who you are. It's so deep in you that there's no way you could be working with the Salieri willingly.

"And that's what I should have remembered rather than losing my head. I at least owed you the courtesy of voicing my concerns in private to the others, not accusing you based on a piece of paper someone left behind for you. To be honest, I shouldn't even have any concerns, but I'll chalk that up to my love for Cherry and my worry at how the Salieri have destroyed everything important to her. How they nearly took her from me when we'd just barely committed ourselves to one another. She is the reason my heart continues to beat. The reason I'm able to keep living. Well and truly, my pulse." He smirked and took a sip from his glass, looking back out into the snow. "People do stupid shite when they're in love."

Of all the deadmen, Mouse was most intimidated by Demon. Other than earlier today, he'd been kind to her. But he spoke very little, and when he did, it was often bitter, bordering on rage. Today, though, he sounded like a man who was one step from broken, working in the direction of healing instead of breaking. Stepping up beside him, her hand to his arm, she clinked her glass to his. "I do love those girls, and I've fallen hopelessly in love with Midas. At my deepest depth, I know that Tribe will help me. Protect me. I would never willingly harm any of you."

He turned to her, his green eyes boring into hers to show her the seriousness of his words. "I promise, Mouse. We will help you, and we will protect you and the girls so that you don't have to keep looking over your shoulders. There's no option because we accept you all, just as you are."

He gave a small smile, one she'd never seen before, and she bet not many people had.

"Never doubt you are Midas' pulse."

They clinked glasses again and sipped their whiskey. Turning to the window together, Demon put an arm around her shoulders, engulfing her into his side, and they stood there, watching the snow fall, until Midas crashed back into the room exactly at the ten-minute mark. Yep. He'd definitely been waiting just outside the door and staring at the countdown on his watch.

Together, they turned to see him standing awkwardly near the door, looking at them. Demon drained his glass and set it down on the table. With a kiss to her forehead, he exited the room. As he passed Midas on his way out, he grabbed his friend's shoulder, squeezing it tightly, and exited without a word.

Midas stared at her by the window. "You okay?"

His voice was raspy with emotion. She wasn't sure if it was for her, for Demon, or for both of them. In the long run, it didn't matter. It was just enough to know that he cared.

"Yeah. I'm good, actually."

"Good."

He held his hand out to her, and after setting her glass down, she moved swiftly and surely into his embrace. Another kiss, this one to the top of her head, and it was as if this one sealed up all the cracks between the puzzle pieces that were Mouse and the tribe.

"You know, drinking with an Irishman is supposed to bring you good luck."

She gave a short laugh and looked up at him. "Is that true?"

"Hell if I know. Just sounded like the right thing to say."

Snuggling back into his chest, she smiled. "Well, I'm thinking drinking with one particular Irishman will bring me good luck. I get the sense he doesn't share his whiskey with just anyone."

"Nope. As far as I know, he's only shared it with Cherry and you. If we want any of it, we have to buy our own damn bottle." Another quick squeeze, and he backed away. "Come on. It's been a long day. You need rest. Into bed with you. I'll be there in a couple minutes."

40

FEBRUARY 12, 2024

Mouse

THE SNOW THAT HAD BEGUN GENTLY THE NIGHT BEFORE started coming down like a force just before eight o'clock and continued nonstop during the day. Midas and Mouse didn't leave the bed during the morning—Midas working on his laptop, arguing with Nova, and Mouse snuggled into his side with a tablet, reading another book from Flame's catalog. At one point, he caught her wiggling and blushing furiously over whatever was on her screen. She'd been so engrossed in the sexy scene, he was able to close the laptop, steal the tablet, and then read it out loud to her, all while she whined and tried to steal it back.

Her embarrassment quickly turned to elation as he proceeded to show her that, yes, in fact, that particular oral technique did work. Afterward, they were both breathless and giggling like teenagers. She didn't think it was possible to be this happy, and she could only imagine that when they were able to completely indulge, it was going to be heaven.

At some point in the afternoon, she'd fallen asleep, tablet in hand. When she woke, the room was dark. The first thing she noticed was that Midas was gone from the bed. She lay unmoving, studying his form as he sat in the dark, shirtless, glasses on, staring at his computer while sitting at the table by the window.

She started to reach over to turn on the light, but his voice cut through the gray. "Don't bother. Power's out. They've got a generator, but they're using it to keep things refrigerated in the kitchen and emergency lighting in the hallways." He didn't look up from his screen as he typed away at it.

"The snow?"

"Yeah. Power lines are down all over the place."

"How are you working if there's no power?"

"I carry extra fully charged battery packs when I travel. Sometimes I'm out places where there's nowhere to plug in, so it's best to be prepared." Without moving his eyes, he gestured to the countertop where the refrigerator and sink were. "Waters prepped ahead last night and picked up sandwiches at a deli yesterday. Couple different choices there if you're hungry. Eat whichever you want, and I'll eat the other one."

Yet another way he took care of her. She always came first. A grin crept over her face as she realized that was true in more ways than one.

Finally, he looked over at her, then did a double take. "Wow."

"Bedhead that bad?" she said with a laugh.

He shut the laptop and slunk out of the chair to crawl onto the bed, sprawling next to her. "Nope. That cute. You're all tousled. Good nap?"

"Don't even remember falling asleep."

"You're welcome," he teased.

With a snort, she picked up a pillow and hit him with it. "No need to be so proud of yourself."

"I think I have every right to be proud of wearing you out. Means you trust me. You feel safe." He tugged a strand of hair, slipping it behind her ear. "I already want to kiss you again."

She gave an exaggerated sigh. "I suppose."

"Brat." There was absolutely no reproach in his voice for her sassy response.

She watched his slow approach, making sure not to spook her. At first, his lips' touch was chaste, but it only took two kisses like that to ramp up the heat between them. "Lie back," he whispered. Once she was flat to the mattress, he ran one finger up and down her arm. "I'm going to try to move over you, okay? Any point it's too much, just tell me."

"I will."

Using his top arm, he reached over her body to place a hand alongside her shoulder. With the comforter between them, he slid one leg over hers, then the second. Once between her thighs, he made sure to keep his hips as light against hers as possible, his arms in full push-up extension so she had room to escape if needed.

"Doing okay?"

She nodded. "Yes, I'm good."

"I'm going to lower myself slowly."

She marveled at his control. His muscles were taut, and there was no evidence of shaking as he lowered himself to where his elbows were bent. His bare chest was millimeters away from her breasts beneath his hoodie that she had once again appropriated. One deep, excited breath, and their bodies made contact. A sizzle passed through her.

"Still good?"

"Never better."

"Coming down all the way." He lowered himself so that contact was made between their torsos, but he still made sure the bulk of his weight was on his forearms. His fingers began threading through her hair, gently smoothing out the tangles as he looked over her face. "So beautiful, *huening meisie*. So brave." He licked his lips. "I'm going to kiss you now," he warned her.

"Yes, please."

His mouth lowered to hers, his tongue sliding between his lips to lick at the seam of hers. She opened to admit him, and they lay like that, lips and tongues lazily playing with each other, and his hips began an instinctive roll and push against her core.

The subtle movement of his hips against her through the blanket reminded her of the omission between them. Worry passed through her. Was she leading him on if she allowed this? It was too late to prevent what everyone saw. He was falling for her as deeply as she had fallen for him. Falling for her would lead to wanting a permanent relationship and expectations of a family, something he'd openly admitted he wanted. Allowing this madness when he didn't know about her inability to have children was unfair to him.

He drew back from her, leaning on his forearms, positioned so that he could look into her eyes. "You totally tensed up on me. Where did you go, *heuning meisie?* Do you need me to pull back?"

She opened her mouth to tell him the truth, but nothing came out. He was giving her an opening to share where her thoughts were. But they were stuck in this hotel. Stuck in this room together since the hotel was completely full due to the storm taking travelers off the roads. If she told him and he withdrew, their remaining time in this space would be intolerable.

Self-preservation prevented her from uttering the words. After the storm, she'd tell him. That way, if he pulled away, she would be able to make a clean break when they went to Washington, DC.

She wrapped her arms around his neck and pulled him back down on her, his weight like a blanket, protecting her from everything bad in her world. Because Midas' body seemed to run at a higher temperature, heat bubbled up inside her own, rolling to a slow boil, and the cold of the room felt like a gossamer net between them, present, tangible, but unrestricting. Part of the warmth was his natural body heat, but she was convinced it was the emotions he evoked in her and the pleasure he stimulated with a simple touch. She needed to be closer to him.

"Hot," she mumbled between kisses.

He lifted his head, his gaze serious yet hopeful. "Want to get rid of the comforter?"

"Yes. Need you closer."

He rolled to the side, pulled back the comforter, and flipped it over to his side of the bed. Briefly, she felt the warmth of his chest against her hands when he moved back over her, but then he rolled them over so that he was on his back. "Let's start with this. You okay?"

Her body was humming now, electrified with the chemistry between them, unlike the powerless room. She needed him. It was a deep ache inside her. Could she be brave, like he always told her she was, and ask for what she really wanted? She had to try.

"Kash?"

"Yeah, Ana?"

"I know if I ask you to stop, you will. Right now? I don't want you to stop."

41

FEBRUARY 12, 2024

Midas

He stayed locked in place, eyes surveying her to ensure she was comfortable. He registered no fear in her face or posture. Just a little anxiety, but he didn't think it was about the physical contact. "You're nervous."

There was a slight pause before she spoke. "Yes, but normal nervous, I think. Not afraid. Never of you. Aren't you nervous?"

"No," he confessed. "Feel like I've been ready for us forever. You sure you're ready? You don't want to wait until we're back home, somewhere more private? More personal?"

"Snowed in during a power outage with a fierce protector who's also a giant cinnamon roll? Flame would be very disappointed in me if I didn't take advantage of the opportunity."

He smiled and laughed softly. "Yeah, she probably would. Okay," he agreed. "I need to get up for a moment."

He slid out from underneath her, crawled out of the bed, and went over to his duffle bag. When Nemo had given him that giant box of condoms, he'd been irritated. When it came time to pack for travel, he'd literally stood in front of the bag on his bed, darting his eyes between it and the box in question. He certainly wasn't taking the whole box. But should he take some? It was probably pointless, but... he'd decided to take one strip of packages. Didn't hurt to have hope, right?

Now he was thankful.

He dug out the strip and headed back, placing it on the bedside table. Standing at the side of the bed, he faced Mouse. Raising two fingers, he flicked them at her. "Come here, *heuning meisie*."

She crawled over to his side of the bed, then rose up tall on her knees. He put his hands on her arms, gently rubbing them before taking her hands in his and bringing them to his mouth, brushing his lips across her knuckles. "I love you, Ana," he whispered. "Thank you for trusting me. You won't regret it. I promise."

A fleeting look of something crossed her face, and then she squeezed his hands in response. He wasn't hurt that she didn't say it back. For him, it felt like he'd been waiting for her forever, and he'd regretted not telling her how he felt before the trip back to the compound. He wasn't going to squander this opportunity to tell her. But her? Her life had been completely upended, so much thrown her way that this was just one more overwhelming piece of information. When this was all over, she'd figure it out. She'd say it, and then it would mean all the more to him.

He placed her hands on his chest, palms flat, hoping that they would feel his body's warmth and it would have a calming effect on her pulse rate. Then he slid his hands to rest around her neck, his pinkie fingers resting on the bottom where they met her shoulders. He didn't grip her tight but instead used his touch as another grounding point for her, his thumbs brushing back and forth between the curve of her jaw to beneath her ear.

Eye to eye, they gazed at each other for a few moments before Midas moved in for a kiss. Soft, sweet flesh met his as their lips touched, working together to explore each other's mouths. Without request, she opened to him, her hands skimming up his chest, across his shoulders, and down to grip his biceps. As their kiss deepened, she kneaded the muscles in his arms, almost as if she were attempting to ground him.

His hands went to the zipper pull on the hoodie, drawing it down slowly until it pulled free at the stop. His fingers brushed lightly back up the center of the tapes, rasping against the teeth's edges, and when he got to the top of the garment, he peeled away the material from her front and over her shoulders and tossed it to a chair when it was clear.

"You're trembling," he murmured against her lips.

"Anticipation," she confessed.

Her voice was strong as she answered, not rushed, nor hesitant, so he continued to kiss her as he smoothed his hands down her sides to span her waist. After a few more minutes of kissing, he reached up with one hand to cup the nape of her neck and the back of her skull, while the other slid to her back. Supporting her like this, he lifted her slightly from her knees, allowing her legs to unfold from beneath her so that he could sit her down on the bed and place them on either side of his body. Only when he thought she was stable did he pull back from her kiss and lower her to the bedding.

His gaze never left hers as his hands reached for the waistband of her panties, drawing them down her legs and dropping them to the floor. When he stood up, she lay before him, not cringing or trying to hide her body. Her arms were at her sides, her eyes were on him, and she was... stunning.

"You are so beautiful, *heuning meisie*," he praised.

He dropped to his knees on the floor, spreading her legs farther for him to get closer. His eyes fell to her core, where his fingers drew gentle circles on the insides of her thighs, intermixed with straight lines back and forth from knee to groin, all meant to prepare her for a more intimate touch. Clearly, he hadn't needed to worry. She lay, back arched, the linens fisted to the point of ripping when his touch reached her more sensitive spots.

"Keep your eyes on me, Ana. I want to see those beautiful honey-colored eyes as I love you." Curving his palms around the muscles in her calves, he pulled her to the edge of the bed, then slid his hands up to the bends in her knees. Grasping her there, he spread her legs wider, placing one, then the other, over his shoulders.

His eyes never left hers as he lowered his mouth to her pussy, already slick with her arousal. He guided one leg higher on his shoulder so he could slide his arm around the underside of her thigh and reach around her hip to bring his fingers to her mound. Using his fingers to expose her clit from its hood, he began his seduction by swirling the tip of his tongue delicately around the nerve bundle, never touching it outright.

Above him, she sighed with pleasure. She loved oral play, both receiving and giving. If they hadn't been in such an intimate, important moment, he might have taken the time to marvel at that, but right now, all that mattered was making her feel good.

He used his other hand to apply gentle pressure on her opposite thigh, opening her to him as much as he could without stretching her legs to the point of pain. Her scent tantalized him. He needed to be closer, deeper, so much so he lifted her pelvis closer to his mouth, allowing him to reach a better upward angle where he could drag his tongue from her clit to her entrance, swirling it just inside her opening to collect the spicy taste of her.

He'd always been a very logical person. Being gifted at math and computers tended to do that to a person. But for the first time, he allowed instinct to take over. Back and forth, he varied his mouth's touch. He didn't count the number of circles around her clit or her opening. He didn't equalize the number of circles to the up and down strokes he made through her folds. Rather, he simply allowed his body to take over his actions, knowing that as long as she was being led to her orgasm, the time it took was well spent.

In turn, she rewarded him with a moan of want as her shoulders writhed against the bed. Her reactions caused his heart to pound furiously. Spurred on by her obvious enjoyment, he quickened his speed, focusing his tongue to flick repeatedly at her clit. The hand holding her right thigh let go and began reaching for her entrance—wet from his mouth and her own arousal combined.

Turning his palm upward, he extended his middle finger to her entrance and pushed inside. She was warm and silky smooth, not to mention drenched with her own fluids, and he slowly began to move his hand back and forth to get her used to his touch inside her. She moaned softly, and he lifted his head to make sure she wasn't in pain or distress.

Her eyes were still on him, a bit glassy, but needy and not hurting, other than wanting more of what he was being so slow to give her. He smiled at her, watching her honey-colored eyes. "Such a brave, beautiful girl. Ready for more?"

42

FEBRUARY 13, 2024

Mouse

Her thoughts were in tumult. All she could do was stare at him, hoping that her eyes could communicate what she needed to tell him. However, with Midas, everything was about her consent. Her yes. Her no. If she didn't find the words to tell him what she wanted, he would stop. That just wouldn't do.

"Y-y-yes," she stuttered.

The smile he wore grew just a little bit bigger. "*Goeie meisie.*"

Holy crap, she loved when he spoke to her in Afrikaans. No clue what he was saying to her, other than she knew it was something with the word "girl" based on when he called her "heuning meisie." Honey girl. The first word started with G. Was it "good girl"? Holy, holy crap!

"Keep your eyes on me, sweetheart."

Eyes on hers, he continued. Looking at him like this, while he worked her body, was incredibly intimate. Embarrassing yet arousing at the same time. Intense. Focused. That was Midas all the time, so why wouldn't it be that way when he was making love?

When he withdrew his finger, she whined at the loss, then gasped when one became two. The slow pumping of his fingers continued, and his mouth lowered to her clit again. This time, however, his mouth suctioned onto the nerve center, and his digits curled up against her top wall as he pulled them toward her entrance. He sped his actions up a fraction, and suddenly she was toppling off a ledge, free-falling into pure bliss. If she made a sound, she had no clue because she was so lost in the sensation and knew nothing else.

As she came back to reality, she heard him still murmuring against her skin in his native language in between strokes of his tongue through her folds and around her clit. Each stroke of his fingers became slower and slower despite dragging across her inner walls, easing her down through the remnants of her orgasm, and he chuckled slightly when she bucked and gasped at an aftershock that passed through her unexpectedly.

When she was finally free of the full-body tremors he'd induced, he withdrew his fingers from her and stood. She watched through hazy eyes as he stripped out of his athletic pants and grabbed hold of his cock. Lazy strokes up and down, she watched him above her, hoping that he'd stop staring at her and move down over her. There was no rushing Midas, however. He worked on his own timeline, and apparently, he was in "savor" mode.

So she lay there. Might as well get comfortable and enjoy the show, as it were. She raised her body to sit up a little taller on her elbows and scooted back further in the bed, never taking her eyes off him. And really, who could blame her? The man was a six-foot-one, brown-haired, scruffy, soul-sucking, brown-eyed mass of muscle. He looked nothing like a technology geek. But put those horn-rimmed glasses on him, dress him in a tight T-shirt, jeans, and sneakers, then put him behind a computer, and he was her very own version of Clark Kent.

Right now, his Superman side was making her pulse rate skip again.

He tilted his head at her as he reached for the condom strip and tore one off. "What's that smile for, *heuning meisie?*"

She heard the tearing of the wrapper as she answered, "I was just thinking about how you're my version of Clark Kent and Superman."

"Hmm. Man of Steel, eh?"

He rolled the condom on, then knelt on one knee between her legs, hands grabbing her under her armpits and repositioning her even more across the bed.

"Mm-hmm."

He grabbed a pillow and put it underneath her head, kissing the tip of her nose on his way back to kneeling above her.

"I don't plan on racing any bullets, lifting any trains, or leaping off any tall buildings, and I definitely can't fly."

She smiled lazily, one finger lifting to trace the outline of his pectoral muscles. "Well, you can make me fly," she teased.

His smile was beautiful as he looked at her. "Oh really? Should we see if I can repeat the performance?"

"Yes, please," she said on an exhale.

The agreement was no more whispered before he lowered himself to kiss the corner of her mouth. He slid his left arm underneath her shoulders, the hand palming the back of her skull in support. His other hand took hold of his cock and lined it up with her opening. Before going any further, he kissed her again and whispered, "I want forever." A brief pause. "I love you, Ana."

A flash of pain went through her, so she slipped her arms around his neck and pulled him tight with desperation, knowing she was eventually going to hurt him. She prayed he would think that her emotional response was one of happiness and not pain.

"I love you, Kash." She hadn't meant to say it. Now she had compounded the problem, but there was no way to take it back. Truth be told, she really didn't want to. She wanted this with him. Wanted his love. Even if it ended badly, she needed him too much.

Then he was inside her, filling all the space, as if he was meant to be a part of her that no longer existed as a single entity but now existed as "them." Once surrounded by her heat, she should have known better than to be surprised that he didn't move right away. He was all about making the most of moments. Noting the details. Savoring the sensations. So now, he was over her, weight back on his forearms, brushing hair back from her face, and just holding her gaze in his.

Gradually, he began to move. She was glad she hadn't pushed him, letting him set the tempo of when he introduced things, as he said he would do, but allowed her the ability to control the pace of the event itself. It made her feel as if they really were a couple, working together to create a future.

His strokes were slow and even, his hips shifting, working to find the pressure and angle she needed. When he hit something good, she could see how proud he was of himself, that he was making her feel good based on the smile on his face, especially in his eyes.

One particular tilt upward of his hips sent a shiver through her. "More, Kash."

"What the lady wants, the lady gets."

He powered his hips faster, driving himself in as deep as he could, while making sure to angle himself toward the top of her pussy and grinding against her clit to give her the friction she needed, inside and out. When she came, he'd built her to that point so consistently that it was actually a surprise to suddenly find herself falling over the edge and soaring into the void. The only thing she was aware of was him reaching his own peak a few strokes behind her.

Together they lay in the dark, their breathing in sync as their endorphins crashed. Mouse felt her body slipping into the edges of sleep almost immediately. Vaguely, she was aware of Midas leaving the bed. As she drifted further and further into the darkness, she felt him slide back into bed, pulling the covers over her. He gathered her close, cuddling her body into his side, pressing her head gently to his shoulder. Then she knew nothing more.

43

FEBRUARY 14, 2024

Midas

AN ENTIRE DAY SNOWED IN ENSURED THAT MIDAS AND MOUSE had more time to discover each other and the physical side of their relationship. Something had changed though. Midas couldn't put his finger on it. She hadn't withdrawn, yet she had. When he asked her what was wrong, she insisted everything was fine, and then she would proceed to kiss him, distracting him into another round of lovemaking. He didn't mind the distraction, but his skin was starting to itch because he felt like something bad was about to happen between them.

This wasn't how he'd hoped to spend Valentine's Day. Yesterday would have been better, but sometimes you just had to take what you got and be happy with it.

The city started to come back alive in the early hours of the third day, and Mythos assured them that Janus, their pilot while Medusa was still healing from her broken wrist, would be able to take off and get them to Washington, DC, in the midafternoon. As they got closer and closer to departure, Mouse became more and more agitated. While things between her and Demon had recalibrated, and the rest of the team had made sure to reassure her at breakfast that they were all good, he wondered if the strain he had noticed was really more her worrying that this step of the journey wouldn't bring her the closure she needed either.

When they arrived in DC, their first stop was the address that Midas had found for Elliott Howard when Mouse would have been a child. During his initial search for likely locations where the general might hide, it had been difficult to locate the address because it was hidden under layer after layer of shell corporations. That told Midas that it was likely owned by the Salieri. He could probably trace it back for a slew more days and still not get to the source, so Waters told him to hold off on continuing the back search. That was something he could work on when they returned home.

Nemo and Medusa went to the bus station to collect whatever was in the bus locker. Demon and TB took a quick detour to Cherry's old home to make sure that things there were good. Gilgamesh and Loki kept watch at the two ends of the street where Howard had lived, while the rest of the Tribe team went to the property. When they got there, they discovered it was unoccupied and had been for some time.

Midas watched Mouse stand in front of the house, her face pensive. Waters and Steel had her back.

"Something wrong, Mouse?" Midas asked.

"Something feels... wrong."

Midas looked behind them at Waters, who nodded. "I've got a tingle going. The air feels disturbed. Someone's watching."

"Cameras?" Steel offered.

"Don't know." The look on Waters' face was not reassuring.

Steel started to step off to the left side of the house. "I'll check the perimeter." He was off on silent feet, invisible almost immediately.

"Maybe we shouldn't take her inside," Midas said.

Mouse started walking down the driveway without a word.

"Mouse!" Midas shouted. When she didn't even twitch at his call, he tried again. "Ana!"

She kept moving forward.

"Get up alongside her," Waters ordered. He tapped his watch to open a channel. "Nova, Code sixty-six. SOS, level two."

"Affirmative, Waters."

Nova went to work patching the team members into the central communications channel.

When Midas pulled himself to pace Mouse, it was to see the blank expression of a blackout on her face.

"Fuck," Midas whispered. "Ana, come back."

He put his hand on her arm, but Waters had caught up to them and brushed it off.

"Don't disturb her. Let her do what she needs to do. We're here. We're aware. We have no idea what happens if we force her out before she's done what she needs to do."

He hated it, but he knew from his own psychology studies that Waters was correct.

"No one goes off alone," Waters ordered. "Stick to her like glue. Everyone, make your way to Howard's residence immediately. Loki. Gilgamesh. Stay put for now."

Vaguely, Midas heard Nemo informing them they were already on the way back. It was the news from Demon that made his heart feel like it stopped. "Someone's been in Cherry's house. Looks like two someones."

"Any idea who?"

"No identifiers."

By now, Mouse had opened the front door of Howard's house. It hadn't been locked, as if the place knew she was here and simply sat waiting for her. She sailed through the door, and their steps echoed on the marble flooring until Mouse stopped directly on top of a diamond shape.

To their immediate right and left were larger living spaces behind closed doors. In front of them was a hallway that went to the back of the home, traveling beneath two side staircases that curved up to a central walkway on the second floor. There was an arch to the actual hallway behind the small balcony, and on the far wall, a huge round window took up the wall. Had the day been sunny, it would have allowed the rays to set through the panes. But because it had been cloudy most of the day, nothing but gray clouds and treetops could be seen from this angle.

Too many things were converging, and Midas didn't like it.

Silently, Waters went left to begin clearing the house. "Stay here," he mouthed to Midas.

While he was gone, Midas stood, weapon drawn, and pointed down the hallway that went toward the kitchen and powder room. Mouse remained completely still to his right. The silence was eerie, yet the atmosphere vibrated with tension. He wished whatever was coming would just get here.

It was funny—not in a ha-ha way but more of a perverted sense of irony—how in moments of finality, there was premonition. It happened in a matter of seconds. Midas would never be able to tell anyone what brought it on. He just knew from his studies that people often spoke of a ghost walking over their grave, or their hair standing up on end, even an electricity in the air that shouldn't be there, cluing them in that something was about to happen. For him, it was merely a moment of nirvana. Understanding in a flash that he'd made the simplest of errors.

Over his earbud, he heard Demon say they were seven minutes out. The voice came as if from a long way away, distant, and like an echo. It was then he realized his wish for an end to all of this might not come about as he expected, and he felt that right now might very well be his last moments. He'd made a classic mistake. Steel and Nemo were constantly reminding everyone of it. Always look forward, backward, left, right, down, and up.

He hadn't looked up.

The English-accented voice came from the center of the second-floor landing. "I wondered if you'd be foolish enough to bring me my prize." Midas jerked his weapon upward, but the owner of the voice also held a weapon in his hand, which was aimed directly at Mouse. It wasn't a large weapon, but it did have a laser sight on it, and that infamous red dot was pointed right between her eyes.

"Drop your weapon, Norton."

"Oh, I don't think so," came Zion's casual reply. "I've come too far and have too much to lose to just surrender myself. What would be the fun in that?"

"I'm not alone," Midas warned him.

"No, but you don't have your full strength with you either. The two idiots out in the street won't get here in time, and the two on their way here won't make it before I've dealt with you. As for the man in the room to my right, waiting to make himself known? My dear, dear nemesis, Taylor Miller? He won't dare move. If he does, my finger might just slip on the trigger and bring about the end of Anastasiya, and I know you don't want that."

Shit! The man wasn't wrong. While they wanted to take Zion alive, they definitely didn't have the advantage in positioning. He really wished the others would arrive and bring him better odds.

"She can't help you with anything relating to Tribe. She hasn't been told anything of importance."

"Oh, she's been an immeasurable help already, Kash Newton. In ways you'll never know."

The fucker was taunting them. Showing how much he knew. He'd played this hand once before with Cherry, and now he was trying it out on him. Well, it wasn't going to work. He would not be distracted.

"Do you honestly think your little group has been her only assignment? When she proved useless in one avenue, Howard saved her from that hell she was put through in Argentina and made her into a weapon beyond measure."

What the hell did that mean? Clearly, it was confirmation that when she'd been taken from that bus station, it had been by the

Salieri for their breeding program. But he said she'd proven useless there. Did that mean they'd been unsuccessful in getting her pregnant? Luck or something else? If she'd been unable to have children, had they redirected her to make her a pawn for other purposes?

Zion continued, "You all are but the last in a long string of assignments that our little mouse has helped with."

Did he know that was her nickname, or was it just a product of their using her as a mole that brought about his word usage? Midas decided to pry for information to try and stall for help to arrive. "I thought women only served as the role of breeders. The Salieri are finally progressing enough to recognize that women have value beyond their reproductive organs?"

The Englishman laughed. "Women are tools for numerous purposes. We may not have many of them in our ranks, but there are some. Anastasiya has proven to be one of the most useful of them all."

"Yurichenkov trusted Howard to protect her if need be. This is how he paid back his promise? By weaponizing an innocent woman?"

"The Yurichenkovs were outside the Salieri purview, but they were far from innocent. Howard had his fingers in many pies as a way to forward the Salieri cause, and one of those ways was connections to the KGB. The Yurichenkovs and their work for Russia were one of those pies. They broke the rules by falling in love and having a child, so he kept an eye on them, figuring he could use their love for her as a means to get them to toe the line, if necessary. When they refused to follow their protocols, Howard turned them in to their handlers. With the acquisition of Anastasiya Yurichenkov, at least it wasn't a total loss."

"She'll never be yours to use again."

Zion smiled, reminding Midas of a bully he'd once had in school. The kid hadn't liked how Midas always made better marks in school than he did. Thought he could scare him into failing a test so that he could take over the top ranking. He'd thought he could threaten to turn Sawyer in for something he'd done. Something he'd likely have gone to prison for, and the smile on his face when he'd presented his threat looked just like Zion's face right now. That bully had made a terrible mistake with that smile. Just like Zion.

"That's for me to decide, isn't it? Have you figured out yet what triggers her blackouts?"

Midas stayed quiet.

"I'll take your silence as a 'No.' And if you can't ever figure that out, you can't stop the programming. Advantage, me. Right now, however, I'll settle for her being my insurance policy out of here. Do give my regards to my niece, will you?" His eyes remained on Midas, but his next words were to the other room. "Come on out, Mr. Miller. You don't want to risk me shooting your man or his woman. Let me see you."

It was a moment before Waters walked out, hands in the air, his weapon in his right hand. There was no apology in his expression, but Midas saw his team leader's eyes flick toward Zion on the balcony.

"Thank you. Now, put your weapon on the floor and kick it over to Anastasiya, please."

Waters set his gun on the ground and pushed it across the floor.

"Excellent. Anastasiya. Remove Kash's weapon, please, and back him up toward his friend."

Mouse turned in Midas' direction, her eyes completely unfocused, yet she reached for his weapon and took it from his hand.

He wondered if they could stall long enough for help to arrive. It certainly didn't feel like time was on their side.

"I wonder what would be a fitting end for the two of you. Anastasiya taking out her new boyfriend seems appropriate, but you, Miller? I think, perhaps, you and I should take a little trip and start where we left off four years ago. What do you think?"

A screech of tires was heard outside. In a matter of seconds, chaos reigned. Nemo and Medusa came through two shot-out windows on either side of the door. Loki and Gilgamesh came through the back entrance underneath the balcony, and when Zion appeared distracted, Waters began a run for the top of the stairs. It was clear that the cornered man knew he was going to have to use his insurance as a means to cover his escape.

As if in slow motion, Midas watched the gun in Zion's hand begin to swing back in Mouse's direction. Without regard to his own safety, he threw his body in front of her as four shots reverberated in the hall. He dropped like a stone, his entire weight falling on her. Two seconds later, he heard what sounded like the shattering of all the remaining glass in the house, a single rifle retort, and shortly after that, a thud.

Then he heard her scream.

44

FEBRUARY 14, 2024

Mouse

Nothing made sense. A loud noise sounded, seeming to wake her from a deep sleep. Something out of the corner of her eye was coming at her fast, and before she could move out of its path, she was lying on the floor in a room she didn't recognize with a heavy weight on top of her.

A man stood on a balcony, a gun pointed in her direction. All of a sudden, there was an explosion of glass behind him. A huge circular window in the wall shattered, his body pushed out as if an invisible force had shoved him, and then he rolled over the top of the balcony rail and fell to the floor beneath with a thud. He lay on the marble floor, his head turned in her direction, his eyes sightless, and blood pouring out from underneath the back of his head and from his mouth.

She panicked. The weight on top of her was crushing her. She couldn't breathe. Using strength she didn't think she could possibly possess, she worked to roll the weight off.

Only then did she begin to process what she was seeing. There was a man who looked vaguely familiar lying dead on the floor next to her. Flashes of the lab she'd been tortured in sprang into her mind. She'd seen this man before. He'd been asking questions, giving orders, while she was strapped to the chair they held her in for what felt like hours on end. She remembered someone calling him Mr. Norton. He'd always been standing next to a man in a military uniform.

She turned her head in the other direction. While she had no sorrow in her for the death of her captor, she didn't want to look at his lifeless eyes and broken, bleeding body. Unfortunately, when she saw what was on the other side of her, the view was even worse. Midas lay on the floor next to her, red liquid leaking from beneath him as well, the wide stain growing by the second. With great effort, she crawled to him, ignoring the slick wetness on the floor she was slipping through, throwing herself on top of him.

A thundering herd approached her, including nails scrabbling on the flooring.

"Kash, you *doos*, what have you done?" Nemo was next to her on his knees, his voice laced with terror.

Looking at Midas, she could see he was conscious, but he wasn't moving. "Kash?"

"Ana," he whispered. His voice was pinched. "You okay, *heuning meisie?*"

"I'm not hurt, but I'm scared. You're bleeding. Where are you hurt?"

"My back. I can't..." His face showed strain, but he didn't sit up. "I can't move."

She gasped. "What do you mean you can't move? Of course you can move. It will probably hurt worse, but you can move." She said it as if her words would ensure it. Panic grew tighter and tighter in her belly. Acid burned in her stomach, fighting its way up her throat.

The ever-growing sound of running feet had stopped and become the soughing of out-of-breath people standing around them.

She knelt in the still-growing pool of blood—his blood—Nemo by her side. Scheherazade lay down at his head, whining, looking at Nemo in confusion. She swiped a wet tongue across Midas' forehead.

"Kash, you need to get up," she implored. "I know you're hurt, but we need to get you help."

"I'm not going anywhere, Ana." He was able to turn his head and weakly raise his hand to her. "He hit me in the back. I can't feel anything in my legs," he admitted. He looked up. "Get her out of here, Nemo. She can't see this."

"I'm not leaving you." She scooted up to his head, picking it up and placing it in her lap, stroking it. She was leaving streaks of blood in the close-cropped hair, but she didn't care.

"Mouse." Nemo reached out a hand to touch her arm. "Sweetheart, we need to get you out of here. You really don't want to see this. He'll haunt me for the rest of my life." His voice was shaking, his eyes glassy.

"What are you saying?" she whispered, her eyes welling up with tears. "Haunt you? No. He's not going to die. He can't die." She looked down into his face in her lap. "I won't let you."

Midas gave her a sad smile. Reaching his hand up to her face, he caressed her cheek, leaving a faint red smudge upon the bone. "I'm not sure anything can stop that now, *heuning meisie*. Go. Please. Don't stick around for this."

More feet came running. Demon. He came to Midas' other side. Hands began to search his body for wounds. "Fecking arsehole," Demon growled low in his throat. "Why the hell didn't you back out the front door, stupid git? We were almost here. He wouldn't have gotten far."

It wouldn't be long before sirens started approaching. Surely the neighbors would have heard the gunshots and reported them by now.

Midas winced as Demon probed his shoulder. "The shoulder isn't the problem."

The medic looked at Nemo, then Midas.

"Where?" Demon questioned.

"Low back. It won't hurt if you move me."

Demon cursed again. "Help me, Nemo." Together, they rolled him on his side toward Nemo. "Why is it the low-maintenance ones are always the most dramatic?"

He began poking at the wound and watching Nemo's reaction. "Anything?"

The blond twin looked up and shook his head.

Mouse looked from Nemo to Demon. Both expressions were blank, but she knew that if Midas wasn't reacting to the medic's prodding, it wasn't good.

"It's just temporary, right?" she whispered. She couldn't keep the fear out of her voice.

Demon looked at Nemo. They seemed to communicate something between them. Then Demon looked at her. "Mouse, I don't believe in sugarcoating things. He's lost a lot of blood. He'll go into shock soon and then pass out. If there's any hope, we have to get that bullet out of him because it's pressing on his spine right now, causing at least temporary paralysis. We have to get him out of here before the police show up." He looked up at Medusa. "I need a path out of here."

"Got it," Medusa said. "Loki and Gilgamesh have blocked the road. That will give us a few extra minutes. I'll go get the car and pull it up to the back."

"There's no road there," Steel said. He came out of the darkness of the hallway, his rifle slung over his shoulder, and stood over Zion's body. He was the one who took out the window, then shot Zion from a tree.

"I don't need a fucking road to drive," she told him. Then she was out the front door to grab the nearest vehicle.

Midas begged, "Nemo, please get her out of here." His voice was weaker.

When Nemo touched her again, she shook him off, her voice

positively feral. "Don't touch me! I'm not leaving him. Not for a second." She looked down at Midas' face. "You said you wanted forever, Kash. I'm holding you to it." She leaned down to kiss his lips. "I love you. You don't leave the people you love if there's breath in your body to avoid it."

His hand reached for her bicep, where it crossed over his body so that her hand could grip his opposite shoulder to keep him in her lap. "It's okay to go, *heuning meisie*. You're not really leaving me. I know you're with me."

"No." Quiet and steadfast.

"Ana." His body began to shiver with cold.

"No, Kash. Now shush." She looked up at Demon. "If he dies, I will shoot you myself."

Demon searched her eyes. Then he smiled. "Such a bloodthirsty little thing. I guess it really is the quiet ones you have to watch out for." He nodded. "Challenge accepted. And if I screw it up, I'll even stand still."

The sound of a truck horn came from out the back door. Waters spoke for the first time. "We need to find a safe place. Police are three minutes, if we're lucky. Our hotel is close but too public."

"Cherry's house." Demon stood up, wiping his blood-soaked hands on his pants. "Grab him. I'm pretty sure the bullet is lodged in the bone, but even if it isn't, we can't risk being here when the police arrive."

Waters and Nemo both leaned down and grabbed an arm, hoisting it over their shoulders. They began to drag the much larger man toward the west-end door and the waiting jeep.

Nemo grunted. "Dude, you need to go on a diet. Or shrink. It's like hauling a frickin' semi."

Midas mumbled his response. "I'll take my size... over your brains... any day, brother mine."

The response was spaced out every few words. It was getting hard for him to breathe, and at any second, he could go unconscious.

They hauled him into the truck just as the sirens could be heard. Nemo raised his hands for Mouse to help her in the back, Scheherazade bounding in quickly behind her. "Know you won't leave him, sweetheart. Keep talking to him. We need him awake as long as possible," he whispered. He ran around the vehicle to the front passenger seat, exchanging quick words with Waters.

Demon jumped in the back. As soon as he was inside, Medusa gunned the vehicle into motion.

Nemo shouted over the roaring engine noise. "Loki and Gilgamesh will stall the blue line as long as they can. Waters and Steel are going to take care of the body. We won't be able to do much about the blood, but with no bodies, they can't prove anyone's dead, and they won't find Midas' blood in any database."

They had put the seat down flat, and she sat with Midas' head in her lap again, smoothing her fingers down his face. His hand held one wrist, his grip tight, but his eyes were closed. As long as he didn't let go, she had hope. He was still with them.

She knew that Demon, Nemo, and Medusa would be able to hear her, but she was beyond caring. She needed him to not just hear her voice but listen to what she was saying.

"I did not survive all of this to be left alone, Kash Newton. You said I was in charge of all the yeses and noes. Well, this is a hard no. You are not going to die on me."

She felt a weak squeeze from his hand.

The ride to Cherry's house was short in distance, but it felt like it was taking forever. She bent over Midas' head, whispering who knew what to him. Anything to keep him talking and with them.

"Ana?"

"Yes, Kash?"

"Don't shut yourself away. Promise me."

"Shh. Stop. We are not talking about this right now."

"Promise me."

She felt a weak squeeze from his hand, and then it went lax, slipping from her wrist to lay limp on his chest. She couldn't hold in the sobs.

"Demon!" she wailed.

"Almost there, Mouse. Hold on to him." He shouted up to the front. "Gun it, Medusa. I've still got a pulse, but it's getting weaker."

FEBRUARY 14, 2024

Mouse

CHERRY'S CHILDHOOD HOME SAT ON AN EXTENSIVE PATCH OF land, so it was somewhat isolated from its neighbors, and even if seen, two large SUVs wouldn't have caused much of a stir in the neighborhood. The house was far enough off the main road that no one should notice them there.

The kitchen rapidly became an emergency surgery. Demon drew the line at allowing her inside while he worked. After the Mythos crew huddled in private for a discussion, they convinced Demon to allow them to call Janus in from the airport to assist since he had medical training from his time in the military.

Had they been in L.A., things would have been much easier. Tribe had its own surgery since they had to keep all of their work out of the public eye. Hard to explain how there was a living dead man on your operating table. They were fortunate to have this space to retreat to, but she worried that he needed an actual hospital.

Mouse stood in the main bathroom, trying to scrub all the blood off her hands. Her clothes couldn't be saved as they were soaked through. She'd just have to work hard at not looking at herself because it was near impossible to think positively about Midas coming out of surgery in one piece based on the sheer amount of his blood that covered her. Even Waters had winced when Nemo pulled her away from Midas on the table.

As she was drying her hands, wondering if another scrubbing would get the slight pink stain still embedded in the lines of her palms, a knock sounded from the doorframe. Demon. If he was here, the news wasn't good. Otherwise, he'd be with Midas.

He was also covered in blood, but his hands and arms had been scrubbed clean. He stepped into the room and leaned back against the vanity, gripping the counter with his hands. She clutched her stomach and undid all the hard work she'd just done cleaning her hands, as they were now once again in the wetness of the blood Midas had left behind on her.

"How bad?" she whispered.

He looked her straight in the eye. "He has four wounds. The two in the shoulder are through-and-throughs. Nonthreatening, and we've stopped the bleeding. Same for the bicep in the same arm."

"The back?" Her stomach plummeted like an out-of-control glass elevator. She could see the past few weeks whizzing by and could do nothing to stop it from eventually hitting the ground and bursting into a million pieces.

"The bullet is lodged in his spine. I have two choices. I can try to remove it. It's the best option for him, but there's a risk of infection, significant nerve damage, and it's possible he could be wheelchair bound the rest of his life. It might never totally heal. However, it's also the higher risk option.

"Lower risk is that I can leave the bullet there. It would take a very long time, but the bone would eventually compress over the bullet. If, and it's a big if, he would ever walk again, it would be limited. Most likely, it would be minimal, and he would be wheel-chair dependent."

"But he'll live?"

Demon's gaze seemed to get more intense. "There's still risk, and it's high either way. I'd prefer if he had a specialist, but... he's stuck with me. He could live, and I could screw it up. Nick something, make it worse. I can't guarantee anything."

"But you were a trauma surgeon. You did this kind of thing all the time. That's what the girls told me."

"It's been a long time."

"He'll hate it if he can't walk again."

"Who wouldn't? But his job with Tribe, the IT portion, is pretty much stationary. He could still do it from a wheelchair."

"I don't care what happens as long as he lives. I love him. I want him however I can have him," she admitted.

"I need you to tell me what you want me to do. I can't guess. You have to say it."

"Why me? I'm nothing to him. Doesn't he have some sort of directive or whatever for if something happens to him?"

"Yes, but... he changed it before we returned to the compound in Egypt. I only know because Cherry was working on it. Nemo used to be his decision-maker if he couldn't do it himself. Now it's you, and he's unconscious at the moment, so I can't ask him." He shifted his arms to cross them over his chest. "Either way, tell me what you want me to do."

Mouse bit her lip. "Take the risk," she whispered. "It's what he would want."

Demon nodded and stood. "Okay. It's going to be a while. Several hours. You should rest, if you can. Medusa and Loki went to the hotel and brought our gear."

She nodded. "Thank you, Demon."

He started to turn away from her, so she reached out and grabbed him by the arm, clutching him with both hands in desperation. "I know you'll do everything you can, but don't feel guilty if it doesn't work out. He'd hate it if he could never walk again, but I need him with me, no matter the circumstances. Please." Her last word was a whisper.

He grasped her hands in his, then pulled her in tight for a hug. "I know it will be hard, but try not to worry. Get cleaned up. Grab some food downstairs. I'll let you know when I know something."

She didn't trust herself to speak, so she merely nodded. She made it to the shower before bursting into gut-wrenching sobs, collapsing in the corner, clutching the bar of soap in her hands.

AFTER PULLING HERSELF TOGETHER, MOUSE STRETCHED UP AND out to the faucet to turn off the water, then crawled out of the shower. Using the countertop as leverage, she hauled herself off the floor. The woman she saw in the mirror looked hollow. Granted, she'd gone into a blackout, done who knew what, was almost taken back to whomever, shot at, and covered in her boyfriend's blood, but she hadn't counted on the physical devastation that was showing in her reflection. She had bruises on her arms and neck from being taken down onto the ground by Midas when he'd been shot. However, it was the lifelessness in her eyes, the dark smudges beneath them, and the deathly pallor in her face that made her look like a skeleton.

She dried off using a towel someone had found packed away and left for her on the counter, then she padded out to the primary bedroom to her small duffle bag that Medusa had brought from the hotel.

She put on a bra, panties, and leggings, then went to Midas' go bag, which Medusa had also brought with her. As soon as she opened the bag, she smelled his rainwater scent and pulled out his rugby hoodie. It was the one he'd worn the night of their make-out session in his bed at Tribe. It was ridiculously huge on her, but she needed to have him next to her skin.

When she opened the door, the smells of fried chicken were wafting faintly through the hall. The scent increased exponentially with each step down the stairs and toward the dining area. Spread out along the sideboard were aluminum pans filled with chicken, mashed potatoes and gravy, steamed vegetables, dinner rolls, and salad fixings. The team was gathered around the large dining room table, no one wanting to be too far from each other as they waited for news from the impromptu surgery that had been set up in the kitchen.

Medusa brought her a plate with a little bit of everything on it. "Eat. I know you don't want to, but you have to."

A glance at the end of the line of food saw a takeout bowl of barbecue sauce, its deep red color reminding her of the blood pooling beneath Midas on the marble floor.

"Breathe, Mouse," Medusa encouraged her. She rubbed light circles on her back. "You're going to have moments like that. Moments where things pop up, and you're going to feel like you've been derailed, but you can't let it keep you off track. You need to find a way to push it back." She steered Mouse to a seat between Nemo and TB. "Now eat. And don't let Nemo steal any of your food. He's been eyeing up that chicken leg since I put your plate together."

"Hey!" he mockingly complained. "Scheherazade's hungry."

The dog looked forlornly at Mouse, then squeezed under the table to lie across her feet. Even the dog knew she needed comforting.

There was silence at the table, each of them straining to hear anything at all from the kitchen, but the solid oak doors hid all sounds. Waters' watch pinged. He glanced down at the text.

"Demon's on his way out."

Janus appeared first, his face a bit gray, his expression one of exhaustion. He limped over to the sideboard, where Medusa handed him a plate, saying something to him where he stood frozen, the words so soft that no one could hear. Mouse's stomach plummeted again, and her heart felt as if it were lodged in her throat, beating at the walls to escape.

Nemo clasped her hand in support. The others projected a distinct lack of emotion, but the tension in the room was palpable.

When Demon entered through the door, he took a moment to stretch, both hands to his lower back as he dipped backward. He winced, obviously in pain from standing so long, then did a quick scan of the room. His demeanor was stiff, but even though he was obviously in considerable pain from all the hours on his feet, she sensed the tension wasn't regarding Midas. "I pulled the bullet. He's stable for now. I'll watch him through the night. I'm cautiously optimistic he'll wake up since he made it through. We should move him back to Tribe as soon as he can physically travel."

Mouse collapsed into Nemo.

"All I can tell you is that if he wakes up, I'm positive he'll pull through as long as there's no infection. We've left the wound open to drain it and keep it clean, which in this unsterile environment is going to be tough. I didn't see any floating bone fragments, but I'll need to scan him in order to be sure, and I can't do that until we can get him home. I don't want anything floating around in there nicking an artery or something vital if it moves around. As for walking?" He shrugged. "I have no clue if or when. No matter what, he's got a long recovery ahead of him. We're going to be out an IT guy for a while."

TB spoke up. "I'm probably next in line as far as most versed in his work. I can help out."

Waters grunted. "Thank heavens for Nova. Did you update God?"

Demon's face took on an odd expression. "He's aware."

Frowning, Waters asked, "What does that mean? Aware?"

"It means, he didn't have to update me. I was already here."

All heads snapped toward the buffet line at a well-recognized voice. He plopped his plate down on the table and similarly fell into an empty chair. "You didn't think I wouldn't be here when one of my team was in danger of dying, did you?" He turned to his food and began to dig in.

"Ho-ly fuck," TB whispered.

Waters and Steel just stared.

Nemo and the rest of the Mythos members didn't even react.

Waters looked long and hard at Nemo. "You knew?"

"Not until I joined Mythos. And I was sworn to secrecy, so I couldn't tell you. It didn't really seem like it mattered, to be honest."

Waters returned his gaze to the formerly faceless voice of Tribe. "For seven years, you've hidden behind an intercom. Why?"

Propping his elbows on the table, fingers threaded together, fork in hand, he finished chewing before speaking. "For most of those years, I was confined to a wheelchair with an injury much like Midas'. When we started Tribe, I didn't believe my condition was fixable, and I also didn't believe that my situation would engender confidence from my new team. Not only that, but what put me in that chair caused me to be a very wanted man. I needed to hide in the shadows."

"You're not in a wheelchair now. What changed?" TB asked.

"It's a very long story, best served for another time. The short version is, I finally decided the surgery was worth the risk. Just before Gem came to us, I left to have the surgery done. I can walk again, but it was a rough go. I only barely managed to evade all of you at the safe house when Nemo was taken.

"Suffice it to say that when Midas was put in jeopardy, I didn't think it was wise to stay in the shadows any longer. I couldn't be there to help you and Sarah in Egypt." His face was grim. "I was useless when Nemo was taken. I wasn't about to not be here, again, when the need was so dire."

To her, this conversation meant nothing. She didn't understand exactly why this was all so important, but it wasn't what mattered to her. Right now, she felt she had the right to a selfish attitude. "He's going to be okay?" Her voice was quiet as she interrupted the bomb that had just been dropped.

"Like I said, if he wakes up, I'm confident he'll be okay. We just need to prevent infection," Demon repeated.

Before anyone knew what happened, she ejected from her chair, barreled around the table, and grabbed Demon around the waist, her head to his chest, squeezing the life out of him. "Thank you," she whispered.

Demon extracted his arms from her spider monkey clutch, then lowered them gingerly to hug her around the shoulders. "You're welcome," he whispered against her hair. "If you want to go see him, you can, but you can't touch him. I'm sorry. He's at enough risk for infection as it is."

She looked up at him, tears in her eyes. "It's fine. I don't want to risk it either." She smiled and said with a slight teasing tone to her voice, "I'm glad I don't have to shoot you."

He winked. "I'm glad I don't have to be shot."

Without a backward glance, she pulled free of his arms and dashed into the kitchen.

MIDAS WAS LYING ON HIS STOMACH ON THE LARGE FARM TABLE. They had done the best they could to make him more comfortable, but it wasn't a hospital bed. Not that those were very comfortable either, but this was basically a hard slab. They had elevated his head on a folded towel and turned it to the side so he could breathe easier. They'd used whatever they could find to strap him down to the table —an array of belts, bungee cords, and rope—so that when he awoke, he wouldn't move and damage himself further.

She had no idea what they could have possibly used for an anesthetic, so the straps would have been to hold him down during the removal of the bullet as well. But then again, he hadn't been able to feel anything from his waist down, so perhaps they hadn't needed anything in the end. A sobering thought.

Quietly, she crept up to the side of the table. She pointedly ignored the open wound in his back, preferring not to see what was below the tented sheet they'd improvised over him to try and keep out dust and debris at least. Instead, she pulled a chair over to the table, making sure to sit more than arm's length away so she wouldn't forget and touch him.

He looked terribly pale, and he didn't stir. She wondered when he'd wake up. She needed to see his beautiful brown eyes to feel as if he really was going to be okay, even if it took time. She had all the time in the world.

"Hello, Kash," she whispered. "I just saw Demon. He says you need to wake up, and when you do, that will let us know you're going to be okay."

He lay still. Not even a flicker of an eyelid or a twitch in his face. She desperately wanted to reach out and touch his face, to run her fingers along the side, to reassure herself that he really was there in front of her. He was so still, she'd swear he was dead.

"Thank you for protecting me," she continued, "although I must admit I'm pissed as hell that you put yourself at risk. When you wake up, you're going to get an earful about it too. Not right away, but eventually."

She hitched her chair a little closer. "You wouldn't believe who showed up to see you today. I don't understand all of it, but your boss was here. Not Waters. The bigger boss. God. Apparently, you've seen him several times and never knew it. Mythos calls him Janus. Kinda makes sense, huh? Apparently, he runs both Mythos and Tribe. Janus, the two-headed god. One face looking backward, at the past. Mythos. Never forgetting. One face looking forward, at the future, making a path to another life. Tribe."

She stopped, her voice wavering. Hands to her face, elbows to her knees, she began crying. She was so scared. Why wouldn't he wake up? She needed him to wake up. To look at her and smile. To tell her everything was going to work out. That he'd always be with her.

Another presence entered the room. His limp was very pronounced, and he looked completely done in, but he came to stand behind her, a hand coming down to smooth her hair from the top of her head down to her shoulder. A very fatherly gesture. "Keep talking to him, Mouse." Janus. Or God. She wasn't sure which name she should call him. "He'll hear you, but you need to keep talking to him. Remind him why he needs to come back to us."

She sat up, teary-eyed, to look Midas' boss in the face. The man was big. Tall and broad, like TB, but with dark-blond hair and cat-green eyes. She stood up, offering him the chair. "You should sit."

He shook his head and declined the offer. "No, I'll be heading up to bed shortly. Being on my feet like this is torture. I now know how Demon feels if he doesn't take his medication." He patted her shoulder. "Midas needs you to stay here with him for a bit. If he finds me here and hears the news, he'll want to kick my ass, and that won't work out well for either of us."

"Shouldn't Nemo be here?"

"He will be soon. I imagine Demon will come in and kick you out of here to get some sleep eventually. Nemo will come see him then." He slipped a hand beneath her chin to raise her eyes to his. "Love him hard, girl. He deserves that. He deserves you. For so long, Midas has been alone. Even when he was with Nemo, he was alone. It's not easy being in charge of people, even if it's just one person. He's had to fill so many roles that I think Midas has always been a little lost.

"Not that he'd complain, but meeting everyone else's expectations makes for lonely work. In the last year, he's started to finally come into his own, and he's going to need someone at his side to remind him to be brave enough to be who he's supposed to be."

She sniffled. "Himself."

Janus smiled. "Exactly. Knew he'd chosen well when he chose you. Of all my deadmen, he was the one I worried about the most. Turns out, he should have been the one I worried about the least."

He turned and limped out of the room. The door closed softly behind him as he left. Mouse remembered his instruction—to keep talking to Midas. She racked her brain for what to talk about.

"I remember the first time I saw you. It was only for a few seconds, but you were larger than life. My body hurt everywhere, and I was scared that the girls had been hurt, or worse yet, left behind. Your eyes were so kind, and for the first time in a long while, I felt safe and not so scared anymore.

"Then I woke up in your apartment. I was convinced you'd been a dream, but you came out of the shadows, and you took my breath away. It hurt to breathe, you were so beautiful. You were a complete stranger, but there was never a moment when you made me feel cornered, despite the fact that I was helpless to save myself if I'd needed to.

"You did everything you could to take care of me." She reached out a hand. Although she couldn't touch him, she let her hand follow the contours of his face in the air around him, sending as much of her love for him through the energy between them. "That's who you are, Kash. When you've felt like you needed to be all things to all people, you were really just one thing. A protector. That's it.

"I knew you were special the day you brought the girls to see me. You knew exactly what the best medicine was for me to feel better, and it was the first kindness that anyone had shown me in a long time, I think. Then you introduced me to your friends. They were so fun. No judgment. Concerned for me, the girls, and just all around good to each other.

"But I fell in love with you the day you took us all to the pier. I saw what I wanted so badly for myself. A family. Maybe not completely by blood, but a tribe bound by love for one another."

She clutched her stomach by wrapping her arms around herself. "I have a confession. Multiple times I tried to tell you, but if I did, I knew I'd lose you. Watching you with the kids, it was clear how much you loved them, and when you started talking to me about your one regret being that you always wanted a big family, I felt trapped in the omission. You talked about wanting kids, and..." Her voice caught on a lump in her throat. "I can't have children. I'm too... damaged inside. From those first years I was missing.

"I should have said it the minute you mentioned children, but I was petrified, and then after that, it never seemed like there was a good time. I know now there's never a good time to tell you something like that. I should have just told you. I should have made that a priority so that you would know and could let me go before your heart got too involved.

"It was so selfish of me, but I wanted you so badly, just for a little while. Something so good and pure. Just once, I wanted that in my life. I think I kept making excuses as to why it wasn't a good time. Still am. But I swear. I'll tell you as soon as you wake up. The timing will be shit, but you deserve to know. I can't keep it from you anymore. Even if it means losing you, it will allow you no sense of obligation to me, and you can concentrate on healing completely."

She felt tears welling up. "You saved my life. If you hadn't jumped in front of me, I'd be dead right now." Tears began to slide out of her eyes. "You're so stupid. Why did you go and do that? I'm not worth it."

"Nothing worth more," he whispered.

The words were quiet and more than a bit garbled, so she wasn't sure she heard him. "Kash?" Her eyes searched his face. Nothing seemed to have changed. Was she imagining his voice because she wanted to hear it so badly?

"The most beautiful eyes I've ever seen," he murmured. "*Heuning meisie.*"

She gasped, relieved to hear him speaking. The tears streamed harder than ever. "Kash! Oh god, Kash, I'm so glad you're awake."

"Don't cry," he commanded her. The weakest command ever given. A baby wouldn't have listened to him.

Relief brought on incredulous laughter, and she wiped away her tears. When he opened his eyes, she didn't want him to see them. She would be strong, be worthy of him, make him proud.

One corner of his lip twitched. "Kids don't matter, Ana." His voice slurred. "Only care about you."

Crap. He'd heard her for real.

She looked at his face and could tell he'd fallen back asleep.

46

FEBRUARY 28, 2024

Mouse

He'd woken up one more time the night of his surgery while Nemo visited him in the middle of the night, for a few short periods the next day, and then they'd almost lost him the third day. He'd had a seizure, which then caused additional damage and blood loss. Demon had to repair work he'd already done, plus do a live blood transfusion from Nemo, and then they crossed their fingers and hoped for the best.

Somehow, they'd managed to secure a hospital bed for him and set him up in what used to be Grayson Bosworth's office.

The teams could have gone back to work, but no one wanted to do so until they knew Midas was out of danger. Janus/God spent a great deal of time sitting with him, so between him, Mouse, and Nemo, he was never alone.

Weird as it was, she worried most about Janus. Mythos was

completely nonplussed by the reveal of his dual running of Mythos and Tribe. However, they'd all known about it. Tribe, on the other hand, had been delivered yet another truth they hadn't been ready for, so it made the tension in the house palpable.

He spoke to no one, just roamed about the large house like a ghost. Early on, he did spend several hours closeted with Waters and Medusa, but when they both emerged several hours later, neither shared what their conversation had been about. The only person he really seemed comfortable around was Mouse, but when she was with him, they didn't speak. Most times, he would silently drift in when she slipped into a nap and be there when she woke up, or disappear like smoke when she fell asleep, and she'd wake up alone in Midas' room.

On day five, when he appeared to be waking up more and more, Mythos went back to work, with the exception of Nemo. Waters, TB, and Steel also headed home, which left Demon, Nemo, and Mouse behind to take care of Midas until he was safe to transport.

One thing that made her mad was that he refused to allow her to help Demon take care of him, which caused their first fight. He apologized the next day, but he was absolutely adamant she was not to be involved. He got so upset with her when she brought it up again, she gave in and let Demon take care of anything he needed.

Instead, she kept him company. Most of that time, she sat in a comfortable chair they'd put in his room, and it reminded her of their first days together when she was the patient. Life really did come full circle.

Mostly, she read to him during the day, starting with book one of Flame's releases. While reading her second book, he teased her about how red she turned when reading the sexy parts, and her response was to taunt him that she was bookmarking the sexy parts for him to study because she expected them to do research when he was better.

At that comment, Midas had gone very quiet. She'd worried that she had been insensitive. What if he didn't walk again, let alone have the ability to make love to her? The latter, well, yeah… it would be disappointing, but she loved Midas. The concept of leaving him over his injury was absolutely ridiculous, no matter how things turned out in the long run.

His twin had also been a bit of a zombie the past few days. Despite the snarking between them and Midas' lingering feelings of abandonment, the brothers really did love each other, and Nemo's concerns equaled her own. In a rare moment of Demon, Nemo, and her being alone together and not with Midas, he was the one who asked the blunt question that everyone was most worried about. "He's going to make it, right?"

As usual, Demon didn't sugarcoat his prognosis. "He's made it this far, so he should live."

"And walking? Will he walk again?"

Here, Demon paused. "Each day he wakes up, there's still hope for a complete recovery. Unfortunately, his level of sensation isn't increasing. Could that improve in the future? Yes. Could he stay the same as he is now? Yes."

Nemo flashed a look at Mouse, then back at the medic. "What about his… functions?"

A bark of laughter came from Demon. "Is that your subtle way of asking if he can have sex? Not really sure that's *your* concern."

"Dude." Normally, his brother was free with his discussions about the topic. Mouse couldn't help but find it amusing that this would be embarrassing for Nemo.

"Dude," Demon imitated sarcastically. "After the concern of walking again, I'd be more worried about whether he'll be able to pee and shit like a normal human being. Are you offering to be there the rest of his life to wipe his ass?" He shook his head. He sighed and ran a hand through his hair, attempting to reset himself. "Sorry. Inappropriate. Look, I don't know, and that's the honest truth. Lots of partially paralyzed people regain normal bodily functions after the most critical portion of their recovery. Right now, neither of those are in my concerns."

"He wants a family. He'll likely be concerned about sex."

She didn't realize she'd said it out loud until Nemo cleared his throat. "He said that?"

She nodded.

"Whoa. With you? Not that that's a bad thing!" he rushed to say. "My blessing isn't needed. I just didn't realize you two were that serious yet."

This time, she shook her head. "Not with me specifically. Just in general." She left it at that. This was not the time to go into why that was never going to happen.

"Again," Demon reminded them, "right now, anything is possible. We need to be patient. Recovery for this type of injury is unique to each individual. I saw people who were up and walking the next day, and I've seen people who never walked again, and everything in between. A lot of that is up to Midas, and I'd be lying if I said I wasn't concerned. Each day he wakes up and realizes he still can't feel anything from below the waist... I see it in his eyes. He gets more and more depressed."

And each day with no evidence of improvement, Midas became less and less receptive to talking about any sort of future with Tribe or her. It didn't help her face her own fears about the relationship. Even when she was with him doing something else, she couldn't stop thinking about his comments over the past few weeks regarding kids. She kept visualizing him with the girls at the Santa Monica Pier, and her heart cracked a little more.

In the end, it was a total of two weeks before they were able to transport him back home. The night before the trip, she cornered Demon in his room and asked him for a huge favor. "D, I... I need to know something. For sure, know it."

He stopped packing to focus on her. "How can I help, Mouse?"

"When I appeared at the compound, the doctor there gave me a physical. Since I couldn't tell them anything about myself, it was pretty extensive. One of the things the doctor told me was that he believed I couldn't have children." The last sentence faded into a whisper, and her eyes pleaded with him.

"Because of what happened to you when you were first kidnapped," he surmised. "Let me guess. You want me to look over the records?"

"Yes. Just to make sure. It's not that I don't trust the doctor, but... I know you'll look deeper. I just... I need to be sure."

He considered her for a minute. "Having kids is important to you?"

She shrugged. "It doesn't matter to me. I mean, I would love to have kids, but it's not going to destroy my world if I can't. There are other ways to have children, but..."

"Are you second-guessing your choice to stay with him?"

"No! At least, not because I'm shying away from taking care of him if worse comes to worst with his condition. I love Midas. I'd do anything for him."

"Including letting him go, right? Because this is about whether or not you can give him the family he said he wanted."

"I've heard him talk about Axel, and I've seen him with the girls. It's obvious he'd be a wonderful dad just by how he lights up around them. If I can't have kids, it's not fair of me to tie him to me, and you know Midas. He'll feel obligated to stay with me, and I won't be able to give him what he wants. But if there's any chance that I could have kids, well... maybe that would be enough to justify staying."

Demon stared at her so long, she began to shift uncomfortably. "You know what? Never mind. It's fine. I'm sure the doctor was right—"

"Mouse. Stop. I'll be happy to request the records from Mythos and look them over. I'll even be happy to run more tests for you when we get back home, but I think you're looking at this backassward. You are in no way an 'obligation' to Midas. That man loves you to his soul. While he might have once thought about having a big family, when we joined Tribe, all of that went away for us. He made his choice already between having a family and not having a family."

"What are you talking about?"

Running his fingers through his hair, he shook his head and muttered to himself in Gaelic. "Has he told you anything about how we all got together?"

"Very little. Just that because of what he did, he could never walk beside me publicly. That I'd be 'alone' because he's technically dead."

"Right. It's a bit more intricate than that, but... yes. The work we do is dangerous. We've been up against some of the worst of the worst —sex traffickers, cartel leaders, slave traders, rogue military. You name it, we've pretty much seen it. When we were recruited, we were handed a folder. If we didn't open the folder, we could walk away, no questions asked. If we opened it, we had to come work for Tribe, leaving all of our family and friends behind, or we would be erased for real."

She felt herself flinch.

He nodded. "Yeah. You'd think none of us would have opened that folder, but apparently, our five dumb arses did. Most of us didn't have family or friends around anyway, so that part wasn't a hardship. Waters and his sister were recruited, Midas and Nemo were recruited together... they were the only ones with living family, so on that end, it didn't matter.

"But then Waters' sister was taken in retaliation for a Salieri operation we flipped. We didn't know it was them at the time, but they raped and murdered her in front of him as revenge. We found him half alive minutes after she died. Our boss flipped out so bad over the whole situation, he told us we weren't ever allowed to get involved with anyone, or he'd put through what we call the final edict—total erasure. Fine. We were okay with that. Sarah's death spooked us hard, and it seemed a reasonable rule, given what we do.

"Then, enter Kubrick. Waters let evil out of Pandora's box when he met Kubrick, so the rest of us have followed his example. Relationships were suddenly back on the table, but families? How the hell could we possibly manage that?

"Enter Axel. TB and Flame didn't get pregnant on purpose, but evidently, TB's sperm are as Dominant as he is, so now, apparently, we can have families."

She was so confused. "Demon, I don't understand what you're trying to tell me."

"I guess what I'm trying to say is, none of us went into this portion of our life thinking that any of what's going on is even possible. We were resigned to being alone. That was the price we had to pay to do this. So the idea of having a relationship, or even a family, if we want one? Those were pipe dreams for us, if we gave them any thought at all. Midas won't care if the two of you can have children of your own or not. He'll be happy enough just to have you by his side because up to two years ago, all of us believed we'd be hunted down and killed if we tried to have that."

"But now he knows kids are possible because of Axel. He'll be able to have that again."

"Mouse. He loves you. He wants you. Do not look for a reason to run. I guarantee if it's a choice between kids or you, he's going to take you, hands down. Both would be nice, I'm sure, but if you can't have kids of your own and you really want a family, heaven knows Mythos has tons of them for adoption. Why not take in Shakira and Ona? They're bonded to you. TB and Flame adopted Paris. Waters and Kubrick are attached to those twin girls. Wouldn't be surprised if they adopt them.

"Will it be messy for everyone adding kids to the mix? Yes. Does it create a helluva mess since we're 'dead'? Yes. Will it stress us all the hell out because we'll be worried if something happens to us or them? Yes. But we all believe, one hundred percent, that it's worth it."

She wanted so desperately to believe that Demon's assessment of what Midas would want was correct, but she couldn't see how it would be. Yes, she knew who she was now. Yes, she was relatively safe from the Salieri with Zion Norton out of the picture, although they weren't sure if the organization would pursue her in his place. What could she possibly offer Midas? He deserved so much better.

"Don't look for trouble, Mouse," Demon warned her. "It comes on its own and doesn't need to be summoned by putting your worries out into the universe. Let's go home and let nature take its course. If it makes you feel better, I'll look over your files, although I still say they don't matter for Midas."

"Thank you." She nodded and went to her room to pack.

47

APRIL 2, 2024

Midas

"I FUCKING HATE YOU, YOU PIECE OF SHIT LEPRECHAUN!"

"Good. Take two more steps, and I'll let you punch me in the face if you can do it without falling down."

Midas threw plenty more curses at Demon, but he took the two more fucking steps. Took an entire minute to do it, but he did. When he got to the end of the bars he'd been holding onto for support, he almost did fall, but Demon was there, stepping under his arm, to help him sit in his wheelchair. Midas leaned into Demon, ignoring Mouse's offer of help. He saw the flash of hurt cross her face, which she quickly masked with a cheery smile.

"Too tired to punch you," he grumbled at Demon.

The medic-turned-physical-therapist grinned. "I figured. Mouse is keeping track of every punch you're racking up for when we can finally meet in the ring, and I will gladly stand still for every one of them."

"I don't need you to stand still for them."

"Ohh, getting cocky, are we?" Demon glanced over at Mouse. "He's feisty today."

"I guess so," she replied. "Guess that means he gets to do the dishes tonight if he's feeling so good."

Midas pointed his finger at her. "Don't you start. It's Tuesday. Cherry's ordering tapas, so there won't be any dishes to do." While the comment could have been read as a teasing remark, there was an edge to it. There'd been a lot of edges to his comments to Mouse.

Rolling his eyes, Demon walked away to start wiping down the equipment they'd been using in the afternoon's session. "Speaking of tapas," Demon called out over his shoulder. "Mouse, would you ask Cherry to double my order. I've worked so hard today, I'm feeling extra hungry."

"Will do!" she chirped. She leaned down to Midas, giving him a kiss on the top of his head. "I'm going to go play with the girls for a bit. See you at dinner."

Midas didn't react to the kiss, and he didn't say goodbye.

He rolled himself over to the floor-to-ceiling windows of the workout area and looked down on the glassed-in patio. Being in the heart of L.A., there was no grass for the girls to play on, so God... Janus... whoever he was these days... had brought in contractors and done the impossible. He'd turned the outside patio into a sunroom with plants, a fountain, and a couple of playground toys so they could be safe behind bulletproof, UV-repelling glass but still get sun and play. Good grief. When did children become part of their jobs?

And yet... watching them was the highlight of his day now. He could watch them for hours out there, reminding himself why he did what he did for a living. That the sacrifices he made were worth it. He loved them and never wanted them to leave. However, they would soon. Would Mouse go with them? If he didn't get his head out of his ass, she probably would, and he wouldn't blame her.

So why was he being an asshole to Mouse and shutting her out? None of this was her fault. Yes, he took a bullet for her. Four of them, actually. He didn't regret it, and he would do it all over again. She was the most important thing in his world, although he was doing a pretty shitty job of showing her that.

Every day, he saw the light in her eyes dim a little further. She'd wake up, her cheerful face on, ready to face the day. She'd literally do anything for him, although he wouldn't let her. And every time he turned her down, she got a little sadder. Oh, she tried to hide it behind a brittle smile, but it got harder and harder for her to do it. All she wanted to do was help him, but dammit! He didn't want help! He wanted to do things on his own. He was supposed to be taking care of her, not the other way around.

It also didn't escape him that he needed to have a long talk with her, one that began with an apology, proceeded to groveling, and ended with... what? A promise?

And there was the problem. What could he possibly promise her? He wanted it all with her, but what if he could no longer give it all to her? With therapy twice a day, Midas was beginning to show remarkable improvement. It was still going to be a long road to recovery, but Demon had told him two weeks ago that if he worked hard at it, he thought he'd be almost as good as new. It was the "almost" part that had Midas concerned.

He couldn't marry her. He could do some sort of grand gesture, he supposed, a sort of commitment ceremony, but it wasn't the same as marrying her. She deserved that. Give her a family? That seemed like a long shot right now. She loved those girls, particularly Shakira and Ona, but she deserved a family of her own too.

"Being a dick make you feel better?"

Midas grunted. He kept his eyes glued on the girls down below.

"She's scared, too, you know."

Again, he didn't respond.

Demon tried one more time. "She thinks you don't want her anymore."

"How could I possibly not want her?"

"Well, let's look at the evidence, shall we? You don't speak to her unless she speaks first, and when you do, it's in the fewest syllables possible. Sometimes only a nonverbal. If it's not monosyllabic or nonverbal, you snap at her at every possible opportunity. She reaches out physically to you all the time, and you don't respond. She would do the worst jobs to help you, but you reject her help. Shall I go on?"

Midas said nothing.

Demon sighed and walked up next to him, his gaze also focused on the kids. Mouse walked outside, and immediately the kids went running to her. He could almost hear their screams of "Miss Mouse."

"All right, let's cut through the bullshit. Is this you being worried about sex? Because we talked about this. You said there was no issue with arousal."

"Nope."

"Have you two...?"

"No."

"But you did have sex with her before the shooting?"

"Not sure why you need to know that, but yes."

"Frankly, I don't give a shit if your dick works."

"Well, I give a shit," Midas mumbled.

He got another eye roll from the medic. "Okay, so if we're dealing with issues right now, your dick works in general, but you haven't tried to have sex with her since the shooting. Have you gotten off at all?"

"Dude!" He felt his face heat. He wasn't embarrassed, but it was weird talking with Demon about this.

"Oh my god, you and your brother really are twins."

He flashed a look of confusion at Demon.

"I'm a doctor. I'm a guy. Trust me. Okay, so it gets hard, but you haven't masturbated, and you haven't tried to have sex with your woman. Are you worried about having sex?"

Midas sighed. "Maybe, but that's not it."

"Then all I'm left with is, it has to do with those five little girls down in the atrium. Have you talked with her about this?"

"'This?'"

"Do you even know if she wants kids?"

"Look at her."

Down below, they could see her playing some sort of tag game with the girls that involved catching them, giving them hugs and kisses, then setting them free to run again. Gem was also involved, but she added putting them at the top of the slide and letting them go down it. Even Scheherazade was in on the act, barking and herding the children back into the women's arms. By the looks on all their faces, even from two floors away, it was pure joy.

"She loves every second with them. How could she not?" he whispered.

"You're making a pretty big assumption. Not everyone who loves kids wants kids of their own. I'm guessing there are a lot of teachers out there like that. I can't imagine dealing with them all day and then going home to them."

"She wants kids."

"You *really* need to talk to her about this," Demon urged.

For the first time, he looked up at the medic. He frowned. "What do you know?"

Demon walked away. "Nope. You. Her. Talk. Tonight. Or I'll pack up her shit myself, move her into my old apartment, and send her with Gem and Nemo in two days."

His heart stopped. He forgot to breathe. Two days? Were the girls also leaving in two days?

Midas turned his wheelchair around and wheeled over to where Demon was sanitizing equipment. "No one told me they were leaving in two days."

Shrugging, Demon replied, "Nemo's been gone from Mythos long enough. He needs to go back to work. Besides that, why would anyone tell you? It's been discussed for the past month. You haven't reported for a single meeting. It hasn't exactly seemed like you cared about what was going on. If you're not here doing PT, you're holed up with Nova. Who you've also been a right cunt to. Never thought an

AI could get its imaginary feelings hurt." He mumbled to himself, "Skynet is alive and well."

"She's not leaving. Neither are those girls."

"Sorry, dude. As of right now, Gem, Nemo, and Mouse are set to leave on Friday." The medic gave him the side-eye. "Unless..."

Midas turned his chair and headed for the elevator. He hated being manipulated, but he admitted Demon had checked him. Now it was time to put this "leaving" shit into checkmate.

APRIL 2, 2024

Mouse

"You can't catch me, Miss Mouse!"

"I'm gonna get you!" she threatened. Ona just shrieked and laughed because Mouse's voice didn't match her words.

Mouse was winded from all the running, but the discomfort of being out of breath chasing after the girls was far better than the lancing pain of Midas shutting her out. She'd known he would struggle with his injury, particularly how slow the recovery was, but she'd hoped that as he grew stronger, he'd become more positive. He'd actually gone the opposite direction.

Friday, Nemo and Gem were returning to Mythos assignments, and their first one was taking Shakira and Ona to a new compound. Waters and Kubrick had announced last night that they were adopting the twins. From what she understood from Cherry, it seemed as if this commitment was a solidifying of their relationship, and they both seemed incredibly happy, not to mention how ecstatic the girls were.

Leaving with Shakira and Ona would be painful. However, staying and being rejected by Midas would break her altogether.

She finally grabbed Ona around the waist and swung her around in a circle, squeezing her tight, much to the child's delight. As she turned in a second circle, she caught a flash of sunlight bouncing off the door to inside the building. Then she heard the calls.

A chorus of "Midas!" bounced off the glass walls directly at her and hit her hard. One more hit might be the one that caused all the shards to break apart into pieces that no one could ever put back together.

Ona struggled in her arms to get down, so she settled the girl on her feet, made sure she was sturdy, and watched as she ran pell-mell toward the man in his chair. Meanwhile, Mouse froze, afraid to take a step in any direction. It wasn't lost on her that any direction she went but one took her away from him.

Ona had crawled up into Midas' lap, and the other children were gathered around chattering. All she could hear was their happy babble—likely telling him about all their adventures today since Nemo and Gem had snuck them out and taken them to a real movie. She wished she could have gone, but it would have meant missing Midas' therapy appointment, and she refused to do that. He might not want her there, but there was no way she was letting him go through this alone. If it was the only way to show him her support, then that's what she'd do.

She couldn't hear what he was saying to them, but after a few minutes, he called Gem over and spoke to her. She nodded, turned to wave at Mouse, called to Scheherazade, then took the twins by the hand and went inside.

He said something to Shakira, and she nodded and pushed him, Ona still in his lap, into one of the shaded sections that had been made for when the sun was at its hottest. She loved how he let them push his chair for him, something they enjoyed doing. He wouldn't even let her do that. A little bit of jealousy pierced through the veil of her happiness, but she pushed it down. It was more important that he didn't take out his frustrations on the girls, and he was incredibly good at that.

Once under the awning, he put an arm around Shakira and took her into his lap on his other knee. The picture they made, him sitting with his arms around both girls, brought tears to her eyes. It felt like the air around her warmed even more with the love he obviously gave them, but her own heart froze a little more.

Whatever the conversation was, it looked very serious. Had someone told him they were leaving on Friday? She hadn't wanted to tell him, chickening out at every opportunity. She wasn't ready yet.

She'd never be ready.

The girls both threw their arms around Midas' neck, crying, and he sat there rubbing their backs, burying his face in one's hair, then the other. She could hear the low rumble of his voice but not what he was saying.

Dammit, he knew. He was saying goodbye to the girls.

The door to the inside opened again, and Nemo came out. Both girls kissed Midas' cheek and left with his brother, leaving her and Midas alone in the atrium.

This was it. Now he would say goodbye to her. Might as well. Two more days weren't going to make any difference. It was over. She and the girls would go to the compound on Friday, and she'd never see Midas again.

He began to wheel himself in her direction, stopping about ten feet short of her. It might as well have been a mile. The silence stretched long between them, and his face was a blank mask, giving nothing away as to his emotions. She wasn't used to that with him. He wore his emotions out in front of everyone normally. The shooting had changed that.

"I hear you're leaving on Friday."

Her throat felt like it had a boulder in it, and she swallowed hard, trying to work around it. Her mouth was so dry, she had to peel her tongue off the roof of it with great effort, and even swiping her lips with her tongue wasn't enough to wet them.

Why was this so fucking hard?

How did she answer this question?

"Gem told me that she and Nemo have been ordered back to work now that you're on the mend. They're supposed to take the girls to a new compound."

His eyes didn't leave hers, but she still couldn't read them. "You're going with?"

The boulder was back, as well as the dryness. She fought to get the words out. "Janus…" She corrected herself. "God offered me a job at the compound."

There. Noncommittal.

He looked out through the atrium windows at the neighboring buildings for a long time. When he looked back at her and spoke, she couldn't have been more flabbergasted if he'd told her he'd sprouted wings. "I've been a complete, raging asshole, Ana. I'm sorry. I know I owe you so much more than those two words, but I really didn't have the time to prepare anything that would even come close to the apology you deserve, so I'm just keeping it simple. I'm so sorry."

This is how the shattering began. The words "I'm sorry" said it all.

"It's okay, Kash. You don't owe me anything. You saved my life. Twice. If anyone owes someone, I owe you."

She wasn't sure how much longer she could do this before she broke down in tears. Why couldn't he just say it and get it over with because there was no way she would ever say them, even if she left on Friday.

"Ana… fuck, this is so hard." His voice actually sounded like it was going to crack.

"It doesn't have to be hard, Kash," she assured him. "Just say what you need to say. It's just me. No one special."

His face morphed into the most incredulous expression she'd ever seen. "Not special? You? My god, Ana, of course you're special."

"But not special enough, right?"

"What—? Fuck, I'm totally messing this up. You think I'm breaking things off with you?"

"Aren't you? I mean, I get it. You almost threw your whole life away for me in that house, and now you're facing the absolute worst challenges in the world. We still don't know what triggers my blackouts, so there's no clue what I'll do or who I'll hurt next. And on top of that, I can't give you the children you want. Demon confirmed the compound doctor's records were accurate, and I know how much you want a family—"

"Ana. Stop. Right now."

She put a hand up to her mouth and her other arm around her stomach, squeezing herself tight as if somehow these two actions would prevent the words and the tears.

His face shifted to surprise, then remorse. "I'm never going to be able to stop apologizing for fucking up, am I? I. Don't. Care. Do you hear me? I don't care if we can't have kids of our own. Knowing my luck, they'd be boys and all turn out like Nemo. Been there, done that, do not want to have to bail them out of jail."

She barked out a laugh that combined with a sob. Oh my god, was there actually hope?

He wheeled two feet closer to her. "I care about you. About us. Fuck, I'm such an idiot. All these weeks, I've been worried I couldn't give *you* the family *you* wanted. It's a lot to ask of you to stay here and then find out we can't have a normal relationship, but I'm willing to take the chance to make it work, whatever happens. All I want is you."

He wheeled to her so that there was only a body width between them. "Yes, at one time I wanted a large family, but I knew it really wasn't in the cards for me. Raising Nemo, even though he's my twin, was hard, and like I told you, I'm glad we didn't have more of us back then. Then, when we were on our own, we were thieves, wanted in several countries, no home to speak of, running around the globe. You can't raise a family doing that. Then Tribe. Who wants to be involved with someone you can't publicly claim?

"Lots of things have changed though. Being here with the guys? It taught me that blood means nothing when you have a tribe behind you. I want you as part of my tribe. The most important piece, actually. And if you'll have me, we can still have a family, Ana. If that's what you want. You love Shakira and Ona. Let's adopt them. We'll make our own tribe within a tribe. That's what I was talking to them about. If I could convince you to stay with me, would they stay with us. Be our girls."

Was he for real? This man was willing to take her, just as she was? A survivor of trafficking. A human weapon used by the Salieri. A broken woman.

She was so stunned, she realized by his next words that he thought she was struggling to give him an answer.

"Want to play a game, Miss Mouse?"

"A game?"

"Yes. Tag."

"Tag."

Inside, she was smacking herself in the head. Could she do something other than repeat what he said to her?

"Yep. Here's the game. You run. If I catch you, manage to touch you within sixty seconds, you stay, and we adopt Ona and Shakira. We get everything we've ever wanted. If I can't catch you, you can go away with Mythos. I'll miss you. There won't be anyone else for me. But I love you that much that I'd let you go, if that's what you want."

She paused, her heart thudding at his proposal. Yet again, the yeses and noes were hers. Always. "Okay. I'll play."

"All right. We start on 'go.'"

"On 'go.'"

"Ready." Pause. "Set." Pause. "Go."

The last word was a whisper.

She didn't move.

He locked the brakes on his chair and worked to stand. It was slow, but he managed on his own.

She still hadn't moved.

He reached out a hand for hers and took it in his. "I win."

Gently, so as not to knock him over, she stepped in closer so that there was no air between them, her other hand snaking around his neck to pull him within a breath of her lips. "No, Kash. We all do."

ALSO BY NICOLE CRAIG

<u>The Deadman's Tribe Series</u>

Good Enough BoCJFSW6LZ

Bad Enough BoCTHZPN6Y

Never Enough BoCZ339NWF

Strong Enough BoF1RBGWHF

Brave Enough BoFPWKBJCZ

Long Enough (Coming April 2026)

<u>Six Paths to Justice</u>

"The Lucky Rabbit" (out of print)

Justice for Francesca BoDTV65N4V

Justice for Elyxandre (Coming January 20, 2026)

ACKNOWLEDGMENTS

Mama Bear & Sissy Bear—These past few months of your mentorship have been what I needed since the beginning. You give and you give, and you ask nothing in return except that I stop kicking myself so hard. When I'm excited, you're excited. When I'm sad, you build me up. Through you, I've seen that I'm not alone. All the things I feel are what all authors feel. I'm so glad to have met you both and call you my friends as well as my colleagues.

SJ—As an author, you'd think I'd have the words to express just how much your help on my books means to me. And yet here I sit... with no words. Maybe that means you know how I feel without me even having to say them.

Steph White, Vanessa Esquibel, and Kat Wyeth—6 books. 7 by the time this releases. Assorted short stories. You make beauty out of the Hot Mess Express.

Nicole Craig's Tribe—Thank you for being a part of my reader group. We are small, but we are tribe.

My ARC Tribe—Thank you for taking some of your valuable time to read and review my novel. I know it's not an easy job. I appreciate your honest reviews.

To Anyone Who Reads This Book—Thank you. You're making a life-long dream come true for me.

ABOUT THE AUTHOR

At ten years old, Nicole Craig snuck into a secret box of her mother's books filled with mysteries and romances. Since that day, she has a book (or five) available at all times. At the age of thirty, her husband encouraged her to try her hand at writing. It only took another twenty-five years of teaching high school and a pandemic to do it, creating the types of books she found in that magical box.

Nicole lives in Southeastern Wisconsin. She is a devout Milwaukee Brewers fan, mother of three furry feline children, and married to The One. After twenty-five years as a high school English teacher, she decided to retire to spin fantastic tales, travel, and live the ultimate fantasy: reading a book a day until the end of time.

Please consider leaving a review on Amazon or Goodreads. It's one of the best ways to thank a writer (besides buying their books!) for the work they've done.

Check out her Facebook Reader Group or any of her social media links to get the latest updates on The Deadman's Tribe series or other upcoming projects.

Facebook Reader Group: Nicole Craig's Tribe
Website: https://nicolecraigauthor.com/
Instagram: https://www.instagram.com/nicolecraigauthor/
Newsletter: https://dl.bookfunnel.com/aoslx3defo